JOURNEY HOME

JOURNEY HOME

PAUL BURKE

This book was printed in the United States of America.

To order additional copies of this book, contact:
Xlibris Corporation
1-888-795-4274
www.Xlibris.com
Orders@Xlibris.com
23335

Contents

CAST

The Band

Danny—Lead Guitar
John—Bass
Mark—Drums
Doug—Keyboards
Bonnie—Flute

Old Timers

Sam—Bar Manager
Eric—Hippie
Wendy—Actress
Louise—Drifter

Young Bloods

Adam
Jessica
Ben

THE MALLARD FLOATS

—

It was a relief the rain came. He was searching quietly, being driven by some unknown force. Hunger, greed, hatred, fear, hopelessness, passion, faith, curiosity, dreams and love where did they come from? And why were they here in our minds? It seems simple enough. The Earth is brilliant in it's spinning of night and day, in it's terra firma cradle and water soul. The Earth, the planet, spinning, floating, spectacularly mundane with forces beyond vision with billions of manifested souls. God like in our consciousness, a step below angles, we curse and hate each other with jealousy, envy and gripping hopelessness. Life and death much the same, understood only for it's horrible truth missing the mark of our better natures and it's better reality. The blue planet spins on.

People crowd each other's dreams with mock sincerity wishing it were them still realizing we are the same but only for our surroundings. And that's the starting point, the challenge, the goal of life itself. Within yourself and not in response to others overcome whatever ails you and grow a thousand lifetimes in a year. Every moment is an opportunity to create or destroy. The Earth quakes, shakes, rattles and rolls in every fiber in every essence and in every stone unturned. Life is going through its transformations and the people too by the billions. How is your truth appropriate for all? Does it matter if it is or isn't? Is it like a shirt that looks better on you than on your sister? The answers you have found are for you alone. The person sitting next to you will find their own answers. Force your answers on him and he will fight you to the death. Because inherently we know this is our journey. Our roads are not all the same. Each of us is looking for our own golden fleece. Get out of each other's way.

The light shines just as understanding passes. The muddy waters of despair overflow and we drown. The dragon flies, with impeccable timing alight on our consciousness. The feeling that feels so complete an elation thundering with motion while you are so still. Your eyes widen, your head turns, you point or gasp or merely your back straightens and wonder can burst through just like anger.

A screeching halt of automobile tires burns out on the street as a young woman is thrown out of a stopping car. She rolls to the curb in one toss and rises. A voice calls from the car, "here have a beer," as a bottle of Coors comes at her brow and smashes against a wall. The voice from inside the car reeks with sarcasm and insightful abuse, "trash," it bellows and without pause heads off. Ducking, a sigh of relief, and a bottle of republican brew smashes into tiny shards of discontent. It shatters its political campaign donations into public hazards. Glass lay all over the street. A cut foot and more blood shed in the road. Human nature I suppose.

The girl picks herself up and steps back onto the sidewalk. A bloody footed boy groans. He looks at his toes and feels the wet blood cool against his foot. His one sandal is soggy. He raises his head, the choice being made, the dice rolling and speaks to the girl. "Are you alright?" No reply. She made her choice. But the problem with choices is that they keep coming, " . . . look I just sliced my foot open. Do you mind acknowledging my existence?" She didn't care but she did turn her head slowly and stared in disbelief. Eyes smoldering she said nothing. He bent over to reexamine his foot. The cars filing by didn't care one bit about them. They didn't care about each other and they might not even care about themselves. In fact no one cared about anything at all anymore.

It was a busy night in this little Florida town outside of Fort Lauderdale. The tourists had found their way inland. They had converted this two gas station and a post office strip into a trap. A cheap trap filled with gimmicks and one liners that would surely bring you down in your pursuit of happiness. The cars at night cruised the boulevard with the locals hanging on the side streets. It once was this out of the way Victorian sea town. The old fashioned kind built far enough away from shore to withstand the hurricanes and the thunder showers that blasted in from the north. Each storm seemed to howl and bring a warning of furious redemption for those who forgot about the forces of nature. The beach was a wonderful place to live honestly and in the face of such force. Man shaken to his knees reminded with window shaking fury that he is merely a part of nature, a small part at that, and not apart from nature. Batten down the hatches and watch the waves boys. There's a blow a comin'!

Now a days the inland waterways were jammed up but good with Bertrams and Chris Crafts. There was more to business than the price of a bushel of clams. They showed off gold plated foreign cars that cost too much to fix and stereos too loud to hear. But that still didn't stop the rain. It just keeps coming down faster and faster. It makes one long sustained rush of noise as the wind set it's pace. It pours down in sheets and pounds a driving continuous beat that makes you forget everything else. A romantic mood gains hold for the lucky few as a loud smack of lightning sends the posers and the wannabes, the phonies and the freaks, the juice and the grifters, running for cover. Everyone gets wet and those inside hide their heads. The darkness and the gale force winds blow fear down the street chased by a salty cold rain. Too scared or smart to drive over the bridge the ghetto mobiles are no better than the suburban rides and everyone goes slower. Bodies tremble with soaked chill and evil rears it's head. Always there, just over your shoulder and in your shadow, fear opens the door and you wish you were dead. So powerful it exceeds anyone's intended involvement or supposed self. No matter what you believe or how you perceive it Mother Nature has just served notice.

They have lost their respect for each other and nature does what she has always done so well. The rain falls, the thunder slashes, and the mallard floats. The driving rain buries it's head. The darkness shrouds it from view. The veil of water drums the sea around in which it sits. Bobbing alone it rides the storm out. Land, water and sea spinning, endlessly alone in space. We float along with the storm.

Drowning wont stop the rain. It rages all around as inevitable as the pride of man, which becomes his undoing. It's all just exactly how you want it to be. Defining your reality by your assumptions, taking chances, making choices. It's all old news unless you forget it.

The girl on the sidewalk has now given some weighty attention to her plight and the bleeding foot is still of no significance to her. "No wonder that guy threw you out of the car!" That got her attention. "So you got away with your life it happens every day." She shot him a glance, quick and mean, but kept her mouth shut. A lesson too few of us have learned. She started to go. She had always left whenever she wanted to, even if it was from a moving car. That had always been her rule. She walked away. Her name was Louise, she pronounced it "Lowease". She was drifting through east Florida and had no idea why she was heading south. Whatever possessed her to come south on A1A she did not know. Life is like that. Intuition. Going with the flow. Playing a hunch. A gut feeling. Call it what you want, but the more in tune you are the choices are easier to make.

The Jaded Lady was a night club across the bridge that spanned the inland waterway. The bridge was beautiful and built with a huge arch so the boats could pass underneath without disturbing the cars. During the day, the sun shone brilliantly off the white concrete and reflected all around. Like some beacon the bridge was there. All one had to do was cross it to get to the other side. Danny, bleeding foot and all was different. He knew what he was doing in town. It was his first winter south and he and his band were making another stab at eating. The band defied description and that hurt sales. No one knew what to call the improvised staccato that Danny played on his guitar. Regardless, things were going well and much better than they had back home. Fleeing the tragically hip and the corporate driven media, the band made its move to Florida. They were in search of an audience that didn't have to be told by the magazines and the radio stations what was good. They were looking for an audience of searches who enjoyed the road along the way. A bunch of rebel loving, NASCAR watching, Skynyrd listening, mullet wearing aficionados who loved Coltrane wasn't really that hard to find. "Hey . . .," Danny called after Louise, ". . . wait." There was a pause and Louise stood silent, shoulders hunched, rain soaked, exhausted, hurt and sad. Danny picked it back up, "you jumped, you escaped, what did I just see there? Should I call the cops? I mean, look, I just stepped out for a quick bite . . . want something to eat?" The choices just kept coming. Louise was half way down the block now, "this loser wants a dinner date," she thought to herself. Louise was not about to pick up with yet another stranger and throw her life into his. It was a mess of a night and his statements trailed off into the emptiness. However, faintly heard through the downpour, his own inner voice emerged and stole his attention. It promptly cut off his vocal chords. His back stiffened and he became reacquainted with his heartbeat. Thoughts ran slower, "what are you doing, she's just some random bitch, mixed up, fucked up anyway?"

"Maybe," came another voice, deeper and familiar but never heard before. Quickly, but quieter other thoughts reached out through the panic from the side not penned in by fear. The fear side came back louder and with more of a shrill, "get real, she's just some whore who tried to roll the John and lost." But still the debate loomed and the side not soaked in fear went deeper than any voice of doubt could go. It went all the way down from the depths of infinity and side to side until it came around again seemingly from the center of his chest. It pushed out from the back of his neck and out his shoulder blades. It formed a vector beyond his head from above and focused down through to his spine flushing his gut. It was a strange familiar feeling he never felt before—at least in this lifetime. His shoulders straightened a split second before his thought was finished. For some strange reason he was remembering what it was like going into the recording studio. How he thought all his friends would come through. They would buy up copies of his disc and with the help from some of those spots they had been playing, things would really mushroom. But those places were too broke to pay and his friends thinned out quickly when instant success didn't appear. Other's resented his minor accomplishments and more than a few showed up to watch the train wreck. Eventually even they got bored. About a month from his first release date the crowds got smaller not bigger, contrary to that old feeling. When they packed their bags to head south for another try, no one noticed they had gone. All they had was each other and the urge to jam. "Toke, did you say toke?"

"Say it again," asked Danny?

"I mean you might want to call the cops or something." Louise moved real slow going from moment to moment like she always did. But she liked to shock people too. Still reeling from the car, a little blood was trickling from some obvious wounds. Pain like an avalanche was rolling unseen. "What's your name?" she asked.

"Never mind," he answered.

"Hiding something?"

"Not anything more than you."

"Is that a fact," she paused. The rain swirled up the street.

"I do that stuff all the time," a huge clap of lightning jolted the vagabonds.

They moved quickly under an awning. Danny still had glass in his foot and that was going to have to be attended to, but in the mean time Louise fired up her joint. Strike, a spark lit up. The red and yellow flash from the match startled shut Louise's eyes. She began to go into a daze. A deep toned hum began to pick up in volume. A low groan echoed in her mind. Another flash of lightning this time closer louder and brighter. It brought some sense into Louise but not much. Maybe she wasn't all right after all. She went down on one knee. The joint still laid on her lip while the match blew out in the wind. Danny reached out and grabbed her by the arm. She looked back at him with that strange familiar look of lost recognition. Human to human. Louise's eyes cleared for the moment, "I'm all right." She got up off her knee, "thanks." She was close enough to feel that Danny's concern might be real. She wanted to turn away from anything at all like that. Her face grew stern. "Where's that joint," she asked, like nothing happened. "Sorry," Danny paused and looked down. It was floating downstream in the rainstorm and out of view. "Lost to nature," she said, looking down with just a hint of disappointment in her voice.

The downpour hitched to a stop for an eternal second and began again. More rain and wind swept down the street. The street lamps were still on but throwing light in a very small circle. Windshield wipers slapped furiously in ridiculous contrast to how slow the cars were moving. The moments kept creeping by. There was no slowing time just our awareness of it. Danny studied her graven face and thought she really needed care, "can I buy you a warm drink at the Jaded Lady," he asked?

"Where," she asked, only mildly amused by the name.

"Across the bridge" he returned her insistent look.

"Yeah, sure. The cops wont do anything for me," she answered absentmindedly. Danny forgot about his foot and they took the long walk back across the bridge.

When they got back to the old whorehouse they looked horrible. Blood was still coming from Danny's forgotten foot and Louise laid up against his shoulder heavily. She was slightly hobbled but rain had washed her outer cuts and bruises clean. They sat down at an inconspicuous table and water ran off of them like a stream. From across the room John looked on. John was a little concerned. He was of slight build except his mind. He stalked the stage barefoot and said little. He was his own man. John got up slowly and made his way over to the table. The lights were low in the Jaded Lady but Danny and Louise were obviously messed up. John could see they were in pain. As he got closer he hid his panic. His lead guitar player disappeared and came back shipwrecked. Pulling up to the table, panic well hid, he just stared in disbelief. "You look like shit."

"Brilliant observation John." The typical tension of a band on the road was never far from the surface. You could never make the road your home no matter how hard you tried. The closest you could get was slightly comfortable before falling off to sleep.

"Foot's bleeding?"

"Oh yeah."

"Hey," spoke Louise. John shot her a glance. The stranger was speaking to him and he looked at her knowing it was her fault. Years of screwed up relationships swelled toward this woman. The rain was probably the first shower she had in weeks. Her skin was rough from exposure. "She was to blame," John thought to himself, and Danny was headed for the slaughter. "Your friend here looks a little beat up," said John motioning toward Louise. Danny returned his comment with a blank stare. "You two trail in here like this?

We've got a job to do Danny and your out screwing up. The only reason you got by Sam is because he motioned for me to fix this mess." Sam was the manager of the Jaded Lady and was not pleased with unwanted attention. "Good. You're going to take care of us," claimed Danny, "get us two hot cider drinks while the ale's still hot."

"Oh great, going for the waffle affect?"

"And get me something to wash and clean my foot out with. Hurry up. We've got a set to do." John went away more pissed than ever but Danny was counting on his uptight side. Louise just wanted some dry clothes. John came back with two scalding hot cider ale drinks and some dry towels. It was a drink of freshly brewed ale with cider spices for flavor. One sip of the hot ale and you were stoned. Sam learned the recipe from his bootlegging old man. His father as a boy learned the recipe during prohibition.

Sam's father used to sneak down into Billy the Bum's basement in Fishtown and get "waffled" as they said in the old days. Sam called it his hot waffle brew. They called Billy, "the Bum" because he didn't work not because he was poor. "All right. Back stage with both of you. Right now." Danny sipped his drink down thoughtfully. A few fans waved hello on the way in, unfazed by their condition. Danny was a rock and roller. He was supposed to look like Keith Richards (cue the horrible cigarette laugh).

Louise fit right in and needed dry clothes too. Something was nagging her at the back of her mind. There was a low rumble of fear and of trouble to come. "What the hell am I doing here," she thought to herself? Her luck had been so bad of late. In fact she had counted her luck out years ago. She knew that just because life is a flow of events doesn't mean they have to be good events. Her luck had to change but it seemed to her that Sister Good Luck had an easier time of changing than Brother Bad Luck. John's voice was rising slightly. Danny just stared at him impassively. His body was getting numb now from the cider, rain, cold and the loss of blood. He was happy seated where he was. In that state he was open to suggestions, but at what level were the suggestions registering with Danny? John was right in front of him, but where was Danny. Louise was having some thoughts of her own. Other than thinking about luck she wanted to know Danny's name.

"Danny's my name," he spoke starring straight ahead. His own voice sounded strange and curiously foreign to him. It came from deep within.

"What," she spoke.

"My name, you wanted to know my name," he turned and looked at her starkly. "Just now, you asked me my name."

"I did? Are you sure?" Danny just wrinkled his eyebrows. Louise had that," I was thinking it but how did he know," look on her face. She was frozen into not admitting anything. Startled and pulling back she made eye contact with John. He had stopped talking by now. "I didn't hear a thing," said John looking directly at Louise.

"It's time we went backstage," said Danny and they all got up and followed each other to the back. "Here I go again," thought Louise, "why must I always fall into these things. They always lead down dead end roads. The last one ended with me kissing concrete." They walked on in unison. The dance floor lights were brilliant loud and rude, but did not register with them. Louise was just rambling on in thought. " . . . my body aches and I feel sick . . . I need dry clothes . . . . luck, I could use good luck this time . . . gotta get going . . . can't stay again, can't stray forever . . ."

While these thoughts were running through her mind she followed John and Danny into a back room. It was down the long end of a corridor. The carpet was soggy from a beer keg. For ten bucks you could drink all the keg beer you wanted. So many people felt obliged to jump in. The floor was a mess. There was an old "Facts About Aids" poster nearby. Someone scribbled the words "Latest Best Guesses," over the "Facts" part and "West Nile Virus," then "SARS" and a "No Fondling Below The Waist" over the "Aids" part. The old door handle on the back room wouldn't cooperate with John. Danny took the key and opened it up in one try. He was unconscious at this point. They walked in. The room was lit by only one small lamp, "this is my favorite room in the whole house." House? A seven story motel is more like it, refurbished with brass lined rails, ceiling fans and the old ceiling ripped down to reveal the original beams. The huge front banister was restored to its original beauty. The dining area was garish with pastels. It grabbed everyone by the throat and wouldn't let you forget that you were in Florida. Beside the audacity of the dining area and a garish dance floor, the old motel was restored to its roaring twenties hay day. It had the original feel to it. There was a lot of back room partying going on at the Jaded Lady. The basement was turned into a wine and booze cellar with huge walk-ins and storage. The attached garage could keep six cars out of the weather. Those hearty of spirit lived at the Jaded Lady. "This is my favorite room all right," continued Danny. "It's right around the corner from the stage and after closing it's a teenage rock 'n roll fantasy!" When they had all three entered the room they sat down on an old brass bed. They were all back to back, with John at the foot. Danny and Louise were off to either side. The three just stared in silence at the walls. Louise sighed and looked out a window and wondered what this brief shelter was going to cost her. At least she was off the street.

The rain had finally stopped just as suddenly as it had started. The sweet tropical rain mingled with the luscious green and started evaporating into the night. It kicked up a mysterious fog hovering four feet off the ground. On the other side of the bridge the night was alive with cars cruising the boulevard. It was the rich fast life. But on this side of the bridge there was only swamp and an old grand fathered liquor license. It had a lonely street lamp and a huge unpaved parking lot. The lot was littered with Grand Cherokees, Jeeps, Trucks, BMWs, Novas, GTO's, Mustangs, Falcons, Bugs and the occasional Dead Sled. They were all here, playing in the Everglades. The Jaded Lady looked like an old shipwreck of a grand whorehouse. It was the first and only thing that greeted you once you crossed the bridge. The old rum runners tied off here before anything else was built. Once they built the bridge the magic of one side mingled with the chaos of the other. In the minefield parking lot of lost suspensions and hubcaps the cars were scrambled like the music and the eggs they'd want for breakfast. The one lonely street lamp shined out front and screamed, "go away" and then "all right come in if you must." Behind the Jaded Lady the green swamp land rose and fell towards an embankment and then down to a beautiful and silent body of water. It flowed right on by. If you stood next to the river and listened very closely you could here it

run. It sounded like an old familiar song. The longer you listened
the more the strangeness of it all seemed familiar. It was the music we
were born with, the music of the river. Danny often walked back here
to get charged up for a show. You had to find your inspiration every
night and he hated himself for going through the motions. He had to
dig hard not to become a parody of himself like an old Vegas act with
the same tricks every night.

A large bright moon looked in on our three companions changing
into dry clothes. Louise and Danny were half undressed when John
started attending to Louise's wounds. Mostly scratches and scrapes
John was nevertheless drawn to tenderness as he applied the peroxide.
Bitter and angry thoughts dissolve when the flesh is revealed. He was
rubbing down her badly mangled shoulder as Danny attended to his
foot. "Damn little piece of glass. Get that light over here." As John
moved the lamp Danny caught the sucker glistening in the light
change. "Got it." He pulled a practically square piece of glass out of
his foot. Louise smiled. She was happy to see someone's pain
disappear even if it wasn't hers. Danny dressed his wound with gauze,
tape and a sock. He looked a little silly but he stopped the bleeding
before too long. John put the lamp back and attended to Louise's
shoulder. She sat with her arms crossed in front of her. Danny got up
and looked at them in the light. John was a dog. "Were on in twenty
minutes," he said as he walked out of the room.

Danny moved through the crowd and exchanged glances with
familiar faces. The band had been doing okay with it's new change of
atmosphere and they had a solid if slightly crazy following. The crowd
returned every weekend, partially paying the owners bills, so
Sam extended their gig. When Danny got to the bar Sam slammed a
Heineken down in front of him. "Sorry Sam not tonight, I need two
more hot ales."

"Messin' with the formula?"

"It wont bring me any bad luck Sam."

"I still wouldn't try anything different with the way things are
building."

"This isn't much different." Before Danny could repeat his thought
Sam cut back in, "isn't much," he bellowed and leaned in quieter to

Danny, "she's poison!" Danny looked on momentarily confused. "The girl you brought in, you big dope."

"Huh," Danny was miles away, "oh her." Sam had seen it all before.

Back in the old dressing room John and Louise had sparked the moment. No longer was she a weathered vagrant. Her eyes revealed a depth, and her skin where not weathered, was smooth and beautiful, soft and round. She gave in because she thought she had to. He came on because he thought she wanted him to. Youth is wasted on the young. There was nothing left to do but follow it. Her breasts felt his hand heavy and strong. They were way past introductions now. John hardened and ached for the relief that would surround his explosion. Neither of them gave a damn and surrendered. Louise's mind was racing. John did not resist.

"That's ten Danny."

"Thanks Sam," he flipped him a twenty and walked away. Danny liked treating people they way they treated him. He headed back to the old room with the two drinks for him and Louise. A knocking brass bead and hard stabs of passion were there to greet him. Louise's back was arched with her head thrown back and her hair flying. John was pushing upward as far as he could go ramming with hard unhinged thrusts. Louise wrapped her legs around his back. John's arms were stiff his fingers digging into the mattress, knees steady. Danny was in the bedroom, "come on, you guys, gimmie a break," he put the drinks down and turned and walked out without missing a beat. Neither did John and Louise. Their heads jerked back and forth. He exploded and she collapsed. John seemed to think that the only way to extract the most out of something was to take it to its extreme. At those times he was wide of the mark. He missed the essential that was still with you after the rush was over. Lady luck had it that Danny was back talking to Sam. "Back so soon?"

"Yeah I got a bad taste in my mouth. How about the usual."

"Coming up," the manager effortlessly opened a bottle of beer. Things were kind of sticky at the moment and Danny didn't really go for that action back in the room. "I have half a mind to go back there and break it up," he thought to himself. But he didn't, instead he walked back to the stage and fiddled with his guitar. "Bartending can be fun if you only work Friday and Saturday nights," Sam thought to himself. Danny liked what he was doing on the guitar so he plugged in and turned up the volume. He had confidence these days and was not inhibited much to the audiences delight. He was using his bottleneck and jumped into an old "Hound Dog Taylor" tune. Back down the hall John and Louise were apologizing to each other. Danny's drummer Mark scrambled on stage knocking a drink over in the process. He quickly fell into a grove behind Danny's playing. Doug, not too far away, went for the keyboards and not his horn. Pretty soon they were playing the blues. Mark managed to get a couple of be-bop to werlybooms in along side of Doug's plink, plank, plankity, while Danny just slid on by. "Look Louise it just happened," John was interrupted by a look from her.

"I know," she grimaced. The apology was different.

"It wasn't so bad," said John as his smile turned up under his left cheek.

"Like cold pizza," she spoke.

"Danny can handle it," John stated matter of factly. They were both quiet now as the improvisational blue notes came tossing down the hall. If you don't tune yourself in you wont notice the synchronisity. "It's Allright," indeed. Oh well, another aspect of life just flying along in the wind. Some aspects pass like up on the North Atlantic up around the pole with torrential winds frigid and mighty and one says to oneself, "self looks like that just blew right by me." Sometimes it's as simple as a thought that might elude you. Or it can be as big as stubbing your toe. So you just grimace and try and walk away. Yet it all boils down to a thought. Thoughts spawning, forming and morphing. Millions of trains of thought, some good, some evil, but most mundane. All these thoughts seemingly from out of nowhere or from some spark of an original universal first thought. One push from the dominoes and the trails are splitting and leaving and coming back in a never ending cycle. The awakening of consciousness. Choices at every turn also mingling, splitting off, turning and never ending. Why are they present? Everyone of them is an opportunity. Time is there to forgive us if we miss it. Lofty ideas and disastrous deeds reach back and come from the same spot, from the beginning of consciousness, a faint inner whisper or loud declaring burst. Whether that whisper becomes a calm voice or an aggravating shout depends on our individual imaginations and sufferings. The labels are in place, over used, and without much meaning by themselves. But they still define the original understanding and the reality of the results of our choices. The choices we make and the choices for which we alone are fully responsible. Perhaps we have no real definition for life. But we seem to grope through it all the while, labeling things as we go. We miss the original and true essence of each thought in lieu of the words we use to describe them. How we handle the situation of life defines who we are. "It's an awful, cold world out there," spoke Louise, as she and John joined the party by simply closing the door behind them. "It is a world that likes to argue a lot and it feels so damn lonely sometimes." The words break down and bitterness is revealed and the argument goes on. But we are not here to argue, so feel better and put some big wooly socks on.

Bonnie joined the band on stage with her flute. She smoothed out the edge and rounded out the tone. The blues rock set wound down as a more traditional folk and jazz sound emerged. Bonnie was the type that wouldn't make it on her own. She learned the hard way but still wanted her own way. I guess she hadn't learned a thing. She wasn't the female balance the band had hoped for. Instead of cooling down the testosterone she was a lightning rod of controversy. A bitch on wheels. Danny eased down the volume on the guitar and Mark switched from drum sticks to brushes. Doug changed the mood of the piano. It was Bonnie's turn to shine and they had been told what to do. They still managed to improvise behind her and to her credit she was able to be spontaneous once she established her mood. In the end no matter how you get there it's fine. Our road scavengers have reached nirvana. Time, the labeled concept, nebulous and pliable, had slipped them into the jam. Danny had slowed his playing to almost a single note now. Bonnie's flute started in on her first ascent. The tones of the flute warmed the atmosphere and settled the crowd. She sensed that and took her time. Her war torn, hidden smile crept out as it always did. Right on cue. It was so non-challant that she hardly noticed it. She was too busy listening. Nobody listens anymore.

John and Louise found a table, "well, should I go up and play," questioned John? He had this very strange restrained feeling and guilt ran over his face. "They started without me . . .," Louise interrupted him. "I wouldn't take it to heart and I certainly wouldn't go up on stage if I wasn't ready." As John thought it over a cocktail waitress took their order. The band sounded almost too good for John to interrupt. The house lights came down as Sam realized the set was going on a bit earlier than usual. The band appreciated that. With the lights down and the candles burning on the tables the Jaded Lady took on this jazzy bop atmosphere. The atmosphere and I can think of no other name for it than that, was rich and heavy. Not laden with smoke but with an "atmosphere" that seems to seep into your pores. It overwhelmed the mood you came in with, lifting it's head up into yours. All of a sudden your in all the way, and just as far a head of the next note, as the musician has to be. You feel connected. The life forces go wavy throughout and within. The whole building comes alive. The band has tuned into the elusive wavelength of collective consciousness. Music is the best way to get at that. Not the only way but the best way. John waited for the wave to waver. Sometimes it lasts a song, sometimes all night but usually only a fleeting moment of crescendo and flash. John sensed the band needed a bass line to hold it together. It was his turn to join in. How did he know? By not trying to figure out when before beginning to listen. Listening for the band to wobble and catching the flow was like merging into traffic sometimes slowly, steady or fast. Then the music takes over with a life of it's own. Existing from without pulled through from within and delivered up to the realm of conscious awareness. No one could miss it unless they weren't hearing anything but themselves. John had to try and park his ego behind his thoughts. He did not want to take over but to join in. He wanted to connect but without trying and just by being, naturally, without forcing the way. Quiet now, forget the past. You and your hands will remember the chords your ear wants you to play.

The band had been playing slowly and had everyone's attention on a pin. Sam was almost laughing at how the mood had changed. John made his way to the stage. Louise sat down front with her legs up on a chair. She kept running her hand through her hair and was genuinely enjoying herself. She would pick another time to leave. Danny looked over at John and counted off one, two, three, four and the tempo picked up taking everyone along with it. The room got louder and louder and was punctuated by laughter. The band swung into a brassy big band swing set. Outside the hot and arid temperatures dried everything in a wink. "It doesn't matter about Louise," thought Danny and John simultaneously.

THANKS

—

Across the bridge the impressionable grooved to the beat of their industry generated, prefabricated dance music. Formula pop music had lost its innocence decades ago and lost its soul. When it ceased being about something, music became nothing more than a distraction and noise. For most, it filled a void and much like television kept us from addressing what needed to be addressed. Too distracted to feel anything about ourselves and the people in our lives, we have become easier to manipulate. Our senses have been dulled with nonsense and noise. People don't care anymore because their art and entertainment don't address the things we need to care about. Thump, thump, thump is all the music says. Television laugh tracks tell you when to laugh. By and large there are exceptions to every rule, but they are in fact exceptions and not the rule. Deep people are a mystery, strange, weird, not normal and shut out because they force others to question what is all around them. Being stupid is funny and hip. Being violent and having a gun is fashionable. Dig deep. The adventure is glorious and the soul is satisfied when it has stretched it's imagination. Dig deep. The feelings are so much richer and fuller. Find your own road and meet the others who travel it also. Dig deep. The laughter is earthy. It means so much more. Dig deep and you'll find your smile where the infinite and finite mingle. The deeper we go the better the garden will grow.

Gold chains and watches over customized BMW's materialism is at a frenzied pace. The wannabes with their tongues pierced look no less ridiculous than the white belts, white shoes, and big lapels of the Seventies. The dance clubs are a haven for the thoughtless who rattle their heads around hoping something comes out. When the cheaters get turned down their night is ruined. Do they go off to wonder why or just to pout? Thumpa, thumpa . . . the music works hard to say nothing. No feelings, no one gets hurt. Turn the bass up so high you bust your eardrums and drown out your inner voice. It's a pretty sad way to go just to lead an unexamined life. But when the emptiness inside is bigger than your soul and it means nothing at all, the death and the dying, are we surprised? It's time to turn it all off and take a walk in the woods. When the love or even just sex doesn't amount to anything can we figure it out? Deep, go deep before your time is over. Yes it all means something. Life becomes a thickly rich experience with each moment dripping with fulfillment and happiness. Life is thick with meaning. Everything washes your senses and satisfies your soul. Get in the moment and stay there and life feels like it will last forever. Life and death are all a part of the same thing. The original spark found in every breath you take and tingling the very surface of your skin. Rich moments dripping with packed days of listening to wind chimes or visiting the ocean with the children. Lovers warm each other with a bonfire as they stare out to sea.

"I love to feel the grass on my feet on a warm spring day," thought Louise to herself. Heaven on Earth. The collective mood of the band intertwined with the music pushing both the music and the musicians further. It took the audience and made some of them think about soft cool grass under their feet. Others had to put make up on and plan their agendas. Mark was thinking about an old egg farm and the friends he had there. Doug was chanting his mantra, "Hip Hop ain't got no soul, kill your mama, call your wife a ho'," as his fingers searched the keyboard for Count Basie.

Back over the bridge and further on down the road, the bright lights and flashy bursts of color charge up the restlessness in our souls. As fashion trends and trends of thought and food fill the void, restless blue jean-clad journey souls, grunge their way forward searching for their truth. They are protesting the unblinking acceptance of unquestioned authority in a members' only decision chamber that was supposed to be built for all. Dreadlocks and tattoos blot out their color, not the light. The angst feeds the wrong and the right flame.

The dance club glistened out in dark reflective glass. The sharp darkness contrasted with the bright silver chrome finish. The dance floor was awash with people. The bartenders were busy and hassled. The sound system was screaming loud with berserk music as the people spazed out on the dance floor. The cigarette smoke ended Eric's conversation with the bartender upstairs. As he moved down to the first floor, drink in hand, pushing past the squealing girls and poser dudes he wondered to himself, "can you go out every night and still have fun?" As he shook his head in disbelief of the frenzied crowd his reflection stood staring back at him in a wall full of mirrors. The vain loved this. Most people stood around that area all night, sneaking peaks and body primping. His reflection was clear but nothing else was.

"I can't believe how relaxed I am," thought Eric to himself. He was no longer looking at himself or wondering. His imagination drifted from a clear vision of himself to the blurred surroundings. Suddenly his eyes livened up and he was scanning the dance floor for his ex-wife. "The only reason I come to this place is to keep her from enjoying herself," he allowed this glimpse into baseness. She deserved it. She totally stripped him of his personality and strength. The things that she most loved about him. He was starting to drown in self pity. Sort of like having a concussion. Once her own insecurities had reduced him to a dribbling idiot, she split. "She knows she can't come in here on Thursday night." Like his old self he had been drinking from the big cup of life and he had eventually made the Lauderdale strip his own. He was not defined by what he did for money although legitimate. He worked with his hands. All the fabulous people of the media generation kept a long line outside. All the clones were there. It was on television. So Eric, being a lover of clones, was there too choking on cigarettes and bad perfume. He knew his ex-wife was one of those people who had to be there and that was why he had loved her. But now, well if he could break her stones at her own game then so be it. A healthy relationship it wasn't.

His ex was no wimp but her instability beat the loving kindness out of him until his soul was like a dishrag hung against the counter. She was no idiot. That's why she didn't go. She would see him and she did not want that. She had changed him into something hideous and not himself. She insisted on the change and then wondered what happened to her man. He gave in to make her happy but what he truly was about rumbled beneath the surface. He gave in all the way until he was gone. Then once totally unattractive to her he became himself once again. He was on his way back but he still had some attitudes to regain. She on the other hand never realized that what she wanted would change what she liked and cast it to the wind. She could live without the club on Thursdays and she could think of a lot of excuses not to go. She was always good at that. He beat her to the punch at her own game and for that she was furious. He was still alive and was doing his own thing. She could not stop that. Yes she made light of it to the friends she had but she still was avoiding him and not liking it. Eric was reemerging. Inevitably his former self was there waiting for the charade to end. His true self buried, it weld up inside him like a steam locomotive getting under way. Once up over the hill and through the tunnel, going over the bridge was easy. The wheels rolled faster and the rails seemed greased. One would think that his ex-wife would charge in one Thursday night and command the show like she always did. Eric was waiting for that confrontation at this very moment but his needs were not going to be satisfied that way. She knew all to well that, like it or not, it was a no win situation. Fat chance she was going into his winner circle. "Hey," he yelled to the bartender, "did you see the fight last night?"

"Yeah, Perez got his brains knocked out!" The bartenders eyes lit up. He was glad for any unpretenscious behavior. The bartender waited on Eric immediately. Eric smiled and said thanks. It was a simple reply and yet it held all the connotations one could read into it. It became one of those words that jumped out by itself and stood there all alone. It spoke of lost loves and cherished dreams. It kind of permeated the air not mistaken for weakness. It sprang forth blowing the trumpet of civilization realized. It belted out a song all loved who dared to sing. The crispness in which it reassured and applauded was magnificent. It was a wonderful word. Just plain old "thanks." The length of the word and the way it sounded pushed forward beckoning silence. Only the equally humble and magnificent, "your welcome," could possibly come after it. Mostly it was greeted with silence and a smile that said thank you for thanking me. The barkeep nodded and the people around them only strayed from their thoughts a moment. The "thanks" kept on thanking even after the roar of the crowd resumed. On a vast dessert island a hemisphere away a fisherman said thank you toward the setting sun. The sun thanked the blue sky and the blue sky said thank you to the clouds as they rolled by. The ocean said thank you to the breeze as it tickled its surface in the gentle gusts of a summer's daze. Far into the night the wind rustled a tree and thanked it for nature's symphony. The brook babbled back a hello. The lonely said thank you to the enormity of it all. They sat silent in the dark staring at the night sky drenched with depth and starry mystery. The stars sparkled back and plunged a few fallen thanks, thanking the people that count them. The waves crashed the beach in a never ending melody saying thank you to all that stop, look and listen. The dune grass bristled, "your welcome." The ocean said thanks to the moon's reflection and the moon said thank you to the soothsayers. The constellations said thank you to Leonardo and Galileo and the Earth said thank you to the rain.

"Wow, is it still raining outside," Wendy wondered to herself? Wendy was another one of those tanned people at "Club South." The latest and greatest club on the strip where all the beautiful people hang together, nosh, schmooze and circulate, darling. She was not having much luck keeping her identity to herself. She was getting work in television, soaps' and soap commercials. Life was treating her well but with her new recognition she had to try harder to stay in touch with herself. The self from before her image was created. People didn't realize she wasn't type cast but that she was doing something called acting. A lost art form for some of todays stars. She was becoming paranoid about who she was and who she was becoming. There she was though hanging out with all the beautiful people. In the midst of more of the same. There were plenty of heavyweights around, fat cats and money bags. As she moved her way around the bar she bumped into someone else she knew. "Wendy how have you been?" Wendy looked up and faked excitement sort of like her orgasms with her husband. "Wendy dear you look so well."

"You look the same," she unflinchingly replied. She had learned to become a bitch. The only one she couldn't convince was herself.

RUM AND PINEAPPLE

—

The splashing rain was kicking half-a-foot back off the street. The hard concrete gave no relief to the endless falling rain. The street life vanished. The cool cats went running for cover. The rain continued its slow rift through the atmosphere. The night grew darker. Out on the beach five wanderers drifted by, four together and one alone, so all alone. Their dark silhouettes shrunk against the sea and the dunes rose above them. Peering from on top of one of the dunes was a great vantage point. Those sand dunes that in the morning soak up so much laughter and flesh, can at night be a great vantage point for the lonely, lust and crime. Yes crime that smelly business of totally ridiculous human behavior all wrong and not seeing the light of day. Another old couple jumped, another beating, it's all wrong. No matter how big and bad, there is always someone trying to take you down. Why would anyone want to play that game? The rain was sifting into the sand. The storm hadn't cleared the beach yet but it was headed that way. Bare feet were caressing the soft cool sand. Two young couples walked. One young girl's blouse was partially unbuttoned as she whispered to a young man. Her friends blond hair picked up with the wind. The other boy was carrying his shoes. His eyes were all red as he was ready to crash. A young girl giggled at him. The rain pushed itself up the street. The darkness increased. The night got thicker. As the rain quickened everyone picked up a step. They picked up a step at the dance club and even across the river at the Jaded Lady. "At least there is this warm wind," spoke Jessica as she leaned closer to Adam.

The approacher was approaching. The young couples were together and euphoric. Their spirits were full with satisfaction and their selves were flying.

What could be more perfect on a warm summer night? The waves were laying perfectly onto the sand. The wind brushed against shorts and flapping shirts. The rain soaked warmly through them. The talk was quiet, the rain no bother and their bodies tanned from active lives. Slash, a blade crashes into the evening sounds. Its hiss audible and pronounced. Blood flows as Adam falls to the sand. Screaming in pain he gets a smashing kick as he falls back. Sand in his face, sand in his mouth, blood on his hand, hand on his stomach. "I ain't fucking around I want your money and shut up," he cursed at Adam. "I didn't cut you that deep," he snarled. "I want your money," he began again looking at all three left standing, "or I'll cut his balls off!" They reached into their pockets as the ocean rumbled on. It remembered the old days when lovers could walk the beach at night.

When they had given up their money and their stash, the little thief was delighted. He grinned a toothless grin and moved closer to the three standing. "Quite a haul I got here," he leered, motioning his knife waist high out in front of him. He waved the knife back and forth slowly under their eyes as they watched the rain bounce off the blade. He moved his face in closer smiling and not afraid to be seen. He laughed out loud. It was a short quirky laugh as the darkness rose within him. "You hang out with some rich dudes girls. For that I'm gonna fuck one of ya!" Jessica lost her breath and the other girl began to sweat. "Fuck you," blurted Jessica.

"Shut up," he swung his blade around. Foreplay. "The one with the big mouth got the biggest tits, huh?" The blade opened Jessica's blouse and cut her bra open in one swift motion. He brought a little blood. He stiffened over her youth. "Anybody moves I'll kill her!" Jessica's eyes widened. A roaring silent pause then the thoughts started running rampant and out of control. They weren't that far down the beach. The heart of town was about a mile. "Adam . . ., it'll be over soon . . ., I don't want to die . . .,God don't let him kill me . . ., I don't want to die . . ., it feels like fucking . . ., I don't want to feel that . . ., it feels like fucking . . ., I don't want to feel that . . ., knife in my neck . . ., don't move . . ., don't breath . . ., I don't want to feel that . . . !" The little man's ass was jerking around side to side. He really felt nothing. Cursed with a small prick he was too embarrassed to let anyone touch it. But his adrenaline was still pumping. His heart beat too fast he worried about getting caught. It was just like jerking off but with someone else's body. He kept looking over his shoulder. A lot of sand got in the way. Tears ran down Jessica's face. The others stood petrified. The little mans blade was in Jessica's neck. He went until he came. Not really that long at all. "This is the best night I've had in a long time," he said while standing grinning pulling his pants back up. They all just let Jessica curl up in a ball. "Yeah I bet," seethed Adam now sitting leaning to one side on his am. The little man kicked his arm out from under him and Adam fell back to the sand. "I'll kill you," he shouted two inches from Adam's face. He got the message.

Jessica was too young for this although she had just done it minutes before. They were horrified and the rain no longer was romantic. It pelted them and was now coldly evil. Soaking they stood there and waited for the little man to strike again. Life always screws itself up. Who knows why? At one point things are fine, even fantastic. Then quick with no warning things are changed forever. Love can be that way. Life just reaches out and gives a subtle nudge and shifts the whole thing around. You just get everything all set up and wham someone or something has changed the game. So you adjust and move to a new town and drift on through. Might be a west Texas ballroom, then poof your floundering with the Mississippi River kicking your butt. Come on life, stand still just for a second! Stop it for a moment so it can all seep in and once it all stops, we'll all pray it starts up again. And if it didn't start up again, what horror. Frozen in time. In the most powerful way possible, man would yearn for his old revolving ways. No borders would separate man's universal anguish. Some would stop and spin in their own circle, like the game we used to play as children.

"You don't wear a lot of make up do you, hon?" Wendy was smiling politely at another phoney. It was becoming obvious that her little bit of fame might be more trouble than it was worth. "Transparent bitch," she thought to herself. "Just like the negatives she's filmed on." Now a tall man, not bad looking, with the hands of a carpenter, was standing in front of Wendy. He spoke, "I bet she sleeps with that eye make up on!" Wendy smiled at that. She had not smiled all night. Eric flashed his smile. It was the same one his mother flashed to get his dad. It worked for him too but only when he was not thinking about it. "There are some people here I want to avoid," said Wendy shaking her head.

"I know the feeling," he answered matter of factly.

"Why do my absolutely worst convictions about people seem to always come true?"

"They think and do get away with it," lamented Eric continuing her thought. They unconsciously made their way to a table by the front door and sat down. Two people came in as two went out. The club was crowded with wannabes. They absentmindedly listened to the chatter and squeals coming from outside the club. The line to come in went around the block. The rain came down on them and told them how ridiculous they were. Their flashy clothes were soaked. Eric was delighted by all that and said, "hey I'm cool. I'm inside," he mocked himself to himself and afforded himself a little smile in return. Eric looked into Wendy's eyes as the street life jumped in and out of her consciousness. The pace quickened at the club. The people were like starlings going from tree to tree. Doors swung open, drinks spilled, and girls squealed hello to one another. The light jumped in and out of the doorway. It scattered like on the sea when the clouds are moving quickly. Wendy could not shake herself from the trance she was falling into. "It's crowded in here," spoke Eric. The silence between them grew but the commotion outside prevailed. Wondering about nothing and everything at the same time Wendy traveled further into the realms of her own mind. She always liked that aspect of thinking. She slipped down the slopes of consciousness and down deep in the caverns of her mind. She peered into the dark vastness of the rippled walls, "why must we be so?" She was floating down the Congo of thought now effortlessly. "I don't know, look at it this way," she told herself and her mind exploded in doubt. "What is going on? Why have I sought the camera? Why is everyone so impressed with a screwed up actress? I need a corner to crawl into. Who is this guy? No kidding it's crowded."

While Wendy was ridding down the river of doubt she just blankly stared at Eric. He was trying to deal. It had occurred to him that Wendy was lost in the crowd roving behind him. But he some how strangely knew what she was thinking. A shiver ran like a wild boar up and down his spine. "I guess they spend a lot on clothes," Eric tossed out this large life preserver of a thought. It was one of those open-ended comments that begged for a response. Harsh or agreeable the life saving purpose did not care. It just had to bring back the victim alive. "They want to be famous," Wendy responded quite frankly. The life preserver had reached its victim. Another pause, a broken glass and the rain rushed up the street. Eric spoke, "they just want to show others they have some worth. They're living in response to the others, constantly worried about what others may think, and just confused." Wendy was furiously trying to swim upstream against Eric's burst of thought. She turned and began making her point. She was not so tired or lost that she could not sugar coat it. "That might be mostly true," she answered, "but don't forget that not everyone is the same. There are a fine number of talented and dynamic people who are just acting natural. The ones quietly in the corner suffering their own hell are just dying for release. They might give a shit about what other people think of them, but look, damn you, lighten up. These folks don't want to intimidate they just want to have fun and some even hope others do to." There was another pause in the darkness of the moment. Eric was beginning to feel persecuted. He got up and pushed himself away from the table. Wendy was really just talking to herself. Anyway, Eric was just trying to stir the pot. He left her with one final thought, "yep," he said and began to walk away, "you gotta be happy where you are."

"Get me a rum and pineapple, will you please," asked Wendy. That empty space in time in the moment that had hung so heavy changed on a dime once again. It hung light now. Eric smiled and went to the bar. He didn't allow his usual head shake till he got around the corner. Hell had disappeared if only for the moment and so did the trip down the Congo. Heavy gray matter realigned itself and the deep caverns of the jungle inside turned to the vastness of outside. Wendy basked in a glow at eleven at night. Eric came back with the rum and pineapple and Wendy said, "lets get the hell out of here." The trouble with choices is that they keep coming. Eric looked on and started to laugh a real belly laugh, "where has that been," he wondered to himself? As the two new cohorts went out the door they did not know what to expect. The first people they came upon were not phony but merely grungy. They handed their drinks to them. They noticed the rain was falling hard. Once outside a car zipped by and sprayed water on them. Their own laughter drowned out the laughter from the car and those around them. They looked at each other and disappeared into the night, towards the beach. Their hearts knew the way even if their heads didn't.

THE CULPRIT

—

It happened to be one of those nights. The kind that reach way down and the lights shut off. On this particular night the sky was so drenched with clouds that no one could possibly see. The stars that were usually out in force were hidden beneath a blanket so thick it felt like you were scuba diving in mud. Occasionally, one lone warrior of a planet would penetrate this quilt of darkness. It echoed on in solitude and loneliness like the single solitary bark of a dog echoing in the northern mountains of Colorado. It was not so much of a bark but a beacon showing how vast the universe was. And the beacon with all the power it could gather was so quiet, so alone, so silent. Standing, nodding in agreement, was the lone listener. A moment accentuated for all time. The silence continued it's deafening roar. And the beacon shone on. The silence never broken, the music stopped, the attention beyond complete, the silence of a quiet universe. Geese fly south with no honking, just the movement of their bodies and their wings through the air. A sort of gentle ruffle of feathers mixing with the breeze can be heard. The darkness of the night covered every opening in the doors, every opening in the windows and every opening in your soul. The darkness poured like syrup through time and space like sweet incense. It wandered on still air. It reached around every source of light and the ocean rolled on. All alone a block away you could hear it crash. The ocean was unforgiving, never pausing, never judging, sometimes raging, sometimes calm. Adam's blood was dripping on the sand.

"Leave us alone!" He shot Jessica a glance, "shut up bitch, shut the fuck up!" The bitterness and the anger stretched past his throat and out his mouth. Jessica's own inner voice was raging at top decibels.

Only her mind kept her under control. Every other part of her body was tearing him limb from limb as she sat there mouth clenched shut. The sky has fallen in upon you and you want to, have to, battle against it but you can't because you know the difference between now and tomorrow. She released the culprit from her view and fixed her gaze on the only star that shined as the storm took hold of the beach. More violence, more carnage, we waste this gift of life. Like spoiled brats at Christmas we never realize the love behind the gift. "My lord," Adam thought to himself, "I'm bleeding to death!" The culprit had moved off now first slowly then turning and running.

Jessica sat up, her two hands behind her. She sat like that this morning watching Adam surf. But there was no sun now. The night had become cold and dark. The sand wet with blood. Crows off in the distance heckled the ground-ridden animals. Romance paused, love cemented. The light vanished from Adam's eyes. The sun was gone and the light from the moon was stolen. The wind and rain kicked up and it seemed the middle of the Earth had just gotten a little smaller. Caught in the moment, Jessica jumped up. She was barely cut, her pride destroyed. She dusted her ego back into place for the moment and blocked the thought of aids. Her head darted back and forth. She wanted to move quickly. She grabbed her friend's Coke bottle still dangling from a shocked hand and shook it furiously. In one movement she shoved it between her legs and blasted out her insides. She spat three times. She looked up at Adam. "I sure hope I killed everything." Her voice trailed off but her words hung heavy. Jessica was like that though. She always just tried to shrug it off. She was undaunted by mosquito-laden beach head. Jessica had the resolve. She had the world at her feet. But now she and her friends were doormats for scum. The world had a funny way of turning on a dime like that. The dark moon looked on. The gulls were silent. Jessica's friends left standing were stunned by the whole picture. They had been shamed into silence and stupidity. But Jessica was forced to process the information faster. She was the victim. She reached out for Adam's arm. The jerk off was miles down the beach by now. The culprit's heart was beating, his head was pounding. He was rushing headlong into a confrontation with himself. Reality would seep through his delusion soon enough. His sleep would be only from a stupor. The evil from this event would be chased from his mind only if supplanted by another more horrible and fantastic event. How would he top tonight? His blood was too hot to care.

Adam stood up with the help of Jessica. Several pounds of Columbian were in the trunk of his car. Jessica being raped and himself being stabbed well they would just have to live with that. No stand offs, no heroics, no cops, just a thinking man pissed by how much he had to loose and how much his hesitation cost him. They had to revel in their score or they could have gotten to business right away. He chose to have some fun before the business was settled or the servant of death would have missed them. Instead there was an eerie chill and the dark cold sea. "I knew this was a bad idea," said Adam to no one as he stumbled back down to his knees. His friends gathered him up. "Don't die," they thought in unison.

"I'm not going to die," seethed Adam as he was being helped back up. "Let's just go." But the reaper was front and center now with his hands on his hips and tapping his toes. "Jesus don't close your eyes," begged Jessica as Adam slouched harder on their arms. In those brief fleeting seconds Adam shut down like a nuclear reactor, completely in a panic and in a frenzy. Quick, everyone get out, oops, too late. The little souls have melted. In the brief and futile time between death and what is Adam knew he would not last forever. "So make the best of it now."

They found their way back to the car and climbed into a nineteen sixty nine four door Thunderbird with suicide doors. The trunk was filled with pot. But they wished it wasn't. Adam was no longer in the mood to celebrate. The front head lamps flipped open and up and the Thunderbird hauled off into the streets. Tires bearing down, windows up laying low Adam's eyes were open. "Nasty wound in the back seat here," rang Jessica's voice. The radio stayed off. "What are we going to do now," pleaded their friends in the front and driving?

"Where can we take him with a trunk full of Columbian," they asked?

"I've been trying to think of that all along," spoke Jessica from the back seat. "He can't wait. There's no time to get rid of this stuff," she hurriedly continued. She looked down at Adam, "don't close your eyes!" She flipped her head back to the front, "he has to be attended to now, damn it!" Her voice was shrill and filled with desperate anger. Adam was wavering. Wandering his body floated. "Well where can we go," he asked to himself. No one could hear him. The view from the rear view mirror was still. The Thunderbird pulled quickly to a stop.

EVENING, THE
START OF
THE DAY

—

The scene was all together and complete. Nothing looked out of the ordinary from the street. The tinted windows locked out the outside world but on this night the passengers knew better. Their world was far too shattered to hide behind windows. Ben stopped at the stop light and searched his memory. It frantically raced through what had been and what was to be. What was going on was so completely in his face he could not believe it. He thought of bars that the bikers used to hang out in. He thought of some famous seaside dives filled with friendly lushes. "Eighteen and I've covered too much ground already," the voice inside his head rang. The car continued west. Out of the city was the only place to go. Hospitals would ask too many questions. Perhaps they might find some roadside doctor they could barge in on. Forcing themselves on some law abiding citizen would be a fine capper to the evening. "Doubtful," was the thought ringing out this time. Adam bled on the back seat. Jessica panicked silently. Stress and blood pressure were having a great time together.

Theatrics was one thing, a vivid imagination another, both fine on their own and even better together. But unless you experience life, you never feel it or see it. So go on, go to it, get caught up in as much as possible, but watch the hidden blows. However unfortunate it might be you can never get too comfortable. Life has an intriguing way of nudging you along. "I know a place we can go," said Ben. Shaking off the paranoid stupidity from the beach he hit on an idea. But paranoia only stepped aside for a second. His voice began to waver. Doubt already crept back in, "it's clear across town, but I'm not sure exactly how to get there."

"I don't know how long he'll hold out," Jessica's quick answer made a statement not a question. Jessica looked down at Adam and back up at Ben. "Shit don't ask me. I'm doing all I can right now to hold the blood!" Ben felt incredibly set up and was running down potential whys and whos. Jessica was wondering about alternatives. She bravely put herself into a position to get what she thought she wanted, only to run back to what she knew. Her instinct grabbed onto what she could control and the safety of what was known. Never mind the bore and the predictability. She somehow could put up with that. Better to go round and round with the same old thing than to step out onto the edge and into the life. The new life, the changing life, the always moving life, where it was so damn hard to try and hold onto something for any length of time. Where you could almost feel the Earth spinning, but miss your soul's desire. Not just the desire's they advertised or she was taught, but the ones that fit like a glove. In spite of all reasoning and rational expectations, her life might be something else. Why was her calling so hard to believe? Why even though it overflowed with fullfillness did she opt for the mundane? There was a dream that excited her. It ran through her veins with the force of an undamned river. She had the dream that was forbidden by those with no dreams. The big dream that reveals too much of yourself to yourself but makes you feel the most vital. In the end you become the storm surge. These dreams were so beyond the mundane that we held them in check. That's what they told us. That's what they said every day. That's where they were wrong. Clear your head and move to your real center. Follow your heart, you know yourself.

Adam was wondering where everyone had vanished to while he was having such a good time. Jessica spoke in an awe struck hush of a voice, "better hurry, he looks pretty spaced out to me," a voice that was laced with resignation. Adam's mind floated in thought, "even if they weren't all here it was just as good as if they were. If they weren't why was I?" It was indeed one of those crazy nights. The stillness of life reached its zenith. The breath that comes out was cold and thick. The light that was seen is so subtle and accurate at first. Sharp and clear, near but far, always present running through you but a ways to go to get there. They would have all laughed if they had been there together but it does get cold. You notice that if you are not all the way there yet. Then again they may have all cried. Somehow it waits for you and your journeys are not in vain. As one waits in time unable to focus in on the blurred boundaries, the quest continues on another realm and the cold disappears. It just keeps going on and on, life and death, a part of the same journey. The poles may shift and the sea may turn brown. You may get older if you're lucky, and somehow the soul stays together. Life as it is, a heartbeat away from the whole thing. Essential all tied together, the here and now with the there and after. Just being nearly a heartbeat away, music gets us a half step closer. Who can fathom how much ignorance we have accepted in our lives as a whole and individually. Life's episodes take off over the road and love is too hard to understand unless it is outside of one's self. In only the short while that it takes in this gold mine and land mine of life if you get love, if you get being human, don't worry about getting anything else. See the thread of unseen reality as it runs through everything as love. The vibration of the empty space between you and everything else is love and the only thing to do with hate is hate it. Love never looses is never lost. It's just in between realization and reality. Breath deep and one catches the pause needed. Don't be afraid to ask "why" because that is the only question worthy of asking. Unanswerable to keep us going. Inscrutable to keep us from ignoring. Forever, time is forgiveness and love always present.

There it was that night, right there in front of Adam, and the lights were on or out as the case may be. The silence lifted the night and the coldness appeared just as it had gone. Once more it seemed like old times with everyone laughing and the porch shaking. The light of some nights is so incredibly rare that the Druids marked the evening as the start of the day. Their moments so vivid still ripple in our consciousness. Curse those times when we don't see it, or be it, or feel it. The crow calls out in exclamation. No sunglasses needed here and your neurons sparkle and fire in your brain. The light of the soul has begun its exit from the body. Leaving its physical trail of furiously excited life, light and love and all the things you shouldn't have done. Adam was looking for the way out and the way in, and all at the same time. No more or less focused than bees in the summer sun. The light was now blinding Adam. One final distraction before the separation. Soon the realization that there is no more distraction and the confrontation of his actions, his every word will be apparent. The motives he hid from himself will be known. All that was him shall be and he will know why. Distractions blown away scattered action and thought merge into a togetherness of seeing through feeling. Here the distractions keep us away from the World and worst of all ourselves. They prolong the mundane and leave the wrong unrighted. They obscure the feeling and dwell on the fear. It was blinding Adam now. He was waking up. A world of distraction shed. Immediate reality front and center, but where was he?

TWO HIPPIES

—

"Hey lets ask those people over there." "What," Jessica's hair caught fire? Ben, in an absolute move of pure stupidity pulled the car over to the curb. Wendy and Eric were on the sidewalk having a mildly intense discussion on the plasticity of life. "Life in and of itself is amazingly clear," Eric was saying, "but when one adds in human consciousness to this soup called reality," he paused and looked over at Wendy, "well you tend to get all kinds of different interpretations."

"And everyone tries to hoist their own beliefs on you. They want you to break down and accept their dogma so that it validates their own beliefs no matter how whackado they are," said Wendy.

"And if its religion they are even more fanatical on enforcing their beliefs, sometimes violently on each other despite the fact that most religions preach tolerance and acceptance of all," spoke Eric.

"What's most frustrating to me is the exclusion of other world views that may have very beautiful, careful and ancient points of view," added Wendy.

"In the name of personal gain they're willing to transgress the very meaning of the religion they hold dear and wage war, spilling blood, on others who see it from a different point of view like people who are passive or just disagree. It doesn't have to be a religion. It can be a culture or an alleged way to act, or an alleged way to sound. When they come upon someone who is only different in sometimes the most superficial ways, like looks or hairstyle, or clothes, someone who truly is free enough to think on their own or from another culture, well it scares the hell out of them and causes them to bring their whole belief system into question. It's patently absurd but I'm beginning to think the more they shout about their convictions the less sure they are of them, deep down inside where it counts. In the place where you have to put thought into action and words into deeds."

"So the more unsure they are, the more violent they get towards those with another point of view," spoke Wendy. "And the more power hungry they are the louder they clang their belief bells if they think it will gain them even the slightest edge."

"So much for helping your fellow man. Let's just annihilate them if they think different," lamented Eric.

"People who are doing them absolutely no harm at all." Wendy agreed.

"People think they have all the answers and the keys to this story called life," extended Eric. "But the only rule worth knowing is the golden rule, 'do unto others as you would have them do unto you.' That's the only rule you need. The rest of it is detail, and the devil's in the details." Wendy loved meeting love a new and so did Eric. It's a time of rediscovering yourself by discovering another thoughtfully and with passion. Thank God we are not all the same. "This life is not designed for us to know the answers. It is a question of questions. It is our life long test and journey to deal with the unanswerable, the quiet source and either live up to our utopian potential or mire down in the quagmire of mistrust, jealousy, greed, hatred and hopelessness. Earth is where heaven and hell meet in the physical plane. What we do with that, what we choose, becomes our individual realities no matter the trappings of material gain, no matter who we live next to," spoke Wendy.

"They are fighting, trying to prove who came first like they made the sun. And their way has to be the only way because they are the chosen ones or the most persecuted or whatever malarkey they have been telling themselves for the past several generations. The smart ones look at everything, ancient and current, and study everything creating their very own philosophies based on their experience and life. No one should be telling anyone what to think," finished Eric. As Wendy was agreeing a nineteen sixty nine four door Thunderbird rolled sheepishly up to the curb. A window came down, part of the way. "Pssssst, hey do you two hippies know how to get to the Jaded Lady?" Wendy and Eric were the only two people on the street. It had been a long time since Eric was called a hippie. Wendy just laughed. They were sort of dressed the same in hipped out subtlety with the coats they wore. They were headed toward the beach but the rain had Wendy and Eric trapped under an awning getting to know each other. First looking left then right then at Wendy who shot back raised eyebrows Eric spoke, "I know where it is." The darkness of the turmoil in the Thunderbird seeped through the night air and infected the night around them. Eric picked up on a bad vibe. This one was strong and the despair was palpable. The conversation and the deed were merging assembling a terrible force of it's own. Good and evil were kicking up sand and it would be trouble tonight. Like a twister bearing down on tornado alley, destruction was sure to follow a very distinctive path.

Ben's words held back the panic but his heartbeat gave him away. Can't fool nature. "Any help we can get we certainly appreciate," spoke Ben. Eric started to give rather involved directions. He noticed Ben kept looking over his shoulder into the back seat. Muffled conversation was drifting out into the night air punctuated by raised voices of a discernable clamor. "Look you have to listen dude," spoke Eric impatiently.

"I am, I am" spoke Ben but his eyes showed he was real lost and loosing it. Desperately he blurted, "could you just get us there, we'll follow you?"

"My car is five blocks away," spoke Eric alarmed!

"We'll give you a ride," pleaded Ben. Jessica gasped out loud her eyes opened wide, "are you crazy," and then in a lower voice, "there is fucking blood all over," but Ben cut her off. "It seems that one of our friends here has met with some trouble," he didn't even try to hide it with the choice of another word. Just then the rain started back up again pelting the windshield of the Thunderbird and pooling off the awning like the Arkansas River. Eric felt a twinge and started to back away. His "don't get involved" voice like an Aerosmith sound check was at a piercing loud holler. That voice had been vanquished in the sixties, raised artificially in the eighties, and festered into an epidemic in the nineties. It was still going strong at the beginning of the century and it dragged down the weak and the faithless. It was an ever increasingly intense struggle of conformity, acceptance and fear. "Well Wendy," asked Eric stalling for time, "how about it?" Wendy had caught the curiosity bug. Later she would regret it immensely. "They need our help." With all this righteous talk Eric thought it was time to put up. He wasn't beyond sizing up Ben as Ben had already done before pulling over. "We'll give you a ride to your car," said Ben again, his smile sincere but broken. Jessica was flipping out frantically in the back seat. She didn't have a chance to really scream at Ben. She had grabbed Adam, not the wheel, and it was going around and around faster and faster. Adam was going south and it looked like he was dragging everyone with him. Eric felt the intensity and caught on completely once he stuck his head inside the car. A bunch of teenagers looking scared and not too threatening. He looked back at Wendy who was ready for a joy ride. Eric was immediately scrambling to cover up. But Wendy had the back door open already and her eyes met Jessica's. Eye's locked. Adam was obviously messed up. Wendy made the split second decision. It was like she was looking at her little sister and brother. Life sometimes has more to offer on the whim. But, "oh my god," she exclaimed and looked back at Eric who had opened the front door and was peering in the back seat with Wendy. She returned Eric's stare. "Are you serious? The Jaded Lady? This kid needs a hospital." They jumped in. If they had thought about it another minute discussed it or if the passengers hadn't looked so young and lost they wouldn't have. Eric was too stunned to not follow through. He was following Wendy. She was already barking directions to the closest hospital. Ben was arguing with Eric as they pulled away. "Just get us to your car. You don't want to ride with us!" It was too late. Headlong into disaster, they made their choices and they were in the deep end quick. Eric turned to Ben and said, "he doesn't look too good!"

In the back seat Jessica's mind was racing and furious, "how could Ben be so stupid?" Eric peered into the back. He could smell death and feel the cool spirit of the soul evaporating with the blood. Ben was just like some school boy chum acting without thinking, praying something right might happen, and taking terrible chances. Eric didn't feel that way. He turned to Wendy one last time. She had not missed the dread he was trying to communicate. No one spoke for a second. The silence was deafening. Adam groaned a low long groan from the back seat. Jessica brushed back his hair. "Lets just take off. Forget my car," spoke Eric. "It's clear you guys don't want the cops." The car sped away into the night. Hell or high water their party night was over.

The old car rattled on and Eric was barking out rights and lefts. Ben had only a vague idea where they were going. Jessica was not enjoying this twist of life. It was some real shit for a change but a lot too real. Eric was past being nervous. His instinct told him he was stupid. But he was pulling the older brother role out one more time for these guys. Ignorance was not a defense and Eric wasn't ignorant. He knew he was their only resource at the time. Lucky to have found him, hippie indeed, he jumped in with both feet. But what amazed him is while he hesitated Wendy came to the girl's rescue first. He couldn't imagine anyone of her actor wannabe status doing anything other than blowing the Thunderbird off. He knew he was a do-good-er. That phrase was a negative etched into his head by a so called friend. "Any excuse to visit the Jaded Lady," he would later say to Wendy. Even if he was aiding and abetting a criminal. Eric imagined he would have been one of the monks that hid Martin Luther after Luther pissed off the Catholic Church. Rules, rules, rules. Your rules, my rules, lets kill each other over man made rules.

"Watch your speed," hissed Jessica.

"He'll die if we don't hurry!"

"Yeah and Johnny Law will be right behind us if you don't cool it."

"She's right," barked Eric as if he had known her all his life. The car slowed down. A light switched to green and the rain let up. Jessica was desperately trying to stop Adam's bleeding. "I knew something would go wrong tonight," she spoke out loud to everyone and no one in particular. "Something goes wrong every night," said Wendy. The situation was beginning to sink in. It wasn't as if Wendy had been free of her scars either. This night, whether she was aware of it or not, she was breaking free of the chains that grounded her to her television image. That was not who she was anyway. And it wasn't anything that she had set out to do. Maybe the break away was stewing in the back of her mind but normally she wouldn't jeopardize a thing. "You care about this little sister and you don't even know her," she locked stares with Jessica. "This is who you are," came the calm voice from within. Eric noticed her silence. When given a chance to break free it can happen all at once. In a flash but that doesn't mean you don't have to work at it, nurture it like a tiny spark just getting the fire started. Ignore it and it goes out. Who were these two mysterious strangers willing to help out? So familiar as to be known, but an infinity of unanswered questions. They might never know their ordinary lives, just the explosion of chance and change in decision. When the hand of the moment presents you with choice, the clock always seems to be ticking faster. It defines who you are. Taking a chance had been alright for Ben and Adam. No big deal. Take a break from the routine and score some contraband. Their girlfriends had faith in them, plus a piece of the action so no big deal. The money was handled and the veil of peaceful, naive, suburbia screened their identities. It created a safe and preposterous harbor to hide in. Where did all that money come from on the intercostal highway?

There was very little traffic on the road to the Jaded Lady and that was a good thing. They were jumping at every set of headlights that came near. Eric had successfully guided them off the city streets. They were now going down a two lane highway with only an occasional street light for guidance. Nature was all around them. On either side, the farmland rolled on unhindered by strip mall suburbia. Fences rolled into lawns that rolled into trees that rolled into groves and rolled into the night sky. It was dark with a dense black sky of moonlit clouds. The high beams of the Thunderbird were blazing down the road. The car rolled along with no apparent urgency. Why should it marvel at human consciousness? All human consciousness could accomplish was an internal combustion engine that needed more care than a two year old child. So big deal man had created the nuclear bomb and could now annihilate himself. That's progress? He had achieved conformity, brainwashing and cultural grayout. The revolution will never come. We are all too busy watching television. We're having enough trouble keeping our tiny environment right and getting along with our neighbors. Revolution, utopia, please. Violence and hatred, stupidity, intolerance and greed are in abundant supply. The whole damn thing will blow up while we're counting the loot. It always does. But life's pretty nimble. More than just a whisper of the larger scheme is laid out before us in absurd obviousness. Still tears fall all around like star dust as humanity helps destroy dreams and build nightmares. "Utopia is possible," hollers the Milky Way slapping its hand on its forehead. But if mankind thinks he is it the ultimate, the boss, the creator of all things; if he thinks he is in charge and the beasts are here to serve him; if mankind doesn't realize he is merely the custodian of this planet; and if he fails to seize this opportunity to prove his worth, to prove he can manage his resources and himself, then he will be humbled and never get past diddling with himself on the outskirts of the universe. Yes utopia is possible but not without evolution. An evolution of mankind from his shortsighted greed, power, lust, death march. So what the hell Eric and Wendy got in the car and were headed off into the distance. "There it is," Ben shouted recognizing the bridge. The Thunderbird pulled up to the light just before the bridge. The river went on by and under the bridge. The bridge went over the river. The Thunderbird idled at the light. Adam rocked back and forth between pain and consciousness. Jessica wondered to herself what they were going to do and how would they take care of Adam?

"They have a doctor on staff."

"What?" she said, startled from her thoughts. Could Eric have known?

"They have a staff doctor." Eric insisted.

"Yep," said Ben half under his breath. He had his head bashed in there not that long ago. "This place is a great old club," spoke Eric. "The last hold out from prohibition all the way through the fifties. You know the fifties black leather jackets, fat cars and where I got my name." Wendy laughed out loud. "And then in the sixties and early seventies, before all of our idealism got too stoned and went out for something to eat, that good attitude flourished here in the face of that war that got both Kennedy's killed. The Jaded Lady is a grand old place and still off the map and off the charts," finished Eric.

"I heard a great band there last time," said Ben turning to Eric.

"Can we make small talk later," wailed Jessica from the back seat. As the Thunderbird moved forward, she squeezed an ever colder Adam, whose eyes had just opened. "Adam," she whispered in his ear. Crossing the bridge from the country road, they passed through a busy intersection. The avenue revealed was crowded with tourists restaurants and cheap tee-shirt places. A few craft stores run by a few hippy holdouts lined the alleys. The Purple Flamingo was still there along with Sound Explosion Records and Tapes now selling CD's. Adam was white, the pale color of nausea, in the back seat. Jessica had stuffed Adam's tee shirt into his wound to stop the blood. The shirt was soaked and the back seat was wearing some of it. The situation, although always apparent to Jessica, was now hitting it's zenith. Ben wanted out and he felt and was acting like he was near escape. The car made its turn into an unpaved lot. It was going to stop soon and Ben could run and blame it all on Adam if he had too. He could still play the "little boy" role to his mom and force a few tears.

They sat in silence and were tossed about as the car slowly made its way through the rutted lot. Almost hitting his head, Eric said, "pull around to the back." Ben followed his order. Eric knew he could take care of Adam if he could just separate him from the car and get him away from the scene of the crime. It surely was a crime that so much had gone wrong so far this night. "Pull right up to the side of the building. You'll see a huge garage door."

"Can we just take him in," asked Jessica?

"No," said Eric dryly, "you all have to wait right here until I go in alone. Stay in the car and kill the lights and engine."

"Well I'm picking a dark spot," said Ben, a little self preserving mistrust coming from his voice. "He's going in alone," Jessica thought to herself. Eric looked right at her. "Trust me," he said. He had felt the flash of tension from the back seat.

"Nobody trusts anyone anymore," said Jessica.

"We got here didn't we," said Eric? And with that he was out of the car before anymore protests could be made. Jessica's mouth was wide open and her palms were beginning to sweat. What had she gotten herself into? But Ben was fine. He had his plan and it would only be moments until he could dump Adam with a doctor and see him next week at the Point catching waves. Adam could have the pot. All Ben wanted was a shower. He maneuvered the Thunderbird into a pitch dark spot and felt good about Eric's reminiscing of old times. "He'll be right back," said Ben confidently as he peered into the back seat. Just far enough away was all Ben wanted and a good spot to run too. Hopefully it wouldn't be a real hard spot to come back from, when it was time to face his friends. Jessica didn't trust anything at this point, including Ben. She wanted Adam well and she wanted him well now. The Thunderbird had trusted it had come to a halt. Eric was walking in a side entrance where there was a small light in an accompanying window. Two silhouettes stood as a third stood up. Ben had his eye on the window. "Anything could happen at anytime," he thought to himself. Although he still trusted Eric, more people were getting involved. He'd hang in until the last moment possible. With several pounds of marijuana in the trunk there was no telling when that might be. The mood was desperate and crazy in that car. Jessica felt it all over her.

She put her back to what happened to her tonight but now sitting still in the car she couldn't get away. The mood was at her throat, overcoming her, and in her hair. Relentlessly it pursued until complete and utter violence consumed her body and withered her spirit away. Her life in an instant had become violent with assaults. No matter what type of magnificent struggle she put up, it would always be there. Her spirit, like a dropped glass, shattered beneath the violence. Jessica had never felt this way before but she fought it off for now. With the rain pelting down again, the garage door swung slowly open. Eric headed back to the car, head down, hands in pockets, quickened steps.

Just then Sam's phone rang. He pushed down line one. "The office, I wonder what's up?" No one hears him say this although he wonders out loud. "Yeah," the voice on the other end spoke up, "Sam?"

"Yeah, what's up?"

"See if you can't find Lefty the Doc and send him down here." The urgency in the voice was masked but Sam knew it was rare that they asked for Lefty. "Okay." Sam hung up the phone. Lefty lived up on the third floor. There was no phone up there but the rent was dirt cheap.

Lefty was a first year intern at the hospital back in town on Atlantic Avenue. The crew in the Thunderbird might have met him at the hospital earlier if only they didn't have thousands of dollars worth of dope in the trunk. Sam headed upstairs. He threw his bar towel over his shoulder and walked by Danny and the band as they were swinging into the Ella Fitzgerald version of "I'm in the Mood for Love." There was a great groove going and the crowd was beginning to howl. It wasn't that late. Sam hustled up the front stairs. Lefty was sound asleep. Sam was knocking increasingly louder on the door, "come on Doc you're needed down stairs." It wasn't bad enough he had to work all day and night at the hospital but he also had to patch up drunken fools that fight in bars. Doc scrambled to his feet and he and Sam were headed down the long staircase and over the dance floor where the band was still playing. Instead of turning down the hall, Doc and Sam went around behind the stage and out a back stage door. The door swung open onto a fire escape. The steel had long since rusted. Lefty was thinking of tetanus shots. "Downstairs," questioned Doc?

"Yeah," Sam said. "I hate getting involved in these things," he continued to himself. When they hit the back lot, they quickly spun into another door and through the back office. "Sorry to wake you," spoke Eric. "They were able to get the bleeding stopped."

The air was thick with the unknown and anticipation mixed with fear. The three of them went through yet another door leading out of the office into an empty warehouse. Save for the Thunderbird there wasn't a thing in this abandoned area. Except for a few hanging lights there was an old car, Ben, his girl, Wendy, Jessica, and Adam. Adam was laid out on a table. The kind you might find in your mom's basement. It was sturdy and useful. Great for the kids table at Thanksgiving but hardly nice enough to bring upstairs. Ben was thinking of his Mom's house swearing he would never leave and pacing nervously. The garage door was shut. He wanted to pose as a lookout and slip away. But he was locked in this warehouse with yet more faces seeing him. He was pacing in wide circles.

Doc immediately went to a nearby closet and got an emergency bag. It was kept around for the occasional glass in foot like the one upstairs used for Danny. The warehouse wasn't active anymore. It had been a place where touring bands tuned up before heading out. But the town went with the cheap tee shirts and booted the bigger road acts out. Gotta have a variance for that kind of noise fellahs. Except for the occasional New Years Eve party, the warehouse was just empty. All it had now were walkins loaded with booze and food. It may not have been exactly like the old days. But the Lady could still crank out some good times. Sam always thought that the land the Jaded Lady was on had to be magical. If it wasn't at first well then the past one hundred years had left a mark. In all its incarnations as night club, cat house, VFW post, bed and breakfast, speak easy, rock club, and yes, even disco for a few months, there had to be an energy created that drew people to the old place. It was sacred ground as far as Sam was concerned and he often thought it might be on ancient Native American burial grounds. He desperately wanted to keep it from being consumed by condominiums and townhouses or whatever the trend of the day was according to the fools who clawed their way into power.

Lately it had been the religious fanatics trying to impose their will and power grab on all of us. Like the explorers who first came to this country, Sam and his friends were fleeing religious persecution by the busload. They just wanted the freedom to live and let live, existing in this reality, seeing with their own eyes and experiencing their own take on creation. All they wanted, like the explorers of old, was to be left alone and interpret for themselves what a big green meadow on a small blue planet might mean. Their fathers from the sixteen hundreds came to this continent, and based on their experience, built into a new country the separation of church and state. No one could impose their will and rule on them over something that is personal and up for interpretation. The real meaning of freedom includes religious freedom to worship without harm as one sees fit. What is religion anyway but a personal journey. It's not a lobby group. But the delusional and power hungry only two hundred years later were at it again. They were trying to erode that hard fought for separation. Even though the examples are all around us today, reminding us of the horror of state sponsored religion and how it splinters and destroys society. It pits brother against brother in the alleged holy land. What's so holy about a century old war zone?

People died to come here and be safe in their own beliefs. Now out on the horizon the big power hungry dictatorships want to take the right of your own opinion away from you. They want to take away your right to journey down your own road. They want to march us all in lock step even figuring out the correct percentage of your tithes. Why are they buying weapons and spreading hate with religious contributions?

Most big religions have always been that way. My way or the highway. That attitude doesn't have one thread of religious foundation in it at all. That attitude flies in the face of tolerance and acceptance that all the wisest of men and women have preached. Some of the most noble religions like the Quakers with their belief of a little bit of God in everyone, and the Native Americans who saw God in everything, coexisted peacefully for years. It wasn't until the juggernaut of a government started to inflict it's moral standards on the Native Amricans that they diminished to a flicker of their enormous selves.

History is full of examples of religions violently imposing their control over peaceful indigenous populations. Populations that were flourishing and surviving in harmony within their environment and within their humanness were replaced with an out of tune, violent, war waging, fanatical world that is still struggling to maintain it's very own civilized veneer. Because of ferverent opposing religious convictions that are at odds with each other's details of dogma we are tearing at each others throats. Only a fight to the death will satisfy the lust of annihilating an enemy. Ah the enlightenment of religion with an army.

Jesus told his disciples not to fight. Separation of church and state is the only formula to defuse that eventuality. From freshly learned, bitter experience it was placed in order to create a better world. Certainly the powers that created us want to see what we can achieve. To see if we have the faith and creativity to achieve it. To see if we have the creativity to believe in a world without cultural black out in which we are all free to be. Maybe because of this doctrine we will get there. Without it, oppression is automatic along with it's rebellion. Separation of church and state is a big key to peaceful coexistence. A big key to utopia. There are no more continents to which to flee and damn little land left to divide. Sam always knew the last stand of freedom was right here where he and the others who felt like him were standing. He would always keep the Jaded Lady running even if it killed him.

Adam was finished being stitched up at this point. A local was all that was needed. Eric, Ben and Sam were talking. "Thanks Sam, we had nowhere to go."

"You have Eric to thank for that Ben we're old friends."

"I haven't done anything like this in a long time," said Eric.

"You mean help out someone you don't know," said Ben.

Sam answered, "you never know who you are talking to." They all nodded in agreement. "Whatever happened to all that trust and brotherhood," asked Ben?

"They ruined a wonderful thing by not believing in it," said Jessica.

"But it's a good thing," said Sam speaking to Eric. "Trust needs to be earned, then it's understood as noble in giving. But to never let anyone measure up to that . . ."

"I don't want to have this conversation again," interrupted Eric.

"How about the one about marriage then instead," asked Sam? He raised his eyebrows reminding Eric of all that spewing, retching blather that he was forced to listen to until Eric got hold of himself. Eric put his head down remembering the months that had passed by as he bared his soul to Sam. "I'm so sorry for that," said Eric raising his head in laughter at himself. However beyond the laugh was another refrain. If one was patient enough and trained in the ancient art of listening and if you tried very, very hard, through the vents and through the walls, Danny's voice was reaching for the rafters of truth. He was singing with passion and spontaneity. "That's what I like about those guys," thought Sam to himself, "they put everything into it."

There was a full silence in the garage as the band echoed through the walls. The band had found a theme or maybe rather the theme found the band and they were hitting it harder and harder each time. It toyed with them, and them with it. The melody rambled and rolled along like a drunken sailor up a steep street. Lefty came over and told them what he told Jessica. Adam needed bed rest and watch for a fever. Sam offered them spare rooms for now. "You folks want to follow them?" asked Sam to Jessica, Ben and his girlfriend.

Ben's girlfriend hadn't said a word since the attack and started to shake her head. Ben was halfway out of the door when he tossed Jessica the keys. "I'm outta here man." His girl friend turned back to Jessica and spoke the first words since the attack, "I'll call you," and with that they were gone.

"Later," said Jessica sarcastically to an empty space and leaned over and picked up the keys. Now she had the blood stained Thunderbird, the bleeding boyfriend, and the pot. When did she get to be upset about being raped? Outside Ben dialed for a cab. The paper trail unwittingly started. "What's the deal," questioned Sam? Jessica slowly eased her way back to the Thunderbird and flung open the trunk. "Whoa," said Eric, his mouth wide open. "This isn't your ordinary lumbo," stated Jessica. Sam reached into the trunk and fondled the booty. The trunk was packed with the tumultuous herb green. The aroma was so sweet that your parents would want to smoke some. It smelled that good! "I've been waiting for this same stuff all night," said Sam matter of factly but still startled.

"Small world," remarked Eric to no one in particular.

"No seriously I sent three vans out around eight o'clock to hook this up at the harbor. I haven't heard back all night and it's getting kind of late. Just a shade of concern crossed his brow as he shut the trunk. Obviously it had made it to the docks but where were his guys? Then he walked over to where Adam was resting. Adam was trying to sit up. He sensed a proposition walking toward him. He had seen this walk before. Sam knelt down in front of Adam and spoke, "did this come in tonight?" Adam nodded back, "just south of the Wharf."

"That's where my trucks were headed."

"We got it around nine o'clock," spoke Jessica.

"It's likely the same damn contact," spoke Sam hurriedly.

"Or one helluva coincidence," came back Eric.

"They ran it ashore in a thirteen foot Boston Whaler," returned Jessica.

"From the cargo ship," questioned Sam?

"It was all pre-arranged," spoke Adam, "they wanted to lighten the load.

"Or get some street value for themselves," said Jessica knowing the situation.

"That sounds about right," guessed Adam. Standing around Sam was Jessica, Eric and Wendy. The Doc was putting his bag back. "That stuff is worth a fortune," said Sam.

"I know," answered Adam.

"We put up some bucks," added Jessica, hands on her hips.

"I'll give you what you paid for it," offered Sam.

"Hell no," reeled Adam, "I stand to triple that."

"Selling nickel bags," questioned Sam to his younger counterpart? The Doc stepped into the conversation, "cool it guys, you'll rip my stitches out. He needs some rest and so do I." The Doc walked off but waited for Sam's okay. "Okay," said Sam with a wave of his hand. "Sorry kid, I've been waiting on this for a month," he spoke and put his hand on Adam's shoulder. Adam's body could not have been anymore tense so he relaxed and remembered how weak he felt. Jessica came over beside him and took his hand. She got between him and Sam and spoke, "we can't go home, not with that wound and all." Sam had suspected they still lived at home that's why he offered them the room. Adam got up from the table and Sam grabbed him. He now had a vested interest in Adam's well being. Sam instructed only his trusted staff to clean up the car. Two Spanish speaking locals cleaned the car with their heads down. They didn't want to see anything or know anything as the others left the room. The only sign of a disturbance that night was a hunched over Adam and a dimly lit Thunderbird getting cleaned. Sam led them up the back fire escape.

Doc looked around the warehouse one last time as if to see if anyone was following. He had an instinct for survival and did not want to be seen with the others. The night so far had been a mixture of rain and heat. The few stars that had managed to appear twinkled a starry hello and then went on back to their business. The front that was moving through casted brooding moods for those on the fire escape. Doc lagged behind.

The band was winding down it's next to last set. Danny, Mark and John were the only ones left on the stage as the lighting went back

down. Five, with Doc following, stretched out from behind the stage
and moved around the edge of a hushed crowd. They were locked
into the music and only the most perceptive perceived all that was
going on around them. They were tranced into the music emanating
from the stage. The low lights and the soft beat had a once wild and
jazzed crowd now sitting down on their rumps. The individual tables
with their candles burning and lights flickering were accenting the
consciousness of those so focused. It was subtle and beautiful and
seeped into awareness slowly like all great beauty. No one noticed
Sam holding Adam or that the others had moved on by. Almost
everyone except for Danny. He knew something was up. Was this one
of the drivers Sam was talking about? Who were those kids? Losing his
concentration Danny fumbled some licks but made a nice recovery
and bowed out of the set gracefully.

Once the lights came back up a bit the band made it's way off
stage. Danny made his way over to the bar and waited for Sam. Doc
made his way around front and headed up the front stairs. He was
slightly more conspicuous than the others. It's always been a matter of
timing either all good or all bad but never in between for the good
doctor. The others were already upstairs and Sam was showing them
to private rooms. Adam had only sleep on his mind. Sam shut the
door, assuring him to rest easy. Jessica slid the car keys under his
pillow case and finally got to a shower. Sam had given her a room with
a private bath. She wept in the shower and now started to think about
what had happened. She washed with the vigor of revenge. Wendy
and Eric declined Sam's offer to stay but said they would be back early
in the morning. Eric felt responsible. The wind and the rain started
to drive down again and the windows of Adam and Jessica's rooms
rattled in response. The band still had one set to go but neither
Adam or Jessica felt much like dancing. Sleep would take a great deal
of effort in each case.

Sam was pondering his situation. Waiting was the cruelest fate of
all. He certainly did not want to leave just yet. However, he knew there
would come the moment that he had to go. He knew he could delay
the inevitable no longer. The forces that compelled him would be too
strong to deny. The war he waged on deep inside his soul, his

convictions versus his fears, slammed against his desires and his needs. All of it swirled together like a hurricane. It swept the idle into motion and delivered them unto themselves. Finally his hand would be forced. There was no resistance. There was no cause, just his own torment that was so like everyone else's. Only he was given the chance to see the eye up front and close. Where could he go? He agonized over the eventual outcomes. Either everything was all right or it was all wrong. He packed a small leather bag.

Downstairs, Danny eventually got around to finishing his beer. Things were in a real comfort zone for him. The band had been gaining a following lately and everyone was real pleased with everyone else's playing. The concentration and the commitment to each other and the music were strong. A real family was being born and Danny could feel it in his bones. However he knew something was up with Sam. They were all waiting for the same thing. "Trouble," he asked as he clunked his mug down?

"It's nothing," Sam paused, "not yet anyway."

"The vans aren't back yet," Danny guessed?

"No one is panicking just yet," Sam whispered as he leaned closer to Danny. Sam was full of shit. He was praying for the end of the night so he could close up. Every now and then you are brought down to Earth. They had an unreal thing going at the Jaded Lady. She was a fine club with a good tourist reputation and a fine local concern. The behind the scenes activity had a home where it bothered no one. Since it wasn't violent, it thrived. "Who are the kids?"

"Danny I can't go into that now," he said impatiently. Danny had never seen Sam like this but he kept looking at him. Sam gave in, "search me," he said with a shrug.

"That's just what they'll do if this thing goes wrong," Danny said sharply.

"Okay, you got a little money in this thing you might as well know."

"Sheesh, like pulling teeth," Danny thought to himself. Sam shot him a glance like he knew what he was thinking. Sam leaned in closer again after the customary look around. "We know the boat came up the coast fully loaded and that they may have had more than one unscheduled stop."

"As far as we're concerned," Danny interrupted.

". . . But after that, anything could have happened," Sam continued.

"What?"

"There could be some real trouble."

"They should have been back by now," claimed Danny, "no call or anything?"

"Nothing," answered Sam solemnly. "Not a hint," he continued, "and if the police come here like they usually do we'll have something more to hide this time." He paused for a moment and waited cheerfully on a customer exchanging the usual laughs.

"I don't want this pressure," he said to Danny as he walked back to him. "The last time they were here looking for any tree to bark up they kicked my ass. I was held up for three days with their bullshit. They kept coming back and leaning on me and when I laughed at them they got pissed. And they'll be all over me again like last time."

"I was hoping to get that tonight," Danny said absentmindedly.

"You may get it after all. The thing is not to panic just yet."

"I could still catch hell. I put up dollars here and if there's trouble who knows what would come out."

"It depends on what the police want to hear," said Sam. "If they have them," reminded Danny. "If they have them they can say or do just what they damn well please." No argument was made there. It was time for the last set. However it would have it by plan, coincidence, torrential down pour or choice that the crowd had really thinned out. Fortunately or unfortunately the heat and the contraband could come in through the door at any time. Danny gave the word to Doug and Mark and they began to strike the stage. Sam was in the front foyer pacing. No one had called and that wasn't right. At least the cab had finally come for Eric and Wendy, splitting the fare across town. Eventually Sam started to lock up. He had a car with a trunk load of the most expensive grass to hit the coast in ages. He had three vans out on the street and who knows what had happened to them. He had no word or no clue as to what had gone down if anything and a bunch of innocent kids lying around like it was a war zone. The kids he cared about. That made Sam a dinosaur.

Louise was drunk. As Sam tried to hurry her out the door John hollered, "she's with me."

"First no stash and now no girl," Danny thought to himself. As he dispassionately hung at the corner of the bar. His back to Sam, elbow on the brass rail, the lamp behind him warmed his neck. "Danny," hollered Sam back, waking him from his self imposed mood. Sam crossed the floor. Before he could get a word out Danny spoke, "I owe you a set I guess."

"Forget about it," and he paid him for the week.

"You wont be here tomorrow?"

"It's anybody's guess."

"Depends on the who and the why."

"That's right. They might close us down. We have a slight edge on them because of Eric stumbling onto those kids. But I expect a knock on our door sometime soon."

"That's if the cops got them," stated Danny.

"That's if anybody got 'em," said Sam.

"Maybe they are just out getting fucked up?"

"Doubt it Danny," said Sam sharply. "I feel trouble," he added. "I have to take care of a few things." When Sam returned he had more money for Danny. He counted out the bills and smiled. It was one of those "nice to know you" smiles. "Now put that truck in the rear and load up. You may have to get out fast." Danny was nodding and heading back to the stage. He had already warned Mark and Doug to load up the truck. So with the rain still coming down, they were backing into the loading dock. They were getting ready for more equipment. Danny had to tell them. He was speaking to Bonnie, Mark and Doug. "What's up boss," asked Doug, "we're making a quick get away?"

"Go back to the band house and get your stuff ready. There might not be any sleep tonight. Check back in with me later but don't get caught milling around here."

"Huh, what now," asked Bonnie? She was getting ready to drop attitude fast. Danny ignored her. It was his best option when it came to dealing with her off the stage. "If you see the cops, just get going to New Orleans. If we get held up here you'll know. If we miss each other go on without me and hope I show up at the next gig in one piece. John and I are staying here tonight."

"What have you gotten us into Danny," Bonnie accused.

"Never mind all the details. I don't have time for that now. Bonnie please trust me. We've got to get going!" With that Bonnie, Mark and Doug wrapped up and slipped off into the recurring storm.

Louise was fast asleep upstairs but back in the bar Sam was speaking. The Jaded Lady was empty. "They probably know we're stewing and missing our vans and all but I'm not showing my hand. Tomorrow we open as usual for breakfast and the crew will be let in to clean."

"Good thing those trucks are falsely registered," said Pancho back from cleaning the Thunderbird. "Yeah but those guys could be in big trouble. I'm not going to go down with out a fight."

"Don't you mean flight?"

"I'll leave here high and dry if I have no choice. I'm not taking the fall. There are too many other people involved. They want big dogs, not us mules."

"Since you're big you run eh?" challenged Pancho. "Hell if I was big I wouldn't have to run," countered Sam with distinction. Sad truth ran down the walls through the bar. The problem was real and Sam and Pancho locked up. Except for the one lamp on Sam's bar the Jaded Lady was dark. Danny and John had made their way inside and John had gone to bed. Louise snored unmercifully in his face. As usual she had no idea of the doom that waited around the corner for her. She was lost in a snarled dream in which she was naked and everyone else was in a suit. They were waiving credit cards at her. Did John hear a laugh? In her next dream sequence she was floating effortlessly through a haze of disco madness and hillbilly rockers. Downstairs Danny stayed up with Sam. Pancho had driven home. "The trucks are registered to someone else?"

"Well yeah." Sam went on to say, "Pancho and I have an arrangement. I don't know if he's their guy to watch me or what, but since I'm above board there is nothing to watch . . . . we just run the club together now . . . that's all."

"Oh."

"They have some phony insurance company set up but when the detectives figure that out, they'll be looking for you know who."

"How do you think they'll trace it all back to you?"

"We've had a long history Danny, ten to fifteen years of harassment. They know who to look for."

"Guilty of having too much fun?"

"I guess you could say that. We've broken some very definite laws though."

"Like noise?"

" . . . and hours, crowds, experiments that went on for days. That warehouse in the back used to shake, rattle and roll. When the reggae bands were happening . . . well you tell those guys they can't smoke their ganja." They both laughed, but the silence that followed was deafening. Danny tried to get the conversation back.

"Still how could they trace the vans to you?"

"They'll beat it out of them. Someone will crack under pressure or they'll trace it down cross referencing some database. The silence poured back into the conversation and the rain was still coming down. "I don't know exactly, but the cops will make up some bullshit to scare the shit out of somebody." Danny frowned and showed Sam that he had gotten the idea. "What they did tonight, meeting that boat and all well they must have been pretty nervous as it is."

"That's no small fish they went after," suggested Danny.

"Right, no question that payload is worth a ton." Just at that moment the bar lamp dimmed as there must have been a power surge from the utility company. A lonely black rotary dial phone sat underneath the lamp with its hands on its hips waiting to ring. You could see the dust settle on the receiver. Pitch darkness surrounded our friends and Danny drummed his fingers on the table. The rain was again pelting the glass on the front doors. It beaded up and fogged over the front glass. Sam lowered the air conditioning. He had his eyes peeled for headlights coming and needed to see through that glass. There still was a chance that the vans could pull up but it was looking bleaker by the moment. Somewhere in the distance a clock struck three and Danny rubbed his eyes. "I'll tell you one thing" spoke Sam, "I don't know where I'm going but my bags are packed."

"I'm headed to the Crescent City," Danny said. He was still slightly psyched about the next venue. "There's room with us." Now Danny and Sam had worked together for two months. The band had a standing gig in New Orleans waiting for them to come in and play back up for some legends. But Sam, although he liked Danny, did not know him well enough to just throw in with him. However, the hatchet was hanging over both their heads. To Sam the offer did not seem so far out of place.

Upstairs the mood was no less sullen but much more violent. Jessica was flip flopping like a fish on a dock. The covers were all torn up and she was forcing her eyes closed. "Shit I've been raped." Her internal dialogue was reeling, "Aids," it screamed!

"If it hadn't have been for that stupid pot we could have gone after that bastard." A deep breath stopped her rage.

"Okay, cool it. Your lucky. Adam was almost murdered."

"Lucky shit," rang a voice from within, "he was only stabbed."

"Raped and laughed at," she fought her ego.

"Herpes," screamed another voice as she tried to come to terms with the situation. She seethed, "that fucking bastard," she cried out loud, throwing herself to the bed and banging her fist on the mattress. "Ahhrghh," she clenched her teeth and spun her head. Her eyes were wide and filled with the hatred of an innocent wronged. With venom like boiled lead, she spat into the air. The flying mass of germs and disease rolled and tumbled through the air until it met the wall by the door. She heard it splat. The darkened rain soaked night was no match for her and paled against her unshared anguish. As lightning slashed the sky she screamed into a pillow with the fury of wild mustangs. "Goddamn it, goddamn it all!" The thought of pregnancy crept from behind the wall of death. "I'll have that fucking kid and cut its balls off. I'll torture the shit out of the little piece of crap," she screamed out loud!

Adam in the other room was having a much different time of it. He was asleep. However his dance partner was immediate, and it dangled ever close to the him. In Adam's sleep there was this rushing feeling. He felt as though his innards had permanently vanished into thin air. He had this amazingly hollow feeling as if his skeletal frame were transparent. His feet felt like they were where his head was and his head was where his feet should have been. "Holy Christ," is what his voice said to himself. His hands folded on his stomach right below his rib cage felt as if they were completely inverted. They were inside out and upside down. His left hand responded only when he tried to move his right hand. He had this light airy feeling that manifested itself and the longer he felt it the stronger it got. His bones reeled and felt as if they were all alone without flesh in the bed. The covers were not heavy as he liked them and his wound was completely numb even though the local had worn off an hour ago.

Then, suddenly there was no desperation in his soul, but a strange fluttering in his belly. He was so light that it seemed he had no physical substance. Something was creating a drag as he went rushing through an atmosphere. His innards were way behind as though attached to some sort of coiled rope or tether. He rocketed through mysterious atmospheres and vapors and finally felt like he was floating down a staircase.

He started to recognize something. To his amazement he was in his home outside his parents first floor bedroom. He floated effortlessly in the hallway. He floated in balance but in hesitation. "Lets go in," the thought just popped into his being," and show mom and dad the new trick I've learned." He pushed through their swinging doors, although his feet did not touch the ground. As he floated in, the light of his mother's reading lamp appeared. She was sitting up in bed reading. "This isn't a dream," screamed an interior voice, "get out, get out now or you'll blow their minds! Do you want them to have a heart attack?" In agreement with himself Adam floated back out of the room. His paranoia fueled his energy as he picked up momentum. It was like being sucked through a giant tunnel. He heard this strange ruffling noise as if someone held a book to his ear and pealed back the pages. A thumb let the pages fly. His airy self went rushing back up the stairs he had floated down. He traveled at an ever increasing speed in conjunction with the pages that flew by his ear. After a momentary pause, his innards caught up with him. His head now felt the pillow again. But the body oscillated once more and he had the strange inverted feeling all over again and twice as intense.

Now a fog cleared and he found himself in a vacant lot. Everything was silver and gray, and a mist was obscuring what lay ahead. Something compelled him to move onward and he did. This time he could feel his feet. They slipped over the empty lot. He was drawn by some force pushing him from bellow and from behind. Suddenly before him, a huge metal stairway presented itself to him. Like the fire escape on any old building, but larger wider and with no end in sight. Very metallic silver and clean, the mist obscured the top from view. He knew he had to get to the top and he started to climb. He still had that strange airy feeling but he felt each of his footsteps against the stairway. He climbed for what seemed like years and his point of view kept drifting from outside observer to a full chorus assembled just behind his own eyes. The whole scene of mist and fog, gray and silver stairs, presented a dreaded feeling of oppressive force that was more than he was willing to contend with. But he knew he had to keep going. He wanted to see what was at the top.

His outside observer saw a very small and lonely figure trying to make his way through an unseen and uncharted climb. The stairs themselves constantly turned like a car on a winding road. Unseen turns surprised and horrified him. Each time he barely missed the turns and now was so far up that the wrong turn would be fatal. If he fell he would fall forever, and he knew that as surely as he knew his name. If he ever did hit the lot below, he would splatter into infinity with his molecules scattered, never to come back together again. Truly this was the ultimate destruction of the self. The sweat was beading up on his brow as he became more cautious. Each step was now measured by the inch and it seemed the staircase was swaying in the wind. Like a ribbon on a breeze, it started to sway wildly in a ripping and rolling fashion. More and more turns would arise and he blindly searched with his foot for the next stair step that sometimes wasn't there. The railing he hung onto he hung onto for life. The railing was cold and gray, dark and wet from the mist that had turned into a forbidding fog. The fog mixed in with his breath and filled his lungs with pneumonia. It was thick as cotton to see through and only revealed snatches of a view. He had no idea where the staircase was leading or where he was going on the mysterious swaying staircase. He could barely see past his own arms. But every now and then the wet fog would clear and he could see he was up and out very high.

Suddenly there appeared a door on a square building but only for an instant and way off in the distance. The vision seared through his eyes and burned on his brain. It appeared far then close and then it was gone. His sweaty palms gripped the rail ever harder as he knew his salvation was in the flux. He hung on for his life. But was this life? Was this anything like life at all? Or was it beyond life. Why was it so very real and so fantastically intense?

This was no dream. There was no spirit lying in bed with his body. That body and that bed were left way behind. All his awareness from all that was him was focused on his hands as they gripped the railing. He stayed focused on his hands not wanting to loose their grip. It felt like he was being tossed about on the bow of a ship in rough waters on an unforgiving sea in the raging North Atlantic. And then suddenly still, his line of sight became clear. When he could see, he knew his destination was at the top. He knew that cold, lonely door was clamped shut tight and that it was his destination and his destiny to pry it open and see inside. It would take all his strength. But the staircase was draining all his strength. When the fog would roll back in after his fleeting glimpses were over, he was forced to put his head down and search blindly for the next step. The journey got harder and tougher as he neared the top. Each step was a life and death struggle as he held on to that rail with all his might. The fog, rain and wind combined was doing its slippery best to shake him from the stairs, blowing him off through time and space on a never ending trip. As the wind howled and the forces overwhelmed, he prayed like a bastard, "oh please lord I've got to get there," and his feet would stretch and search in every direction and it seemed like days until he found the next step.

As he struggled to keep his grip, he became totally physical again. There was absolutely no notion of a dream or a dream like state. His full concentration was needed or his soul was damned to slip and fall and start the climb all over again. In his universe there was only his destination and his struggle to get there. He was totally soaked in fatigue sweat and fog. His shirt hung heavy with water. His hair was cold and wet, completely slicked back. Yet the fierce wind still blew it about. The moisture of the rain and fog were mixed in his eyes with sweat and the salt stung. Like a blind man he stumbled and swayed. The rail was so wet the danger was that he could have slipped and slid all the way back down to the beginning, only to have to start all over again. It seemed as if that was just what the wind and the rain wanted him to do. His searching foot dangled in the vastness looking desperately for the next step and it was an eternity between each one. He never knew how he kept finding them except for the fact that he could never give up trying. Once he considered staying put and just holding on, but he was so close to the top he knew he had to keep going. Somehow he knew that if he had to start all over again the very fist step would be as hard as the last. He had to continue. He prayed to the God of all things, of all thoughts, of all possibilities, of all creation and theories and lives. He prayed to the God of all breath and the God of all struggle and the God of all hope. He prayed to the God of everything imaginable and unseen, all the while searching desperately for the next step. "I can't stay here and I can't go back. I will go on," he bellowed, "no matter what the wind and the rain throw my way!" And the struggle for the next step continued.

Suddenly, just as the moment of realization hit he was there. At the top of the stairs. He was on a very narrow platform. "Don't look down," were the words that screamed through his being. They were vibrating in his soul with such resounding force that it brought him to his knees. Then a loud boom crashed all around his head twice. Just as he noticed the flash and what seemed like lightning, he had moved effortlessly to the door. In an instant all the weather had stopped and everything was still. All that could be heard, and all that would be heard, in that stillness after the mightiest of uproars were the dew drops falling. A lone floodlight could be seen adjacent to his left on the roof fastened slightly behind the wall and the door he was facing. The building was a cold gray cube on the outside. Somehow he could see inside while still standing outside. It was a square room, brick building, steel girders. He was now inside. But still not through the door. The daunting imprint of facing the door to open it was still with him. Now, forever, and it seemed that way but only for a moment, and it seemed that way too. He pondered how to get in. He must get in.

What else was there to do? And then as if triggered by the mere release of the force and conviction of his thought, he was in. Blink, just like that. Once resolved, he was all at once resolved. Fully realized and now inside, the door was shut behind him. Floodlights were shinning everywhere. One from each corner. The room was brilliant awash in light. There was a source in the center that bathed everything in a brilliant white light. It was contained and centered and perfectly round like the sun. It floated above the floor and hung the same distance from the ceiling. It did not obscure the other lights of the four corners but rather was the same. It was a part of all the light that was shown in the room. It was brilliant but not blinding. Like a waterfall all the sources of light were coming from the same source. As if they had found their way into the cube somehow from without but from within all at the same time. And like a reminder from the life struggle before, a whisper of a slight fog surrounded him.

The ceiling was high and the girders visible in this completely square room. He stood there drenched, drained, exhausted but secure. "Why such an epic struggle for this security," he wondered? "Fear, was fear a good thing as a driving force?" He was all alone now more than ever in his whole entire life. Where was everybody? He wasn't afraid. He was just glad he had made the climb. It was amazingly clear inside compared to the dark, murky outside. It looked brand new inside but he knew it was from the dawn of time. An eternity had passed in what seemed like moments and he just stood there in one spot, turning round and round. He looked in every corner and at all the walls. He especially gazed into the four floodlights, each one for an equal length of time. And he remembered the one on the outside. It had stood like some sentry guarding a fort. Even in the thickest fog that spot shined a light sometimes focused, sometimes diffused and scattered. At all times the vision was clear, even when he couldn't see. And then he saw it.

Bathed in light and sparkling like the most wonderful, tasteful image imaginable, lights everywhere with all the colors of the rainbow surrounded and filled one corner with presents and a tree. A magnificent tree, alive and filled with colorful lights with snow upon the branches and the ground. Enormous and with presents wrapped

in beautiful boxes of all shapes and sizes, and all with colorful paper
and bows and name tags. Name tags for every being that ever was. And
he knew they were all for him and for all of everyone else at the same
time. A never ending cornucopia of dreams and wishes for the asking.
They were waiting to be opened by those who found the room. Each
present a dream fulfilled so completely as to not need open but one.
Yet your other dreams were also there and it was also fine to open
them, even desired by the love that had put the presents of dreams
there. All at once or slowly one at a time the presents opened by just
thinking about them. Each present came to Adam and overwhelmed
him with its complete fulfillment of his innermost dreams and wishes.
Each opening bathed the room in happiness and joy. He realized all
at once that it was okay to have more than one dream, one wish and
that they were all there for him, each as satisfying as the one before
and none greater than the first, second or last.

Danny had long since gone to bed. He was involved but had no
fear. Maybe he was ignorant but then again he could do nothing.
Sam's head lay underneath the lamp on the bar. He was asleep but no
dream for him tonight. This was a quick rest. He was on the alert and
thought he would have to run come sun up. Sam had been through a
lot in his life and was no stranger to being on the run. Back upstairs
Jessica had forced herself to sleep. A shallow uncomfortable sleep.
The rain splashed against her window. The electrical part of the front
had passed. Dawn was just around the corner. The planet was right on
cue. No impending doom could hold up its journey. The sun shinned
continuously on the Earth. A new dawn each day, each moment, each
year was forever in our time.

Jessica found herself suddenly awake yet she had not recalled
falling asleep. Though she tried to get up it was as if she was chained
to the bed. An understandable feeling if you are a woman. One thing
for sure, this was not the same room she was in when she had laid
down. There was no large white wall like the one she was starring at.
Realizing this she turned her head away in fear from the unfamiliar
and looming wall. Yet she still seemed motionless, "this is not where
I am," she thought to herself. But the wall blew open and appeared a
window like a bright summer morning a gust of wind, a slight gentle

breeze came through as the windows opened out and sheer, white curtains danced on the breeze. The fresh air rung the wind chimes that hung from the window frame and the flowers from the window box grew outward towards the meadow and the full green rolling hills. Blue sky and sparse white clouds filled the horizon as far as the eye could see. The wind chimes played a harmony of sounds briefly. A bell choir of chimes and tones followed the light burst of a breeze and turned her head back around. Again she looked back at a wall, "shit the damn thing wont go away," her sight shifted with her thoughts as her body lay still. Try as she might she could not move. The large white wall was on top of her like some speeding Mack Truck closing in. But it shimmered and hung in the balance of that ferocity.

Springing out from nowhere, and to her demise, there were three men standing over her. Her heart ran a little faster. They were the most evil and oppressive men she had ever seen. One had a patch over his eye, another had a scared face, and the one in the middle wearing a dark coat had a gun. She could not move. She was paralyzed with fear, frozen and entrapped. She was already immobile. She did not need the added fear. It was as if she was tied down or sealed shut. The turmoil increased as her thoughts turned back to the white wall. Now where there wasn't one before hung the window again. And it flew open outward one more time. A beautiful meadow laid before her with monarch butterflies, bluejays and all of mother nature present. To move through that window and that opening was the key but she could not get free from the bed. The three men waved the gun back and forth. Suddenly she was behind a night table in the opposite corner of the bedroom. She was blown farther away from the meadow. The barrel of the gun loomed large inches from her face. She pleaded for them not to shoot. The fat one with the gun pulled the trigger. The gun exploded but she was not dead, only embarrassed and ashamed. "That chamber wasn't filled," she hollered although no one in the Jaded Lady heard her cry out. The three villains laughed and bent over to peer at her closer, their breath on her face. She cowered beneath the night table. In a rush of anxiety and adrenaline she lunged out at her tormentors. The fear of the gun and the burn of a bullet were so great that it forced her to her feet breaking her chains. She pushed the fat one in the middle in his stomach and swiped the gun but returned behind the table and cowered just a moment longer. "Well at least you've got the gun," her tormenters laughed sarcastically invincible and unharmed. However Jessica realized that she had regained her mobility. She looked at the gun again but in an instant sprang through the window of the white wall. In the next moment she was free, clear and clean. Only in the meadow for a moment all things in her life and her self were clear. With enlightened determination she struggled awake and returned to the plain wooden walls of her room. Instead of wandering over the horizon of the meadow never to return, she lay silent in her room and felt her body breathing. The air went deeply into her lungs. She took full, deep breaths instead of the typical unconscious, shallow breathing we usually do. Slowly she turned around. Now she felt her body and the bed covers. The men were not there to be seen but the mood of their oppression was. The night table was there, although she could not recall noticing it before. As she lay still, quiet and calm the moment passed. She wondered if that was the end.

The horizon was getting light now and the birds were stirring. Jessica was wondering if she had gotten any sleep or not. She was exhausted. In the next room, Adam was in a pool of sweat. His sheets were drenched and he was pissed that he was back in his room alone and cold. The beautiful feeling of fulfillment and realized self gone. The horrible, glorious struggle and the heavenly wonderment had been replaced by the mundane and the return to three dimensional consciousness. Even though his present circumstance on terra firma was anything but ordinary, he was still just a man on a planet.

ESCAPE FROM
OBLIVION

—

The morning brought back a sense of balance and calm. It all seemed quite ordinary and yet we know that our existence is out of the ordinary. The sun rose that morning like one of the Greek gods was splashing paint on a canvas. The sun's rising flare sparked in a hue of red and orange. There was no low moody horizon to obscure this morning. Sam still had his head on the bar asleep. The one bar lamp was still lit. The morning light was streaming in through all the shutters. There was a knock on the door. It startled Sam awake from his sleep. Unfortunately, his head had just hit the bar moments ago. "The door . . .," his mind raced. "You've been waiting all night," another voice in his head rang. "It might be the cops or the boys. Didn't those guys have a key?" Sam pushed his body up from the bar. The tension arched his back. His eyes peered through the sleep and saw two figures at the door. The knock came again, only this time louder and more urgent. Sam recognized his friends and the relief that washed through his body was real. He walked to the door.

"Sam you're still here?" Eric questioned. He was waiving the morning paper in Sam's face. "The headlines Sam, the headlines." Sam tried to focus his eyes on the paper. And there it was in blazing black and white headline news, "BUSTED!!!"

"Vans Caught Loading Drugs!!!"

"Holy shit," said Sam as he read the paper.

"You guys weren't the only ones to send vans out Sam," said Wendy.

"Sammy, you didn't tell me how big this was going to be," blurted Eric!

"I didn't know" he replied quietly. But as his head rose from the paper his voice raised also, "look we gotta go. Those kids, Danny, and Doc are all upstairs asleep."

"Okay,"said Eric, "I'll get them up," as he raced up the stairs. Wendy looked at Sam. He knew what she was thinking and said, "I'm not sticking around."

"What about the kid," Wendy asked. "Get him out of here." They broke away from the main entrance. Doc came down from upstairs.

"I've given this a lot of thought," said Sam. "I was up all last night."

"How is he," spoke Wendy completely ignoring Sam.

"Oh he's fine. Who are you?" What the hell did Doc know? It was back to work for him and another mind numbing shift. "Wow," Wendy thought to herself, "someone doesn't recognize me." Not everybody was glued to the boob tube after all. Still she had to be constantly aware of her status much to her disappointment. "We gotta move him now Doc. What do you think," asked Sam?

"No problem."

"That was damn good of you Doc," said Sam and for a brief second a civilized society made it's return. "But look, you have got to leave. This place is going to be under siege in any second."

"I'm surprised they're not here already" said Wendy.

"Hey I'm on my way out. Don't worry Sam, I don't know a thing," he said with a smile. Doc took a few steps to the door and turned back around to Sam and Wendy, "It's nice knowing people can still help each other without getting sued." And with that Doc walked out the front door. Sam was sick to death of losing track of people. Friends always seemed to be coming and going and he never got used to that. At least he didn't think it was his fault anymore.

"One down," said Sam. He and Wendy went up the stairs. Danny and Louise met them in the hall. They all turned and went into Adam's room. Jessica and Eric were already there, talking with Adam. Eric was speaking, "you can't go back to your neighborhood and sell pot."

"Besides,"countered Jessica, "you know how those people are."

"Small town mentality," spoke Adam.

"They wanna know your every move," reminded Eric.

"Well what are you going to do" asked Sam? No one spoke for a dreadfully long second. "Look," started Sam again. "Sell me the trunk load. It'll be off your hands and you and your girl friend can go back home. But quickly now you've got to make a decision." Life was like that. Pushing the issues, creating the situations, and the need for making a choice kept right on coming. "No way, I invested a lot on this one," Adam showed his age.

"Well I can appreciate that," spoke Danny taking the edge off an already heated situation. "If you want to kid, you can go with me."

"I can go by myself. I got wheels," shot back Adam feeling much the victim. "Look dude, he's got a place to go," said Eric trying to cool the attitudes.

"Definetly," spoke Danny again, "we all can hold up in New Orleans cool as a breeze. And you can stay at the band house, move a little pot and get on your way."

"I'll make more money that way," said Adam.

"I don't give a crap about money right now. I just want everybody out and long gone," hissed Sam. "Jessica," spoke Adam almost stripping gears emotionally. She guessed and she spoke, "I can't go home without you. They'll be wondering where you are."

"Then we go together," said Adam without giving it anymore thought. Attitudes changed on a breeze, smiles were lost and regained. The pointless consternation obscured the reality of the moment until the next words were spoken. Remarked Jessica, "what's back in that little hole anyway? You always said how you hate it so much." She looked accusingly at Adam. She knew he thought it was the safest thing to do. But she continued her attack, "the same boring people doing the same boring things, repeating the same boring stories, living squarely in the box." Jessica took a breath, "too scared for an original idea to take hold. Those are your words Adam."

Wendy interrupted, "I'm going with you."

"But why," turned Jessica?"

"Same reason I helped you last night. Same reason Eric and I came back here this morning. We care about our friends. Weird, huh?"

Eric wasn't sure exactly where all this had been leading since last night but he was following Wendy's lead. "I'm with you," he said trying to stay true to his vision. "Okay lets go," she said, "let's get out of Dodge." And with that, Wendy, star of hand soap and tissue commercials, was finally in a real drama. It was not her first and not her last. John had since stepped through the doorway and met everyone at the bottom of the stairs. Louise was behind him greedily sipping down a coffee. "I don't have much of a choice," said Adam to Jessica. "I'm not giving up the score. If we can flip this stuff for a real profit. I mean Ben already bolted. True friend that he is the first sign of trouble and he's gone. I'm sure he'll be dogging my name to the first person that asks. Jerk. We'll take his cut. I hope he asks for it someday." As they all moved away from the stairs each contemplated the latest cords they were cutting. The world kept turning. Louise had no clue what was happening. She was the real drifter. Then came the band. There was another vicious pounding on the front entrance. Everyone looked up at Sam, "get out, get . . . the back way, everyone into the Thunderbird." Decisions were made, choices were had, and all in a heart beat of time. Danny and John looked at Louise. She shot them a glance back that said nothing to loose. "From one mess to the next," said Danny, looking squarely at Louise. "That'll be the same until the day I die," she answered.

So that was that, and Danny, John, Louise, Eric, Wendy, Adam and Jessica scrambled out the back. Sam had to see what the situation was and ran back upstairs to peer out a window. It was dark in the old Victorian. The bar was all refurbished but not a dime was put into the back rooms. Still from Doc's room you could see the front door clearly. The hallways were empty now and the dampness seeped in from the corners and surrounded Sam. As he entered the room for a moment it felt like he was entering a cell. He peered cautiously out the window what he saw was Pancho's car and not a cop in sight. He looked up and down the street. Going back down stairs he let Pancho in.

"Sam jeez did you see these headlines?" Pancho was talking before he had gotten all the way in the door. It was now about seven in the morning and the sun was bright. "Pancho you don't have to be here."

"I'm paid to be here," he answered stoically.

"Not by me."

"That's right," he said with a raised eyebrow.

"There's no way I'm taking the heat for this. The only reason the cops aren't here yet is because those vans weren't registered."

"They weren't the only vans there," said Pancho.

"But someone will yap sooner or later!"

"I'll be here," remarked Pancho coolly.

"They'll work you over pretty good," advised Sam.

"Hey I'm just a bartender cleaning up. You're the one they'll be askin' about Mr. Manager. I'd get the hell out of here if I were you," he said.

"I'm on my way. But what are you going to say after they rip this place apart?"

"Me? I'll just quit and keep a low profile." Pancho was being calm out of habit and for Sam's sake. "But in the meantime we're opening as usual, only we might just need to hire another manager." Pancho smiled, "you did a great job for us." In all the years Sam had known Pancho he never heard him talk like that. Hell Sam hired Pancho. Sam just shook his head and shook Pancho's out stretched hand. At least the company was giving the patsy a chance to get away. But Sam knew all the signs would point to him and he was hung out to dry. He took off for the garage. "Hey," shouted Pancho after him. "I got something for you," and with that Pancho pulled a wad of money out of his pocket and handed it to Sam. "Road money. They told me to give it to you if you were still around."

"You mean get lost money," said Sam as he took it without saying anything more. It was quite some roll. These guys must have wanted to make sure Sam got lost but good. "So long Amigo," and with that Sam turned his back and left. The Thunderbird pulled out of the garage. Danny and Louise had gotten into Danny's Jeep and waited for Sam. He stuffed the money in his pocket, grabbed his bag, and headed out to the Jeep.

The Thunderbird with Jessica, Adam, Wendy and Eric at the wheel pulled out onto the street with the Jeep behind them. Sam and Danny said goodbye to the Jaded Lady and hello to the road.

The world is too much like the road. Hello and goodbye. To get anywhere, to do anything, one has to be in constant motion. What can anyone understand if they are too busy trying to figure out which exit they need? Try to do something different and you invite disaster. If you make those around you question just which way they are going, what they are doing or what they haven't done, even though they had the time, the means and the dream, if you draw this sharp of a picture and challenge their lethargy or their complacent view of things, get ready to be blasted even by the one's closet to you. Because maybe they didn't take the time to put their dreams into action. Frittering away their precious time of this reality they lacked the convictions to believe in themselves and their dreams. They never took the time. The time that dreams so richly need. Maybe they did not have any dreams? Or dreams took too much effort to unfold and pursue? Or maybe the people they trusted the most envied their dreams when they took shape. Worse yet, maybe they ignored their own dreams as being unrealistic and failed their whole life to ever take a chance. Playing it safe, frozen by fear, holding the shinning stars at bay, they burn with the pain of unfulfilled lives. They then in turn project this fear on each other and blame each other tearing the dreams and the dreamers down into a nightmare of petty wars and hatred. They miss the simple beauty of heaven on Earth and stumble through their own personal hell, bottling up their pain until it has to be unleashed on one another. They piss away the dream of utopia in bloody back stabbing, power grabbing, envy. They fail to seize on their moments of enlightenment and are doomed to repeat the cycle of lives. All the world lays passionately open at their feet and they remain huddled in self doubt, faithless unto themselves, denying their calling, caught up in the mundane, frozen in time, and jealous of those who break free. Instead of measuring themselves against themselves they measure themselves against each other, and they remain vain or bitter. Dust off the imagination, arise sailors of the sea, make your way through to your dreams and delight in the trying. It is the only noble way to live on such a noble Earth with such noble creatures in a fantastic world of immense beauty in a deep universe. We have just barely scratched the surface of existence. The answers are withheld, so the journey continues.

Well their lives mattered, whether they knew it or not. Their beauty could be found in smaller things than in designing national defense mechanisms or raising campaign funds. Days do occur in which the winds of fateful choices whisk their way through ones vision, questioning time, place, and reality, only to leave in its aftermath plain simple truth and delightfully enticing simple opportunity. The thoughts become painful as one wonders what might have been if one only did this or chose that. True sailing is dead to those who wont risk the trade winds and set sail. Simple fears of doubt and hesitation, not trying what beckons, doing something different than the norm. Listless, ignoring the listening and the energies that drive them and not daring to reach conclusions on their own. And so it is, the pavement is hard.

Dreams die into asphalt paved over by necessity hardened by lies and broken by failure. Life is hard with the detachment of those that do have to have. They insulate themselves against those that stand back. The chorus of "boos" is heard loud from those without courage to do but with the ability to sneer. Why do they care to voice their opinions? Opinions are easier than well laid out plans and mean nothing. Vindication is not often swift or even noticed or even taken, for in reality, it is a soul's satisfaction that matters instead. Days and moments pass and then finally one is dead and this whole particular experience of transitory reality is over. But are life and death really separate events or part of the same thing? Isn't the idea to live life and to do the things that others think hopeless unrealistic or a waste of time, foolish or improper and unnecessary. Perhaps to help each other and then to find that mysteriously you simply end up helping yourself. The universally and globally thin atmosphere that gives this planet life is all around us and only miles away. Reach for it, and pull it into your soul. For the magic that exists all around you is the magic that is you yourself. Delight in existence and the world is yours regardless of material accomplishments. Overcome the daily distractions and love something outside yourself. It is not always a measurable thing but it makes itself known. Life welling up like a wave pounds the shore with great realization from moment to moment. The infinite and the finite mingling on Earth. Few say thank you for the day or give the sun a nod of thanks along the way for continuing to burn. What makes it burn? Where did those combination of gases come from? How lucky or divine we are to be not too close but not too far away from the source and just the right distance. Isn't that amazing?

Lift your heads up out of yourself and really carry reality with you. The amazement doesn't go away, just the awareness. So it goes and those that can step outside themselves are those that can risk the comfort of convention, ignore the selling of fear, and see the beauty that is all around them, including the stars, to the forest, to the sea, and even the person evolving right next to them. The hunger, the pain, the fear have not diminished this reality but enhanced it. Sail the seas of chance and dreams. Forgo the tired selfish routines. Lucky are those not scrounging for their next meal horribly inflicted with disease and pain. What burden do they have that keeps them down, but doubt? How petty is that to the blind and the sick? Make your noise and not one of excuses.

The Thunderbird and the Jeep high tailed it across Florida. Our friends sat silent in their respective gas-guzzlers. The hot pounding Florida sun white-washed the road and glared in through the windshield. They sped on to their collective and separate destinations. Danny was enjoying the twist of events despite his involvement. He was a surface player but still had a real fear of retribution. The authorities can charge you with anything they want and their little community of prosecutors and judges are mostly aligned in lock step. Drunk with authority they have control and power strapped to their name or their belt, for lack of anything else. So Danny was back on the road again and a far cry from his stifled hometown back east. Here he felt he was beyond the petty jealousy and cynicism that pervades a small town or too tight a circle. Here, away from all that hurt, he was just looking forward to the next gig.

Playing gave him that extra special feeling. It was like being in love with someone. One could get lost in the melody but not lost in a negative sense but more like lost and found. Playing was freeing. To Danny it was a very selfless experience if no ones ego was trying too hard for the spot light. Let the music take the bows, then that whole harmonic effort can permeate into the crowd. Danny thought that if the collective egos are supplanted by the music, then what makes us small creatures can be transformed into an understanding that reveals our kinship and likeness to one another. Instead of capitalizing on our differences, something that we do every day and in every way, music can brings us together. And if only for a moment, well then what a moment it is, and you can take that moment with you, no matter where you go. Danny loved music and music playing because of this affect and effect. Music was not just another distraction of the body but it made the soul grow. What better service to one's self and friends could there be? Music can transcend the barriers of communication and specific languages. Its creation of universal moods and feelings convey simply to everyone. That's why it has been with us for so long. A driving tribal rhythm section galvanizes one to its roots. A slice of Beethoven or Bach fuses together the complexity that is our world into a fluidity that is the understanding of the mingling of the intricacies. The arrangements only hint at the very complexity of our reality and blend it all into a harmony. Showing that part of ourselves beyond moment-to-moment awareness back to ourselves.

Music awakens us and moves us out of the mundane. It hints at the wonder of life and delivers. It points the way to the fulfillment of existence in it's infinite variety and finite reality. It is an escape from oblivion and tunes us back into the amazing. The amazement of this tiny planet that sustains us in this horrifically vast universe. The harmony that must exist in unison, that keeps the Earth spinning and this life growing, despite man caught up with himself. All the while certainly not keeping in mind his real place in the universe on the outskirts of an enormous galaxy, alone and fragile.

So let's mess with genetics, pollute the planet, poison the food chain, and burn holes in the fragile atmosphere that holds our very existence. We are not cognizant that the Earth itself is the miracle. What more proof do you need then that we are here and that which is all around us? We have the audacity to take this world as granted, our lives as granted, and each other for granted. We don't get that the miracle is us and the world we are in. Stomachs and dicks are all we think about. No, no music moves us beyond that and shows us that there is something larger than meets the eye going on, and forever and a day it is constantly all around us.

Danny had the wheel of the Jeep as all this was going through his mind. Louise was next to him running her hand through her hair. She was reading the morning paper and rethinking about going off in this direction. It was much better than being tossed like a salad from a car and damn near getting run over. "But why had this guy Danny stuck his neck out," she thought to herself? Every time she stuck her neck out it got cut off. Hadn't Danny learned that lesson? Perhaps he had but still chose to ignore it, "to his own peril," she concluded.

First he helps her off the street and then helps another stranger out by offering him a place to stay till he gets it back together. He might just be clueless she allowed. At least she was on the road and happy with that. After all she had a fine time last night, "so far so good." One step ahead of the law and living on her own terms made her strong. She was with the band and was still in one piece. She had dry clothes and food in her belly. What more could she ask for? Not a bad fate seeing how far she had come and now headed back to New Orleans. Maybe she and John would work out, but she really didn't count on that. The human spirit needed one little thread of hope to hang onto to get through the day. So she continued searching for it secretly.

Sam was in the back seat worrying about the speed limit and how high up on the road he was. On one hand he was trying not to be so paranoid and on the other he knew that the authorities would be looking for him. It was an awfully big bust. John stared out the window. Not only had the three vans gone down unloading a ton and a half of pot, but several others had been busted. The freighter had unloaded at certain points along the way. There had been several busts along the beach way before the damn boat even docked. The police and the DEA were probably on this from the beginning. A lot of people were going down but those on top were nowhere to be seen. Sam was now slouching down in the back seat. "Those guys are going to hit the Jaded Lady hard," he thought to himself. The police didn't want the lowly drivers and they would make that very clear. If he could disappear for a while he might be able to get back to his beloved Sarasota. "They'll tear her apart," his thoughts flew by with the white lines of the highway. The problem was that if they caught him he couldn't tell them anything anyway. He was the poison pill on a need to know basis. He was the patsy, the fall guy, the Oswald. "Ending up dead was better than doing the time," he thought to himself. It wasn't the first time he had thought about this. "Shit, I gotta get out of Florida," and then out loud," don't bust the speed limit kid."

"Don't worry chief, we'll get you out in one piece."

"Do you guys need a manager," said Sam half heatedly. John raised an eyebrow, "was Danny going to take Sam in too," he wondered?

"Not one as hot as you," shot back Danny immediately. Louise laughed and gave the front page back to Sam. She kept the sports section.

The Thunderbird was three cars back in traffic suspiciously doing the speed limit. If the heat was hot in the Jeep because of the Jaded Lady then it was just as hot in the car with the runaways, stabbing victim and contraband in the trunk. The people in this car were a wreck! But Eric was in his glory riding a little lower to the ground. If he'd been still married he would be home right now emptying the trash and arguing with the drunk bitch. Oh sure it was alright for her to go out with her friends, but she didn't like Eric's friends. He hated playing that stupid game. She was everybody's favorite, a smart broad who played it sweet and innocent up front. But she had a fuck you, back stabbing attitude if she didn't get her way. For a while before they got married she acted like they were having fun especially in front of an audience. But after he was hooked, the fish was landed, she hit the booze every night, and it caught up with her fast. She was a bitch to him twenty-four hours a day. There was nothing he could do. Eric gave her a long time to come back around but finally they divorced. Then the war really started. He would venture out and there she would be, really putting the victim and innocence into action. She worked overtime slaughtering him behind his back because she knew she was vulnerable to the truth. She played people like suckers because she thought she was smarter than everyone. The guys all knew they had a real shot. But they didn't get in too close. They knew they'd just end up the point of her own self loathing fears and petty issues.

But Eric was solid underneath. With her he wasn't allowed to do the running anymore or there would be hell to pay. To deny himself to satisfy someone else's lack of trust hardly seemed to be the point of life. To rock and roll and play together well that seemed more like it to Eric. After their divorce he started getting back to his true self. All it took was a trip to the Jaded Lady and a room full of blues. She would never go with him. He could only imagine how she would have reacted to this latest entanglement. "Leaving for New Orleans for a few days . . . sorry honey, I can't tell you why." Yeah that would have gone over real big. Still he wished he could have sprung it on her. But it was all changed now and that stress was gone. He was at the wheel of a sixty-nine Thunderbird. One of those cars that make you want to drive. His window was down and he had a smile from ear to ear. He had his shades on and the bright Florida day was warming him up. He didn't know why he felt so good with so much trouble looming, but the adventure was back in his life and Wendy came with him.

Wendy had her own turmoil to deal with, but nothing as bad as being henpecked into boredom. She was quite familiar with Eric's story. Wendy had heard it through the grapevine when she would go out to the clubs. She met Eric on the dance floor. But not dancing to retro disco disguised as street hop, but rather Sinatra. Summer Wind was playing. Eric had requested it. Wendy noticed Eric's ex making a damn fool out of herself on a nightly basis. She thought she understood. There were filthy rich people everywhere, some even had a little bit of class. If his ex got lucky she could latch onto someone else's coat tails and ride out life. But she was a ruthless bitch and kept so much of her real feelings inside you could feel the steam coming off of her. She carried herself like she was going to explode. Wendy always rooted for the underdog. She knew what it meant to live and die and breath fresh air. She loved the natural wind at her back. She loved the animals and knew they were god's creation as much as she was, and as much as the sky, sea, planet and sun were. All things were holy to her as well as all manner of life, from the Sierra Nevada's to the Blue Ridges. The trees, the birds, and even the people were holy, yes even the hateful ignorant unenlightened people. It was all creation as far as she was concerned and it was sacred alive and revered, magical and mysterious, amazing and delightful in it's magnitude. To harm it in any way was a crime against all of reality, humanity and nature. To her, every day was the Sabbath and she tried to bring that spirit to bear anyway she knew how, no matter how many tried to define it any other way.

She was seen weekly on a local soap, sang the national anthem for the local baseball team, put out a few CD's and made several commercials. She definitely burned Eric's wife whenever she made a big fuss over him. She enjoyed bringing his upstart wife down a few notches. It was hard to find a deep person anymore and she had talked long enough to Eric to know that she liked him. So there she was, on her way to New Orleans, leaving everything behind. But with all of creation still around her, and the eyes to see and the heart to feel, she didn't need anything else. Wendy thought to herself, "won't those people be wondering about me," and allowed herself a laugh, "if they notice Eric is gone too, oh boy." Walking away from her contracts and disappearing would give all those bloodsuckers plenty to talk about. She thought about law school. But before joining that costly overcrowded unemployed group she thought she'd have some fun first. She wanted to go where people didn't know her, or how much money she had made. "How are they going to write me out of the script," she wondered to herself and then laughed out loud again?

Eric looked at her and smiled. He had a good idea what she was thinking about. It's not every day you have enough guts and faith in yourself to chuck it all. He understood the hypocrisy of making it and having no real friends. Wendy thought on about traveling with a band and the fun in visiting New Orleans. After all, she didn't have to hang the lights and unload the trucks. She had been working so hard with no chance to travel or even spend time with her friends. Her old friends, her friends before she had become an over-night sensation. Well it was vacation time now, and she had plenty of ideas. When they got to New Orleans she and Eric would take off together. They had been coming onto each other since the day they met. Eric knew enough to have patience but now was the time.

The mood in the back seat was decidedly different. Adam had to unload his stash and quick. He was wondering who he would sell to. He'd decided to trust Danny but that left a lot to chance. He chose this path and he had to see it to the end. It wasn't nineteen sixty-five anymore. He was going to have to have his guard way up. The early sixties remained a spark and a guiding force in millions of people's hearts but by the late sixties everything had been marketed and there were phonies everywhere. They were dressed just like each other but they didn't get the picture. It wasn't about dope and weird music. It was about being a human being. People went out of their way to help one another, driven by the quest for love and peace. Selfless acts and idealism in practice gave a generation a whiff of what this life could be like, fully realized. But power and greed quickly swung it all back one hundred and eighty degrees and fear drove the sales pitch. It didn't matter who hurt who, robbed you of your lunch, or banned your book Huck. How much you can get away with has now become the true measure of success. It was very frosty these days and humanity was being fumbled over what to care about and how to act. The misinformed and the nasty led the dialogue and Democracy was sold to the highest bidder. "If you want to feel like a man, act like a man," Adam's grandpa always said.

Danny was one who never gave up on what he believed, even if he wasn't sure of what he believed in all the time. Even if what he believed in was constantly changing, he still felt like an artist molding the clay of his soul. He molded his life with his beliefs and kept an open mind for suggestions. He knew he was a work in progress, "based on what I've seen, heard, and felt with all my senses, all six, seven or however many there are I trust my gut instinct above all else," he often said. Those instincts aren't a so called friend with a hidden agenda. Those instincts have evolved over eons of time and kept him alive and on his way. He was trying to reassure himself. He fought to stay positive. It was too easy to go negative. Anybody could be a jerk. In the face of overwhelming odds he just got stronger.

Adam had no way of knowing this about Danny and his blood was running hot and then cold. He was young. He had problems and he even worried about his parents worrying. That's how he knew he was in real trouble. "Hey Eric," he called from the back seat," when we pull over for gas I need a quiet moment to call my folks!"

"Okay," said Eric laughing to himself.

"I just don't want anyone to think I'm calling the police."

"It's your neck."

"I know," he said heavily. There the conversation stopped and the obvious danger came out in force. The way moods can swing like a storm front. Rolling in the energy comes up off your chest and freezes your face shut. The result was Wendy and Eric weren't so relaxed now. But Adam and Jessica were because they now had some support in helping them worry.

Jessica was the one most alone. She was so preoccupied with thoughts of running that she didn't have time to think. That is until now. She fought off tears as the highway clicked off the moments of her life. Her one love had been stabbed. Why did she have to be the cool one? When the pressure hits and we're thrown together and the spot-light swings around to you, what do you do? None of this would have happened if they were the nerds. Hell, the nerds just did well in school and got the good jobs after graduation. Not going to the prom had its rewards in the long run. Adam never had time for that way of thinking. He fell right into step with the "cool" kids and never noticed that they were either being busted, getting pregnant, or flunking class. He did notice the politics of living and the wasted energy of trying to out-do your neighbor. "Didn't people have more important things to talk about," he wondered to himself? What a load of wasted energy trying to keep up with the minutia of existence and what clothes to wear. Following like lemmings and keeping up the ridiculous envy of the hallways. It seemed to Adam that much larger issues were at play in this world. He had no idea what his neighbors were up to as long as they were not bothering him. He had no idea who the coolest kids in school were as long as no one mistook him for wanting to be one. "Take a look around," he would say to his friends, "wake up and smell the ganja!"

But Jessica's thoughts were different when it got to the ganja part. If they hadn't been out on that beach she wouldn't have been raped. But who was she kidding they were always on the beach. What is life if you don't get in some beach time? "Aids," a voice screamed in her head. She had been utterly and completely penetrated by the evil that exists in our world. It was unimaginable to those that have never lived through it and beyond the definitions of hell. If she dwelled on that for too long her whole world would collapse. "Aids, STD, herpes," screamed the voice, and there was no escaping it. Like lightning it ripped through her skull with deadly force, never breaking a sweat.

All those years nurturing something so important as her body, the temple of her being, only to have it raked over and treated as a toilet. She was powerless from ever removing the presence of the simultaneous and reflexive associations of despair, the vulgarity and the wretchedness. What Adam would think of her dominated her thoughts. Would Adam thrill in the singleness of their beings once more? Or would it all be shattered knowing that the outside world had penetrated their singular oasis easily and at will? Are we all so powerless to prevent evil from happening or do we justify and rationalize it all somehow? If only her mind wouldn't focus so hard on the negative. But how could she prevent that when she was surrounded by filth, unchecked rage, and polluting evil. She knew that only the strength of her mind and soul would pull her through and she was determined to have her old kick-ass attitude back. But she was afraid she had used that attitude all up last night. She was wondering how long it would take to come back or if it ever would. Sometimes we have to reach down with the kind of resolve that only the gods have. She had to shatter the events that would shatter her life. No one could do it for her. She had to bear the burden in order to break free.

"It was the act of a loser," she told herself. A poor wretched individual who would never get any long term satisfaction out of it. The quick, reckless act, the negative energy, what's dished out is returned. Each horrible act draws you closer to the dirt that lines the landfills. The victim suffers horribly but the aggressor sleeps in a shroud of evil. Once awake, the culprit needs another act to obliterate the last act from consciousness. Each waking breath was breathing in and out the turmoil and the wretchedness. Everywhere the culprit goes, and everything he touches, dissolves and reeks of sulfur and sludge. He is radioactive and polluting all that he touches polluting

the ones that he loves and the few that love him. The wretched
motivations of evil seep through us all and through the bowels of our
consciousness. Lives are wasted and wash up on the shores of our
streets. They are covered up by attitudes that mask the fear of nowhere
to run and no way out. The violence pummels into our collective
souls. It is both unconscious and conscious. It spills from our pores,
relegating the positive to the ridiculous and the sublime. The serpent
eating its tail and the long spiral down through hell is the war that
wages on in the souls of us all.

Jessica will tell herself of these things as she fights to shine on in
her beauty. It is something that can never be taken away but only
overlooked. The beauty is always on, with its own strength, quiet, not
with furry, diminishing the results of the damned with the twinkle of
an eye. At this moment, and it is always a question of which moment
our heads are in, she hadn't the time to reach any conclusions. She
knew however that she wouldn't let any "asshole" ruin her life! "Why
go back home now," she thought to herself? "What's the use. Nothing
will be the same. How can I possibly care about that routine? I'm
alone, damn it, and no one will ever know the depths of my experience.
Five minutes and my god damn world is completely changed.
Everything is different. I've been so far catapulted over and beyond
all of that high school crap. I can't go back and pretend that everything
is the same again. Besides," she continued to think to herself with a
wry smile, "I've never been to New Orleans."

Jessica realized she could not go back until she had time to
straighten the whole thing out in her mind. If she went back, killing
herself might become an option. When she was younger she didn't fit
in with the cheerleaders and the prom queens. Saturday nights at
home alone she felt the rage of rejection and would sit and cry on the
kitchen floor. To turn that rejection onto herself by her own hand
became a desperate, harrowing option. The realization of what she
means to those that love her saved her. Fortunately, her parents told
her everyday how much they loved her. She had good parents. And
missing out on all that this world had to offer was quickly ruled out as
an option. But besides the music, the love, mother nature and the
simple pleasures of this physical reality, besides Van Gogh and Walter

Anderson, Andrew Wyeth and Rodin, besides rooting for and watching the underdog win, besides childbirth, and a rich full life and even besides all that, was horrible cruelty. Somewhere along the line she realized that without one, you couldn't appreciate the other. However, this was little consolation in the belly of her despair. "Don't do anything crazy. Let your wrath go down with the sun," her soul would shout. And tomorrow had always been a better day. Unfortunately the higher the pile of shit that came down on her head, the more sunsets she needed.

In the distance on some nearby beach, the ocean continued its pace washing wave after wave ashore. The thought of her safe little world made her cringe and feel sick. What a phony unreal existence. It was filled with fallacy and assumptions. But what did she really know of the lives around her? She knew from somewhere deep inside her that when it became clear they would all have to deal with the spectrum of horror sooner or later. "It has its days damn it," she said aloud. Wendy turned round and met her blank gaze with a frown. She had every right to be hard and angry it was part of the process. Letting go as all things pass was yet another lesson of this life. Would she ever see her way through to not seeing through it all again? Jessica turned her head and stared out the window as the road rolled by.

"How about some music," Eric asked? Just then Danny reached down and turned on his radio in the Jeep up ahead. The Rolling Stones fell out of both radios in both the Thunderbird and the Jeep. The collective hmmm of interesting timing was at work and once again unknown to those involved. The caravan of two wound its way through the afternoon. No one had too much to say. They each wrestled with their own thoughts and hesitations. It was plain to see that the happy people outweighed the miserable, perhaps for the first time ever. Despite the press clippings, the happy people weren't idiots. They just didn't let negative concern override positive possibility. Like always though, there was plenty of misery and doubt to go around for everyone. It was just a matter of who could channel it the best and separate concern from possibility, and turn dreams into actions. At the moment Eric, Wendy, Danny and Louise were doing a better job of that than Sam, Adam and Jessica. When they reached the state line,

Sam was complaining from the back of the Jeep, "hell it's almost dark and were just reaching Alabama?!"

"Florida's huge," said Danny for the fifteen hundredth time. He knew how much pressure Sam was under, and nobody was looking forward to the trip through Alabama and Mississippi. Danny had never been through this before. It was clear to him, and subtle like an axe to the forehead, that if he wasn't careful he would end up in very deep. The potential was that both sides could squeeze him pretty hard on this one. Danny grimaced to himself. There he was again, right smack in the middle. Although he had been in Florida for some time now and had gotten to know Sam, Danny wasn't going to sacrifice the band for anything. He had worked too long and hard and his patience destroyed and regained a hundred times. To help someone on the way down while he was on the way up, well that wasn't very street savvy of him. The fact that he was helping at all and genuinely concerned was definitely out of character, for the "nasty is cool" world.

Right now the band was doing well, much better than anyone back home would have guessed. They were getting some bookings, and a weekend at Tippitinas was no slouch gig. Austin was next and there had been some talk of playing in Los Angeles. Of course Danny wanted the gig in L.A. to be in a real roadhouse, not some trendy upscale nonsense. Denver was another possibility with a little side swing through Boulder, but none of this past New Orleans had been nailed down.

"Alabama," drawled Louise with a thick drawn out accent. "Y'all better go the speed limit or we're going down the shitter together."

"No kidding," hollered Sam, wrenching his voice and his body in the back seat of the jeep!

"This is no time to be freakin', honey bunch. You be a hunted man. But don't get your butt all up in the air. You ain't no Billy The Kid."

"Cut the accent woman. I don't feel like being reminded about how these God-fearing Christians get so righteous about their man-made law."

"Slow down," Danny jumped into the verbal sparring, "first of all we know how much trouble you're in from both sides of the law, Sam.

Right now if you would have stayed behind you'd be in leg shackles. You're their fall guy, but the law just isn't looking for you. Acting like some maniac isn't going to help anything at all. Besides, the pot's in the trunk of the Thunderbird and it belongs to Adam," he emphasized. Louise turned around and looked Sam right in the eye. She waited a few seconds till his brow unknitted itself and he sat still. Then she spoke, "I was just trying to make you laugh." She turned back around and sat down.

Louise had always taken a lot of abuse just at the point in time when she was either trying to ease tension or being completely sincere. It was an unbelievable set of circumstances that always kept her jumping. Just as she was at her most sincere plateau, the person she was dealing with would holler, "bullshit." It was aggravating as hell. She always just figured a little soulful righteousness was too much for people to take. Today everyone was preaching their twisted points of view at ever increasing volumes and no one was listening. The important thing to her is that she just kept on going. She hoped that eventually her mysterious road of travel would bring her to people who understood and grasped the ideas that she held so dearly. Even though they may not be so clearly defined. How else could she explain that deep river of impulse that kept her happy despite millions of things being wrong? How could one explain that upbeat attitude that kept her ticking in the most severe of times? How could one explain and make people realize what was inherently resilient? How could you, if you couldn't even get them to laugh when you were trying. Or they got mad when you wanted them to be happy and said "bullshit" just as you were uttering your most heartfelt truth and understanding. Why keep on trying?

Well she didn't know. All she knew was that she didn't give up. And that one day all the separate rivers of her soul would merge together. Until that day she would nudge and pull together all the grooves until they resonated in one note that was herself. Then she would move off the face of the Earth leaving behind only what was created. Selfless existence and mutual human respect were the goals. Utopia was the name of the game. She had a long way to go but she wouldn't stop until she got there. Even though she had no idea where "there" was, she would recognize its lack of pollution and material possessions. "There are other things to desire in life," she often thought to herself, "like warm summer nights and hearing the trees sway in the wind."

The eight-wheel caravan was headed for Mobile now. Sam had taken a reprieve from paranoia and Danny cranked the radio a little louder. "I long to open up underneath cloudless skies," spoke Wendy quite suddenly. It was getting darker now and Eric flipped on the headlights of the Thunderbird. He looked over at Wendy and motioned with his hand palm up. It was a line from a show she had done in college back when everything was most important. Society wants you to think you were a naive child in those meaningful days of your struggle for truth and clarity. Like the slacker wanting you to be a fool so he doesn't look so bad. Society wants to hide its lack of care, involvement and initiative. But Wendy and Eric were putting their foot down. Enough was enough. Going along to get along might be the ruin of us all. They were not as they appeared. Rivers ran deep within the two and a change was at hand.

"What does that mean," Jessica asked repeating, "I long to open up underneath cloudless skies?" Adam was surprised she had broken into Eric and Wendy's conversation. "It can mean anything you want it to. In fact the meaning you give it describes perfectly the person you are."

"You mean it's full of shit to the people who are full of shit," spoke Eric.

"And beautiful to the people who are beautiful," said Adam looking at Jessica.

"To me," answered Wendy, "it's like there is this wonderful creation that we trample over every day but that we don't really see. Just to have a chance to lay back with someone you love and take time out on a grassy hill. To me it means the desire and realization to feel the Earth spin as you breath, slowly, laid back under a blue sky. Just to lay there, no questions asked, centered with no preoccupations or a cluttered mind of a weary restless soul. To be alone together but with everything and nothing to gain except the feeling, the air, and the view. You and your lover in perfect harmony with no eventual outcome in store and no position in life to gain."

"You mean society don't you," interrupted Jessica.

"That could be," continued Wendy "but it's more like laying your soul wide open and not being distracted by the oh-so-convenient distractions of everyday life." She paused and looked back out the window into the falling night, "understanding through absorbing and trying without trying," she closed her eyes and listened to the quiet underneath the noise. No one spoke for fifteen minutes.

"No doubt that's pretty intense," started back up Adam, "but I'm on a completely different wave length right now. In fact my world is over. I might be able to sneak back home but I won't be and it won't be the same. My girlfriend has been . . ."

"Don't remind me, interrupted Jessica, "I'll never forget," she said plainly. Adam went on, "I've been stabbed and now I'm boxed into this corner. I can't waste time pondering the meaning of it all. You people are along for a joy ride. I've got my back against a great big wall."

"You wanted to be a big time dealer," stated Eric mater of factly. There was a long pause. Adam stared vacantly ahead. Outside the green highway signs sparkled the recognition of yet another set of headlights. Speeding cars with souls unknown, the illuminated highway pointed the way. Eric looked in the rear view mirror. He could see Adam mulling over his words. "Look," spoke Eric again, "It's not all fun and games. The stakes get higher, the pressure mounts, and things can go wrong. There is always that intangible unknown factor that has the most impact. Where I come from the dealers were the sons and daughters of the people who ran the town. Nothing was ever allowed to go wrong. The cops never bothered anybody. But then one day the F.B.I. came in and cleaned everybody out. Do you know the people had the nerve to act surprised. The point is, no matter how good a thing you think you got going, the unknown, the unaccounted for, the impossible, and the unimaginable will eventually show up like clockwork."

"Makes for some nifty wake up calls," answered Wendy.

"Yeah if that crook on the beach had never come along we wouldn't be in this mess."

"The unknown factor," answered Eric back to Adam.

"I think you're wrong," said Jessica to Adam ignoring Eric for the moment.

"Suppose we would be home now? This is a monster score for us. With the way word spreads like brush fire at school and with all this crap in the news we'd be very vulnerable. Anybody you have managed to piss off in the last couple of years would be drooling to see you go down. Anybody who was jealous or you made look bad wouldn't wait ten seconds to rat you out."

"It wouldn't be as dangerous as this," Adam fired back!

"Would you rather be on the move," asked Jessica," or a sitting duck at home?"

"That's a tough question," answered Adam and he thought about it. Right now he could have been back home with the phone ringing, dealing on campus and moving the stuff quickly. Or someone he "boyed" could dime him out for not being half the man he was. Whatever his conclusions were he had made his decisions in life and there was no getting around that. He knew the heat would be on at home. But he had no idea as to what awaited him in New Orleans. "We'll be alright," Jessica said after a moment.

"How can she be so strong," Adam thought to himself. Only the entire rest of the world knew she was faking it. He turned toward her and his eyes said, "with what you have been through, your calming me?" Things have a tendency to be reflective that way. The dichotomy of reality is in a parallel relationship like currents in a circuit traveling back and forth. The sender and the receiver have to be righteously clear for it to work. "Ah the old role reversal coming through again," thought Wendy. She knew Jessica had been raped. Eric just kept his hands on the wheel. Adam felt a little stupid since his wound was only skin deep. Jessica toughened mentally and put her head back and grabbed for some peace. Adam pealed his eyes to the road and watched the darkness darken. Eric dropped one hand from the wheel and put it on the back of Wendy's hand. They drove on.

Up in front, the Jeep had passed several cars, including the Thunderbird. Louise was telling jokes and talking to Danny about

Dolphins. He forgot he was talking to a homeless woman, which was a good thing for both of them. He was laughing out loud at one of her best dirty jokes. "Where did you learn to tell jokes like that," Eric said.

"Hell, if I didn't know any better I'd say you've been hanging out in Vegas."

"I spent time on the strip," she answered, "people can be very generous!"

"Okay," said Sam, realizing that this was not out of the realm of reality.

"Seriously," Louise spoke, "I spent three years as a caddie."

"Spare me your life story but why did you quit," asked Danny?

"Why does anybody quit anything," she asked?

"Because they pull up lame," came back Sam.

"Because they can't make it work or make it to work when they are supposed to," added Danny.

"Not me" said Louise. "I was at my best back then!"

"Oh no, here we go," laughed Danny.

"No seriously, at first it was a little unorthodox but Dad had been the one to take me to the golf course when I was a kid. Eventually Mom got used to the idea of me hanging around the caddie shack. I was making some money but there I was a bohemian in the middle of all this wealth. These people were rude. Like the world should bow down to them because they were there. They were all trying to outdo each other and get people to kiss their ass. They were all screwing each others' wives and the women were twice as bad blowing off their rotten kids and boozing it up. Judges and lawyers fixing fees oh man it was unreal. Their views on everything were arrogant. But not everyone was so bad. There were people who knew how to act and they were the ones whose children had careers. But the lowlifes were too much. Bitch all day about each other and then sit down to dinner together. I just decided I wanted no part of that anymore. It was so absurd and hypocritical. People trying to throw weight around that they didn't have at home or at work, and all us poor working stiffs stuck in the middle. It was funny as shit but it pissed me off!"

WELL ADJUSTED MANIACS

—

When Jessica awoke, they were crossing into New Orleans. "Wow, a real city," she sarcastically thought to herself, "with tall buildings, violent crime, smog, noise and light pollution." You weren't a real city unless you had overwhelming noise and light pollution. "What more could a person want?" Actually Jessica wasn't always so sarcastic. But she had a few different ways of looking at things from time to time. They had driven straight through. They had been on the road for nearly fifteen hours. A few stops along the way for eats and gas, and once to switch drivers and then back again, as they neared their destination. Seven hours into the drive they had stopped and Louise handed out black beauties. Those little pick me ups come in handy after one has had their fill of coffee. "I need a joint to take the edge off, not this shit," said Eric as his stomach groaned.

It was well into the night when they crossed the bridge into New Orleans. It was a hot humid night, typical of this southern port's weather. Their caravan rolled into the city with urgency and expectancy. Here was a city that was loose. Everything went and has been going on since time began. Still Danny was trying to make the curtain. Bonnie, Mark and Doug had left Florida before sun up. Their three-piece jazz arrangements would be perfect in the Quarter until Danny and the other ones had arrived. Danny wanted to keep the band working. Money was always an issue. Luckily New Orleans was one of those places that did not get going until late. There was no curfew and some clubs did not start swinging until midnight. This was fortunate for the band. Danny was sweating all that and everything else, including the speed. The jazz combo could swing through a jazz set until he got there. They would probably start off slow and mellow. Needless to say, the whole sound of the band would change, but the group would appreciate doing something different. They were performing at a club called the Chamber. It seated a very large crowd and had three different bar areas. It was a cross between an old coffee house and a slick new bar. It mirrored the old road house Ol' Man Rivers.

Ol' Man Rivers was a club that was so hot it burnt to the ground in fine Louisiana fashion. The Chamber wasn't open until nine and closing time was somewhere around eleven in the morning. They served breakfast. Danny's band would be the featured house band when they arrived. On the weekends, bigger named acts would roll through and they would back them up. It was great to have the weekends off but they would rather sit in with the Johnnie Johnsons and Katie Websters of the world. Within the framework of the New Orleans sound, which was as much gumbo as anything else, the band could really step out. Their core blues rock sound would always be, as long as Danny was around. But if his feet weren't there, they could always play traditional jazz.

"Did I miss anything," wondered Jessica aloud?

"Just Biloxi," answered Adam. With time to think, Adam had decided on a very mellow approach. If he took his time, he might get something set up long term. What it was, he did not know. "Oh damn, I guess we passed Ocean Springs."

"What are you talking about Jess," said Wendy from the front.

"Walter Anderson!"

"Who," asked Adam?

"Walter Anderson was this way-out cat from the old days," answered Eric. "He had this incredible lifetime burst of creativity that made him row out to an island during a hurricane just to see what it would look like."

"That's messed up," said Wendy, she meant it in a good way.

"It's like so many other stories you hear," said Jessica chiming back in. "The man was incredibly talented but he was seen as different. If it doesn't validate the status quo, it's rejected. If it makes you rethink or question the supposed norm, well then it's not safe and therefore dangerous. "A society that doesn't want to live in balance with its own mortality doesn't have a place for sculptors, painters and poets," answered Eric. "Unless someone validates it for the masses, no one notices. If we are told it's hip, then we act like we are thinking on our own. Original artists just get passed over unless something sensational, controversial or shocking happens," spoke Adam.

"It was the same for poor Walter. A life time undiscovered . . ."

"Until after his death," interrupted Wendy. Jessica started back in again, "an all too familiar story. Real talent sits out there in the land undiscovered. Life gets shallower because a few consolidated corporate heads are deciding who, and who doesn't, get distributed through their tightly controlled media outlets. These men are good at making money and identifying homogenized marketability, but they are pitiful at judging talent or originality. They have no taste at all for art or music." She paused, "Walter's work is so beautiful. He had this room he painted from floor to ceiling that is filled with so much incredible energy. He talked of the magic moment right before sunset and how that illuminated the subtle nuances of the world and his work. I wanted to go there and pay my respects to a true American hero." She paused breathing deeply and continued, "he pushed on with his vision and work in spite of everything. He stayed true to his vision. Despite the avenues of discovery that were closed off to him by the unenlightened few he continued to work with spectacular paintings, rich with color and vibrant. The man was a true knock-your-lights-out talent. Although unknown, he deserved rich accolades from all of us. To spend five minutes in that room would surely sooth my soul, anybody's soul, who was smart enough to see and feel for themselves."

"It's that good," said Eric. "It took me two seconds to realize it while I watched a brief bio on the man. He deserves a national tour of museums and all he got was the Warhol fifteen minutes of fame as a side note on another story. Warhol knew how to work the media."

Back in the Jeep Danny's eyes were wide open and Sam was commenting on the ghetto. It reminded him of every city he had ever

been in and so he felt a bit more comfortable. Louise knew the streets.
It didn't matter what city. She did not waste time feeling comfortable.
She knew most of these people were stinking rotten poor and laying in
wait for each other and the hapless tourist who wandered off the beaten
path. Danny knew right where he was going. He moved the Jeep through
the streets with ease. It was not that hard to find the French Quarter.
Just follow the trolley tracks or head for the river. Big muddy, mighty
cajun atmosphere, and all the time rain. No snow, rain and flood waters
and the constant pumping of them back into the river.

Then there is the occult. It washed over this city like the water. It
sprang forth up from every dark alley, poor and affluent. Voodooism
along with friendly devil worshiping was as common as going to church
on Sunday. The heritage and history of New Orleans was a melting
pot of religions, strange and eerie, permeating the air. It is said the
first witch was burned in New Orleans not Salem, and with the dead
buried above the ground who could argue. Sailors, conventioneers,
tourists and lovers arrived amongst the naked titties and queers
dancing all night long. They lined the streets of downtown as the
hookers and the fags in drag competed for attention. These
transvestites told San Francisco to take a hike. New Orleans was the
real deal. Key West forget about it. Every night was all hallow's eve in
New Orleans. The ancient druid priests would have loved this place
lined with the pagan realities manifested for all the world to see. It
was one big show of circus freaks and creativity that dug deep at the
understanding of the world around us. The jazz flickered and the
steeples stood unwavering as the chains remained on the whipping
posts in the long ago mansions of wealth and war. The French Quarter
is only part of it. The old plantations with their slave quarters and wall
shackles give material proof to the evil that exists. Not to be taken
lightly or messed with unthinkingly, it all gave New Orleans almost a
medieval feel. The graveyards were creepy and more horrible even in
the daylight for those of thin skin and active imaginations. The city is
haunted and shrouded in mysticism. Drunken debauchery is only a
part of it. With this in mind, the caravan pulled off the road and into
a back lot behind the Chamber. During the course of a month one
may find the talents of a Tinsley Ellis, Chris Cain or Lucky Peterson

playing here. They are drawn like magnets to a vortex of creative energy both positive and negative. Now even our traveling heroes, bystanders and villains have made it to the Chambers famous alley. The pagan festival was on-going, and only a healthy respect for all the forces at play could render the night rich, sly, deep and fun and bring the dawn on safe.

The suicide doors flung open simultaneously and Eric and Wendy jumped out of the front seat of the Thunderbird. Jessica popped out from the back and reached around to help Adam out of the car. He got out gingerly. Danny and Louise stepped out of the Jeep casually and stretched their travel weary legs. Sam climbed out of the back seat, a step ahead of the law. Eric tossed the keys to Adam as he stood on the black top, "all yours now," spoke Eric. Wendy reached out and grabbed Eric's hand and they began to walk away.

"We'll be here every night this week," Danny reminded them never expecting to see them again. "We'll be back," assured Wendy.

"Come back for breakfast," pleaded Danny to the dwindling silhouettes. Eric and Wendy had stepped off the curb and onto Decatur Street. Adam looked a little paranoid, but Danny tilted his head in his direction and motioned for everyone to go inside. Sam knew he was on his own. Adam felt that same feeling really come home. Beside Jessica who could he trust? Sam and Adam would have to be friends. Louise had moved around to the front of the Jeep and had her hands stretched out over her head. "Wow," she spoke, "what a fantastically clear night." She wanted to go with Wendy and Eric as she watched them disappear. The five of them moved towards the door, "what's behind this one," thought Louise to herself. Adam stopped to check the trunk and make sure everything was locked up. Jessica noticed him do that. At least for the moment everyone was paying attention. Danny had his hand on the cold knob of the door and knew he would have to be on stage at any moment. Sam was wishing it was morning and he had an early edition Florida newspaper. He couldn't take the chance and call Pedro. He was on the run but good. His destination would have to be Mexico or Canada. Since Mexico was closer, that would be it. He might try to find Buffet down in the Keys but that wouldn't be cool to do to his old friend.

Eric and Wendy had left that tension behind them. For the first time in a long time Wendy felt free. She had so many obligations when she was younger. She had waltzed right into her modeling career. One day she was laying on the beach, stretched out, a youthful beauty, and the next thing she knew she was modeling clothes. Law school fast became history. Beside hardly anyone wanted to be on television or make lots of money. The whirlwind had her in front of the camera before she had a chance to think about it. Lately she did think. She wasn't so sure she liked being herded around with no mind of her own. It was her time now and she headed into the Quarter sky high.

Eric had his own cross to deal with. His major break with routine had occurred when he left his wife. She had told him he would waste away. Well every now and then he got wasted, but he sure wasn't getting stagnant. This excursion to New Orleans was only more proof that all he had needed was room to grow and not a wife telling him what to do. Eric and Wendy held hands like school kids. Their feet rushed over the pavement. They were on a dead run down a tiny musty street with their souls clacking over the cobblestone. The walls that surrounded them were fermented with moss and pee aged by endless days of rain. They were dried in the summer sun, then soaked through with humidity and more piss. The pavement was buckled and there was litter strewn about. But they didn't notice that. They didn't notice the French styled architecture or the gingerbread design rolling through the rails that lined the porches and the balconies. They didn't notice the giant ferns. The street melted with the curb their legs melted with the street and their hearts melted with each other.

They stopped with a jolt when they reached Washington Square. A brand new crescent moon's dark side was all lit up silver and gray. The open skyline obscured by the buildings and porches went unnoticed until they hit the Square. The civil war was over, but like everything else that's a kin to belief and routine the memorials and remains rage on forever changing in perspective and significance. One can never wipe out a real culture especially one that is rooted in the land. No matter how many overthrows there are, no matter how many wars are waged, the people go on. Eventually their culture surfaces again and again. Nothing can be destroyed that already exists. Nothing can be controlled that can't be defined and the spirit rages on undefined. It rages on through the dark veils that try to shroud it in silence, and it turns that silence into mystery. History rambles over its obstacles in the long run. Though fools mistake it for current events. The essentials win out. The things that are common to all eventually rise to the surface, the land, the independence, and the faith. The spirit of free thought determines for itself, not being told what to do by those that would manipulate the thoughts of others. We all blend together in fantastic reality, whether you like it or not. The details are the things that divide and separate us. They are the minor, man-made facts and they do not matter.

A version of Mississippi John Hurt's "Satisfied" came rolling out of a pub on a corner of the square. It fermented with the evening air. Wendy and Eric sat down on one of the benches that faced St. Louis Cathedral. The lush greenness born of a hundred-thousand hot days and humid nights misted the air. It intertwined with the clear twinkling sky and the soul of the soft clear voice of Mississippi John Hurt. It sent wave after wave of shivers up Wendy's back. Eric studied the Cathedral doors and followed the facade all the way up to the heaven bound steeple. Pin-pointing the direction of all creatures hurling through space the steeple looked as if it went on forever. "Lets get a drink and something to eat," spoke Eric. They never asked where but followed the music instead. They walked in and sat down at a bar in the Quarter. The bar was long and lined with a mahogany top and walnut foot rail. There was a Hawaiian hula lamp draped with plastic beads that eerily shed light on the bartender's massive hands. Wendy and Eric both ordered the same dish. It was an oyster combination that was poached in a bay leaf sauce and then deep-fried in egg batter. It sure took the edge off the roadside burger spoons that had greased their stomachs so far. "We're on vacation now," said Wendy as she cocked her head to one side. The night moved effortlessly and the music rolled right on through the dessert and after dinner drinks. After a while Wendy and Eric found themselves back out on the Square. They walked down to the foot of the Mississippi and stared at the mouth of the river. It's enormity and powerfulness was not lost on them. "This cuts right through the middle of the country," Eric spoke with reverence and awe.

The river was splashing and tossing itself against the banks in constant battle with the city itself. Its lengths of water reached up and tried to pull them in. On a calm night it was like a storm surge that wanted to lasso you back into the sea. More than once Eric and Wendy jumped back. When they were back far enough Eric's hand reached up and touched Wendy's cheek. Wendy had a peaceful felling as his easy hand felt her smooth skin. His fingers traced her cheek and moved under her chin. He pulled her to him with his last remaining touch. Their lips met in a subtle, soft kiss and romance was born again into both of their lives.

The door swung open at the Chamber and five tired bodies moved through the darkness and the smoke. Two lonely spotlights were trained on the stage. Doug was on the piano and Bonnie was stretching and probing the smokey atmosphere with her flute. Danny stopped for a minute. The bouncer recognized him and waved all five of them through. They found a table off in the corner. There was business to take care of and Danny reassured everyone that they would have a place to sleep that night. Whether it was all together or desperately alone only Louise seemed to weigh that option. "Hey Danny, I thought you'd never make it," bellowed the club manager.

"And let you guys not pay me!" The club manager motioned with his head toward Bonnie," she thinks she's at the Village Gate with Herbie Mann." Danny didn't know how to answer that one. And before he could the manager was pushing him on stage, "get your ass up there and pick up the pace," he half growled and then laughed. After all day and half the night on the road Danny was tired but ready to work off his stress. Mark walked by and patted him on the back. He was headed up on stage. Danny went for the band coffee machine that was stored by the empty road cases back stage. He helped himself to a bottle of Jack that had been waiting for him when he got there. He poured a healthy splash into his Java and went to find his guitar. Funny how some nights he could walk right to it and feel excited like he was meeting an old friend. Other nights it seemed heavy and cold and hard to tune. Tonight she was warm and fuzzy and waiting on her guitar stand just for him. His stack was all set up on stage and he went to plug in. At this point John was easing the bass line. Doug and Bonnie thought they were breaking for a while and let Mark work the percussions into Doug's piano scape that he was trying to end. But sometimes the music wont let you stop and you just keep on playing. Bonnie was getting ready to wind down and even had her back to the audience when Danny came bounding on. He quickly plugged in, made eye contact with Mark, John and Doug, and slammed into the opening chords of an old Elmore James song. The lights changed up. The crowd let loose with a jolt of adrenaline. Bonnie jumped off the stage in fear of her life. Sam grabbed Louise's hand and immediately spun her around. Everyone jumped up to dance. Jessica brought beer and healthy shots of Old Number Seven back to the table. The New Orleans night was in full swing.

The bar was loaded down with weirdos, near-do-wells, well to dos, wannabes, fags, sailors, psychos and an assortment of well-adjusted maniacs. Grunged hipsters mixed with environmental warriors, old time bikers and pierced punks. The fags were dressed cleanly with polished nails. The city folk had on suits with matching red eyes. The college kids were a mixed bag of bandannas and torn up blue jeans, worn just as proudly as any Harley man and his colors. The other assorted tourist and locals sported a wide range of hawaiian shirts and cotton. The young girls were the only ones dressed better than the fags. The blacks were cool and calculating. They weren't shooting up or shooting at anyone. They were VIP's in the finest tradition. Mutual respect was paid just by everyone being there and having fun. Here in the South everyone knew and remembered each other's twisted horrid history. Everyone had a heritage not forgotten. New Orleans was beautiful that way.

Jessica was loving the drag queens and they were loving her loving them. She gave a stab at an explanation that was not necessary, "they don't want to blend in," a glass shattered on the floor, "they're so frustrated by the limits of society and they can't make a living as poets and artist."

"As if there is any mystery left in the world," Adam interrupted.

"Not the industrial world," Jessica continued without missing a beat. "Everyone has to be the same so this is how they rebel and show they exist and that they matter."

"Or spread a gaudy vibe," countered Adam. Jessica and he looked into each other's eyes and said at the same time, "a very gaudy vibe," and laughed. They sat silent for a rich, strong, moment and Adam sipped his whiskey slowly, "it's not out there," and he made a sweeping motion with his hand, "but in here," and he held his hand flat against his chest, "right now." Jessica got up from the table letting Adam have the last word. Sam and Louise were still spinning around on the dance floor. An empty space that had hung heavy when occupied was now hanging light. Sam ran over to the table and slammed a shot in a frenzy. Then he grabbed Louise and she slammed hers down. It was time to loosen up and everyone was right on schedule. The floor got slimy as drinks were spilled and feet stamped in time with the band. At this point the band was smoking on an original Allman Brothers tune, "Every Hungry Woman."

"Greg doesn't get enough credit as a writer," Danny thought to himself. He gave up trying to imitate Dickey and Duane, "that was impossible." So he just played from the heart. That was the idea anyway. John was ripping his bass runs trying to match Berry Oakly's unsung brilliance and Doug was trading guitar licks with keyboard chops, half rhythm and half lead. The drummer, Mark, felt and looked like "Animal" from Sesame Street while trying to play both rhythm parts. They all loved music, and especially what the Allman Brothers Band did to it.

SHADOWS FROM LIGHT

—

What's a home anyway? Should it just be where we hang our coat and hat? Is it a closet to hide in? Is it something that rewards us for our time and struggle on the outside or is it more of the same? Is it our sanctuary? Is it our fortress from all the oppressive powers that rankle our lives? Is it the one true place we have left to shut out the evil and the insanity? Then why do we bring the evil and the insanity in the front door with us? How much control do we really have? We are playing with a stacked deck. What human can endure a constant struggle twenty-four hours a day? We know tomorrow will be here soon enough but the bickering grows like a cancer in our homes. We attack our loved ones with more vigor and determination than we attack those things that need to be addressed in society. What a waste of time. Why prolong our agony of the day? Why not extinguish our anguish in the love and understanding that suits us best? So perhaps the battle is not won by five at night. But the night has come and the enemy sleeps. Don't let him ruin you by entering your camp. The world is tough. It is a battle. Don't bring it into the last sanctuary you have. Beating children is not the answer, nor a relief, but the further victory of the precarious detail you have nagging at your heels. Be it money, or lack of fulfillment, or whatever imagined monster that breaks down your door while the banks are all closed. Get a good night's sleep and come out strong in the morning. Downing a quart only gives the enemy more leverage. It doesn't pay the bills or feed the babies. They'll be there in the morning along with a terrific headache.

What does it all amount to? Surrender, give in, take the abuse or fight back, pick yourself up and move, lean away. Scramble, leave, scat, get out, book, skedaddle, scram, exit, gone, split, stage right or stage left. Pow! You find yourself back on the street and the enemy has you by the throat. No sanctuary, no peace. Or not. Maybe alone is best for some. You don't have to stay. Living in a home with drunken rage, complaints and negativity is a waste of a life. Eric was glad he left. How long is too long to preserve a bad marriage. Perseverance has its limits.

A whispered voice pushes through the sweet night air and moves warmly to the heart, "you've been starring out there for quite some time. What is it that you see?"

"I see everything I need to see, Wendy. The water and the stars. I can feel this massive reality welling up from a depth within." Their eyes met and the intensity moved from wandering to wondering to a smile so deep and wide as to curl the eyes. Warmth spread through their hearts and their lives were saved for now.

The walk to their next destination was filled with inspired talk of things to come, plans and realities. The stars and the truths are there, however hidden they might be, revealing the realities of it all. Let me tell you about this dream that I have and this dream that I had last night. And oh lord, the rush was unbelievable and it's getting to the point where I don't tell anyone about my deja vu experiences. I am hardly taken back by them any more. Can you believe people take them for granted. The solar winds echoed through a choir of angles and sounded so familiar. Do you hear it too? Danny does when he plays his acoustic guitar.

Wendy was filled with oysters as well as inspiration. It was a change from the typical blown dry personalities of her life. She loved being ga-ga. It had a cyclical effect that fed off of each other and grew in strength. Eric was just happy that he made someone happy. It was nice to have an ear that not only understood but said so. Wendy, well, just her presence was bringing out all these beautiful and complete thoughts by Eric. He was inspired by her compassion and her ability to listen. Her being able to give that to someone was finally being appreciated by someone. She preferred that instead of being some slab of meat or talking circles around the obvious and the eventualities, the hoped-upon outcomes or the obvious conclusions. The real self was getting a chance for some self-expression now. Not "yes sir" and "yes mam boss" or whatever happy horse manure they had to put up with at work, but some realness of original thought, and it was not competing with anything. It was merely playing in harmony and symphony with the stars as they sparkled in the night. They had their room key for a luxury suite.

1875 was no shabby date in architectural design. One built with their hands and was an artist. A fountain in the middle of a court with plenty of lush foliage made for romance. It was Spanish and French all at once. They wound their way through Gothic entrances and wrought iron gates. They walked over cobblestone and passed by history of immense proportion. The lushness and scent of the evening reached into their bodies bringing home to them the good Earth. The natural connection was made with each breath. As they wound their way up through the interior walkway past open terraces and closed tight rooms they walked past an ever-elevating view. The view from above showed the patio below with now empty tables and chairs askew. They found their room. As he slowly pushed open the door they entered a dimly lit room which featured wooden-pegged floors and smoothly stuccoed walls with well placed cracks and settling marks. Age was seeping in through where renovation was only temporary. Playing on the antiquity was a king sized brass-framed bed with a light quilt. A large window looked out over the courtyard and the sky was visible. It was quiet and dark outside. The enemy sleeps. It was warm and thick with air inside and the nurtured spirit awakes.

He stares compassionately into her eyes as she pulls him toward her. She brushes her hand along his face and stretches her hand out firmly against his chest. She runs it down as far as her arm will go. He wraps his arms around her and breaths softly on her neck. The kiss that followed was soft, warm, moist, and full. Her chest was pushed into his chest and he could feel her as she breathed heavy with satisfaction. Her scent was so familiar. She could feel his stiffness through her skirt and against her thigh. His hands slid down her back and squeezed her behind softly then harder and full of passion. She reached down passing over his stomach and felt him grow in her hand harder and harder as she squeezed. He reached up and undid her shirt. It fell open and revealed more of her cleavage and bra. She ran her hands up and down his thigh and reached to unclasp his belt. He pulled her shirt over her head as she raised her arms. He gazed at her as she stiffened pushing through her bra. The room was hushed in a warm light and the fountain could be heard in the distance. She undid her snap from the front as her chest was revealed and released. He tore off his shirt and they stood a brief but eternal moment peering at each other. Then she reached back for him and they pulled each other strongly and passionately together.

They felt their bodies together for the first time and their skin sighed. The fullness of her chest felt so warm and soft against him. He ran his hands down her back and up and inside her from behind. He leaned his head down at first teasing and licking her chest with his tongue and then trying to swallow her whole with his mouth. She smiled and stretched throwing her shoulders back. As they fell to the bed together he felt her soaked cotton panties and ripped them from her body. She reached for his pulsing hard-on freeing it from his pants. He stood there naked, stepping out of his trousers as it throbbed up and down. She leaned forward and slid her mouth around it, sucking it into her mouth as far as it would go. Her tongue circled and flicked its shaft. The wetness of her mouth was warm and hot. It bathed his passion. Then she pulled back quickly and just licked the end of it tasting the sweet juices. She leaned back onto the bed and slightly spread her legs in anticipation. The wait was killing them but he hung poised above her, throbbing. It's head still jerking back and forth. He sunk his face between her legs and kissed slowly softly her inner thigh. He licked and kissed her moist folds and plunged in his tongue with his lips lightly upon her. She moaned with delight as he probed her flesh. He backed out and tongued her clitoris and she quivered and grabbed at his ass. He had three fingers in her now. As she withered her eyes rolled up. Slowly he slipped his fingers wet and sticky in and out. Her body shivered and thrashed. She arched her back and he let her go. She fell back to the bed as he mounted her. He licked her warm supple breasts and then sucking deeply he let them fill up his mouth again. Slowly moving the tip of his cock up toward her she felt the hardness and excruciatingly anticipated his thrust. He met her soft opening going in slowly, pushing in tight, feeling his aching, throbbing hardness engulfed. It stretched her wider and deeper until finally all the way in and then thrusting back and forth. It fit perfectly. Too much bigger and it would hurt. A little smaller and it wouldn't hurt enough. He then quickly stopped and slowly pulled back and she contracted around his hardness and then he went back in a little faster this time. In harder and faster out slower and slower. He was banging her hard now as fast as he could. His genitals were slapping up against her ass driving her wild. He held her arms out away from her body by her wrists and she loved it. He stopped half way in and half way out and then started up again watching her tits bounce. Deep in ecstasy their hearts raced and the bed shook. Her explosion came slowly from across state lines and his came from another planet. He jammed furiously as he let go again and again and again and again and again.

When it was over they laid in a tangled heap. He rolled over numb from head to toe. She loved that he had given his all. Love was what made it special. Not needing to be reminded of that and not forgetting it either they curled up with one another. Their legs were draped comfortably and relaxed hearts were still pounding. Expressions content with head on shoulder they talked little but other than "wow" and the breathing was heavy. They drifted off to sleep. All time was engulfed in those moments. The hypocrisies and the lies of the world with its deranged societies and misguided fanatics was washed away. Personnel demons were exercised if one truly knew how to let go. The fear and doubt were obliterated. All the politics and fanaticism and self righteous posturing of my religion versus your beliefs, blah,blah,blah, pale in comparison to the self evident truths that nature gives us and places right at our feet. It's as clear as grapes on the vine and the weed in the ground and the love of two people who see life all around. Not dead and dying but rich vital life was teeming everywhere. It was filled with dynamics and mystery enough to shake the drudgery and doldrums loose from even the most cynical or pious. It is a vibrant world. The magnificent beauty of the natural wonders of the world go marching triumphantly onward forever, regardless if you can see them or not.

The power-hungry, glory seekers claim that the moon and stars, which the creative forces used to paint the sky, are symbols of evil. In spite of the fact that they fire our imagination and propel us to discovery. Fools, paranoid and dangerously misguided dismiss and exploit nature. There is nothing more and nothing less than the nature that sustains us and enables us to survive. Without a healthy environment we perish. Have we become so arrogant as to believe otherwise? We are provided with all the questions and wonders we could ever imagine. No fabricated institution, no matter what its political or accepted modes of behavior are, will ever produce something as massive, intricate and complete in it's balance, as the Earth. So live on and be free in your thoughts and desires. Know that the forces that created us created us with all of everything else. It is us who cloud everything up with our daily drudgery and fatally flawed misinterpretations. It is us who, with our separate cultures and doctrines, slay each other. It is us who destroy the kindred spirits and the animals who share this Earth. It is man who made up all the rules, religions and doctrines to hold up as a means of control and to organize. But the moral details are just ingredients for disaster. Before all the madness were the simple truths of reality, unclouded by interpretation and the lust for control. The rivers still flow onward and the Earth still spins around the sun and the Milky Way. The stars shine and the seasons change and the basic truths of reality will never be altered no matter what you call them or how you try to manipulate them for your own gain. Your self-absorbed self can never deny them. Put the bread on the table. These final thoughts ripped through Eric's mind in a kaleidoscope of feelings as he drifted off to sleep.

Across the dusty street that cracked with age and worn-down cobblestone, and down the darkened roads that were quiet without Fat Tuesday, the transients, artists, and affluent slept quietly. They were more confused and unprepared than any other generation. They were surrounded by the roots of the mysteries of reality and drawn to the Crescent City with its veils of witchcraft, voodoo and the occult. The dark forces gathered here and danced in the air with corpses. They mingled across, and through not-so-ancient times of slavery, wealth and war. The ravages of time left no mark on the bog, or the swamp and a big muddy river. Swaying in the breeze, the reality just is. Here is where the Mississippi, like the Nile, Tigris and Euphrates, spawned a civilization as deep and mysterious as the water and the sky from which it came. Children swung over the river from a rope tied to a tree. Life went gleefully on in all its bliss. Traded goods from the ports of the Caribbean and South America converged on the water highway. All have to deal and live by the mood of the sea. The rush of the mouth of the river overflows like the Nile, "well damn the whole city then." Some say the whole city is damned. Hell is only four feet below sea level. Myths, folklore, the birth of jazz, paddle wheels and gambling on the bayou. Life imitates gumbo and gumbo imitates life. Crossing from one side of the French Quarter to the other side can really make one think. History reign's supreme and the lessons are real. The battle of New Orleans if lost would have split the continent in half more than the most horrible political agenda.

Across town, back at the Chamber, the last note had been struck. The crowd was thinning out in an exhausted sweat-drenched aura of enlightenment. Louise and John were huddled in the corner weighing their new relationship. Adam and Jessica were still at their table. Adam did not want to stir too much. He was exhausted with booze and the road, both mentally and physically. Danny was wiping the neck of his guitar down with a purple dishtowel from home. Mark, Bonnie and Doug were at the bar slugging down ice-cold Dixie long necks. It was the only way you could drink that beer. Sam was wandering over to Adam and Jessica. He motioned to Danny to join them.

"What's up," asked Danny hoping off the stage?

"I think I can get us out of this jam and right now," said Sam looking at Adam and Jessica. They all stared back and forth at each other. The flame on the candle flickered with energy and then, went out, leaving Adam and Jessica less illuminated as they sat at their table. "Well," spoke Sam finally, "maybe not all the way out of our jam but definitely a little easing of the situation, especially for all of you."

"Do you have a buyer," asked Adam intuitively.

"Yeah," answered Sam slowly.

"Do you know these guys, Sam," asked Danny who thought they could do this patiently through known characters? "No, but I figure if

I can help Adam and Jessica unload it and quickly," his voice changed in tempo and confidence, "well then maybe they can head back home." Everyone was weighing this burst of information from Sam when he leaned in looking right into Adam and Jessica's eyes. "You two don't need to be out here on the run with me. If we're not careful then this whole trip is one long spiral downwards."

"You two don't need to be busted runaways," said Danny.

"I don't plan on being a hooker," came back Jessica. They all paused and took note of the power of her voice. "I can get a fair price and it will be off your hands," spoke Sam getting down to business. "And how much do you want for moving the stash," asked Adam? He didn't like Sam from the start. "Not a cent. I just want to start cleaning up this mess as quickly as possible. You're going to get the money and hopefully go home." Just as Adam was about to grill Sam a little harder, Jessica said okay. "Lets get rid of the bustables and have some cash."

"When and where, I'll be there," answered Adam in false bravery.

"Hold on dude, this is going to be tricky enough without a wounded man to look after." Adam was bought off by the word "man." Sam continued, "just give me the keys and I'll get this together. Better I meet them alone instead of us traveling in a crowd. Nothing concrete is worked out yet." Adam just nodded his head. He felt he had enough on Sam to protect his end. "Wait a minute," interrupted Danny. "You don't know them. You're taking a big chance. We can move this slowly over the bar through the employees."

"Too slow and too many people. I think we're all taking a bigger chance holding on to it." Sam turned to Danny and said, "how long do you think it would take before word got out, if you tried selling this stuff piecemeal from backstage," he paused for a moment?

"I don't know Danny," said Adam, "that would be risky."

"But we've done that before, Danny pleaded." Eric just shook his head no, "not with this kind of heat." They all just looked worried.

"Don't worry so much Danny," said Jessica.

"That's my strong suit," he answered back with a smile. "We've got to at least check up on those guys you're talking to Sam."

"Okay you check up, ask around, but only to a few people. We don't need anymore attention," and with that Sam walked away. He didn't need any negative thoughts in his head while this might be going down. He'd been in this situation before but back in more innocent times. "He's fine," spoke Jessica.

"Let him go," said Adam. Suddenly he didn't care if he got his money back or not. He had come dangerously close to death the night before and that scare was still with him. At this point he wasn't sure where he was going next. Was he going with the band, home, or to the Gray Bar Hotel? If he went with the band, how long until they got sick of having him around. Eric and Wendy were already gone. Who knew if they were ever coming back? Would that be the last time he would see Sam? Home was always an option, but the longer he stayed away the harder it was. Questions would fly at him from all angles and he might not be able to answer. And the more lies he told the farther from the truth that was himself he would be. He had this deep running instinct to protect Jessica and not ruin her life. He had to get rid of the pot even if it meant throwing it into the Mississippi. But how could he do that? He had risked his and her life on this investment and it would be foolish just to throw it all away. He needed to make some money. Sometimes principles had to come in last. Or did they? He wondered and toyed with his ideas. What was he trying to do anyway? Why had he risked his life in the first place? Was it just to make money, or what he was going to do with that money? Now he was telling himself all the noble things he would do with the money. But the truth of the matter was all this might have been just an act. It perpetuated some kind of image that he and others projected on himself. An image that was perpetuated by his peers and by trends. But Adam was enough of a man not to blame anyone other than himself. After all, they were his actions and he knew only he was responsible for them. At one point it gave him some kind of power in a world in which he had no identity. It was not only deemed cool by his peers but it also was a very easy shroud to slip in and out of, that is until now.

Anyway, he realized that his choices were severally limited since he had given up his car keys. "What the hell does Jessica think now," he wondered to himself. Jessica turned to look at him strangely on cue. Adam paused for one snap of a second. Then she spoke, "look we'll get the money and get the hell out of here. There is no one to look after us now. We make a move and go to California."

"Yeah it's nice out there," said Louise just now coming back to the table. "I've been there," she continued, "saw the Grateful Dead outdoors at the Greek Theater in Berkeley. Man, what a bunch of freaks in that crowd, but you know I never felt safer in my whole life."

"Right now I don't feel too safe," spoke Adam. He had always played a kind of macho role. It was getting tougher to break out of that role, but unusual circumstances brought about unusual results. Not that long ago he and his best buddy were busted back in junior high. Adam could hardly afford to go down again this time. Back then his buddy cried like a baby and blamed Adam for everything. He was young enough to get away with it and his old friend played the sorry child to the hilt. Everyone forgave the crier, but Adam's personality was no act. He stood straight and tall and maintained his course in the face of the establishment. He would never rat a buddy out or make excuses for his actions. He wasn't used to giving up on a friend, but his old buddy tried to act like nothing happened. He choked when the heat came down, and didn't take advantage of the time Adam bought him to toss the contraband from the car. He hid that fact from everyone. But Adam knew he was just greedy and thought he could hide it in his sock. The betrayal was a slow burn and a tough lesson to learn. His words he meant, and that was rarely true for most his age. His main hanging out buddy was a poser much to the confusion of Adam.

Jessica wasn't phased tonight. Somehow this situation turned her into a pragmatic. Aids would be left to a blood test and dealt with later. All the time until then, if she let it pray on her mind, the not knowing, it would eat her alive. She only used to worry about getting pregnant. "We are completely out of sync with nature," she thought to herself, "who needs anymore proof than aids?" She shook her head and looked down at her hands for the moment.

Back up the street, in this surrealistic town that Salvador Dali must have dreamed up, Wendy and Eric rolled over. Back at the bar, Danny was wondering why it always seemed to be him that looked after people. He never got the answer to that question. "What's going on Danny? Sam's talking to some scary looking dudes," probed Mark. "It seems we've got some pot for sale," answered Danny.

"Christ on a crutch Danny, don't let us go down in this city. Southern hospitality goes out the window for Yankee drug dealers."

"Good point Mark. See the guy doing all the pointing and talking?"

"The one with the expensive shirt and sneakers?"

"That's the one we need to find out about and quietly," said Danny. He headed over towards Bonnie and Doug. They were talking about the blues influence on jazz for the thirtieth time this tour. They were boring some poor unsuspecting bartender. Danny got a beer from him and asked about the guy in the expensive shirt. "Looks like a cop to me," spoke the bartender. "Now those drag queens over there are much more of a tourist attraction." A couple of laughs latter Danny hadn't found out much. The bartender was filling in for someone, or at least that's what he said. Sam came back up to Adam and Jessica. "It's set. I'll be gone ten minutes."

"I'll be right here waiting for you. Don't fuck up my car." Sam had this silly grin on his face. He always enjoyed straightening things out. He loved being the troubleshooter. "I'm just going down Decatur Street and meeting these guys two blocks from here just so you know, okay?" Adam shook his head yes. Danny approached the table, "according to the bartender they might be cops but he didn't say for sure."

"A little too cleaned up to be undercover in this place," said Sam trying to let Danny know he thought about that already. Danny just raised his eyebrows and frowned. "We can't hesitate for a moment. They'll be looking for that sixty-nine Thunderbird after their parents file a missing persons report. "He looked back at Adam and Jessica, "when they pull you over and find that hooch you'll be sunk."

"Okay Sam," said Danny," but you could be sinking us right now!"

"Don't worry," and with that he flashed his gun, "I got it covered."

"Hell," seethed Jessica with her teeth clenched, "don't get any wild ideas. We don't want that shit coming back on us, Sam!"

"I'm just showing the guys that we're not getting taken."

"Okay then all right," said Adam, unfortunately impressed by the gun. Just then the jukebox kicked back in. The late night and early morning crowd was starting to arrive. Of course the held overs were holding over. "Lets get a really nice place for the night," spoke Jessica. Wendy woke up momentarily and kissed Eric on the cheek. She pulled herself closer to him as they lay on their sides. Eric reached back and let his hand fall lightly on her leg. Back at the bar, Jessica pushed herself away from the table and told Adam she would be right back. On her way she ran into Louise. "How are you," she asked?

"Fine," she said without having to give it much thought.

"Who's clothes do you have on?"

"These are John's," said Louise. There was a slight pause and Louise felt the need to explain. "When I came into the Jaded Lady I was soaked from the rain and well . . ." she stopped short of a full explanation, "I haven't had a chance to hit the mall yet." They both had to laugh at that. "Poor lady," Jessica thought to herself, "hey look if we get some extra cash we'll hit the mall together." It was a moment of compassion. Jessica was like that.

"Don't waste your money on me," countered Louise, "first of all who ever has extra bread," and she raised her eyebrow at her own thought? "Besides the roads not too kind to designer wear."

"Well," Jessica thought out loud, "we'll get you stuff that you can use. You shouldn't be so homeless that you don't have your own clothes," Jessica grimaced at her own abruptness. Louise looked at her with the compassion that Jessica was trying to show Louise, "I'm not homeless, I'm just a little transient right now. I'm not mental, and I've had some damn good jobs. I'm a damn good worker. I was on my way to settle in Florida when I rolled into Danny. If we hadn't of crossed paths I wouldn't be here right now."

"Is that good or bad," asked Jessica sincerely?

"Well, good I suppose," she paused. The jukebox was playing Ronnie Hawkins' version of Matchbox. "I was getting my head punched in pretty bad when I ran into him."

"He saved you," Jessica asked incredibly.

"Well not exactly," again she paused, "let me put it this way. I didn't have anything better to do."

"Is everything you have on your back?" Louise could detect the disappointment in Jessica's question. It wasn't a disappointment that was critical but rather sorrowful. So Louise made up a lie to spare her new friend some hard feelings. Louise had always paid for those lies. The lies lived on longer than the time it took to speak them for those that did the remembering. She knew the truth was different and it dug down deep. "I have a place back in Florida." It wasn't her place at all. "And a checking account honey," she forged her roommates checks. "What about you Jessica? What are you doing here," she said changing the subject?

"The same as you. I'm on a bad roll. Luck of the draw. Adam's a great guy but we don't need this. The whole problem is," and she pushed her face closer to Louise, "this fucking reefer. He's so attached to it. We could have left it on the beach or thrown it out of the car window. If we sold it to Sam last night we would have been home by now. He's got his ego totally wrapped up in this thing. We could have split instead of going on this joy ride."

"At home you would have had to explain the knife wound."

"That would have been easier than explaining away all the other things." Jessica stopped short of telling Louise about the rape. She didn't want to tell anyone about it and by not being home it would be easier to keep it quiet. Being on the move the depression doesn't get a chance to settle in so far. But when it takes hold, and you are not home, the depths of despair become enormous. She knew she had to find another way home. There was a Creole swing number coming from the jukebox now. Jessica made her way to the bathroom. "For every debt there is a payment one way or another," spoke Louise. Jessica was still within earshot and just nodded her head.

Louise found her way back to the table. The flickering candles still burned. Beaten children beat their kids, and beaten children let themselves get beaten by their spouses. The cycle perpetuates itself. You have to be of strong character to break the wrong pattern and start the thing rolling in the right direction. We find ourselves in this loop of perpetuating the modes of behavior we have been taught, some good, some bad. The trick was to know the difference and what you were imitating. To break free of the pattern is to be an individual.

Knowing the difference between mimicking and self-discovery is required. Jessica had returned to the table and sat next to Louise, "I just hope we can get rid of this stuff. It's like an albatross hanging from our necks."

"Without the wafers," added Louise. Jessica didn't hear her, "and then we could get home." She turned to look at Louise and sighed, "and deal with the rest of this shit."

"Home is right here," Louise pointed to her chest, "don't let anyone kid you about that. Unless you realize that simple truth you'll be wandering and searching forever."

"You're still searching aren't you?"

"Oh yeah but it's not like I'm searching out there for the answers. I know they're inside of me. I'm just hoping that one day I run across something that releases them. And then maybe I'll know what they are. Look, all I am saying, and it is simple, is this; the answers to those questions that come part and parcel with birth and the human experience, well you don't have to go to California to figure them out. You don't even have to figure them out. If you look beyond yourself and see your spirit residing in your body then you have seen it all. Your body is just a temporary vessel for the spirit. If your life doesn't feel right, then you have to step back make a plan, and do something about it. I chose the nomadic way. Okay, extenuating circumstances and opportunities keep all of us hemmed in at one point or another, but no one meets a situation or circumstance or problem that they can't overcome. The stronger you are the harder the test. You just have to believe or have the drive, the power, or the will to overcome. Hell most of the stuff we worry about is just superficial garbage compared to what is really real." She took a drink and Jessica looked at her cautiously. "The things that are common to us all, no matter what our culture, or what beliefs we create, are the threads that join us. But we are so obsessed with our self-importance we don't think anybody else deals with these same questions. If you take a look around, humankind has been struggling with these questions since time began. Why do you think we have all these different religions all claiming to have the answers. Maybe, just maybe, there are many different ways to unlock the door.

No one method is right for everyone. An individual has to go about it their own way. If you waste your time going through the motions don't be surprised if you come away unfulfilled. You can't sit it out. You either laugh, marvel, or listen hard, and I mean really hard, to what is going on around you, and within, or you cry. So know it and feel it. All these large institutions are set up because people want other people to tell them what to do. People desperately want an answer to the human condition. They'll commit mass suicide they are so desperate to be led spiritually. They need to think for themselves and find the answers within. The questions are so basic, who am I, what am I, how did I get here, how did we get here, that it cuts right to the core of existence and becomes so large and unclear that people are just spazing out all over the place."

"But some people are really sick," spoke Jessica quietly.

"Right and it's because of a lack of identity that these questions and doubts become so overwhelming. They can't be ignored. The damn thing surfaces daily and creates havoc even for the healthy person. Others shove their head in the sand and still others break down completely. But no one can mask the toll of the unexamined and unfulfilled life. No amount of drugs, booze, money, sex, or any other common variety of distraction will work. It's all been tried."

"So who's fault is it."

"Again with the fault, the blame game. You are responsible for your situation and your choices. That's all there is to it. It's no one's fault. Society needs institutions just to survive and function. It wouldn't be a credit to society if we all just scrounged around pissing in each other's well water. The intention behind the progress, behind the words that are spoken or written, is what it is all about. Are we just for ourselves the drive to survive so the ego can pound its chest? Or are there other reasons at play that are more noble and less selfish? We have become too comfortable with technology and thinking that the latest invention will give us fulfillment or help us reach nirvana. We have lost the art of solitude. The joy of being alone and feeling the rich, thick moments of our life fully and completely as they move on by. It's a lost art. We can't relate to each other or our surroundings anymore. We run from distraction to distraction trying to fill up the void inside and we never do. The progression of technology is not the entire justification for our being."

Jessica was starting to squirm in her seat. Was she listening to a mad person or was she making too much sense? Louise went on. "Life is like a maze. It's meant to confuse, to offer us choices, time and time again. It's meant to give us the opportunity to reach beyond the glorification of self, and to partake and to help the whole of all being. It doesn't matter which way you go. There are more than a million galaxies worth of choices to make. In my opinion only that you go beyond the limited attitude of self is all that matters."

"So why are you here," asked Jessica again?

"Life is an adventure to me. Like a giant sandbox. I'm here to see how far I can go. When I can go no farther here I'll pick up my gear and go elsewhere and see how far I can go there."

"Been down a couple of dead ends, I bet."

"A few, but every road eventually stops and becomes history. There is no end to the number of roads you can take."

"Some aren't very physical either," said Jessica throwing her drink down.

"Well you can never tell for sure about them. I mean you might know, be absolutely convinced, but in trying to share that spiritual path with somebody, well, you lose something in the translation. That's why religion is so personal. Unless you are trying to convert someone to your way of thinking and brainwash them into your cult in order to manipulate them, there is no reason to hammer away at dogma all day long. Share your thoughts with your congregation, but respect that other people are traveling other roads to enlightenment. In fact I'm convinced there is a different road for each and every person. Those that believe there is only one way, road, or path and that their way is the only way, well that leads to blood shed. And it's amazingly short-sighted considering the incredible examples and the diversity that is around us and that is us. So why are you here?"

"Like I said I couldn't leave Adam behind, and I sure couldn't tell him what to do. Guys are messed up like that. It's like his whole life depends on this reefer and it almost killed him."

"Yeah, all this status-driven, action-hero baloney drives me crazy too," said Louise. "Hey, big deal, I'm a dope dealer. Look at me. I have to sleep with one eye open and one day I disappear and no one knows where I went."

"But it's not his fault that I'm here either," said Jessica. "I guess I've got some of you in me. Hell, I figure this might cure him of some of his cowboyness. We're in it good now and this is no time to bail on a friend."

"No and you shouldn't give anything up until it starts to hurt you and what you have going on inside of you. As long as you keep your foundation and sense of self strong you should be able to withstand anything life throws at you." Jessica looked back across the table at Louise. Half of Louise's face was covered in shadow. She had this really healthy look on her face for wearing someone else's clothes. The laugh lines were deeply cut around her eyes and she proudly displayed her weathered hands on the table. Her hands revealed more of her journey than her age. The road was worn into her. Her hair was straight and pulled back with an old piece of leather and the flickering candle reflected in her eyes. They were deep and dark. Her expression was calm. Jessica spoke, "so that's how you do it."

"That's how I do it. No matter what is going on around me, I never loose my sense of self. That doesn't mean I'm not open for influence. I know a good idea when I hear one and I draw from all the truths in this life that surround me. But I'm not perfect and I waiver and forget, obsess and worry like anyone else. But I take time to be alone and listen to my breath and calm myself. I usually wake up fresh. There's not much carry over with me. Each day is really special and filled with opportunity to right a wrong, work on better choices and search for new ones." She looked back at Jessica," but I fuck up a lot too."

"Well since it's obvious that I am here because of some ego ridden man," Jessica continued choosing her words carefully, "could you have the same problem?"

"Sure," the word came out slowly and with dignity. Louise didn't think it was wrong to do things because of a man. After all men do a lot of things because of women. "But your independent and a drifter. What's up with that?"

"The boys were kind to me. I'm wearing John's clothes. Danny tried to help. Besides I like to be held and made love to and I prefer men over women."

"How unfashionable," Jessica said in mock disdain. They both cackled like two crows on a wire. "Then you don't think less of me for following my typical male boyfriend around being his typical girlfriend."

"Think less," Louise marveled at the thought? "Hell, I'm envious, and if anyone gives you attitude about your happiness, whether your involved with somebody or not, they're just envious too!" They both mulled it over for a second and Louise picked the conversation back up again. "Look what does it matter? What other people think is irrelevant and leads to confusion. Does it make you feel happy inside or is it causing you pain? You have to listen to your insides for your whole life, every aspect. Are you just using each other or do you feel it fulfills you? Even if you're just using each other that can be all right too, but I wouldn't recommend it because feelings grow. The question is does it hit that gut mark and fill you up or do you feel empty inside? The other person can do that for you but only if you let them. It comes down to you the individual and what you are capable of and understand. Besides I don't think either of you are typical. I mean, I just met you, but if you're out here with me then you're not too typical. It takes a lot of guts for your friend to be in the situation he's in now. All his money is tied up and someone tried to kill him. You're the only one he can trust and I wouldn't betray that trust. Trust might be easy to give but it's impossible to get back once it's gone."

"Stay with us for a while Louise."

"I do better alone." With that Jessica reached out and held the hand of the drifter. Funny how beauty always comes out so much stronger when it comes from inside. Louise put her hand on top of Jessica's, blinked, smiled, and moved away. As the pace of the music on the jukebox quickened so did the mood.

Sam silently slipped out the backstage door. It was the same way he had come in and the darkness was as complete as it could be. It met with the humidity to create a dark soupy atmosphere. Dark and thick was the night. The streetlights spread a dim yellowish light.

Each particle of light struggled. Like sunbeams through a dense forest, the light never reached the ground and barely showed the way. We are scared and blind. That's why we chop the forest down, proving our ignorance and furthering our own demise. It seems this civilization has a suicidal tendency for self-destruction. We know what we are doing, but we do it anyway. Sam's shoes hit the pavement hard. Knowing the contraband was where it should be he opened up the drivers side door of the Thunderbird. It creaked open, old, rotting steel. The solitary noise reverberated down the alley. He was around back now and the noise of the club was street side. He turned the engine over and pulled out onto Decatur Street. He didn't have far to go and drove very slowly. Sam was a pro. He adjusted his mirrors and scanned both sides of the street. Just a block, a turn down another street, and then up an alley and he would be there. His headlights, old and faded struggled to find the road, but Sam knew his way around these streets. The night and the darkness crept into his soul. The clatter of the engine and the shaking of the car ran up his legs. He learned to ignore apprehension. He made his final turn and cut his lights. He decided against idling the engine. The old Thunderbird was too loud or the alley was too quiet he couldn't decide which. His heartbeat was the only thing he could hear. The mist moved through the night air. He got out of the car and checked his watch. A match struck farther up the alley. Sam struck his wooden match. It cracked against the silence and darkness with fire. The light lasted for a few seconds and then died out. Sam heard their footsteps and muffled talking as they approached. Way off in the far distance laughter could be heard. Sam was counting on some more people moving about. He'd just have to ride this one home. Sam stood motionless.

"Where's the stash bud?" It was one of the guys in the bar.

"In the trunk. How 'bout the cash?" With that a sudden thud hit the hood of the Thunderbird. A flick of a lighter and the unzipping of a small road bag showed neatly packed U.S.A. dollars. Sam did not allow himself a smile. Any amount of money within reason would be good. He did not count it but looked in the bag for bogus bread wrapping paper or monopoly money but it all looked real to him. Sam reached out from the darkness and handed over one trunk key that had been in his hand. He did not want to have to reach into his pockets and raise the level of tension or force a search. "They don't trust me either," thought Sam to himself. The trunk swung open while Sam was still at the front of the car. He had the money and was going to slip away while they unloaded. He'd come back for the car later. He didn't see any vans or other cars. He didn't see any other alley doors swing open. The two guys at the trunk exchanged conversation. Sam was backing away slowly. A piece of gravel directly behind him was crushed by an inadvertent shoe stepping off the curb. It was not Sam's shoe. He hadn't had a chance to look directly behind him yet but he was just about to do that. He sensed a presence. He moved his right hand slowly toward his pistol. "Damn, it was dark," he thought to himself. He started to turn his head to the left so he could see behind him with the corner of his eye. Nothing was there. A cold, sharp edge dragged slowly across his throat. The presence had moved right along with him and stayed directly behind him. Blood oozed out hot and moist. Sam's right knee buckled. He fell forward bouncing off the car. He landed on the street on his back as a terrible rush shook his body. His hand never reached his gun. He never heard the conversation that followed next or more of the distant laughter.

Danny had just finished talking to another guitar player that happened by the club that night. They had agreed to work with each other, as the band would do a sound check over the next few days. It had been a half hour since Sam had left. "Any word," asked Danny approaching Adam and Jessica at their table.

"No and I'm worried," said Jessica, "I've got a creepy feeling. He said ten minutes right?"

"These things take longer than that," spoke Louise walking up behind Jessica, and meeting Danny at the table at the same time. "It might be time to go poke around outside," said Adam.

"Right," said Louise with a wry smile, "and what better person to do it than an unsuspecting homeless chick with guys clothes on."

"I'm going with you," said Danny. Jessica was glad she wasn't going.

"We could take the Jeep," continued Danny, "they might be half way across the city by now."

"If they are," spoke Louise, "we won't find them. Besides we don't want to draw attention to ourselves. Lets just take a walk together."

"Be careful," Jessica spoke out, "I think I miss the suburbs." John approached the table, "what's up guys?" He sensed the tension.

"Come on. We need another body," spoke Danny anxiously and with that the three of them went out the back. Once out on the street Louise filled John in, ". . . and we decided to walk. If he's not around here somewhere, he's out spending the money and it's just all out of control."

"This is getting a little nuts Danny. How do we manage to get into these situations all the time?" Danny just shrugged his shoulders. "Don't look at me," spoke Louise, "lately all I've been able to do is get into trouble, not out of it."

"I know it's bad," said Danny, "but I still have to manage this thing so it doesn't affect the band."

"Too late. Bonnie's all pissed off," said John.

"Yeah well she's usually pissed off about something," answered Danny harshly, "I had to beg her to come out with us this time. Can you believe that with the way she loves to show off?" They walked up Decatur Street and turned off the main drag. Now, back behind the dark alleys they dropped the whole subject. The three of them began listening intensely. They slinked up the street more mindful of their presence the noise they were making, and kept looking. The steps the three of them took became more measured and deliberate. "She says you're a fuck up, Danny."

"Latter. I'm not going to get my ass shot off arguing about her."

John stared down at the street. He wondered for a minute about where he was. Right in the middle of everything like the rest of us. Louise tugged at Danny's shirt and put a finger to his lips. They stopped. No one spoke. All that could be heard were dewdrops from the rain gutters hitting the pavement below. The street noise was way off in the distance. They cautiously turned up the dark alley where Sam was supposed to be. Danny wasn't quite sure what Louise had seen but he knew she had better street instincts than he. John was strangely aware of his body his beating heart and how loud he was when he moved. From the other side of the street the rear of the

Thunderbird slowly appeared out of the night way up the alley and with its trunk wide open. John's head was screaming run but Louise was moving toward the car from the passenger side. There was no sign of activity. Slowly, and in the moment, it seemed like forever, they arrived at the trunk. It was empty. Danny's head was on a swivel but no one was around. Louise didn't know what she was looking for but her head was screaming, "watch out." Danny walked around to the other side and saw the driver's door open. His head was telling him be afraid of this. When he knelt down beside Sam to get a better look, shock and a blast of reality washed over his entire being. The darkness had engulfed his friend. He knew Sam was dead but he reached down to check his pulse. No breath, no pulse, just blood streaming over his favorite shirt. "Shit," John was standing right behind Danny. He started to throw up and hurried off the street. Louise grabbed the keys and was pulling what little they had out of the back seat and glove compartment. "What are you doing?"

"Look Danny I know he was your friend but now more than ever we gotta clear out of here." Danny had frozen, "well let's just call the cops."

"They'll be here soon enough and you'll be answering lots of questions."

"I just found him I didn't know." John walked back over and said, "think Danny. They'll probably lay this all on you, especially if you can't blame someone else." Louise gave him an example, "who are you, how do you know him, why was he here and why did you leave the Jaded Lady together?"

"They are not going to deal you a good hand," said John. "You don't want to get anymore involved with this and right now whoever did this doesn't know who you are."

"And that's a good thing," spoke Louise.

"It's my fault he's dead right now. I should have gone with him."

"No it's not and that's not the point," said John impatiently. They both looked at Danny with pleading eyes. "Okay, I get it. Look under the seats and lets haul out of here." So they went into high gear and Louise searched Sam's body. "What the hell you little street bitch," seethed an offended John.

"Look this is no time for self-righteousness. It'll slow the cops down if he doesn't have any id on him." As she spoke, she pulled out a load of dollar bills and it surprised her. "This was a weird robbery. I guess they just wanted the dope. But why leave this for the cops? We'll split it up later."

"We just can't leave him lying here a John Doe," begged Danny, "what about his folks?"

"We're not calling anybody," whispered John.

"Here put his card in his pocket," countered Danny digging through Sam's wallet. "It's from the Jaded Lady. That'll send the trail back to Florida."

"Not likely," said Louise, "when they find out the same band is just playing around the corner they'll swoop in on you guys like a virus."

"Well I'm leaving it there anyway so I don't feel like a schmuck leaving my friend dead in the gutter," stated Danny.

"Leave the watch and rings," said Louise.

"Great," said John sarcastically. Starting to hate the fact that he fucked her. She knew what he was thinking about. Quickly and when they thought every possible clue was taken out of the car and off of Sam's body they fled like the crooks, cops, and vultures they loathed. Shadows from light they bolted down the street. Sam lay there unceremoniously with a Jaded Lady card stuck notoriously in his pocket and near his heart. They tossed his id and wallet in a commercial dumpster outside a restaurant. Finally, back at the Chamber, Louise, John and Danny entered trying not to look too freaked out. When they found Adam, Louise gave him his keys and sat down. "What the hell does this mean?"

"Sam's dead," she answered staring intently into his eyes. "He's laying all over the street in his own blood." She handed him the car's registration and insurance card. "Now either you go back to that car and drive away now this very second or we'll throw the tags in the Mississippi."

"Sam was ugly," spoke John as he slumped in his chair.

"Fuckin A," remarked Adam unemotionally.

"Now what," said Bonnie who was also at the table? Doug stood by her side. Mark wandered over. "It's time to start gathering up our instruments Mark. It's time to go again," spoke Danny.

"It won't take too long for the cops to put all this together," agreed John.

"Great, fucking great," Bonnie was completely pissed. "What are we doing with all these people? Were trying to be a band!"

"Shut up Bonnie, we don't need to hear your shit right now," slammed John.

"Well, I'm out of here," she went on, "pay me. I'm on my way back home. I don't need this! Everyone back home told me I was crazy to go with you Danny and they were right. Everything you touch goes wrong!"

"Go ahead bitch," said Danny, "what the hell do you care? Go on back home! Go ahead, get the fuck out of here!" Bonnie stood up but didn't move. "They'll welcome you back with open arms!" No one said a word.

"Bonnie," said Doug trying to get her to back down, "the band's been through some strange times before." She held her tongue. Danny and Louise got up with Adam and Jessica who had been whispering to themselves. They all went outside together and let the band scream at one another and trash and defend Danny.

"We don't need any more witnesses," said Danny to Adam as they got outside. Still dark the night didn't get any brighter. They walked on back toward the Thunderbird as Adam turned to Danny shaking his head," I knew this was going bad. We should have just left the Jaded Lady when we had the chance."

"Well now you have a second chance," said Louise.

"Danny we're gone," he answered. And with that Adam put out his hand and said good-bye. The dice had been rolling hard and they were fighting the seemingly inevitable. They gave up trying to figure out how it was supposed to turn out and just decided to go. Louise and Jessica hugged. "Look," spoke Louise, "this money was found on Sam. I know he wanted you two to get back to Normal Life U.S.A. before it was too late." She pushed the money into Jessica's hands. Louise smiled and said, "the mall will have to wait." They hurried now back up the street as all became silent again. When they found the alley and approached the car, Sam still sinfully laid there. Late enough into the night and far enough up an obscure alley no one had been by. The cops would be there in the morning when the businesses put their trash out. The night couldn't keep this crime out of view forever.

Sam's life on this mortal coil was long gone. The blood was drying. Jessica took a full moment and stood over him while Danny slid the plates back on. She thanked him for trying to help. No tears fell from her eyes. Adam just stepped over him shaking his head as they made haste. Danny and Louise turned and hustled back down the alley. The sixty-nine Thunderbird's engine turned over quickly and sent a roar after them. But Adam didn't turn on the lights until he was close to the main drag and out on the road. Darkness hid the blood from the curious and Adam and Jessica headed for the interstate. Before sun up they would pull over to eat. Nature keeps rolling right along.

Back at the Chamber the mood was somber. Heads were hung and the instruments went quietly into their cases. The gig was history. Bonnie didn't care how much Danny hurt. Louise did. They decided to wait for Eric and Wendy as the sun came up over the horizon like any other day. They had steak, eggs, beans, grits, sausage, beer and bourbon for breakfast. "Must misery follow me wherever I go," wondered Danny to himself bumming out completely? Louise stayed close to his side. John and Bonnie talked about the possibility of another gig and if it would last longer than one night. "Damn I was pumped for New Orleans," said John.

"No one here knows where our next gig is right," questioned Bonnie?

"We didn't have a chance to tell anyone," said Danny thankful for small favors.

"Well we're out of luck here," Bonnie continued in her tone. As the sun rose up it turned behind some clouds. A bright day was halted and the rain drizzled down. The temperature dropped to sixty-five degrees. Inside Eric and Wendy's room the enemy had been shut out from the night before. Romance was brewing as the two lovers entwined passionately. They explored their passion deeply and pushed their love intensely like an artist attacks his music or lays furious brush strokes to a canvas. The rain fell slowly at first and then pounded the streets. On the outskirts of town the Thunderbird's lights were struggling to see the road. Sam's body was being washed from heaven above. Soon his body would be rinsed clean. Would he become another lost soul wandering between the infinite and the finite haunting New Orleans? Would he be tormented in agony forever doomed by the mystery that covered his death? Would the tombs above ground reach out to him with the restless and wronged? Or would Sam's last act carry him like a wounded soldier to a place of peace, a place where the mind's eye of creativity would flow in full realization all around him? Or would he just rot in the street?

Wendy and Eric strolled toward the Chamber for breakfast. In and out of the drizzle and downpour they came. Inside the club, the band and Louise waited. Louise was ready to slip away. They all tried to appear relaxed, but waiting on Eric and Wendy had unnerved them. It was close, too close, and the cops, although without the Thunderbird for evidence, still had that business card in Sam's shirt pocket.

"Relax," hissed Danny," give Eric and Wendy another fifteen minutes."

"If another cop car goes down the street I'm gonna scream," said Bonnie. With that Wendy and Eric made their entrance.

Eric just knew. He had the feeling when the second cop car went by outside and now seeing everyone on the edge gave it away.

"You're all here," he asked?

"But where's Sam," asked Wendy?

"Shh, we'll clue you in later," said Danny.

"Where the hell have you been," demanded Doug beating Bonnie to the punch.

"Out being normal, obviously," spoke Mark.

"They're here now, can we go," seethed Doug? Bonnie had been cooking him up all night about Danny. "Just where the hell are we going," asked Bonnie, "this is ridiculous."

"Just what the hell happened," asked Eric sensing the urgency ever greater.

"Sam's dead. We gotta go," answered Danny matter-of-factly.

"I thought this was going to be a good day," spoke Wendy.

"I got an idea where we can go," said Eric. "I was thinking about this last night for Wendy and I, but it might work for all of us."

"No motels, they'll nail us for sure," spoke Doug.

"Some place where we won't be involving any more people," pleaded Danny.

"Finally you make some sense," bitched Bonnie. She turned her head to Mark, "I'll get the cops myself," she threatened. Eric stared Bonnie down. He didn't even know her. "We don't have time for this shit. If you want to run out on your friends get going already." Everyone got up and made their way to the Jeep and the musician's van. "What have you got in mind, Eric," asked Danny?

"Well," he said in a much lower tone than the one he used on Bonnie, "we've just got to get out of the city first. I know a good place outside of Baton Rouge and I think we can head out that way. If not at least we'll buy time until we think of something else."

"That's it," questioned Bonnie to Doug incredulously?

The band walked right out the back door and never looked back. Mark, Doug, John and Bonnie got in the van. Eric, Wendy, Danny and Louise were in the Jeep. Twenty-four hours had gone by and it was time to leave. New Orleans was like that.

THERE'S NO MOOSE IN LOUSIANA

—

The rubber was smoking along the interstate in a mad panic. What had just happened blew their world apart. Their world mind you, not "the" world. For surely as they were reacting to their own consequences the world was still doing it's own thing. The maniacs had reached them, rocked and garbled their reality. The choices that were to come were a result of the choices they had already made. The damn thing kept folding back over on itself. Every time they thought they had moved beyond some twisted version of a smash-up-derby called life, more alleged destiny and fate brought them back to face their decisions and themselves squarely in the eye. There was no way to look away and nowhere to hide. It stared them down and made them shake. It wasn't some preordained set of circumstances that a great god in the sky had laid out before them, but rather a perfectly linked set of reactions resulting from themselves and their decisions, and their motives, and their agendas; right down to the souls they encountered along the way. No this wasn't some bad dream god had inflicted on them to test them. These were their self-inflicted choices stacked up like rush hour traffic bogging them down. It was the same for each of them and all of mankind together. It was convenient to blame fate. It was their will and their moves that had landed them straight where they were. Blaming someone else for their predicament was the ultimate denial of self. As if they didn't exist. As if what they did, every second of every day, didn't matter. Jessica and Adam were not about to relinquish that responsibility of self just as surely as they bolted from New Orleans.

The beads of rain that remained on the glass moved slowly across the window. Now headed in the other direction the noon time sun was bleaching the pavement dry. The sixty-nine Thunderbird and its suicide doors pulled in for gas and a grizzly road lunch. Their stomachs howled in protest. "Jessica, look at this," Adam flashed a newspaper at her from inside by the counter. In only the second day headed for the third night the headlines screamed, "Twenty Seized In Drug Bust." The screen door from the station slammed shut behind them as they walked off their lunch. "It's all over the paper," stated Jessica. Adam turned for a pay phone, "I have to call that dumb ass Ben."

"All right I'll see what I can learn from the radio," and off Jessica went to the car. He dialed Ben's cell but it was turned off and he didn't dare leave a message. He dialed Ben's home but the phone rang continuously without picking up. It rang with no sense of urgency. It should ring faster in times of trouble. He hung up and dialed again. Adam desperately wanted to make this phone call. It seemed like each ring rang out slower. They stretched like a balloon about to burst. Each moment was enunciated reminding him of how many moments make up a minute, an hour, a day. "If each moment had a ring, a subtle tone, a note, would we still waste so many of them," he thought to himself? If we felt the moments and really felt the time, and were aware of it's passing so much so that we were immersed in the depth of each moment, wouldn't life then be different? Wouldn't we go much slower and be more measured? Wouldn't we drink more deeply from this fountain of time and light? Perhaps we would then realize that all that has come into being is sacred, right down to each breath? Finally the phone picked up. It was Ben's mom. She told him to hang on. "Hang on," Adam thought to himself, "was she kidding?"

"Yo," said the voice on the line.

"Ben," Adam questioned?

"Adam?"

"Dude," don't let anyone know it's me!"

"What's going on? You okay? Where the hell are you?" Adam broke into the one sided conversation. "Have you called my place looking for me? Do you know anything about what my parents are up to?"

"Yes, I mean no, I haven't called, yes, your parents called here. Adam they called the police." Adam felt his gut drop and roll. Somehow he kept his head as he took a rush of adrenaline. "Ben . . . ?"

"Dude, I told them we were at the Jaded Lady together and that we left before you did."

"You told them we were at the Jaded Lady! It's all over the paper."

"I know, I know, but that's not your only problem. Jessica's dad is on a max freak. He and your old man filed missing person reports on both of you."

"Christ on a crutch both sets of parents banging heads over this, great," said Adam loudly.

"Everyone is hassling me to dish the story. It's crazy."

"Like what Ben? What do they think they know?"

"Hey word travels dude. People know you were at the Jaded Lady and now you and Jessica are nowhere to be found for over a day. Get home dude and make up some story but don't bring that weed back here."

"Thanks Ben, your concern is overwhelming I can assure you we dumped that stuff. It's off our hands."

"Oh yeah, you got my money?"

"Ben," he hollered incredulously, "we were lucky not to get shot. It's gone and no one made a dime." He marveled at his lameness.

"Dude, chill out. I was just asking. People are pressing me about you so when you get home just say you and Jessica decided to hook up for a few nights at a resort or something. That's what I've been telling them probably happened."

"We'll have to think of something better than that. Just keep your mouth and your girlfriend's mouth shut."

"What were you expecting Adam?"

"Not this."

"Look if word . . .," just then the phone cut off and that annoying computerized voice came on interrupting the call for change. "Yeah, yeah, thank you," Adam hollered back at the computer after dropping in more money. Ben's voice came back on but Adam didn't tell him where he was or where he was going. Partly because he didn't have any idea where he was going next. He hung up and walked over to the car. It was idling with the doors open. Jessica had her feet up on the dash. Why couldn't they just go back to the beach he wondered to himself. "Forget the beach," said Jessica, in a tone that suggested an answer to his thought. She put the paper down and gave Adam a stare. "I think they got that son of a bitch who raped me!" It was the first she spoke of it. She had been reading a related article about a man caught on the beach. He was carrying a knife and the police were questioning him about the type of weed he was carrying. "That was our pot," said Adam, "he's telling the police about it all."

"People don't give their drugs away. Sharing is way out of fashion, he'll have to tell him he found it to avoid trouble but I wouldn't count on him being that smart, or the cops that dumb." Jessica was starting to freak, "it's all over the paper Adam." She showed him another article. Full details of the raid at the Jaded Lady jumped out at him and how they locked the place down. "This is huge . . ." Adam didn't let her finish, "that's nothing," he said putting the paper down with both hands, "your dad filed a missing person report and Ben told him we were at the Jaded Lady." He looked at her momentarily and continued, "that means they know what we're driving."

"Well that's just great," said Jessica kicking the dashboard.

"It depends on who they want first. We're not the big catch here."

"But we might be their best lead."

"Yep." Ever notice how the conversation gets shorter and ends when the truth is realized. "We picked the wrong places to go all night long."

"Just another night in America."

"We have to call home," and with that Adam walked back to the pay phone, not wanting to use the cell phone. Jessica shut the car off.

The phone rang back at Adam's house where the carpets were vacuumed and the dusting was done. The garbage was out and the refrigerator was full. The sun shined through bay windows on a beautiful Florida morning and the whole house felt like it was about to collapse. His mom answered the phone and then his dad got on the line. "Just come home," was all his Dad said. Adam's heart was pounding at this point. He was talking louder and pleading with his father to cancel the missing person reports. Life continued to weave down the road, drunk and on a binge. Adam hung up slowly. Nothing had been resolved. Only that his parents knew they were safe for now. How could they get back to where they were once before? How many similar beautiful Florida mornings were they going to miss now that their lives had been so thoroughly derailed?

Strangely beautiful they were free, and just like that another ball pops out of the box. Adam and Jessica knew what they did and what they had to do. Adam's father comforted his wife by reassuring her how easy a sixty-nine Thunderbird with suicide doors would be to spot. As long as suicide was not an option. "This is incredible you should read all the evidence they seized. They say some big bling, bling wanna be with Big Hands Perone organized the whole mess. Perone's got the Jaded Lady and the bling, bling wanna be's got the truck rental place."

"All legitimate businesses right," sneered Adam. Jessica put the paper down, "great phone call with your folks?"

"Oh yeah super. Dad won't call off the cops until we're home in one piece."

"How can we go home? They know we were at the Jaded Lady."

"To tell you the truth, I don't know if I can bluff my way through this. There's just too much to cover up."

"We're all screwed," slammed Jessica, "how can I act like nothing happened? We'll both hear the whispers, 'they were busted,' and they'll know I got raped. Ben and that bitch, she's got a huge mouth. They're already talking," Jessica was so pissed she was out of the car now kicking a suicide door shut, "this bullshit is monumental!"

"The school will probably dime me out to the cops before anybody else does," said Adam picking up on Jessica's death spiral, "you bet the police are doing their thing, asking for names, times, dates, persecution, prosecution and there's evidence to spare."

"It's not the kind of thing I want to deal with," said Jessica as she stared back out onto the highway.

Meanwhile, across time and space, the rain had let up. They were only one hour from the city. Eric and Wendy, Danny and Louise, Bonnie and John, Doug and Mark were making their way through the woods. Insanity surrounded them. The woods were deep, too deep. All those trips to the health food store didn't prepare them for the reality of a dense forest. "Are we there yet," Bonnie asked in mock amazement as to what she was putting up with?

"Don't you have any damn patience," John was so pissed he could hardly form a coherent thought. "Patience for this shit, John?"

"Yeah Bonnie, this shit!"

"Look, I can appreciate how terrifically normal you are, Bonnie," said Danny, "but for the last time, shut up and go if you have to!"

"Where the hell am I going, Danny?"

"That's your problem," he shot right back.

"Straight to the police," spoke Doug, "you know like when you used to rat on us when we were kids!"

"Cute Doug," was her answer.

"Hey," hollered Eric and then more softly," you want to keep it down please? I am trying to listen for the waterfall."

"Where are we going and why," said Bonnie? She did have a point. The brush was so thick it felt like they were trapped. The recent rains didn't help. The footing was sloppy as they mucked deeper into the density. The band, with Louise, Eric and Wendy along for the ride, had been trying to reach New Orleans all yesterday morning. Now they were backpacking through the flatland of Baton Rouge trying to get away. No sleep, plenty of coffee, and much edginess provided the atmosphere. Throw in a splash of running from the law and you got a gumbo fit for a king. It didn't take more than an hour to get where they were and only Eric knew where that was. They weren't leaving much of a trail. There were no registrations at a motel and no suspicious license plates out on the highway screaming, "hey, pull me over here!" Hell, they were so paranoid and careful that Eric was ready to camp out for a week, but they didn't have enough food and water. At least where they were headed there were no tourists or urbanites getting away for the weekend. Vacationers spend millions a year trying to retreat to mother nature, but throw cigarette butts out of their car windows. Well at least this part of the planet belonged to it's rightful owners. Not the tax payers, not the state, not anyone, it belonged to the wildlife that roamed it and the trees that engulfed it. Although there was surely a paper claim to the uninhabited land. "I'm so beat," whispered Wendy to Eric, "how much further do we have to go?"

"I haven't been here in over a decade but I remember this trail. I was on it many times back then." They continued heading off slowly and together. Eric turned back around to Wendy and spoke, "in about three miles from the giant boulder that was sitting by itself, we split off onto a barely worn trail. That will take us to a nice sleepy clearing." Farther back in line, more words were grabbing for reason. "Look Bonnie," Mark was saying, "we have to get buried deep in the woods to find out where we're going. We're too hot for the road right now."

"I haven't done anything and this is not my fault," she said.

"Doesn't the music mean anything to you," asked Doug from the front? Bonnie just glared at him," it doesn't mean this much."

"God forbid you won't be able to go shopping today."

"Eat me Doug!"

"You're running out of allies," spoke John drifting back into the conversation. Eric and Wendy were still leading the way. Danny and Louise were right behind. John, Doug, Mark and Bonnie were following. With the trail beginning to become less worn and the crunching of brush and vine becoming more and more apparent, they all knew they had gone farther than most. New trails were being forged over the others that were easy and convenient. "Seems to be my life's motto," thought Danny to himself. He allowed himself a sarcastic smile. No one was having fun.

John and Louise were barely looking at each other. She still had on his clothes. They were now walking in front of each other. One behind the other, crossing through the forest in single file. The trees were getting larger and the moss was hanging in their faces. Scurrying through the underbrush the weight of the situation was tap dancing on their collective last nerve.

John had always been loyal to Danny even back to the days of their garage band, but never really thought that something positive might happen. John had one foot in the dream and one foot out unable to get by skepticism. It all took time and time was sort of like love. It kept on, no matter what, and was always forgiving you with more time. It wasn't often he'd given Danny a real chance to make it happen. At times he wasn't focused on the music and he showed up late for gigs. John hated himself for getting caught up in the bullshit. He was guilty of having a rock star attitude without being one or putting in the work. Danny just wanted to jam.

It just seemed like John deep down didn't believe it could happen. Some might say that was realistic. But you had to be committed to a dream. It definitely wouldn't happen if you went about it half assed with doubt and fear and hedging your bets. The music wasn't enough for him. He needed more and some sort of guarantee. He was losing the knack for sharing or even appreciating the human experience. Acceptance and cooperation were damned hard to pull together, but it still wasn't enough for him. He sought the attention but he'd been guilty of character assassination one too many times. What a wonderful ugly sound jealousy and envy make as the words tumble from our mouth. John knew he was just bringing it all back around on himself. He was using Danny and now look where it got him. He was now hopelessly insignificant and weak. The orchestrator of his own demise.

"Is the band made of rubber or glue? Everything that is said bounces off of them and you. Everything you needed to know sticks like glue but that you already knew." Louise was having a brilliant simple time with her internal dialogue. At times it made her smile with creativity both dark and light. But other times the dialogue turned more vicious. It badgered, threatened and doubted her every move. "My own goddamn inner voice is pressing me onward through any means available either to perfection or raging indecision. I must do better. What will the neighbors think?"

What a waste of bleeding energy this confrontation is with the other and the inner other. We threaten, insult, and doubt each other and ourselves. It being all the same. Living a life in total response to the other and it is only a strange voice from within or a stranger walking by. It's confusing at best when we worry about what others think. "Sam could have easily been you," shrilled her consciousness! And at the perfect moment Danny reached out and touched her to help guide her over some rocks in her path. He held her hand as he made eye contact. Simple really but he had the look that reached beyond his own self and entered her. It passed her outer wall of assumed identity and seeped through her skin. It burrowed through her bones and lit a smile upon her face. It reached right down to where time stood still, perfectly realized in the moment and where the soul lived. He didn't even have to ask. "Yes, I'm all right," she said. It came from somewhere deep within the hidden source of self. Slowly the words came out in a low tone and strangely unfamiliar in a typical way, but never truer to the source that was entirely her. They were definitely her own words and for a moment her fully realized self. How lucky she was to have zeroed in on at least one authentic moment of her life time. It was surreal beyond it's expectation and it's obliteration of all the superfluous clutter that we gather and mull over in this lifetime. It was the momentary culmination of the self. It seemed to be the sum of all her past, present and future lives, speaking with one voice from all the previous moments of her entity's existence. It was who she was and where she came from. It was where she was going and it was all at once. It was a beautiful fleeting moment fully known through every fiber of her body and existence. Then she had to duck a swinging branch, and like a shower of stars flurrying by in a snow fall, she was back on the mundane plane, but with a rather significant and infinite glow.

Bonnie and Doug were at each others' throat. They were playing that stupid children's game of one-upmanship, insult and laugh until the laughter becomes vicious. The object of the game is to find the other person's buttons. So of course you always end up stressing and losing. "Look you asshole, you defended Danny, that bigger asshole, and what the fuck for? I knew this was fucking bullshit from the beginning."

"Bullshit," said Doug, "you don't seem to think so when the spot light hits you."

"Oh right and you're not out there hamming it up. You're just as big an asshole as he is!"

"Why did you even bother to join the tour?"

"Fuck you! I've known Danny for years and was playing with him before you ever came along."

"And you're so damn supportive for being such an old friend. At least I treat him like a human being, and don't freak out because he doesn't want to fuck me!"

"Shut up Doug!" And the more pissed off she got the nearer to the truth he got and nobody wins when the truth is spoken in anger. Bonnie and Doug looked up just as they were about to run into Eric and Danny.

"Be quiet," hissed Danny.

"Or what Danny, are you gonna kick my ass?" Bonnie was always hair trigger ready for Danny. "Perhaps you have forgotten the deal here?"

"You're the one who is in a deal here not me. You're always fucking things up by not minding your own business."

"We don't need any extra attention," Danny said. And stung by the truth he turned and moved on.

Doug walked by Bonnie. They were usually allies, but they had their differences. Selfishness was the winner. It was not a rare moment. As the others trudged on through the woods Bonnie held her ground. She was going to make them all come back and then tell them off. But she realized she better start walking, albeit slowly, and keeping her eye on the last guy in line, John.

Eric and Danny were now way out in front with Wendy and Louise. Nothing like a little physical exercise when you're pissed off. John, stripped down of his past mistakes with self realization knew he would have to keep it together. At this point it was too much to risk, hoping the others would bail him out. He knew if he wanted to save himself he would have to save them. He couldn't let it to chance that each one of them would be thinking clearly. It was a gamble to think they wouldn't make the same sort of wrong headed decision, like the ones in anger he had made in the past. Regardless of what the others may or may not do John was realizing he had to take a larger view. They were his friends, despite all the wounds and turmoil. They had shared time together.

As they moved off ever deeper into the woods, Bonnie lagged behind feeling sorry for herself. She was now shedding a tear. Was it frustration or fear? There was a crack in her armor, but was it any good if no one was there? She didn't have the keys to the van or the jeep. How the hell did she get in this situation? She didn't feel it was her fault, but only she knew her real intentions. She had been so consumed with the verbal volley that she wasn't sure which way to go to get back even if she did have the keys. She could barley see John's white shirt through the branches as they move ahead. She thought about running back to the road on her own. But they were a long way from the highway. She didn't pay attention to how she got where she was. She quickened her steps with realization as fear surfaced and warned of demise. One moment passed and then another. Her heart rate accelerated. She was stubborn and impatient but her instincts were starting to ring the alarm bells of her central nervous system. Then she heard a loud snap. A broken branch startled her, "what the hell is in these woods," she said out loud and then ran. She was running now and running really hard. "Damned woods," she thought to herself, tripping over what lay before her. She stumbled and fell and then got up. She stumbled again this time sprawling and making a mess out of herself. She was scattered now and her foundation cracked like so many lies against the wind. She was rattling around in her head so much that she lost her bearings. She couldn't feel the ground let alone focus on the center of the Earth. She was a long way from forgiving herself because it was never her fault. She was mad at the band, mad at Danny, and really mad at herself. But she kept that last part hidden from her ego.

The blazing sun was making its way towards noon, just like it always had. The surrounding bog was burning off its surface moisture in a repulsive smell. The morning dew had long since vanished, but would be back tomorrow. Bonnie was finally gaining on John, "they waited for me," she thought to herself triumphantly. She immediately slowed up. She had time now all the time in the world, and she prepared her tongue lashing for them. They were going back home and back home now. They could cancel all their gigs and chuck it all. She was quitting. As she slowed up to a stroll she caught more of her breath and tucked herself back in smoothing her hair. This was as far as she would go when it came to straightening herself out. She now felt in control and started to key herself back up for confrontation and moved forward. Shaking her head back and forth defiantly while looking at the ground she was careful not to stumble in front of them. She looked back up with building indignation ready to blast them with her opinions and gain her bearings.

She was alone. She stared directly at a single white shirt ruffling in the breeze. There was no one around. She was strangely not surprised. She let her opinions go. She touched the shirt slowly and finally stopped to listen. The sun was blazing hot but Bonnie's hands were cold and clammy. She had thought she had seen the others but did not want to start off in the wrong direction. She tried to take solace in the fact that John left his shirt for her but then again it was a ratty old shirt and could have been anybodies. "Hold on girl," she thought to herself," you know this is his shirt but which way did they go?" There was still a whole afternoon left in front of her. They had taken so many turns. Time for another choice in life. The choices just kept coming faster and with more fury. Was the shirt a marking point for where they had turned off the trail? Or had they simply gone on ahead and was John just making sure? Whatever the situation was it was not going to be resolved standing still. These thoughts crashed back and forth like lightning within her mind, and then her inner dialogue cried. "Damn Danny! He's got me in this jam and it's not getting any better. I never wanted to do this. He sweet-talked me into coming. I'm as good as dead in this forest. Fuck him! I had to go off to Florida with him?" She was panic stricken and obsessing. And she was at the point where she either went forward or backward, but without any clear direction. Backwards or forward, it was starting to all look the same. There was no more playing it safe. She was sure home was a sanctuary and unchanged but the way back wasn't. She had to break out even if every step she took might be folly or fatal. Her intolerance of the outside world wouldn't keep her safe now. She was all alone and in the whole of the outside world.

Home, what a joke. The people there spray painted some poor girl dumb enough to hang out with them. At gunpoint they forced her to have sex with a dog. Then they killed her and buried her just four inches beneath the ground. Her neighbors were freaks and amped out on meth. No wonder people stayed locked behind their doors. Home is where the heart is and right now her heart was stuck in the middle of the woods trying to get out. Jammed air waves, mud slinging politics, blaring sound systems, thoughtless words, and televisions steal our time just to sell us stuff. We wonder why we lead lives unfulfilled with too much hate being spewed and not enough words about love. Of course as soon as Danny started getting a band together others wanted to join in and grab the spotlight. But even though she joined the band she never stuck up for him and acted like she was doing him a favor. She had her own interest at heart. But somehow through out it all the music pulled her in another direction. She realized her playing suffered when she wasn't soloing. The band forced her to try and play just as well within the framework of the band and within the total sound of the group. She had through her playing become more selfless. She had to or she was out of the band and with no more solo's. The selflessness had begun to seep into her off stage persona, but this just blew it all back apart.

Bonnie was lost in the backwoods of Louisiana and in spite of her circumstance she was soul searching. She was too concerned with what other people thought of her. It froze her and made her confused. From whom did she need approval? It was all just a bunch of wasted noise. She broke free to join the band, but did she really? They were largely the people she grew up with. She thought breaking free was something that had to do with her surroundings. She didn't figure it was something she had to resolve within herself. The time had come hundreds and thousands of miles away from home to set out on her own without a support system. Was she sick of it yet? Sick of herself? She was down to the two choices that matter. Curl up and die or try. "The hell with them," she said in a burst, "how could I have given in so easily. Only love should have that kind of power over me!" In fact she concluded to herself, "the only power her personal demons have is the power I give them." And with that her fear and self loathing dissipated a little and a new sense of control took a tiny toe hold. She didn't care how she looked, she needed those guys. She would rather die trying to find them then to die running away. In a moment of realization, which didn't come very often for Bonnie, she saw that she was clutching John's shirt to her chest. "They were talking about breaking off the trail," she said to herself. Was this the point they turned? Did they go left or right? The possibilities were endless and the end of all possibilities was close at hand. Bonnie began to walk the fine line between success and failure. She broke off the path, and with that step she left a world small enough to be a king in, but a king without wisdom. It's a safe, small, world but Bonnie was on a different path now. It was a path with different people who looked familiar. It wasn't safe and it wasn't sure. A vast wasteland of easy answers with blame and excuses lay at her feet. Bonnie hadn't realized it yet, but it was good to have an unanswered question or two confronting and shaping our ideas and collapsing our boundaries. There are no guarantees. That's what keeps us honest.

What a neat trick. A puzzle so complex that even with most of the pieces seemingly there, it is only partially done, and the full picture unseen. Assumptions, presumptions, unfounded conclusions, very few certainties, and the baseness of our motives drive the mystery away. Turning blind eyes and indulging in the distractions and the pointless man-made greed, lust, envy, hate, hopelessness and corruption turned the mystery off and viewed the mundane. Try looking at the moon through binoculars and maybe it will bring it home. The dimensional reality is exquisite if you just let it wash over your senses. Some how we are driven to abandon our instincts and to stop digging for the mystery, searching for the stars, or hearing the sounds that surround. Our separate points of view are never confirmed, but shaken and scattered on a winter wind. It leaves us all at the same place wishing for another chance. People are dying to know and no one is really sure if it matters at all. The choices you make, the lies you tell, the life you take, even if it is your own or in the name of some hateful god or belief, all add up. But where and when? Is it at every moment or at the end of this time around? Perhaps both and one in the same. We are all with different names and different points of view, different details to fit the time, place and setting in our culture of now.

Separate religions with their dogma built up over time have their intensity of belief warped and misdirected. Instead of focusing on contemplation they defend and argue their separate points of view to the death. Violence makes any religion wrong. Unless it is a religion of violence. He/ she/ it/ creation, throws us on the canvas of life. We are separate splats of color deftly painted with eruption and energy, and fine tuned with intricacies. The whole picture never seen by us until we take a step back and begin creating for ourselves. Different points of view fitting time, place and setting, so closely interwoven as to defy detection and we are all images of each other. We define ourselves and others with our thoughts, words and deeds. We create the definition. We create the meaning. Why then create a definition and meaning of destruction? Bonnie wanted love, but first it had to start with herself, of herself.

She had to take a deep breath. The brush and vines were tearing at her clothes and face. She was trying to think about which way to go. But thundering thoughts kept pushing her reason away and she went blindly forward, west with the sun. About five miles into the brush she came upon a burned and rusted out car with old beer bottles broken and strewn about in the back seat and the floor. The rusted springs sprang forth from the old stuffed seats of a baby blue 1957 Chevy, which was sinking under its own weight. Animal sacrifice, extinct species, heavy metal thunder, plowing along the interstate, driven through the woods and land sunk. Jerry Lee blasting on the radio, raging energy pulsing, love making back-seat heaven, passion, music and power all rolled into one. The battery was long gone but the energy was still there. Further on down the road, Danny and the others walked on. They were deeper in the woods now and the path was faded at best. Louise turned to John and asked him where his shirt was. All he had on was an old Rolling Stones tour shirt. The tongue and lips were faded.

"That bitch Bonnie," Danny said to Eric, "I had to beg her to be in the band. She acted like I was asking her for money. All she ever worried about were her solos. She never considered what anybody else had to deal with!"

"Give her a break Danny she followed you to Florida."

"Only for the solos."

"Maybe there was something else," said Wendy. "Do you know how many phonies I come across in a day? Hell even the crew and stagehands take on that Hollywood, rock 'n roll wet dream persona. Everybody's chatting each other up for a reason and it's sickening."

"Well that's Hollywood for you," Eric started to say, "everyone's . . .".

"Hold it Eric. You can't tell me about Hollywood. Can you imagine how hard it is to stay true to your vision, when what you have to do to just perform is prostitute your talent and yourself. If it wasn't loaded down with so many untalented but ambitious people it might be better. But those without a talent to perform have a talent for power and they don't let you forget who is who. The successful ones develop a second nature and look right past the bullshit. But that doesn't mean it's not a constant struggle. It's too hard for me and that's why I'm tagging along with you," spoke Wendy.

"You mean you prefer the old hippie sticking his neck out for a cause to a prissy prop girl."

"Any damn day of the week," and she reached out hooking her arm with his pulling him closer.

"Well I'm real happy you two are here because I'm out of answers," said Danny.

"You can't be expected to handle this whole situation by yourself Danny. "I'm just surprised the band is sticking together."

"We haven't had a chance to talk about it, but the thing is I keep taking these situations on and I can't run everybody's life."

"You're not," spoke Wendy.

"Keep pushing Danny."

"Thanks Eric but I've got a drug bust going down and a man I loved like a brother dead. I left him in the street for the jackals and my bandmates are ready to kill me. If I don't get some breathing room soon I'm gonna flip. I should have called the police."

"You think so," asked Eric? "Don't get hung up on doubt Danny."

"But at what price?"

"Your friends will find their way."

"But they're following me."

"That's their decision," spoke Wendy.

Cutting through the forest, the sun was inching it's way down toward the wandering souls. They had been walking all day after being up all night. Funny what a little adrenaline will do for you. The vines and brush kept tugging at everyone's sleeves saying, "hey where are you going? Get back to the pavement." Their destination was an old clearing overlooking and adjacent to a small but wide and full waterfall. There they would set up camp and maybe get some rest.

"Have you seen Bonnie," asked Louise to John she was sensitive to the plight of the missing?

"No, I haven't, and frankly I'm worried that she took off."

"Split?"

"Yeah like try to go home or worse . . ." Louise knew he was thinking police.

"Is she capable of that," asked Louise?

"If she's mad enough she'll leave."

"Like a bum leaves a box car," said Louise looking back up at the sky.

"I suppose that's wise," continued John," maybe we should take a clue from her? Things are getting a little sketchy."

"Isn't Danny your friend," asked Louise?

"I'm just worried about Bonnie. I don't think she's all there. The stress is getting to me and I'm sure to her," he paused and continued, "I just don't want another dead body on our collective heads."

"She'll be all right," said Louise." she seems like a tough one."

"They can be the most vulnerable," answered Doug.

"Poor Sam," John said aloud to no one in particular and with that he tied his bandanna around a tree limb.

Bonnie's each step was measured. The idea of the police was paled in comparison to the fact that she had not seen a trace of the others. The old car was out of sight now and she had no bearing back except to try and pick up her footprints. She was not on any trail and only headed into dense forest with the sun on the later side of the day. Now the thoughts of what Danny was all about, and where to find fault and place blame, disappeared in light of the fact that she had to get herself settled for the night. Who knew what animals roamed these parts and slithered or stomped through these woods. She was no granola eating, trail hiking, Earth Mama. She was a mall rat. She was going to have to rely on her seldom-used instincts of survival. Fortunately for her a few years of modern society could not wipe out millions of years of evolution. Not yet anyway.

With the sun went her hopes chasing them over the horizon like tumble weeds. The real holy war had started. The holy war a person wages with themselves in order to survive, and come to terms with what confronts them. The war to define what is real and what is imagined. The awful, mundane, agonizing, posturing, of society and the relationships between individuals, groups and nations, waned like the moon in comparison to handling a situation where the mind has threatened the body. No longer could Bonnie reach back to some prior event and blame someone else. This time it was all her, and she knew it, so things were clearing up for her even as the sun was setting.

It didn't take Bonnie long to start begging for forgiveness of herself to her god, whatever she perceived it to be. She felt like she was at the gates of heaven and realized she wasn't getting in. There were no footprints to follow, no broken twigs or branches, no settling dust and dirt from a moving herd, no noise other than her pounding heart, and no human life except the burned-out car. Funny how things retain their energy and seem to amass it the longer they prevail. So Bonnie turned and headed back. Each step added to the hopelessness of her situation.

It wasn't that the others up front had forgotten Bonnie. They just didn't know how unraveled she had become. John was beginning to suspect this and was trying to lag back for her but not loose sight of the others. His day pack was getting lighter.

"Think she'll pick them up," asked Louise?

"She better," stated John," if she doesn't find them then somebody else will."

"John they'll follow us right here!"

"I hope I didn't mess up but I had to do this. I gotta feeling she'll figure it's easier to swallow her pride than hit the road by herself."

"The roads a lot easier on credit cards," spoke Louise, "Hell, all she needs to do is get to the airport and she . . .".

"Go to the airport?"

"Go to the airport and she's home."

"That's assuming she wants to go home."

"At this point I bet she'd rather face the locals than deal with the cops."

"You know how easy it'll be to find her if she goes home. I mean the police once they find out who was in the band . . .".

"If they look that hard," interrupted Louise.

"If they look that hard and they might," countered John," then they'll nab her at home."

"She hasn't thought all this through, John."

"Which is worse because on impulse she's gone and it'll be easier for a stranger . . .".

"Or a cop."

". . . to track us." There was an overly burdensome silence followed by the realization that if Bonnie didn't show up they would have to be moving again in the morning. "If the others find out that she's gone, let alone you tried to mark the trail with red bandannas and tee shirts they'll be freaked out."

"It's one of those things Louise. I couldn't wait for her and get lost. Besides I'm not ready to run out on Danny. I haven't really done anything wrong," he was rambling now. "Just trying to keep the band together," questioned Louise sarcastically? She stopped and looked at John, "and how were you going to do that by sleeping with me," she asked accusingly?

"If this mess hadn't come along I'd be dealing with that mess," he said. Look I'm not perfect. I've made huge mistakes but when it comes to the band I'll do what it takes to keep it together. Besides you didn't put up a fight."

"You can't compare the two of us or our situations," answered Louise. "We happen to be passing at the same time. It'd be nice to find a decent friend for a while or even a moment."

"I know you have no idea about the politics of the band."

"I'm beginning to find out. But I'm no Yoko and I'm not playing that role."

"It was too hard to get the band started and get it off the ground," said John. "This is as far as we've ever gotten. Missing those gigs in New Orleans is going to kill us. Let alone we'll need a new name now. But in any event I had to leave Bonnie an option."

"It sounds like that girl has too many options. People are bending over backwards for her. She should get on my level and maybe appreciate she has friends that care."

"About all kinds of things. Sometimes I feel like, you know, Danny and the band, well, we're the last people who give a shit about anything other than ourselves." Louise gave him a suspicious look. "I swear Louise we're like the only people we know that give a shit."

"About the music?"

"Yeah about the music and the way we treat each other, what we spend our money on, the Earth, politics. It all starts with the music and goes on from there."

"Danny seems like a good man."

"No doubt Louise, and we definitely run into some great people. But damn, as a group and I can tell you from the conversations we've had that we feel pretty alone out there. Fortunately, we attract like-minded people and every now and then we get a real good crowd and that makes it all worth while. We all, and I mean the crowd as well, feel like we can accomplish anything. It's overwhelming, but if you don't put it into action after you come off the stage, what are we really accomplishing? At some point just having a good time becomes unrealized accomplishments and a lifetime wasted getting stoned. That's why I'm fighting to keep this thing together. For the rare moments when we accomplish something like voter registration or the Clean Air Act."

As they finished talking they came upon the camp sight. They wearily unpacked their day packs and sleeping bags. The quiet was all around them except for the symphony of nature. The sounds of the waterfall took them out of their weary misery for a moment. The sky was still barely light. A brilliant sunset splashed colors over the pale blue sky. There was still time to gather wood and get a fire going. "I'm counting on her to make the right decisions," said John.

"For you or for her?"

"For us."

"Her path may not be the one you're on."

"I know but for now I hope she sticks with it and picks a safer time to leave for all of us." Out in the distance the night sky revealed itself. Bonnie's immediate concern was her immediate concern. No matter which way she turned it didn't matter. She wasn't thinking about anything but her survival. And for the first time in her life she was right to be so focused. John gave Louise a nod of agreement. He had known Bonnie a long time and he was counting on her intuition to realize his actions. It was one of those situations where if he had gone and asked her to follow along, even if he had begged her, she would have said 'no' for spite or to change his mind. She could be so unreal as if playing a role on some empty stage in an empty theater. It was a role that no one liked, but she had the ability to force you to deal with her. Those were the situations she liked to create. With Bonnie some decisions were better left uncoaxed. Realization just had to be realized. This was just the worst time for someone to be lost.

Reality being survival sure made leisure time look unimportant. Society at its unhealthiest is openly violent. It's present high-water-mark for healthy is suspicious, jealous, mistrusting and assuming intolerance towards differences. True individuals scare the daylights out of most. But society pushes merrily on. Each new generation shocks with its ability to come up with something different. Always some new culture of appearance rises up from the oncoming generation. The bible stompers rattle and the establishment shakes it head. The gen-Xers just want a green Earth and a safe place to live. The gen-Yers just want 'like' a little more emphasis on being human to each other, thank you very much. Hooray for the disenchanted, the tattooed and the pierced. Keep speaking your truth as long as your truth is love. Look out for paranoia and the seduction of power. Look out for those unrealized souls who would drag you down. Shine on in your corner of the universe.

Jesus, if he ever reappeared, would flip out that they use his name and the bible for politics. They'd eventually use the bible they wrote in his name against him. They'd test him and make him prove himself. Those who claimed the most faith the loudest would be his biggest critics. Organized religion would hate him because he would do away with their organizations. The temple is in the body, not some building. That's where you'll meet your maker in your own world and in your own mind. It will be in your soul filtered through your own thoughts, assumptions and fears, experienced through your own actions, desires and doubts.

Wasn't Jesus's lover a prostitute? He wouldn't stand a chance against the corrupted machine and those that have gained power. Their alleged higher moral ground and their duped minions would marginalize him and twist his words for their own gain. Jesus would be wise to stay away and not come back until man doesn't need him.

We've had, and continue to have, our chances through eons of time but we wage war in the name of our individual institutions, gods and self-appointed leaders. We all claim to be right and everyone else to be wrong. We end up trying to persuade each other by force and we march peace, love and understanding out the door, every time. And we still don't get it. It's a disgrace that we have learned absolutely nothing from the first visit. I doubt we'll see him again until this is a peaceful, caring, tolerant-of-each other world, and the weapons are antiques. As long as we are using religion as a tool for power, either individually or collectively, and as long as people are maimed in the name of a god, any god, and used for political power, well what would you do?

Jesus isn't going to come back and waste his breath on intolerant, non-listening, close-minded, fanatical, blood thirsty hate mongers. Until hate is the collective enemy, we are on our own paths to gain enlightenment and grow as people individually. Then the nations will resolve themselves and then the world. It better be a world of compassion, tolerance and freedom. Jesus isn't coming back until we calm down and evolve. Until we recognize what it means to be a part of the whole Earth and not apart from it. Because, like it or not, the life force makes everything and everyone. We are the stuff of stardust, galaxies and planets. Millions of people as a chain of consciousness with unseen ripples of faith and belief, hatred and anger. Where individual thoughts of hate breed mass hysteria and love conquers all. We are the leaves on the single tree of life, the stars in the sky and the light in each other's eyes. All of what is in the universe is what is in each of us. The challenges that befall us are the challenges we make for ourselves on our individual roads back to the center of creation.

Bonnie was taking the first step by being honest with herself. Her mind was racing now as these thoughts overwhelmed her. She thought about Danny and John, her life back home, and her mom and her dad. She began to measure herself against herself and her thoughts and ideas. New ruminations were now consuming her mind as she searched the woods for clues. Unchanneled energy and jammed circuits bring down the world as well as the individual. The right mindfulness can make walking in the woods the right meditation. The intention behind the action is the driving force of the reality and that from which we are measured. The avoidance of the unexamined life is a worthy goal. Consumed with distractions she had left so many friends behind. Consumed with distraction she let pride drive away real love. Consumed with distraction her body only told her when she was hungry and horny and nothing else. Her instincts were numb, her philosophy base and her intuition mistaken for uneasiness or a fault of character. She never saw it as a signal, or energy from the surrounding thoughts and vibes of others, or that she was a sensitive. No sixth sense here. She was unable to read her real spot on this Earthly plane. Her listening capabilities were only tuned-in when playing her music. However, the music was strong and led her beyond the superficial. Now those instincts, developed through her playing, lead her on the unmarked road. She took each step slower and tried to feel her way.

"Well this is it folks, Eric's little hideaway. I haven't been out here in years but it still looks the same."

"Oh you mean you're happy it's not a dump," said Mark standing by the cliffs edge. "Yucca Mountain it's not," chided Louise.

"You got something against nuclear waste piling up daily with no way to dispose of it," John said kiddingly with his hands on his hips. Having reached their destination they afforded each other a smile, but Louise knew of John's trail markers. He didn't feel like a hero. In fact, John was even more worried now that they had stopped. Everything hinged on Bonnie's decision. Was she going to be rational or insecure?

At this point Bonnie had given up. She started to retrace her steps and felt fortunate that she reached the clearing where the Chevy lay rotting. She hesitated and turned both east and west. She had tried to follow the others but to no avail. The light was slipping away. In the hours leading up to this moment she thought she might disappear forever and send her soul on it's way. All that had happened would be a memory and an inconvenience. Bonnie knew John was trying to help. She knew what turning her back on herself would mean to her family and her friends and finally mean about herself. She went on her way, her very own way.

Doug and Mark were off getting firewood. The waterfall rushed on oblivious to the main event that was being featured on it's northern plateau. The water was tumbling off the rocks like Coltrane and Monk trading improvisation. Louise remarked that the sounds of the Earth were not "like" music they were music. "A babbling brook and a rambling staccato have a lot in common," answered Wendy.

"Garcia," Eric jumped into her and Louise's conversation. Wendy put her hands on her hips, "Wow you must be really old."

"Don't give me shit hammerhead."

"I'm not," Wendy stammered.

"You're warming up to it."

"I just thought you were more of a Kenny G man." Looking on from behind the tree line Doug thought Eric moved pretty fast for an old guy. Danny was laying out his bedroll as Eric and Wendy sprinted by. Then he walked over toward Louise by the cliff's edge, "they're having fun."

"They're not in love."

"Oh, said Danny a little taken back.

"Much too soon in the relationship," explained Louise.

"Expert, eh?" He looked at Louise cautiously, "does that come from jumping out of cars on rainy nights." Louise laughed, "I don't think I thanked you for coming to my rescue."

"No need."

"If I would have gone back to that apartment he would have been waiting for me."

"What got him so angry in the first place?"

"The usual. I didn't come across."

"That's ignorant," stated Danny abruptly.

"But not that uncommon."

"That's no excuse."

"Sometimes that's how the rent gets paid. It doesn't make me feel all that good. I never hang around for long. It's not the worst thing that's happened to me."

"That's not the point," said Danny.

"What's the point then?"

"The point is that you're human and deserve respect."

"Danny, respect has nothing to do with falling out of moving cars."

"My point exactly."

"Look here's a guy that helped out for a couple of weeks. I've been down for a while, but Danny I've been that way primarily out of choice. The past two months have been harsh and low on bucks. You know how these things can compound themselves. That guy happened along and helped set me back on my feet."

"Don't you mean your ass," Danny interrupted?

"In a few days I had gotten a shower, food and slept with him. It meant nothing."

"It always means something, and what it means or doesn't mean extracts a price."

"There's always a price."

"Exactly, and do you think Eric has one?"

"Sure do."

"What then?"

"To help himself escape."

"Escape what?"

"I don't know. Why don't you ask him?" Danny paused and then changed the subject back. "It's none of my business Louise, but thanks for sticking this out with us. Feel free to stay as long as you want."

Louise laughed out loud. "Great. Is that before or after the cops catch up to you?" Danny just shrugged his shoulders. That last remark sounded a whole lot like Bonnie. He couldn't blame Louise for being cynical. "No strings attached Louise. You wont find yourself flying out of cars with me."

"Who knows, Danny, I seem to have the ability to piss people off." The corners of her mouth turned down, "but thanks, I got that right away from you," and she reached out and gave him a long embrace. She looked good in John's clothes, everything all loose and comfortable. Careful Danny boy. Some are still claiming that premarital sex is a sin even though god gave us the tools in the first place. Ah, the dark ages, they're over right,—suicide squads, inquisitions, unplanned parenthood and shooting doctors? Forcing your beliefs on people is the evil. Danny smiled broadly and walked back to his tent. Eric had Wendy pinned against a tree, "okay you got me, Dead Head now what are you going to do?"

Mark and Doug were joined by John, "how's the fire-wood hunt going?"

"Fine," answered Mark knowing that John was much more concerned about something other than kindling. "Just tell the other's I'm headed off to find Bonnie."

"Whoa," spoke an alarmed Doug," she left on her own. You don't owe her. She made her choice, John."

"I know, Doug, but I still kind of feel I've got to do this. It's been gnawing at me all afternoon. She could be in real trouble."

"Or making trouble for us," said Mark.

"Or that too," said John.

"That spoiled bitch wouldn't think twice about playing the victim and laying blame on all of us."

"Look Doug, I don't give a shit how you feel. I just wanted to let you know in case I'm not back in a while." He looked at both Doug and Mark, "okay?" They nodded.

"If Danny is wondering just tell him I went for more firewood, and to make sure that no one is following us."

"More like praying she's following us," spoke Mark?

"I can't let her alone out there, it's getting dark."

"What if she didn't follow us," spoke Doug? But John had already turned and was walking away.

"Don't get lost yourself, sir," called Mark after him.

"I'll be back. I've just got to try," he called over his shoulder. Mark turned to Doug, "I don't know what to feel about this."

"I know it's hopeless. The girl doesn't get it. First sign of trouble and she splits, good friend that she is. I'm sure glad I helped her out when she needed it," said Doug sarcastically.

"Well it's not quite the Ritz out here in Bum Fuck Egypt."

"What's that got to do with anything," asked Doug, "compared to the situation were in?" Mark just shrugged passively.

The rain from the morning had long since stopped falling. The moisture had evaporated in the noon day sun. But John still felt a heaviness in his chest as night closed in. Like the rain his concern came and went. He knew he was counted on and somehow he had earned the role of a leader. Danny never would have left Bonnie behind under any circumstances. At least he was consistent. Bonnie however, was doing her level best to drag the group down to where the focus was on her. The others could loose control from time to time. Doug had his temper but John would always be there to calm the situation down, especially if it was him that was late for a gig. Was Danny just trying to call Bonnie's bluff? Or was he finally at the point of being fed up? The stakes were way too high to be playing that type of guessing game. The pain they would feel was huge, especially for Danny if they never got the band off the ground. Like some leaky faucet the idea of not getting it done dripped drop after drop after drop on the back of Danny's consciousness. Forever, forward it pushed him.

John wasn't the only one in the group that recognized Danny's talents. Bonnie knew. John saw that in her ass-backward way she loved the man. Instead of being direct, she weaved this pathetic, attention-grabbing, drama, so tight that she was the only one who got caught. Danny was outwardly oblivious and annoyed. She ran circles around him. But somewhere on another level, just below the surface, he had to know. Somehow this whole hidden love affair would play itself out.

Bonnie and Danny were like two old souls meeting again to work out some unfinished business. John knew all this as he set out to find Bonnie. Doug looked at Mark, "good old John, always looking to keep the baby chicks in the nest."

"You can't just walk off by yourself like that," answered Mark.

"You can try but you better be ready to answer to the ultimate one," said Doug.

"Whose that, Allah, God, Jesus," asked Mark?

"No you idiot! Yourself!" Doug gave him this complete look of horror for his ignorance. To Doug we were the judge and jury. Each one of us individually. Doug knew that within all of us and inherent in the plain fact that we existed, along with everything else, was the true sense of how to be. The difference between right and wrong was known to all without doctrine. He felt that our collective consciousness was tapped into the great universal truths and was one. And that was as plain to see as a tree when you are peeing on it.

Doug crossed back over the waterfall, putting one foot in front of the other. Mark just stood and felt himself disappear from Doug's consciousness. The times have always been tough. Life's a challenge not an entitlement. Mark was disappointed that fleeing from responsibility was a major option taken by most who chucked values for trends. Looking out for number one, but at what cost? Help others and then you help yourself. He wasn't prepared to tear down the growth he had made in the face of ignorance. He wasn't going to diminish other people in the hope of elevating himself. The end result he knew was just a lessening of his own stature and enlightenment. Mark's goal, whether alone or with all, was the development of his spirituality. "What is life," he often thought, but a series of incarnations in order to become a more perfect being. He worked on the conflict within himself first and then his friends and foes. He hated getting caught up in the distractions and details of the every-day struggle. He didn't want to succumb to pettiness. But he knew with a rye smile to himself, that was just where everyone on this trip was headed, unless individually and collectively they reached down inside themselves and summoned the best in each other. Bonnie was searching for the best in the survival of herself and in the face of her fear. There was hope, Mark thought, and John went to help elevate awareness over both of their fears, hatred and envy.

Doug didn't have time for all that. Life was simple as far as he was concerned. It was an unglamourous struggle for bread and survival. The table must be full and the cards are dealt. Some bluff their way through it for a time but eventually they must face themselves truthfully. Mark could care less about being the "King". He felt his choices defined his character and that his character was his fate. The situations presented were the turns in the river of his destiny. The reasons behind the choices were more important than the choices themselves. He greeted each new day by trying to be honest with himself and seeing the magic that is the world and it's reality all around him. Mark moved ever closer to the water's edge. The spray kicked up in his face and for the moment it replenished exhaustion from a long hot Bayou day. He waited for it to happen again.

Doug was crashing through his head now, weary of the chase and the fact of being chased. But that still didn't cause him much pain. He was somewhat ambivalent to what was going on around him. Sure Sam had been brutally murdered and for what, to get high, a few dollars? The slice of life the culprits were gambling on was enormous. To kill would always leave that element of the victim's soul in the murderers mind and his being. There, like the vacant playgrounds of the city, like weeds through the cracks in the personality, the victim's energy would seep through and overwhelm the black-topped veneer of the culprit. The desperation and the feeling, whether hunger or passion, the weight of the dead seeps into the consciousness, robbing it of its remaining fleeting peace and beauty and strength. Their own souls crippled, the culprits must go out and catch the breath of another death to keep them from going insane. They can feel and fight the insanity creeping in moment by moment. They flee the world and turn off the conscious knowledge of right and wrong. The dark energy to kill again comes forward. It may take years, it may take months, and it may take days, but the steamy hot blood runs down the back of their hand and over their entire being, washing away all other considerations. Lost in the deed, the rush is on, taking their souls with them never to regain their full and complete selves again. Only the finality of their own death releases them from the nightmare. They are imprisoned and praying for release from the death spiral, hoping to begin anew again. Drugs, gambling, larceny, arson and destruction are no match for the intensity of terror, the unholy unleashing of crumbling floors in an earthquake of horror due to the loss and taking of a life. The plunging knife over and over again releases rage against the lack of control, sexual frustration and dark confusion. The light is obliterated from their souls for the moment, but the curse of knowing the difference between right and wrong turns slowly back on. Ever brighter, they struggle harder to conceal it, only to enlarge it more each time. There is no escape from responsibility. There is no blaming one another. There is no ducking from the truth. There are just the extremes one would go through to hide from it. Agonizing they don't have the decency to ask your name. But they never forget the look on your face or the steam from your body. They think they have a cause, but Doug knows that the cause has them. It makes you forget all but that which is your immediate self. But how terrible the nightmare screams in defiance and you want to make it scream back. Shed a little darkness of your own. Maybe if we all scream together in horror, agony and war we can blot out the light of the sun? Doubtful. We can only blot out ourselves. The cause for which you are fighting manipulates you more than the enemies you seek. Look no further than yourself. Hell is in your heart. Until faced, no killing of mother nature's golden child will ever win the battle in your soul. As you refuse to look within, you turn your terror and fear outward, you forget, you deny, you fall in the battlefield. You fall in the alley. You try to retreat from the battle within any way possible. The cowards run from themselves. The heroes know that what is to be conquered is within themselves. "The choice is yours," babbled the brook.

The water passed the banks and splashed by the rocks, playing with velocity, gravity and depth. It passed beauty and truth, woven together in harmony for all to see, hear, feel and breath. It made life rich and people whole. But it has been ignored, wasted and destroyed by those who look for richness and wholeness elsewhere. You have to see artfully what is all around you to know that it is connected within. After all everything is all together in this realm. Doug brought logs to the campsite that would burn forever. "What the . . .," laughed Eric out loud.

"Oh, he's big and strong," said Wendy with her best school girl act.

"What, are we going to be here a week?"

"We might," said Doug answering Eric as he let the logs drop with an Earth worn thud.

"Good job, Doug," spoke Danny looking up from the front of his tent. He jumped up and gathered the logs. Danny was trying hard to maintain an equilibrium. Eric and Wendy were fine but their glibness was starting to piss everyone off. Danny had put Bonnie out of his mind.

Wendy had success. But she couldn't figure out why anyone would want the spotlight. What's so great about stalkers, weirdos and phonies vying for your time? "It was one night Eric," said Wendy, "these guys just barged in on me in my Jacuzzi. One was a writer who thought he was hot shit, and there was a photographer, and one television middle-manager type. I was horrified and screamed at them and they still didn't think I was serious. And that was that. Ever since then all I ever wanted to do was get away from that business. I just want a nice, quiet life."

"Tucked away in the woods somewhere," interrupted Eric.

"Exactly." Wendy paused, "if there are any damn woods left in this country"

"Don't get me started on that," said Eric, "they're subsidizing the corporations to harvest our national forests with tax-payer money. They sell the timber at a financial loss overseas. It cost's more to tear it down, process it, and pay these guys than they get back for the wood and the pulp. Not to mention the pollution of the waters around the pulp plants, and the cost to clean that up."

"Brilliant," Wendy said, exhausted at the stupidity. "They should take all the loggers that they are trying to help and give them the money directly. Give them jobs in helping to manage the national parks and the old growth forests."

"Only it's not the loggers electing the government, it's the corporations."

"Still if we're going to subsidize them we might as well do it directly with a mandate to protect and preserve. It's what the people want. Instead we are increasing short term profits for a corporation that is in effect acting as a middle-man between the tax payers and the loggers."

"Selling off our national forest at a loss isn't what the tax payers want," asked Eric sarcastically?

"Give the loggers some biology training and have them track migration, keep the trails clear, plant, and clear out the underbrush that's fueling these massive forest fires. They'll have full-time, year-round jobs and the tax payers will be delighted not to have their houses burned and our National Forest sent overseas, at a loss, for an end table."

"As it is now every time they cut down a tree they're taking another step closer to unemployment," said Eric.

"Exactly. The loggers can do watershed management and watch for soil erosion. This is a big country the potential for job creation is enormous. They could help urban areas revitalize by replanting and managing. Look, when it's bloody hot in the summer, don't you want to be in the shade of a big tree," spoke Wendy?

"The cities swelter. They could use more trees. That's something else the tax payers would gladly pay for. Loggers would have jobs and forests would be properly preserved for the long term," Eric stated.

"The tax payers don't want their hard earned money going to enormous salaries for the super rich, but would be delighted if it went to the loggers who protected our forest instead of stripping them," answered Wendy.

"They are clear cutting the cure for cancer," spoke Eric, "we haven't discovered everything yet and won't in thirty lifetimes!"

"Imagine urban areas with trees, more livable, thereby bringing people and jobs back to the cities. It's a win, win situation instead of subsidizing the ultra, uber rich's salaries," answered Wendy.

"Who better to manage the forests than the loggers who call it home," stated Eric?

"And all the biology and geology trained college students could have jobs teaching the loggers the science they'll need," spoke Wendy happy to talk about something else for a moment.

"By selective harvesting we wont flood the market, or flood the plains, and the price of lumber will go up," said Eric. "Then we can sell for a profit like they do with the diamonds. Homebuilders can get their lumber from tree farms. Everybody wins and wins big. If we manage our resources, and the tax payer's resources intelligently, we get a healthier environment and the money spent on health care is less . . ."

"It's just a matter of breaking the old mind set of strip it, sell it, cash out and run away before the tax payers realize what has happened," finished Wendy. Honesty was out of fashion. Greed was king. Foresight was gone.

It was darker now and the moon had already been up for hours, spying on our friends. "If only the damn thing was brighter, I could find Bonnie," thought John to himself. But Bonnie couldn't even find herself. John kept passing his cloths, "well superman," he chided himself, "you leave these out and anyone can find us. It'll be midnight by the time I get back to the Van and still never know if she followed us, is lost or dead. Damn her. She wants Danny's attention so bad and all he can think about is Sam." John was talking out loud to the woods in hopes that Bonnie might hear him.

"Looks like Danny's musical career is going to come to a screeching halt," he spoke out load again. Still he was determined to keep looking for Bonnie. He had an obsession for tying up loose ends. "Bonnieee," he hissed. He had put himself in this situation. His options were many but his choices were none. It was black out and he was feeling way too vulnerable. The air had cooled. He was cold and hadn't eaten since the morning. He stood in the same spot for what seemed like an eternity. The moon overhead shone down on him. The woods took on an eeriness and power, bringing to bear the true realization of where we are and what we should be doing. He started to trace his steps back to the waterfall. He was quiet now and humbled and listening for clues. He felt small and alone and uncertain. He needed the others and his feelings for Bonnie grew even more worrisome. He hightailed it back to the campsite.

The brooding facts of the mysteriousness of this reality make it all that much easier to blame some larger symbol. The mysteries make it easier to deny that the source of everything, and the way in which it is all perceived, comes from within. How we feel about ourselves is how we see the world around us. Bonnie kept trying to blame it all on Danny. "Now," wondered John, "does she blame herself?" Standing still and alone again, he was surrounded by the power of the trees. They are the lungs and the lifeline of this physical existence. He peered into them as if looking into his own soul. Each layer of bark etched with time and the years of life that had gone before. Like the lines on an old man's face the tree bark appeared with experience, revealing time and whispering of eternity, all from weathering the storm. Some laugh their way through it and others cry. Some not worth mentioning waver in between never knowing why. The woods echoed on surrounded by the rock and the water and the air. Together they brought and sustained life so we could be here. As he gazed skyward an immediate and overwhelming feeling passed through him. The enormity of the sky and stars reached down through him as if the depth of his being went on forever. The blackness of the sky through the night reached him, overwhelmed him, and seeped all the way in as if he was transparent. The stars and their patterns of light brought him out from the vastness and depth and put him solidly on the ground again. There he realized the magnitude of everything. It was an everything, that was everything that could be, and an everything that was going to be, with or without him. The totality of the universe forged itself on his mind and spirit, like lightning on tree bark. But he was not born again, or overwhelmed, but comprehending. Not lost, but found. He did not feel sorry for Bonnie's ignorance, but through understanding tolerated her and wanted to find her. He did not feel sorry for her as one would pity a maimed animal because her wounds were self-inflicted. They were born of pettiness and were short-sighted. He understood why she could get lost and how she should get lost. She's only human and the damned forest is so thick.

The more that is understood the farther it goes. It seems like it's meant to be messy with all its vines pulling and tripping. Getting your skin all cut up and your clothes all dirty seemed to be the way to go.

Especially for John's clothes, which were laying all over the trail. He decided he would get them tomorrow, and if the day came then it brought hope. Hope was a living thing. He continued on through the woods. His head was down looking for where his feet went. He found his way by using all his senses. Enveloped in a shroud he fought the darkness off and heard the crackle of a fire. Then he smelled the smoke. "See I beat you to it!"

"Crazy spark," the smoke replied, "the wood makes you fat."

"And the wind makes you full, but the rain takes us both away."

"Whoa, stop throwing on all those dried leaves," cried the night as everyone's eyes filled with light. John came into the clearing. The fire showed three standing and one sitting. The waterfall reflected moonlight. "Thank you for reflecting with me," spoke the moon. "John is that you," hissed Danny?" He had been standing too close to the fire to see but still heard as John pushed back the brush to come into the clearing.

"Where the hell have you been?" Doug looked surprised. He didn't think Danny had noticed. He felt sure Danny had stopped caring. Mark knew that Danny had noticed John was gone, but also figured Danny had stopped caring. The water cried out, "come in and wade to the middle in order to see which way to go."

"Which way to go indeed. You have a lot of nerve," hollered the wind.

"The course has been set through the ages from a time long forgotten by all but the Earth. It is here where we are, it is from here where we came, and it is from here where we are to go," said the mountains and the ranges.

"But what about us that are moving so fast within the spinning of the Earth and Sun? Where are we going with the life running through us in our veins?"

"Nowhere but where we are all headed. For in movement without effort there is peace much like the falling snow and the quiet solitude of the Rockies."

"So in movement there is peace," questioned the waterfall?

"Everything has been moving from the beginning," spoke the

mountains, "it's easy to see from up here. Even as people sleep thoughts like stones skipping water, ripple through their souls."

"And in movement without effort comes the stillness of the soul. No more distraction as grist for the mill," spoke the waterfall knowing all too well, just flowing.

"The still uncontemplated moments of joy are sustained through response, not calculated or devious, but responses pure in motion and then fulfilling," stated the mountain.

"Like a child," spoke the river.

"Like jamming," thought Danny.

"Like painting," thought Van Gogh.

"Freedom through action of unfettered thought. The mundane and the distractions put on hold while concentration takes us past all that would weigh us down.

Thought giving action to our ideas and action giving creation to our thoughts," spoke Giacometti.

"We loose ourselves in and through the concentration of our creation right Alberto," spoke Vincent?

"Creation is meditation. Through the motion of creation comes the stillness of the shame and drudgery of life that man has so masterfully complicated. Creativity moves freely through the act of creating. The artist becomes one with the work, and the work takes on the soul of the artist. As the collective creative force gains manifestation the pure artist knows that it is not his doing," spoke Vivaldi.

"We are just conduits of the flow," spoke the river. "In action there is stillness of the preoccupied thought. The purity of reality which is creation, and its process, through and through, takes us to the level of enlightenment we wonder why we can not reach."

"Because we are wondering," spoke the mountain.

"Like making love," answered Danny.

"Like making art," spoke Vincent.

"Pure movement is art," spoke the waterfall.

"And movement the quieting of all that is not," spoke the mountain.

"Life fully realized is art," spoke Danny.

"And art is life," whispered Wyeth.

"Thank you Andrew," said Chagall.

John approached Danny from out of the woods as Danny began to speak again of the cluttered distractions of a conscious mind trying to organize an unconscious reality.

"Why is the door seemingly shut on the collective conscious? We know it is there, . . . and Bonnie's nowhere to be found right," asked Danny? Doug and Mark looked at John with mutual surprise and shrugged.

"Yep," said John, just glad to be back at the campsite.

"You know what that means? We've got to head out first thing tomorrow." He shot a glance over to Eric.

"Do you have any ideas," whispered Wendy into his ear?

"Where's the next gig," asked Doug?

"You can't go there," said Louise somewhat surprised, "the cops will be waiting for you."

"Or get there soon after we start playing," said Danny.

"Would that be so bad," spoke John, obviously fed up.

"You'd have a lot of explaining to do," said Danny.

"Like why Sam was with you in New Orleans," barked Doug. Danny put his head down shaking saying, "what a mess."

"Couldn't we just explain everything to the police and get on with the show," spoke Mark?

"Look," said Wendy," the cops hear enough bullshit in a normal day to make anyone sick. You start layin' this story on them and they're gonna beat your heads in with nightsticks!"

"I don't know that I'd blame them either," said Danny.

"But they don't have anything on us, not a thing," said Doug exasperated," we explain and go to the next gig."

"It's not that simple," spoke Danny again. "Let me put it to you this way . . . one of the main drops was going to be my apartment. One van was to unload there . . ." They all looked at Danny with disbelief except Eric. Danny looked everybody over in silence and then continued, "you got paid every night, right? In spite of the crowds or no crowd, right?"

"I wondered about that," said John," but I thought we were just pulling a straight fee."

"No way," said Danny, "the door."

"Why didn't you tell us," asked Doug.

"Because it was hard enough to get you guys to come along in the first place."

"We put that much pressure on you . . ." asked John?

"Truth be known, you were assholes. The first song I taught you guys you ran off and formed a band without me. That pretty much sucked," the venom hissed from Danny's mouth.

"No wonder you were playing like a mad man every night," said Doug.

"No way," countered Danny, "nothing ever polluted the music." He looked around at everyone and they were all waiting for more. "It was a perfect set-up with Sam. I broke it down into dime bags and the bartenders moved it back to the locals. We got paid for the risk."

"So it would look like it came from the band," hollered Doug.

"We had to make the deal to keep the money coming in and to play there for as long as we did. You all said you were sick of the road."

"Mother Mary," spat Doug fuming now," we all take the fall.

"We needed a steady gig Doug before we swung through the southwest. You know that. We don't settle down again until we get to Sacramento. That's in two months."

"Are we selling dope to keep our jobs there?"

"You really thought we got such a good gig because of a few good reviews?"

"Danny I don't know if I would have taken such a risk," said Mark.

"It didn't start out as a risk Mark," he paused. "That may have been my downfall. It was a little too easy."

"You're such an ass Danny," spat Doug again.

"You turned a blind eye Doug so don't give me grief. You never turned the money down."

"I'm not going to jail for this Danny!"

"No you wont Doug. I have no intention of bringing anybody down with me."

"Get real," said Louise jumping in on Danny. "The cops will bash in all our heads if they feel like and throw us in jail and throw away the key."

"Oh yeah down south right," said Mark.

South, north, city, small town, look at them the wrong way and get the wrong cop and kiss your ass goodbye!"

"I don't want to go to the cops you guys. One person identifies me and the next thing you know I'm Sam's boy. Either way I go down hard."

"Anybody got money for a lawyer," asked Eric trying to lighten up the situation."I'm counting on you guys," said Danny. "You can all leave and go back home. But if they want to they'll find you there and then it's front page news in the local county gazette."

"I'm not going home this is just getting good."

"Thanks Mark," said Danny. Doug walked a few steps away. He couldn't believe what a jerk Danny had been for fronting for Sam. How can you make your dreams come true if you keep adding the ingredients for disaster? "Of all the stupid, unthinking shit you've done. I can't believe you would let the band, your precious band, become so vulnerable." Doug shook his head paused for another breath and turned and looked at Danny square on, "you come off so righteous and then wham you've got us all in jeopardy out here."

"Still thinking of yourself Doug," came a voice from the woods.

"Bonnie," exclaimed John jumping up as the others turned their heads. Danny sighed and looked down.

"You've got a lot of nerve bitch," spat Doug.

"Yeah well in case it's not clear to you Danny did this for us." The others were caught between going to welcome Bonnie back and not interrupting the conversation. They stood slack jawed and wide eyed.

"Sure Bonnie did it cross your mind that he probably kept most of the money while we all shared the risk?"

"That doesn't sound like something Danny would do but it does sound like you Doug. How typical and naive just because you steal doesn't mean everybody else does. And you," she paused for a breath and turned on Danny, "just because you're an idealist and care doesn't mean everyone else does!" Bonnie raised her arms in exclamation. "There might . . . just might be some people who want to take advantage of that." Dropping her arms back down, "you've got to see people for who they are Dan not how you would like them to be." She only called him Dan when she was really trying to get through to him.

He understood everything she said but only heard the way she called his name. John was smiling. Wendy and Louise just looked at each other and shrugged. Bonnie turned her focus back onto Doug, "you seemed to enjoy yourself at the Jaded Lady Doug. The shit's hit the fan lets just figure out what to do," she just walked by Doug towards the cliffs edge. Doug was too stunned to say anything but he was thinking, "well she looks like Bonnie."

Eric turned to Wendy, "he's not the only one. I'm sorry too Wendy. I'm no better than anyone."

"You were going to the Jaded Lady to score," she asked half knowingly?

"Yep and to make matters worse a lot of the people we left behind at the dance club were expecting me to come back."

"And I left with you!" She could feel the level of anxiety rising in her gut. She had carefully worked her image to be cool but above it all. She had walked that line between knowing but not doing because she didn't want to cut herself off from the players. The past was one thing and we all know that but she had worked pretty damn hard to keep her image clean and still have fun. A hard thing to do in the public eye.

"Eric my executive producer was there."

"One of my bigger customers."

"Just great." Two seconds before Wendy was about to blow her top she remembered something. She hated those people. But she wasn't going to let Eric off that easy. What else hadn't he told her? It takes time to get to know somebody she reminded herself.

Danny walked up behind Bonnie at the Cliff's edge. She turned and gave him a big grand hug the likes of which he had never seen from her. John came over to see how she was and tossed her an apple. She practically grabbed it with her teeth. Then she untied the shirt that was around her waist and handed it back to John, "thank you for loaning me your shirt."

"I was wondering if I ever was going to get that back," said John. They smiled knowingly at each other and all three walked back to the fire site.

"Alright, alright, so I'm a total schmuck but if my calculations are right we got two hot people here that we don't have to be with," said Doug.

"You mean we could be safe at home," said Mark.

"Right," Doug paused," something like that."

"We still have to come up with a plan," remarked Wendy calmly but with enough intonation in her voice to let Eric know she was steamed whether she was or not.

"We could change the name of the band," said Bonnie.

"That would be a start," said Eric but I don't think it would help much."

"Well you've been leading the way so what's next," asked John tired of the balancing act? The relief he felt from Bonnie being back was enough and running through his body like a locomotive. It drained him completely. Eric looked up at the stars and took a deep breath. He had been thinking all along about what he would do next. But he was hoping that it was alone with Wendy. They were still too close to New Orleans.

"I've been thinking about this," Eric spoke turning his attention from Wendy to the group. "I've got another spot we could go to way up in the Rockies."

"Colorado," said Doug, "they're going to miss us at Antone's. That's Austin just a little west of here and not so much north."

"We've been through that Doug," huffed Mark.

"Well maybe that's where we should go," hollered Doug and then softer, "act like nothing happened and maybe find another guitar player if Danny wants to hide out."

"Hey I thought of that," answered Danny. If you all want to go on to Austin that's fine but I can't. Too many people can identify me. I'm sure you could pick up a great guitar player there."

"Yeah I bet Gatemouth would tour with us" laughed Bonnie.

"Look Doug," stated Mark, "whether we like it or not we're all in this together. You don't think the band minus Danny wont be harassed by the cops? They'll probably get to Austin before we do. Hell they might be there now. Sam's dead and they are going to want some answers."

"They'll never accept a random killing," spoke Danny, "my finger prints are all over this and with how sudden we disappeared from the

Chamber. Then there's Adam and Jessica," he asked knowing full well the implications? "If they get caught well they're just kids," answered John.

"Babbling brook my ass," said the wind, "it's more like thundering hurricane," he bragged.

"That will tie a few things up for the cops. But I don't think they'll back off until they find out why Sam and the band ended up in New Orleans together," said Louise. She took a breath and her eyes darted back and forth before she went on. "They still don't have all the pot. Adam and Jessica's cut they may not care about but they have a lot of money on them for kids. So who bought it? They don't know New Orleans wasn't a part of some original plan. They'll want to trace the national network down as far as they can. They'll check all the road houses and try to connect the dots. They'll want to know who killed Sam? Maybe we're the buyers and maybe the killers!" She paused again and said, "and all this wrapped up in a rock n roll band?" She shook her head.

"The cops must be drooling!"

"Oh right were a part of some big syndicate working out of the back of our van," steamed Doug beginning to lose his mind.

"Just the part we're responsible for," sighed Danny.

"You're responsible for," spat Doug.

"Look the best thing to do is split up again," answered Eric. "You had a role Danny and they are not going to let you get away without a bunch of questions."

"Especially if they can't get anyone else to take the fall," said Wendy.

"If they can't get anybody with all the press this has gotten they'll hang this on the band," said Louise. "They always go after the weakest link."

"If the truth gets out about you running for Sam they'll have your plates on every computer network between here and California," said Mark.

"Looks like you'll be living like me," said Louise low enough for only Danny to hear. Danny turned his head slowly and whispered back, "I already am."

"So that's it? We split up and take a truck each," questioned Doug?

"Whatever you decide Danny I'm going with you," said John. With that Bonnie reached out and squeezed his hand. Danny looked around at his friends with a sense of desperation that only caring can bring. "The cops gotta figure I made a play and made some bucks and split. They're not going to let me get away with that," he said emphatically. "You had a real role," said Eric solemnly. "They'll come looking for all of us."

"So we have to be careful."

"Throw yourself into the limelight down in Austin like nothing happened," said Doug again begging this time. He wanted the band just as desperately as Danny. "That's some chance I'd be taking," Danny said looking down at his feet and wagging his head.

"So that's it then? We split up and take a truck each," said Mark pushing for a decision.

"Sounds good to me," said John, "the music's over." Danny nodded his head. John squeezed Bonnie's hand back. She understood about John. He wanted like hell to straighten it all out. But things were way beyond his control. Wendy was now feeling all alone Eric had disappointed her and she was feeling betrayed. Quietly she thought, "all these people have roots together. I should just go back home. What's the worse that could happen to me a little questioning? I doubt the police are even that thorough. Half of Florida was just busted."

Wendy looked around first at Louise. The fire had a strange glow on her. The anxiety of the night was nowhere to be seen on her face. Louise was sitting now warmly absorbed. A bed roll was spread out beside her. She clutched her hands around her knees and slowly rocked back and forth. In the distance the water fall fell forever onward. Louise was watching it even while she was talking. Wendy's gaze moved over to Eric and he was intently watching her. He had built up her trust and spent one night in a place that he might never get back to even in a lifetime. He looked sad. He did not look sad for himself though but rather by the lack of trust he had built back into her heart. Emotionally it was an eternity between last night and right now. "I'll take you back to Florida," he stated slowly drawing out each vowel and syllable. "What makes you think I want to go back there" answered Wendy to shut him up. With that Louise climbed into her bedroll. "We best be smart like her," John said as he went off to sleep. Bonnie followed behind. Mark and Doug threw sand on part of the fire and headed for the soft floor of the constantly decomposing and mulching forest. "It might be softer under here Doug?"

"Yeah, yeah, yeah."

Wendy and Eric talked into the night until the last embers were fading. Danny told them to get some sleep. Meanwhile John asked for his clothes back. "I gave you your shirt already," said Bonnie, "but I've got to tell you without you I'd be dead."

"Nah you wouldn't be dead you'd just be alone and sleeping under some tree.

"Great . . . lost in the wilderness in some overgrowth, wondering when some moose was going to eat me."

"There's no moose in Louisiana . . ."

HOW QUIET THEY SHOULD BE

—

There is definitely a hook up between the spiritual and the physical worlds. Don't ask me how, suffice is to say that it exists. Walls become doors and passageways are hallways. Unrelated physical events are synchronistically joined. It all impacts rather feverishly on the fragile human psyche and soul. The soul is strengthened by these events, and institutionalized faith is shook. People get scared. If you cannot relate an experience with what has been written, you will. And if you have, well then batten down the hatches, because there is more to come.

Here and there are joined together momentarily scorched on the singular mind of the unsuspecting, human consciousness. The subconscious world joined completely on all levels is only momentarily realized and comprehended by the conscious mind in the physical state. All this changes in the spiritual state. These brief glances are but a tune up for what is yet to come in all its terrible glory, and with its horrifying ambivalence towards our daily distractions. It is the ultimate sojourn. To travel free is the best but a price is always paid to get there. Don't be fooled by the roadblocks, the turns, the challenges, the apparent and impending doom. Be forewarned and aware that decisive headway is being made and the road is a gas, even though some may spill on you and burn horribly. The ultimate glory is hard to say. We are here and not there, but life and death are of the same thing. How could it not be since both were brought into this cycle and realm together? Some of us are near completion and some are just starting out, but time is there for all of us. We are learning what it means to be a human being. A step below angels, we struggle with forgiveness and harbor contempt. Ask the Native Americans. Their struggles are so extreme but paint the obvious for us to see, even though few care to look.

We make our choices based on guesswork and reasoning, attitudes and perception. No matter what the outcome, we suffer knowing deep down that these are wholly our own choices. They define us specifically, even if we claim we don't know who we are or what we want. In an existence of eternity we casually forget our past incarnations and relationships only to resolve the unresolved next time. We draw on them subtly and have them impact us blindly. Ignorant and not knowing, we wander aimless and clueless about the past. Even in our recent and present form, we suffer all the while, never learning from our lessons, and blaming coincidence. It's different for each of us. Some tune-in but others prefer to remain closed to the possibilities of the varied layers of phenomenon and the many chapters in the book of life. The enormity is large and the possibilities only limited by fear and doubt and the choices that follow. So we shrink it down to the immediate and turn a blind eye to the greater realm of reality. It's safer and it's smaller. But is it smarter or even better than being cognizant of the entire contemplation? Why is there the nagging lack of fulfillment when the distractions subside? The fear of the enormity is unfounded and the safety of the seen fleeting and mundane. Find the magic. It turns through the smallest blade of grass to the mountain side and back again. There the drudgery of the finite drops its shroud and the mingling of the infinite can be felt and seen. Listen and become more sensitive. Feel the frequency on a gust of wind, just as you are making your point. We either stink it up or shine it on. There's damn little middle ground as the spiritual and material worlds mingle effortlessly like an ocean and a breeze. So raise your sails or keep them in their bag. I'm sure it feels safer to ignore it with the comfort of self imposed limitations. Give yourself the pause of time and with it note each subtle flaw, or skip on down the road. You're accountable for it all. The fog is thick. Until it clears, you have only the vaguely familiar in which to deal. But something whispers and insinuates there's much more out there than greets the eye. You won't know it until it happens or after its over, which may be too late. That makes it all the more intense, even fun. The choice confronts us to either contemplate or ignore. Worry about what others think and act spiritual for show and confusion will follow. You cannot make anyone else's choice for them. It's designed for the individual to grapple with, even though it may seem you have made no choice at all. Not making a choice is still a choice. It's the why that matters. It will seem clear when you get it right or wrong.

Fate does not exist. If we make the wrong choice we will have made the right one. It is the choice we needed to make because of who we are and to bring ourselves into focus. Maybe in this time we will learn this world and the fulfillment that it could bring. Maybe next time we just learn to help each other and . . . oops there's utopia. Even while plunging off our own personal cliff of doom and self-destruction we have named the poison. Those cliffs are usually pretty deep with anguished rocks and crushing blows. A lost soul provocative in its own right is just another romantic escape. Time is there to do this and time is there to get it undone. Time is the great forgiver. Time is the healer and the second, third, fourth and fiftieth chance.

Do not get captured. Those who ramble on, sucking up souls, are wasting their time not confronting themselves. They do not have your answers for you. They may have some giant injustice to rally against, but their goal is to put themselves in power and to line their pockets. Some bored rich kid playing bratty god with an army of searches never looking inward. A sibling rivalry for fame and headlines. A deluded brother beyond recognition. And though they help no one but themselves unless it fulfills their agenda, time is still there to forgive them, waiting patiently for the folly to end. Time shines brilliant and doesn't offer parlor tricks to persuade. The fact that it is . . . is enough. Even when the ultimate warrior or champion is wiped out, time is still there with the opportunity to go backwards or forwards. The opportunity to start again is there every moment of every day, presenting itself always. But still one can embark on the right path and end up going the wrong way only to finish at the beginning. Fault lies only in the motive of the choice. Fate is the invention of those not willing to consciously choose.

The only thing that burns in hell is what an idiot you feel like after spending an eternity in what you thought was heroic independence. We slay and we capture and hold only for ourselves. How easily we could have avoided that mess by finding peace of mind in helping others. For Danny that peace of mind would be the big jam in the sky with a grin and a full heart. For Louise it would be pretty much the same. She would be at the edge of a beach gazing at the beauty with a full stomach and plenty of corn on the cob. Eric would just want everybody dancing all night long with that infernal band. Just once he wanted everyone to walk out after the show together arm in arm and lovely for all eternity. John would just like everything to be organized and for everybody to be all right. A tall order indeed. Mark would never want his questions answered completely, but if they were, then to have the answers pose more questions. Questions even worthier of being pondered and answered than the first ones. Questions all traveling in a never ending spiral of knowledge. Then all at once, beauty would flash needing no expression. The flash would be so overwhelming even to the most unseeking and followed by the loudest and most complete belly laugh of all creation. A laugh perfect in its humility but not frivolous or diminished in its journey. For Bonnie no paradise is available yet and Doug can't see a thing past himself. Wendy, like most of us, just wants to know real happiness and who conspired to shoot JFK, RFK, Martin and John Lennon. The Manchurian Candidate indeed.

There is so much bullshit to deal with in the waking world that everyone's agenda is in conflict with the whole truth. No one is digging for the truth. The newspapers have given up on in depth reporting. Slaves to the bottom line. Once folded twice, well-respected, left-coast rags now have staples but no balls. They continue on grossly like their other media partners underestimating the publics tolerance, loyalty and desire. Politicians lying with statistics spin them like tops until they teeter and fall. And none of it is real truth when dealing with a loathed but unchanged system. Democracy is being sold to the highest bidder and that is scarier than the backroom giveaway's. Opinion makers are unable to grasp ideas that really mean something. Like the Earth's livestock requiring more and more antibiotics, our immune systems are depleted against the horrors of the world. "We have guided missiles but misguided men," said Martin Luther King. Speaking not on the advancement of science but on the decline of spirituality. Who was Martin named after and why? Everywhere the important lessons of history are lost.

There was a generation steeped in idealism. They were second only to the founding fathers in pulling off their goal. They stopped a war with no violence and are written off as a fad. They are portrayed as ridiculous with their accomplishments of peace and lessons of love. We are sold ideas that perpetuate the status quo but not the ideas that would make us better. Ideas are but simple facts of life. Meaning is what we want. Fulfillment is our need; sages to sooth our psyche and minstrels to rock our souls. The lessons learned by experience are lost to the immediate stupefying distractions. Details disputed by opposing panels of experts until the smoke obscures the reality. Do figureheads really matter except in the role-playing and in the dissemination of misdirection? God forbid we look at the political corruption that develops policy, and lines the pockets of those who develop the policy, as intensely as we focus on a blowjob with a beret. Look behind the camera and between the lines.

We want the animals to survive because on a level deep down we know that if the world is uninhabitable for nature then it will become uninhabitable for men. We are one in the same. We are not separate from nature. We need clean water and fresh air, and protecting and enhancing the environment is the only way to do that. Pollution fills the skies and asthma is on the rise. It's not that hard to see the obvious. With the cost of health care, pollution becomes the ultimate drain on the economy; the serpent swallowing its tail. The free market economy demands oversight. There is a specific and intricate link with humans and their environment and that includes the heavenly bodies. Why do we love the stars and our pets? The status of the environment reflects precisely on our health as individuals both physically and spiritually. This is not a great mystery but an obvious truth.

So how about it? Do we know the truth and are amused at the folly? Or have we become mesmerized by the bells and whistles? Hypnotized by the flashing lights and the pace of marketing. The message is buy more stuff, get in debt, keep working longer hours or two jobs, and don't get off that treadmill. If we do, the treadmill makers will loose their summer homes on the Riviera. Is it really necessary to put blinders on and walk in lockstep so that when someone else tries to skin the cat another way we shout them down? Only if your net worth is tied directly to having everyone walk in lockstep. Those completely in the box don't like those who put even a toe outside of it. Why? Because it makes them think there is another way. Staying on the treadmill is easier if you believe that is the only way. It applies to all cultures and their alleged modes of behavior. If those in power aren't making a dime off of it, they'll legislate it out of existence or slit your throat in another culture. All that we know should be used to help and assist one another. Bringing plumbing to the third world would send the world economy into the stratosphere. We are creation by our very existence. We are that which has been created. Our bodies are little universes in which our souls reside. Each one of us has the full spectrum of feelings, thoughts, desires and emotions running in our veins and our consciousness. What we choose to do should be guided with that in mind. What we choose to rely on from within guides us. What do you want for your world? What do you want for yourself? Then it should be the same for each other. Take care of your side of the street and then one day all the side streets will be taken care of. Do it for yourself. Set the example and others will see. They will make their own choices or not.

Are we in a funk, or in it all do we see the humanity? Is the humanity there? Is it the pain between the lies? Is it glorious in all its imperfection? Does it stand apart from all the noise somewhere on the outside of the box? What is truly fine is that the beauty of it all may be seen and felt for the peace that it really brings. So what is within the realm of possibility? Wendy would like to know, so would I, and so would you. With our imaginations we can make it all real. It depends on what we imagine for ourselves and each other. Even the base and the contemptible are an intricate part of what defines our choices and what becomes the whole. "How much enlightenment can you have? Is it not in a flash of understanding rather than in miles and miles of text?" Danny didn't know. "How am I supposed to give up my dream," he wondered to himself?

"She's pretty cute," thought John. He could never see her beauty before, although the basic parts were all the same. Something now from within had been added. The glow was unmistakable and hopefully not fleeting. For now it was all there in Bonnie. They sat together at the waters edge. Life was transformed and held precious again. The days were going to be new and the nights alive but all this had yet to happen. There was however hope and closeness and human desire and the upfrontness of the situation. Tomorrow it might be all different. The last two days were a blur of spontaneous combustion. But in this moment life was moving slowly but not so slow as not to be noticed. Life is the hurricane we need to live in the eye. We are driven like the rain furiously onward and over everything in our path. Choices abound opportunities leap forward again and again. This is time showing it's love again and again and again. "How do we move ahead without so much destruction," asked Bonnie? John took Bonnie's hand and spoke," wait for this to clear."

The stars at night were writing a story of their own. With each breath that John and Bonnie took they drew closer together and yet hardly moved at all. The waterfall fell forward. They sat near the edge. The cool water vaporized in a mist that brushed upon their faces the cool realization of the moment. Nothing more powerful than the right moment and nothing less. Time is the string of moments one moment at a time. Waiting is always such pain and tomorrow may never come. Is patience a virtue or is it the total immersion of one's self in one moment? Or is it both? Each flowing moment is just another separate and complete entity unto itself. The only pay off is in the total immersion of the singular moment. Small wonder why sex is so fulfilling even though brief in the language of time in a universal sense. The stars played out their silent symphony to the whispering Spanish moss. The gator yawned for food. "You know Bonnie those were some timely words spoken to Doug."

"He doesn't know for shit John. Remember when we were first trying to start this band and all that noise he was layin' on everybody?"

"I never understood why Danny put up with all that," answered John.

"I mean," Bonnie continued," who did he think he was fooling playing those games?"

"After Danny goes to all the trouble in setting up the gigs and reserving studio time Doug is hollering to throw him out of the band." "Unbelievable," answered Bonnie," remember when he threatened to kick Mark's ass?"

"You bet," answered John, "what a joke. Marks the best . . ."

" . . . and," jumped in Bonnie, "he really listens."

"Obviously that makes him a wimp," laughed John.

"There is only so much Doug anyone can take."

"True but you were right in there with him. I mean just as jaded and bitter . . ."

" . . . selfish and self centered," John nodded and Bonnie continued, "I think the word is bitch . . ."

"You said that not me!"

"I know but its time to come clean."

"You mean act like a human. Love something outside of yourself?"

"Well I wouldn't go that far." Silence interrupted the conversation. Doug and the others were off in the distance as the flame of the evening drew to a close. But here by the banks of the fall an unseen flame was glowing ever brighter. The only clue were the stars in their eyes. "You know the strangest thing about you," said Bonnie and John turned his head, " . . . is when you say something that you really believe in you can see it in your face. Its the most amazing thing. Are you hiding anything? I don't think I ever noticed it before." John just shrugged and smiled a long satisfying smile.

"I can't believe I never noticed it before."

"You were never this close," spoke John quietly. He leaned over to her and planted a big wet one. As smooches go it was a very long smooch. There were several o's in smooch making it either one long smooooooch or a bunch of short and long smooches with their hearts pounding. John came up for air after he had sucked all of it out of

Bonnie's lungs. He stared into her eyes. She did not look away but rather down towards the ground. His mind flashed to her picture perfect body. Its strength and beauty he remembered from the beach all those summers ago. "You know Bonnie you are as beautiful now as you were when you were breaking hearts all over town. Bonnie, Bonnie puddin' pie kissed the boys and made them cry."

"That's what my mother used to sing to me," she exclaimed!

"I know," he said. In the not so distant past Bonnie would have bitched at him in full denial. Now she burst out laughing. The laughter only made the moment that much more. More what? I don't know you pick the word. Wonderful? Real? Full? Fantastic? Complete? Whatever it was to Bonnie and John it was more because of laughter. Her arm slipped up over his shoulder. Her breath fell on his neck. John hugged her back. "You saved my life." She almost cried. "I never thought I could count on anyone or even just have fun with anyone anymore and you saved my life!"

"Oh, that again," said John in mock humiliation. But then switching gears he pulled away from Bonnie and looked at her squarely. "Old friends," he paused, "remember?" Its hard to say where the soul comes from. Our bodies surround it somehow. Bonnie knew it came through the eyes. She believed in soul and owned a few Otis Redding albums. "Don't pull away from me you jerk." Bonnie reached back out for him. They had let go of themselves and parked their egos. All that was left to do was feel good. They were in that space. Somewhere between the hand touching the skin and the soul touching the soul. The skin is the soft road on which our souls travel, like a road we take to reach a destination. It's a meeting ground raising the spirit of the Earth and raising the spirit of each other. Such a magnificent road can only lead to a far more beautiful place. Most get lost along the various spots along the way. Whether they are imperfections or quick sand for the senses the greatest joy is in the flight to the end. The forever moments that by the clock on the wall are an eternity disguised as seconds. The forever moments of bliss and passion. It's no wonder we spend so much time talking about sex and thinking about love and trying to get back there. Being preoccupied with paradise is not a fault and an understandable obsession.

He pulled her shirt off over her head. Slowly the perfect flesh showed itself as he caressed it's softness. Much more quickly they grappled for each others belts as their clothes slipped away. John sat upon his blanket as Bonnie climbed on for the ride. At first they were two. Johns hardness imploring to seek refuge in the space that was her's to give. Such giving is usually taken for granted but not by these two. He held her as close as possible and felt her softness push against his chest. Her eyes were clear and brilliant and her bare shoulders round and perfect. They both gazed off at the stars repeatedly and at each other. The stars brilliantly sparkled their approval. The waterfall rushed on through their minds and rushed through their souls and filled their hearts. The mist lay upon them gently. The crickets reminded them of how quiet it was and how quiet they should be. How perfect in the night under the stars and by the waterfall they were. All of nature and all of creation outside and two as one. It was perfect and romantic and sultry. Silently with furry they both came again and again and again. They stayed together. Mounted they dared not move. They reached for their blankets and together forever in a moment they were wonderful, sublime, happy and fulfilled.

Time is a moment that has its own depth and its own place. Eternity is a moment that lasts forever. Love is not in an annual budget and love isn't a climb up the social ladder. Love is a moment that feels like forever. It is that and only that which you can take with you anywhere you go here or there. Even though the circumstances might change love is always there waiting to be felt. Love always is but only to be seen and to be felt and to be heard by those that would and when they do because love is all around us all the time. We are the problem and the receiver of our conscious mind has been shut off by distraction, fear and doubt. Why can't it be? The proof is all around us. Tune out those that want to focus our attention elsewhere for profit and self gain. The sky is blue and the grass is green what more do you need to know. Isn't it lovely?

We move from the moment in an effort to manipulate. Love is manipulated only by the person who is giving that love. We are too busy with our distractions and self to see it as something eternally present in our lives. We end up thinking it is fleeting. At least we do know it is something to be gained and something to be treasured. We are preoccupied with the gaining and not the treasuring. We fail to see that love is ignited by our very own perceptions of where we are in the universe and where we are on the Earth. We are constantly thinking about the idle and overstated realities of our lives. Who has time to notice because they are stuck in traffic breathing in exhaust. We solved the air pollution problem. Sure we did. Just watch a bus accelerate up a street next time. Does it feel good in your lungs? Why are we sweating looking for some shade to hide underneath and dreaming of a meadow lying in the grass? I like melting in one hundred degrees worth of molting, stanky, asphalt, especially with an old truck chugging horrible, lung clogging, exhaust in my face.

Instead we try to ignore it all, flip the air-conditioning on, put the windows up, lock the doors and put our heads down. Isn't this a slightly more pressing issue than a celebrity sighting. We pass each other in the street without flinching. It is a strange and beautiful world it's just the people that mess it up. Wrong headed decisions clearly show we are not the stewards of the planet that we should be. Even though it's essential to our survival. Without real love and appreciation for our life in the vast darkness and silence of space everything becomes just a game of spinning our wheels and wasting our time. True survival on this planet, this window of sound, air and light comes to those who love, their work, their home, their family, their life, their friends, their animals, their garden, their schools, their books, their art, their music, their play, themselves and each other. For now Bonnie and John could see the creating spirit in everything.

Morning was working its way over the swamps of the bayou. The music had slowed down but not stopped. The birds took up their cry and vigil for food. They loved the night and loved the day. They were birds from the moment they were born. Through each moment they were eternally conscious of what they were about. They were perfectly adjusted even when drenched in a down pour or an oil slick. The trees clung to the Earth like they had for centuries saying that they liked their job and looked cool doing it, "we don't mind just hanging out." The wind tickled their leaves or pushed them over in a storm. It all moves on. This side of the Earth spun back into the warm glow of the sun. The waterfall has not missed a beat. Man and his science of toxic waste would poison man. He would die from what he created never learning to discern the difference between his knowledge and how it was put to use. What would it result in if it was applied to help one another? What would it result in if only applied to self? The difference between utopia and Armageddon is a fine line. The choice is there to be made and forever in each moment to make it.

Eric and Wendy had spent an uneventful night. Wendy fought for sleep. Eric pondered the love that lay sleeping and lost to him through a conscious word or two. Many would call that unconscious to begin with, "you dumb ass," he said quietly to himself, "had to open up your mouth. Two steps forward and one step back." How are we ever going to get there like that? Or are we there already? Louise rolled over and stared at a sleeping Danny. "Well the struggle continues," she thought. Thinking she had found refuge in John's embrace and Danny's dreams she only found time. And now she must move on. This is just another dead end on another endless series of roads. Few are brave enough to venture on unsecured and uprooted, "you'd think I'd get a moments rest somewhere along the line," she said to herself. She gathered her things and stole off into the dawn. Wendy with one eye open smiled goodbye. Louise reached over and touched her hand and then she was gone. Not a sound and not a broken branch and like a whisper she was gone.

Mark sat up with his back against a tree. His legs lay straight out before him. His arms were folded and his head back. His baseball cap with the letters G.P. rested on his sweet heart head. He realized that unlike some of his friends he still had two strong legs. Doug was unconscious. He spent most of his life screaming to get what he wanted and he was always able to drop off to sleep. After all it was just a game to him. All the posturing and back arching and strutting just a game to play. He never really wanted to do much of anything and hated ambition in other people. But he had delusions of grandeur anyway and was a control freak. Here was a person who literally thought his shit didn't stink. It was hard to figure why Danny had him along.

Another keyboard player could be found and if he wanted an asshole well they too were all over the place. Doug's main goal in life was to do as little as possible and cause a little trouble, nothing new there. However, his method of screaming at the top of his lungs while standing a few inches from your face was an annoying approach to say the least. It had worn thin even to himself. Although he had always threaten to "kick ass", as he was fond of saying. It was obvious that he had never been in a fight. "One day soon," Bonnie had remarked, "someone big and terrible is going to rip his face off." Danny's reason for keeping him on board was not even clear to him. A misguided loyalty perhaps to a school chum or a promise he made to Doug's folks. "Do you think he'll ever come around," Danny would wonder out loud. But he took him on anyway. Doug had it all schemed out in his mind but Danny was a constant reminder of a different way. Somewhere locked in Doug's head was an agenda for one. Unfortunately the end result was that he just got wrapped around his own axle.

The dawn arose and woke our vagabond friends. Only they did not scurry from the light. Sure their circumstance suggested that they were beneath contempt. They were musicians dealing drugs with the fresh blood of the innocent and murdered stinking in their trail. The thundering right of hypocritical reality would feast on their tale of woe. They would use them as a model of corruption banning them from libraries and burning the paper that binds them. From some lofty unattainable position they would deny all that was real. They preach that they know but what they know is only to further themselves. They take the simple joy of living and turn it into evil. They beg money from the poor and accept money from the powerful to keep themselves so. They fall way short of what it means to be in the world of human beings. Those that see this reality as an oasis understand our place as caretakers and the sole givers of voice in the vast silence of space. What words we use, what we say and the way we say them reflect our understanding of our place in the universe. Ours is the unique opportunity to be the sole voices in a silent universe. No wonder the sick hear so many sounds. All that dead energy that has gone on before trying mightily to express themselves and find their way back into this three dimensional reality. Fragile minds operate on a frequency overwhelmed. A universe full of celestial bodies and alternative dimensions and only the physical realm which we occupy is given voice. All of that energy and vastness is silenced except for human beings on this tiny outpost in the corner of an enormous galaxy. Make a joyful noise indeed!

There are those that live and let live and who hold that truth higher than all the rest. But others use words to gain for themselves. They cloud the religions of the world with dogma and use belief against each other missing what is truly holy. The individual path to enlightenment needs a free mind. To experience life through your own eyes and draw your own conclusions was Danny's goal. These friends though flawed were following their dreams and dealing with everything life had to throw at them. Love is wrong because it involves sex? Language improper because it expresses raw fucking emotions? These were real human beings answering the calls from within. No one could tell them to shut out what was in their own heart. The discoveries of their consciousness the journey of their life was theirs to live. They didn't want to make the mistake of buying in so completely to the alleged norm that they tuned their own selves out. If anything was worth exploring it was what was inside them. They didn't need the validation of the masses to believe in themselves. Perhaps they failed at the defined world of success. But be careful of that definition and who defined it and why? Was it a dream perpetuated by those who would most benefit by the dream? What did that matter if you were enough of an individual to have your own thoughts and build your own life as you saw fit? The trappings are not the goal. The pursuit of happiness and the freedom and liberty to live your life the way you see fit is. To think your own thoughts and to do unto others as you would have them do unto you was the only approach that would ensure survival.

Danny and the band, Wendy and Eric, even Louise created their world out of a love for life. To drink deeply from the fountain that is this consciousness, this opened window of thought and word, deep in the vast reaches of the dark silent universe. Defining what all this means through the words and thoughts of love was the noblest expression they could achieve with this universal anomaly. They pursued happiness and not just for themselves but also for those who came to hear them and those that came to be with them. Nothing else is worth doing in comparison.

The souls that take advantage of the faithful in using them for their own gain will die a hundred deaths more unimaginable than the normal death most must face. No our rag tag bunch did not scurry from the light. They outstretched their arms and sought to bring the warmth of realization of another day unto each other. To feel the Earth's strength and worship its sustaining reality, its air, its water, its soil. No, these musicians were not in it for the money. They were in it for the life. They were constantly after that rejoicing splendor of nature deep in the moment trying to hit the note and letting the note hit them. It was present in everything we do, see, hear, touch, feel and understand if we're lucky enough to flush it out and bring it into our consciousness. They say go climb a rock. Stick your head in the woods. Go swim in a lake. They say arrange the laws to benefit those who need it. They say arrange the laws to preserve that which is our home and sustains us. They say save the planet and we save ourselves. They marvel in creation and try to feel it. They look at the whole Earth as a sacred temple. They don't throw garbage in the ocean.

In the quiet of the morning as the choir of birds begins to sing the light shines through the stained glass window called the sky. It gives sight to the voice of the daily service that is life. It happens each day. There is almost nothing to take the place of a fresh dawn in the woods where the spirit awakes from a needed sleep and see's everything in perfect harmony. Truly nature unspoiled by the hand of man is what paradise is and meant to be. But still there is time waiting in the wings eternally forgiving. It waits until we get it and holds a periwinkle out for us to discover to help cure the cancer we have caused.

Bonnie stretched upward after sitting up. Her natural body stretched toward the sun. She did this without thinking. The sun shown upon her flesh and the early morning chill cleared out the cobwebs better than any cup of coffee or cigarette. "Look at that waterfall," spoke John rising also.

"It really lulled me to sleep," said Bonnie.

"I've got to go in," exclaimed John! On the ridge Eric and Wendy embraced and Danny looked for Louise. "Stop staring," said Mark to Doug. Doug farted, "that's my girl he's sleeping with."

"Give it a break will you," said Mark. Even Doug couldn't muster much hate at this moment of morning. Bonnie and John made their way to the waterfall. They weaved their way along the trail over rocks and frogs and flowers and plants. "They're naked," said Doug revealing his keen insight. Mark just looked at him with that are you for real look. At this point Danny was up on his knees, "gone," he thought to himself about Louise, "bedroll and all, not a sound, good god, hardly time to know her."

"She'll be fine," spoke Wendy resting her hand on Danny's shoulder.

"She sure didn't want to stay with this mess," he said out loud. "Where was she last month?"

"She would have left at this point no matter when she had come along."

"Well of course you're right Wendy. Besides who can blame her. She felt the need to bolt and that's a bad sign for us." Wendy looked down with a perfect compassion born from experience. The experience of being human. "Still I wish she could have stayed," he spoke.

"Rabbits's come out of hats in magic shows," said Eric perceiving the situation quickly. But this life and world is magic better go check your hats. Meanwhile Bonnie and John were submerged in the waterfall. "Freezing," hollered John.

"Brrrr!" Bonnie wrapped herself around John and John wrapped himself around her but it was still great. Doug climbed over to the edge of the cliff. His jealousy awakened. Didn't they know the mess they were in? Indeed they did. "Roll with the punches Doug," said the squirrels, "you have to plan for winter." Doug didn't hear them. Bonnie and John were still rubbing each other to stay warm. No soakin' and pokin' today. Doug turned from the sight enraged. "Why not start the day with a healthy dose of controversy," he said out loud. No one was listening. "So she ran out on you, huh," said Doug at Danny about Louise. In Danny he saw a much more vulnerable target. "Don't you take a break," shot back Mark. He turned his head toward Danny and said, "he's just pissed because John scored Bonnie and he didn't. Eric just smiled. He and Wendy had only been with them a few days but Doug was an easy read. Danny turned and faced Doug, paused and walked right by him. He was headed for the waterfall. Bonnie and John waved him down and the three of them went under water. It looked like fun so Wendy and Eric did the same. Pretty soon they were all laughing and jumping up and down to stay warm. Except Doug.

"You don't get it," spoke Mark on his last ditch effort of the morning with Doug.

"Your going down there too?" Mark just shook his head. "I need a shower you know." Mark looked at him closer and said with feeling, "they're our friends." Doug turned away.

ACCELERATED ACCELERATION

—

A whole generation of assholes! It was inconceivable that a whole generation of assholes could bloom and flourish after the sixties. Wasn't anybody listening didn't anybody care? Pollution of the environment, body, spirit and mind became irrelevant and in replacement stood the almighty dollar. Although it's way too easy to blame the dollar. One should understand that the dollar alone has nothing to do with what happens, why it happens or because of the dollar itself. It is the motivation of the person directing those dollars, rubles, pounds, quid, whatever. But instead we have a culprit that can remain generic and everyone can stand back and say it's the system, it's the nature of the beast. But we can't put all the blame on so small of a green back. Sadly we are the beast man and woman too. Our goals of control and greed are bred out of an ego driven lust for power, insecurity and fear. Money is just a piece of paper, coinage. Not everyone is born a sniveling, grubbing, back stabbing shitfuck. Oh no behavior such as that must be learned, groomed and be brought through a complex system of reinforcement. If any dare stand outside the cherished rites of ignorance and display some original free thought well then that one is banished from the group. The group chortles in an excited frenzy reassuring everyone that each others learned patterns of hate and selfishness are quite acceptable and our free thinker goes merrily on his way. Solitude and peace of mind is the price for not validating ignorant behavior and scrambling out of the box. But the game remains and the ignorant excel. It may all get nuked and blown out of sight but that doesn't give them pause. They are consumed by the petty and do not know their place in the world or the universe. So we scorch the surface and pollute the hand that feeds us. A whole generation of money oriented assholes with big fat mouths saying really stupid things. Aren't they bold, aren't they funny, ha, ha? They reinforce societies ignorance by the day. Confirming the serotype because it is the only role they have the balls to play. They perpetuate a fraud with the web they weave. Their souls end up chaotic and have to relearn the basics. They know who they are and they know what they deny and it gives them fleeting pleasure. But then the pleasure runs out and the demise they have sought for others has landed squarely on their doorstep. What goes around comes around. They're not paying attention. Do something to make it a better world. Say something positive and not about the "bitch you fucked last night" frat boy! There are bigger issues out there than your dick. A whole generation of assholes. What kind of behavior are we spreading how can it be good. Of course the end result is we have a bunch of selfish, ego centric politicians and we act surprised. That's the society we are pulling them from. That's the behavior we are rewarding as we clamor after the rich and famous. I have a feeling the Earth can't wait until we go. I know the dolphins feel that way.

Tolerance, forgiveness, respect, love and patience are necessary to share the Earth. That male driven ego gone astray accomplishes nothing for himself through chest pounding, saber rattling, stubbornness and hate. The Earth belongs to the Creator. We are just the keepers of this blue jewel in the sky. A squabbling lot of school children we have become. Hate is the tool of self destruction. Greed replaces passion.

They stood in the life giving waterfall. Their nakedness was of the soul and not of the skin. The one who turned away may see but does not feel the same. Kindness and compassion are in the realm of joy. Denial of the mystery is so much easier at first, simpler, easy and more comfortable. But in the end mortality forces it's contemplation. And so he stood there alone with the things that he thought he knew. If only he could reach out to them and tell them what was in his heart. Our fragile existences wrapped completely around one another and affecting each action thought and deed with the slightest of movement, the slightest touch, the slightest feeling. Each ripple of energy affecting all while largely unnoticed. The sun bursts forth from behind the clouds when revelation comes upon us. Do we notice?

Yes even Doug was capable of these thoughts. Even though he didn't know it himself. From where he stood it seemed that the whole world had gone mad and left him standing there alone. Obviously these fools in the waterfall had no clue what kind of danger they were in. But beyond that they did not seem to care. How far did this not caring go? Doug was just the type to find out. He would have made a great zealot believing money made him right. He did not notice the rustling trees. He was too busy with his hands on his hips sizing up his friends. "They're weak," he thought to himself. Good people are always weak," Doug assumed. Doug's focus was tunneled into his ego. He didn't realize that happy people suffer also sometimes more. It was just how they responded to the suffering. To some it made them stronger and more determined to be positive. To others it made them weak and confused. No one gets out alive and the glad don't have it better they just look at it differently. But Doug was jealous of their supposed ease and wasted his life trying to get even. He had this vision of these frolicking people in a waterfall all living and loving and it made him crazy. They were stupid idealist unable to see the misery of everyday life. He was wrong. Their happiness was boiled down to ignorance as bliss. He was wrong. What he saw in that waterfall was entirely up to him. Short of seeing Bonnie playfully strangling Danny he could not hear her cursing him out for his stupidity. She was lamenting the fact that he had not come to them about the money. But Danny was standing tall a victim of his dream. He was trying to make his dream happen with people who had made no previous effort beyond the immediate. But the musical process and Mark, John and Danny all knew this, lent itself to communication of the utmost without words. Lyrics are a veil in which the thoughts and ideas are spoken. The audience is the interpreter subjective with a million

different points of view. They read into the sounds and vision which
brings us back to Doug. In spite of his overwhelming talent he could
not communicate with anyone without music. He knew how he thought
he wanted to be. Society told him that. No matter how hard you try you
can't live life as a generalization. Society has painted a myth and Doug
thought being an asshole was all right. He looked outward and
constantly measured himself against everyone else twenty four seven.
Being better gave him a lift. Being worse tore him down. He batted
around like a hockey puck in the crease. He would never settle until
the play was whistled dead.

Eric and Wendy knew the myth. They worked with the main
promoters of it. God how many times did Wendy go to a party and feel
like she was in a television commercial. A beer commercial to be
exact. Everything was perfect everybody's hair was perfect but the
conversation strangely enough never quite lived up to the fantasy.
The harder they tried the more the air went out of the room. But oh
how they tried to be so right. Right wing that is and when that is out of
fashion left wing. The mindless masses a drift on the leads of people
who don't care about them at all. They would rather have a witless
blindly accepting society to run circles around in order to bank the
profits quietly. Doug had no idea how manipulated he was and how
far he had fallen into the stereo type. His opinions came from the talk
radio station and the evening news and the headlines. He hadn't an
original thought in his head. He was a caricature imitating what he
saw. Talking to people was like replaying the talk shows from the day
before. He looked out for number one. He wanted the job that paid
the most money. He bought the cd's they played in heavy rotation. He
argued the right's point against the left and the left's point against
the right. He never worried that someone he would never meet was
grabbing his tax dollars. He never thought that he wouldn't be
welcomed at the super riches table. Trickle down my ass. Doug's
opinions shaped so precisely that he thought he was on the side of
the winning even though his stock options were worthless. Well just
fine. We play King of the Hill until there is only one person standing
on top. Like inbreeding how can that be good for the economy?

And what do you suppose they'll be standing on after the cut throat, win at all cost bastards get done bludgeoning each other to death? I'll tell you what. It will be a rotted old city with polluted water and a nuked out skyline. But hey good for them they'll be in charge. Did you see how fast they scurried out of Washington, D.C. on 9/11 leaving the rest of us to die?

So the people in the waterfall were far from perfect but they would stand together forever to protect each other and that which gave them life. They knew all too well that it was the Earth that gave them life. It bathed them and sustained them with the food that it grew. It restored their spirit in a sunset. It coaxed their understanding like a bottle nose dolphin nudging us from behind imploring us to play. Imploring us to live but not to destroy because once we destroy them we are next. The truth is easy, the truth is clear, the truth is simple. But people like Doug from all walks of life, from all corners of the Earth see themselves separate from the environment from which they live in and from each other. They are immersed in their own self pity, ego and arrogance to such a degree that they hold themselves separate from everyone and everything. As if they can live without it. It is the very thing that sustains them. Hair trigger attitudes and hate ridden souls. Falling in love? Never, they don't know who to trust. They think everyone is trying to burn them the way they are trying to burn each other. Wendy took falling in love every day over not being able to trust anyone. Very human, warmly human, lovingly human, she was a wonderful human being. She was the one with the clear eyes and the clear thinking. She was the one listening to the music within. If you look closely enough those like her are the ones smiling at strangers. They are the ones laughing too loud. Not the ha, ha superior laugh of the terribly vain and bitter but rather the "sanity claus" laugh of the Marx Brothers. Happiness for some is just the expression of their resentment. Mad like giant boulders falling to the sea they impact with all the force and hatred they can muster. They delight in destroying what others love and it makes them happy for a moment. To the vastness of the ocean they hardly make an impact except a brief and annoying noise. Time and time again the water takes them in. Kindness is a perceived weakness along with understanding, patience and knowledge. Their mortality ignored it silently eats away at their souls. They don't understand their journey. What would you do with your remaining time if you knew you were going to die? But you know that already? You are going to die. Doug never contemplated spreading his arms out for a hug. His love was only hidden in some room for a few brief seconds. Then to roll over his back turned away. He was unable to face his partner and soon to find fault. When you can not face love you can not face yourself. When you can not face yourself you can not face love.

Doug wanted to move on. He could feel the knot in his stomach tighten up. He knew they were all on borrowed time. His pulse quickened. This time he heard the trees rustle. "Hey forget something fuckhead?" Smash a black blur cut across Doug's eyes as a stunning blow to the head put him on his ass. The dust rose up as he bounced twice with his hands scraping along the ground tearing skin. Before he could look up one of John's shirts was being tossed into his face. When he could clear the shirt from his face he got a massive kick to his thigh numbing his leg. There was a gun in his chest. The heat from the revolver's barrel was burning a hole through him before he knew what was going on. The heat felt like a fire poker left too long in the hearth. The waterfall kept going not even noticing. "Don't move a motherfucking inch you piece of shit bastard." Doug flinched.

"Don't move," the cop screamed the blood washing his face. He was licensed to protect and serve the public. Which public? Was it the ordinary people public or was it the political public? Or were they serving themselves with a license to do anything?

"Hey Melon," came a voice from over by the cliffs edge.

"What," he screamed still looking at Doug.

"We got all the fish in the barrel." Doug heard this but he only saw a slew of blue swarming through the camping gear. "Damn we didn't get far," he thought to himself.

"Watch ya looking' at fagot?" Officer Melon did not have a southern accent. He handcuffed Doug around a tree. This was as close to nature as Doug wanted to get. His eye began to swell. "You're an idiot Melon. Why do you keep leaving marks on these guys," said another cop? Doug's senses started to come back together. Down in the waterfall they were about to lose theirs. Five of the tightest assed state troopers with guns drawn were getting ready to strip search our stripped friends. "You don't have to point those things at us" yelled Danny.

"Who asked you to say anything asshole your mine now. Get back up there?"

"Where?" demanded Bonnie.

"Big tits, big mouth. Get your gear miss you all under arrest for murder." No one said a thing. Danny looked at Mark and shook his head. "What are you shaken your head for," screamed a cop.

"I got water in my ear," said Danny stepping up and onto the rocks.

"Another wise guy. Yo Melon did he follow you down from New York? Melon was on the cliffs edge hanging around waiting to get them all together. "What's going on," Doug yelled. He watched his friends march up the trail. Wendy wanted to get her clothes back on. "You're wanted for murder boy just keep your mouth shut," and the cop thought to himself, "they're not putting up much of a fight they gotta be guilty." Then he turned to Eric and said, "a little outside of Baton Rouge and you thought you could have a party. Are you all underestimating the state police?"

"This is stupid," spoke John, "what are your talking about."

"Plead your case elsewhere son its time to go see the judge," said another cop. "Who's shirt is this?" John bit his lip. Everyone just stood still. Nothing moved.

"They were reaching here," thought Danny to himself, "no one killed anybody."

"That's my shirt," said John.

"Thanks for the trail idiot."

"Why are you trailing us" Bonnie spoke up again?

"I'm akin' the questions," said Melon. He was transferred south because he shot an innocent woman. He unloaded his revolver and spit on her. That part wasn't in the report. Then he searched her for money. That wasn't in the report either. He got caught so he had to go. "No one here killed anyone officer," said Danny.

"Still got water in your ear son? Shut up!" Another officer stood behind Danny with a huge flashlight on his shoulder. He was ready to snap it over Danny's head. Or so he wanted Danny to think. It was like some rookie training film on how to be an intimidating asshole. Of course the other side of the story would be that the state police were tracking dangerous criminals and they were lucky they weren't all shot to death by a bunch of naked musicians. Doug was bleeding hooked to a tree. Wrong place, wrong time. They dressed under an armed guard. "Why are you drying off? Did I say dry off? What are you two talking about over there? Are you faggots or something?" Mark had bent over to see if Doug was all right. "I'm just seeing if he's okay."

"A couple of fags," said one cop and Melon laughed. What is it in this world that keeps good people down? Why does this world seemingly reward the evil that men do? How is it that the oil companies can go into Alaska and do whatever they want? How is it that they can put their own political cronies in place? How is it that the timber companies get joy from strip mining an entire old growth forest? How is it that the tax payers money goes to them to do it without a whimper? How is it that the loggers stay loyal when the companies leave them broke and living in a ghost town? How is it that we let them get away with it? Where is everybody screaming at the injustice and the annihilation of our planet? Why is everyone so docile? Is television that good? Or is the war on drugs a complete farce and the population as a whole is stoned? We are lulled to sleep while the greedy and the absolute get away with tearing down what is sacred. Sacred not only to our beliefs but what is absolutely paramount to our survival. How can these robber barons not see and understand this? They are slitting their own throats as well as ours. How does this corruption get so out of hand? How and why is doing wrong justified? Why are people perpetuating lies? What are they protecting?

The business world could probably operate more efficiently if run more equitably. All we are rewarding is the fat and lazy insiders. Why is our western society on such a decline? Because we are trained to look the other way and not to ask questions. Mind your own business. If you make waves you get the boot to the street. Karen Silkwood? Lynn Ray Hill? People with real concerns about people they do not even know. That would be us the public unwittingly lulled into a false sense of security. Asleep at the switch while the corporate machine spews cancer into the environment and subsequently into us and themselves. We pass these chemicals into our nursing babies. Each one of us is totally integrated into the environment. Try not breathing for thirty seconds. The price of freedom is constant vigilance.

What the police can get away with they will. Here's to the guys that do the job right. But why have they let the corrupt overrun them? Violence for violence sake? Raping runaways in Pennsylvania? How is this all rewarded and tolerated and when is the day of reckoning coming? Jesus himself has got to be pissed off. So pissed off that he can't see straight. So pissed off that god has Samson holding him down. An explosion is going to occur and it wont be very nice. Wouldn't you be pissed if you were god and honest hard labor and smarts and a good attitude weren't good enough anymore? Wouldn't you be pissed if you were god and your wonderful beautiful perfectly integrated Earth was being raped by greedy morons? Or is god just waiting to see what mankind does with this opportunity? Will we live in Eden for eternity or slash and burn it to hell only to walk right into hell itself. If you were god wouldn't you just say, "see ya later, good riddance"? Have fun in the short term because in the long term there is going to be an accounting for your thoughts, words and deeds. Brilliant theory we humans developed to maximize profits the ends justifying the means. Anybody hear of sustainability? What good is the villa in France when the Mediterranean is so polluted that the pollution is running up river. What good is your townhome in Vale when it is bathed in radiation from unchecked uranium mining? Why do we need all that uranium anyway? Oh yeah to point Earth ending weapons at each other.

Let's see if we have this straight. We need nuclear weapons so we don't interfere with each others corrupting power blocs. We leave autonomy to the power structures of each country and not the people so that absolute power corrupts absolutely. We should have pictures of our corrupt leaders on buildings everywhere. That way we'll know what an asshole really looks like. Let's define asshole as a maniacal blood thirsty dictator who's only interested in lining his own pockets and someone who sends innocent citizens to die to protect his interest.

Smack! The flashlight came crashing down on Danny's head. "Your a shit head dope dealer," yelled Melon. Actually Danny was a slightly misguided dope dealer more of a dreamer. What he didn't know was the varying degrees of belief that his friends fell under. How could he if they didn't talk about it? "I don't need much to be happy," Danny often thought to himself, "just some steady gigs and the chance to play guitar." Danny bled from the head in waves. The blood loss was much more than Melon had bargained for. "Shit! Now look at what you've done. I told them to ship your ass back to New York!" Melon shot his partner a glance, "that's nothin' he ain't gonna fucking die asshole!" Eric jumped on Danny's wound with his bandanna. "Damn it we gotta get this guy stitched up!"

"Shut the fuck up! I'm giving the orders here . . ."

"How fucking typical," thought Wendy to herself, "why do the most inept want to be in charge?" The others had dressed in horror of what might happen but now unnerved they moved as a group to lynch Melon. The other cops had to move in quickly. Doug cuffed to a tree had to watch Danny fall. The blood splattered on Doug. Eric was practicing medicine with a bandanna. An unidentified plains clothed policeman started to pull Danny away. Bonnie went to move in to take care of Danny shrieking, "You fucker!" Six foot four two hundred and fifty pounds of blue uniform stepped in her way. "Step over here mam." The officer strong armed her away. While Danny laid on the ground the police grabbed the rest of them. Melon went over to uncuff Doug but he stopped at Danny first. "Get up boy you're not hurt get up." It's hard to explain fear unless you have really felt it. Fear will make you respond in earnest to the most ridiculous situations. In all his life he would have laughed at Melon. He would have if he had been standing from a safe distance. Or if Melon had been just a guy in the street he would have struck back. But the badge, the gun and the radio in the car made the playing field lopsided. It took his manhood away and gave an unbelievable power surge to and put larceny in the hearts of dishonest men. It was in fact only the honest who feared authority. Danny stood up. Without losing a step Melon walked over to Doug and took off his cuffs. "All right we're going back through the woods single file. Pick up your stuff and move it." Danny got escorted by two cops. It was his lucky day. But Doug had the wonderful officer Melon all to himself. "This shouldn't have happened this way."

"You talking to me boy?"

"Why waste my breath?"

"You better be nice I can help you." It was like a funeral procession. Innocent until held over for a grand jury. Life seems to keep throwing spit balls. The harder Danny tried the rockier the road. The night he told everyone he was going to get married his girlfriend went back to her ex-boyfriend. Love had passed him at break neck speed. He wasn't sure if the river was muddy or if he could see clear through it. The pain etched across his face in lines off lost hope and faith. He kept trying to get the wind back into his sails. There was always something to flood the keel or cloud the sky. But he kept sailing, paddling, swimming and treading to stay afloat. That was his choice. As they filed away from the camp site all that was heard was the gravel beneath their feet. Danny's head was wrapped in Mark's shirt. Melon had a sick sense of humor. "I guess you had nothing to do with it," spoke Melon in an altogether inappropriate voice of concern? Doug didn't notice that Melon was playing good cop bad cop all by himself. "No I didn't have anything to do with it." Doug spit the words out. "So run," Melon barked abruptly.

"Huh?"

"Run," repeated Melon. He stopped and stared at Doug.

"Run?"

"Run," Melon said nodding his head. Doug looked back into his eyes.

"Where," asked Doug? If there had been a house Melon wanted to enter without a warrant he would have said, "into the house!" In fact that almost slipped out. He had used it so many times. "Away," Melon motioned with his head. Just then the iron tight grip that Melon had on Doug's arm loosened. The contrast was overwhelming and startling. "Run," Melon said quicker, louder and closer to his ear. Doug regained his own footing and off like a jack rabbit he went. Melon smiled and allowed himself two whole seconds of fulfillment. He couldn't believe another idiot fell for it and then off he went charging after Doug. Two more cops fell into line doing their obvious duty. They joined Melon and poor Doug in the chase. "He's getting away," Doug heard someone else say. Danny wished him luck but he knew he was dead. Wendy sighed, "Oh no." Bonnie didn't see it. She was in the back with a cop's hand on her ass. "Christ on a crutch . . ."

"Settle down bitch." He dropped his hand and grabbed the back of her neck. He glared into her eyes. Bonnie backed down. Sometimes a few seconds can seem like an eternity and the days can just seem so much longer. It's funny how a year can go by so quickly and that the months seem to drag on. Moments tend to galvanize meaning in a more complete way when utter panic and rage come into effect. It's funny how time heals. But at those moments of utter surprise and hysteria something permanent takes hold. Running from the law is like this. Just ask any Eastern European who made a dash for the wall. Running from violence and a power unchecked is much the same thing. Doug was learning this with an alarming rate of accelerated acceleration. Not even waiting for a breath the mind was calculating and still negotiating the terrain of the chase. He did not know what route to take or what limb to jump or what road to turn or what tree to hide behind. How was he going to make it? All his life he wondered aloud these questions. But he never had the villain materialize right behind him breathing and shouting at him. What dreams to believe in? What woman to believe in? All that was supremely irrelevant now. Questions of love and trust almost completely meaningless in the face of survival. Questions of semantics, ethic and decorum all lie wasted from irrelevance. Only to get away from the predator the goal to escape from authority gone mad. The only goal to live another moment. Only to be caught from behind.

When lunged at by a two hundred and twenty five pound body you hope it misses. Because if it hits you and you are in the process of running the impact and the force is doubled. First your arms, elbows and body hit the ground. You stop somewhere around your knees. The pain shoots back up your body and chases the wind out of your lungs. If you loose the wind in your lungs you feel like you're dying. And the dirt in your mouth doesn't taste very good. All Doug could do was wince every time he was kicked which was seven times. Now seven doesn't seem like a large number but tell the blood in Doug's mouth it was no big deal. The corpuscles were leaving town. They

said something about violent eruptions and lava flows and on their
way they went.

"Look at him laying there with his mouth open," Melon squawked
as the other two officers caught up. It wasn't a long chase but it covered
a lot of ground. Doug didn't know what to feel besides pain. As he was
pulled to his feet he spoke. Now why he spoke is a mystery to this day.
It did not matter what he was going to say. The cops had their plan
fixed in their heads. They knew what they were going to do. It did not
matter what was the truth and it did not matter to them what was
believed. They were on the trail of dope dealers and murderers.
They had an iron clad case or they could make one up. Why waste
their time bringing innocent looking people to trial? You can spot an
honest man a mile away, right? This was a tailor made bust. The words
came out of Doug's mouth slowly without force and unfortunately
without thought. "Helluva way to treat a suspect." He spoke so clearly
and calmly that the one officer actually heard him and laughed. Then
he jammed his night stick into his gut and doubled Doug over.
Seethingly he spoke, "whatchya run for asshole?" Doug couldn't breath.
He started gasping and didn't straighten up. "I asked you a question,
look at me, look at me," the law enforcement official screamed. Doug
lifted his head. To protect and serve. By now the others were getting
closer. Danny could see everything. The long black flashlight that was
to protect and serve went back in a forty five degree arch. It came
forward with such speed as to be just a blur. Trust and hope and faith
were dealt another blow. Doug was on his back. Eyes closed. Danny
hollered and ran to Doug. The cop that was with him reached out but
just missed him. "I want your names," shouted Danny running forward
and your god damn fucking badge numbers now!" As he got closer,
"call an ambulance you fucking son of a . . ." Danny never got the rest
of the words out of his mouth. To officer Melon he looked like a
charging elephant and fair game. What an easy target. One bullet
through the middle of his head and down he would go.

Danny saw the gun. No amount of being right would stop a bullet.
He felt the hole in his head that Melon was aiming for he could feel
it singe and burn. He came to such a quick stop he almost blew out a

knee. He didn't move. He barely breathed. Another officer was behind him now and just as nervous. "I got him Melon," that's all that he said. But his eyes screamed, "put the fucking gun down." Danny never saw Melon reach for his revolver but at the last second he saw the sun light bounce off the barrel. We *are* the horrible creatures from outer space.

THE BAIT

—

Poor Doug. When he finally came to he was hand cuffed again and in the back of a police car. You know the kind, windows up, doors shut, cage in your face. Next to him was Danny. Danny's blood was all over the window to Doug's right. It was also all over the car seat. He looked over at Danny and saw his head was tilted all the way back. "Doug," his voice forced a raspy sound out. "Danny? Are you all right?" Now Doug wasn't going to win any beauty contests. The first blow had swollen his one eye almost completely shut. The last flash light blow had made his ear bleed down on to his shoulder. Danny raised his head. He looked at Doug and smiled, "I'm sorry."

"Oh man don't even say it Danny. These assholes are in big trouble for this."

"No they're not Doug. They can get away with it." Doug reluctantly agreed and sighed a breath of resignation. "You got a bandage on your head Dan they patch you up?"

"While you were passed out, twenty seven stitches. The paramedics have already come and gone." Now its funny what a common enemy will do to even the most hardened adversaries. Danny and Doug had always been fine one on one. But it seemed to Danny that in a crowd Doug didn't want to take the chance of being his friend. Doug didn't have the courage to be friends with someone who might be controversial, someone who might loose or worse yet not live up to his potential.

"You looked funny," whispered Danny. "The cops had to carry you and they were pissed at each other."

"Funny!??!"

"Well you know what I mean sorta like Caesar had too much to drink and Bruits had made off with his lounge chair."

"How can you laugh," asked Doug remembering why he hated Danny. Danny just ignored him. "They looked you over to."

"The paramedics?"

"They just put you in the back seat. Seems you were coming out of it."

"These damn handcuffs."

"Don't pull on them they just tighten up."

"Too late."

"Yeah," Danny laid his head back down and closed his eyes. It was bloody damn hot in that patrol car. The windows were up but at least the front doors were open. The paramedics made the cops do that. Doug looked back around. He could make out the others sitting on the ground. Melon was off somewhere that he couldn't see. Some police were taking down statements. It was a muggy and hot afternoon by now. The sun had flew by eleven and was headed for two. No one was even thinking about lunch. That is except Melon. He was off in the woods going back over the trail and back to the campsite. He and three rookies were going to make a sweep of the area and turn up more evidence. A murder weapon would be nice and so would some dope.

The others were told to wait. No back up was called and Melon was going to get results soon. The longer he kept his captures away from the barracks the longer he could keep the Miranda rights and lawyer calling from happening. The longer Bonnie, Mark, John, Wendy and Eric were kept in the heat with no food or water the sooner their mouths would start flapping. Hell they'd admit to killing Kennedy before too long.

Melon figured Doug and Danny were half dead. But he had shown the others what would happen if they didn't cooperate. Melon had sent the paramedics away without any delay. There was nothing for them to do but treat Danny and Doug and get out of there. Melon was guilty of grandstanding. Hell his own partners were afraid of him. Everyone sat in the sun. Mark wanted to check on Danny and Doug. "Hey where are you going," one Melon wanna be said?

"I'm just checking on those guys. Can't we open their doors for some air if we're gonna sit here?"

"Yeah but sit down I'll get the doors." Doug and Danny didn't notice until the doors were open. Mark got up anyway. The Melon wanna be shouted after him and was about to throw him on the ground. "It's alright," an older trooper spoke. Let him check on his friends." Bonnie got up at that moment too and followed Mark. No one bothered to stop her. "You know," continued the wanna be, "he's back there looking for the murder weapon." Mark looked back at this youngster and saw a scared soul who was afraid to go against the group. He spoke out loud and directly at this brain dead idiot, "he's already got the weapon on him."

"Smart guy huh. Who do we have here Dirty Mary? You wanna end up like your buddies in the back seat?"

Wendy was starting to miss her phony cocktail parties. The ones where you stand in the corner alone with your wine glass and pray to god no one talks to you. Because the ones that end up talking to you are usually the biggest phonies. Their tripe is the most contrived. But today she would put up with a whole roomful of phonies if she could somehow trade places. Since she had met Eric she was getting more confused. One minute bliss the next agony. Deep down she knew her life had always been like that. She couldn't really blame it all on him. However at this moment it was hard for her to be rational. She kept confusing her own mind. She kept going back to this dream of what she thought her world was. It was safe but it also was hard. Her old boyfriend beat her. Why she thought she could go back to him was hard to figure. She really had some wonderful fresh times with him originally but the abuse started only after four months. It seemed she cared too much about things that he thought were silly. He couldn't understand her preoccupation with the art side of what she did. He always thought the dance classes were a waste of time. But she was working steady in her field. So why did he want to mess with what was working? The fact that he had no dreams of his own was mostly the problem. Going with Eric to the Jaded Lady was long overdue. But now she was being held in connection with a murder. When they found out who she was they'd have a laugh. But then it hit her. The paparazzi. Fear worse than ever shot through her. This was really it. Her spine buckled. If the buzzards got a hold of this she was ruined and done for. There would be no going back. She didn't want to loose that option because of a group of strangers. Wendy started to babble. "Getting that down." "What miss, what?"

"Its all his fault," Wendy shot a glance at Eric. Now just at this second every light went off in Eric's head. He knew what she meant but he couldn't believe she was falling apart. "He talked me into coming," Eric hung his head. Nothing could have been farther from the truth. She came and she went of her own free will. That's what Eric loved about her. Now all of a sudden she had changed her mind. He was at this very moment as out of luck as he was ever going to be and she was putting up the white flag. What did she want? Did she want to go back to her old boyfriend the one that called her stupid? The forever wanderings and wondering of a foolish heart. How can someone keep making excuses over and over again? "I know with just a little more love," crash his hands hit her on her face. "With just a little more time," crash the gift from her sister smashes against the wall. "He really is a good man deep inside," punch another blow to her stomach. "He's just down on his luck," smack a back hand across her face. "I can't leave him he has nowhere to go." Rip, her blouse is torn open. "My love is stronger than his hate." A sullen numbness takes over her body but her mind is still active. "If I love him just this one more time he'll change. I can make him change." As long as her ex was getting what he wanted, someone to vent his anger on, someone who will not fight back, someone he can control and someone he can take anytime he wants, he never changed. "Leave him," her friends told her. But no she is playing a despondent role she grew used to. The martyr indeed is great. His love is only what he feels when he gets what he wants. Her's can conquer worlds or so she was told. He wants the power, the control, the fear, the status of god. She thinks her love is strong enough to alter personalities but it can't even change herself. Only when he breaks her a final time does he realize remorse. Only when she finally leaves does he beg her to stay. And the words have no meaning they are just desperate lunges at keeping control. Actions are the truth. She must go and realize there are other people out there more worthy of her love especially herself.

Only a long time gone teaches the heart and the mind, the soul and the body that a persons love bestowed upon you is rare and not to be taken for granted or a burden. Surrender to love and sex and fun with someone doing the same. In spite of all the devastation the world spins on forgiving and understanding and hoping that at least some of us feel it moving. Watch the children love and laugh and play it's as close to god as we come. No one can pry another's soul open. They have to release it themselves. No one steals romance it walks off on it's own accord and is either lesser or greater for it depending on why.

Eric knew in spite of everything that what was true was true. There was no compromising the obvious. The end feeling was so real for him. Yes there were those who had other experiences. Convenience and lies are the products of the games we play. Giving up the higher ground they were mired in hate. They had no vision about their love or their life. A lot has changed in a short amount of time and good and truth are completely out of fashion. But love is still the same. What remains is that if our thoughts are not in tune with this aspect of creation then we are doomed to play acting. In shallow waters we never feel the gravity of this planet, the enormity of the Earth or the miracle of the ordinary.

If we do not think that the gravity of this reality warrants steadfast honorability then skip along the surface of this life's water like a stone. It has it's moments but eventually stops and sinks. Wendy went belly up. At that moment she decided that what she had been shown was what she was always going to see. Eric knew in spite of it all not to loose sight on the next moment of hope or the next day or even the next year. He knew in his heart whether things worked out perfectly or not did not matter. All that mattered was the joy that was felt in his heart when he realized where he was. He was aware that in all the deepest, darkest, reaches of space and within the infinity of the universe a few layers of air kept us alive. Just a sliver of atmosphere in the grand universe of space keeps us alive and we aim and spew a vast poisonous group of chemicals and pollution at it day after precious day and with all our might. It is an array of chimneys, smokestacks, and exhaust pipes that we call progress. While the so called ignorant beasts live in harmony with their surroundings.

The signs were all too conclusive for Eric yet Wendy was shaken to her bones. She cried in the night. She prayed for her dreams to reveal the truth that her eyes could not see. The life and the world never stops it just keeps on going. Eric knew that whatever he accomplished in helping others would fulfill him even if people did not. Wendy kept looking past herself for others to fulfill her. She did not realize that she possessed the essence of life on a conscious level. The life that Eric had led only told him yes there were stumbling blocks and some were mighty. Yes there were diversions but when his head was clear the inspiration of simple reality was overwhelming. How could he put this to Wendy and she realize it permanently. He hoped that the obvious was not hid. He prayed that night that her love for him would last. Eric felt he knew what Wendy was going through. He recognized so much in her that it scared him. But his faith in his own awareness and perception lead him forward. He was determined to stay on the path of hope and life. It didn't matter who or what tried to knock him off. Not everything had to turn out like some bad soap opera. Perhaps this time he had found a real warrior. Perhaps this time he had found a real human being.

Wendy was hooked on an old vision. Eric understood his vision with Wendy had not even had a chance to materialize. Most would rather stick to the mundane and speak of the mighty truths of water sealing their driveway. Life was what we make it and love was the essence of realization. How wonderful the energies wasted on love, even with it's pain and rust of belief. The feeling Eric had toward Wendy at the moment she crumbled was not scorn or hatred but disbelief and then hope. Because everything she did made him feel and understand her even more. For some unexplained reason he saw her actions in the context of who she was as opposed to his own point of view of being sold out. The world was much more patient than he. But his love moved in the way that it did and did in the way that it moved. He understood being framed by Wendy was good for her and excellent for them. It gave them both a chance for forgiveness and the coals that stoke the fires of love.

The cops thought they were Perry Mason and Joe Friday. Wendy babbled it all and it all made perfect sense to Eric. But the cops had no idea. They couldn't understand a word of the rambling doubt. Something told Eric to hang on. He was not going to join in with her mood. It was too easy to be a pissed off asshole. The words that she said hurt and they cut through him but he loved her still. So Wendy spilled her guts and everything came out. Everything! But then again the cops were not concerned about her personal choices. Oh they tried to keep her to the facts, "just the facts mam." But Wendy had a world of guilt between her worlds of illusion and delusion. Her little faux Hollywood world, her abusive romance and now this joy ride that blew it all apart where was the truth? Where was her true self? Who was she? She was still the searcher and there were merits in her ideas. What had she accomplished as an actress? Was she really an actress or a high school cheerleader playing bit parts with a cute smile and a perky nose. The paparazzi had left her alone but her recent success with some meatier parts had the hounds alerted. They were sniffing for blood on the fingers of those skeletons lining her closet. Hell what did she care she wanted to join the peace corps when she was seventeen anyway. "The hell with it all, the hell with it all?"

"The hell with what honey? What the hell are you talking about?"

"What do you care you pig sucking bastard just go home and jerk off. Millions dying in Ethiopia, Bangladesh, New York City, just piss off, go home turn on the shopping channel. Can't fight city hall? Wake up," she hollered! "You don't know shit playing cop busting our heads,"she sighed. Eric looked at Wendy like a hurricane veering off course. "What has this got to do with the Jaded Lady woman," the cop in front of her yelled?

"Everything you fucking moron!"

"The fucking bitch is on drugs," said the other officer pulling him aside.

"Made perfect sense to me," said John. There is always something happening. There is always a moment to moment reality with breathing and feeling and being. The choices one has to make are so complex and yet simple. The truth is constantly dangled like feathered casting flies in a stream. The bait of choice is dangled. Which one do you bite. Will the bait remain or will it fade away into yet another choice. The courage to live up to your convictions is at stake especially if you don't have any. The pure energy of life dragged into the dirt of the Earth. You jump to the bait and hope the hook that is so well hid doesn't kill you. It takes you to another place. Only to find yourself facing yourself squarely again. You turn at once but there you are again. There is no avoiding it no matter where you are, how far you have run or how slippery you may be. Life will provide the diversion but all roads lead squarely back to yourself. Any road will take you right there paved with your schemes, plans, wishes, maneuvers and dreams. There is no avoiding the eventual outcome of looking squarely at yourself. You deal with your presence and who and what you are. You deal with where you have been and who you have been with. You deal with how this all got you there, where it is you are going and what bait set the trap. You came to this point in your road because you wanted to. There you are standing there. Held in a spot in which you chose to be held. Only to move on again. If you are in tune you'll look squarely at yourself and realize hand to mouth to steps where you are, and how you got there. If you are lucky it is a long look and it last a lifetime.

Eventually you come to terms with all the traps and furrowing brows that have befallen you. Alleged misled intentions find you fulfilled and finally you are on your own terms, though others may try to define you. But always the next move is yours. It's all yours alone, if you are honest with the one who counts, yourself. But the bait is still there and you know it all too well. It is the bait of your choosing. The bait you have set for yourself. You choose not to see. But you know yourself and you move on, unto your own being, defining self. When you are finished with the distractions you see that you put them there and that they are very easily removed. Your unknown will power is finally engaged. You stop wishing and start doing. It's just you and the surroundings you have chosen. The energy you project comes right back at you filtered through a turning world. Judge for yourself what is right and wrong. The suggestion of something being out of reach is left only to your knowledge of self and why that might be. What is within reach? Yourself, your knowledge and your sense of well being are contained fully within your reach.

Your heart is shared as you wish with others. Or it's hiding, denying and lying. But the gravity of life is always there. The stars shine and the water reflects with the wind and the sky never hesitating in their phenomenon, but rather only in our consciousness. It's more amazing than we can realize or choose to imagine. So much so we don't even try and write the poetry it deserves. The water runs over the falls, babbles the brook and crashes upon the shore, every minute, every second of the day. Beauty as creation, the canvas of life ever changing and yet the same. Do we see it all? Do we see anything at all?

Louise sat in the woods alone. She was surrounded by herself with all that truly belonged to her. Her world was the landscape that surrounded her. Her day pack full but light. She had the woods, the deja vu and the fallen hawk feathers to let her know that yes, she was on her sacred journey. The track that had always been there for her and preceded her. But she wandered off of it just as a human being would do. She was born into a linear progression for her eyes only to see. It arrived slowly or sometimes in a flash, but the choices and the distractions kept on coming. Only through the intent of her intentions could she reemerge on her sacred journey. There was no being off the path, right or wrong. The mistakes were made to find self and to find the journey home. When it was right it felt good, and she earned the feeling of being. Being was what she felt in her heart. Being was what felt right, truly right and deep within. The recognition of the recollection is only a street sign saying you are here at this point, where you knew you would always be. Your deep self knows your true place, no matter how out of touch your present self becomes with same. The man made world is a world of misguided selves pursuing anything but themselves. They compete with each other instead of themselves. And it only takes an instant to see that original self, to gain full sight, to take the bait, and let the bait take you. Your path is there for you whenever you decide to walk within it, with it, or away from it. And so your path reveals you are on your path with a feeling or a flash of synchronicity. Deja vu you can choose to deny but are not at liberty to ignore. Leave your path and you are still on your way.

Louise had time to make a choice, but not for long, because another moment was coming. Oh, she heard the commotion. She heard the noise and she saw the glint of the gun barrel pointed at Danny. She hid behind the brush and she steered clear of the havoc. It was her instinct for survival not to get caught up in the mayhem. Another trail split off in another direction. She was trying to learn to recognize the right choice when it would be first shown to her. She knew from experience that if she let the moment go the next time the consequences would only loom larger. She was alone in the woods but the band looked more alone. They were beat down and bloodied. They were going to be wrongly accused. They were surrounded and roasting in the noon day sun. They were choking on the dust.

So many times she looked away only to continue to return to the same point and eventuality. The damned opportunities kept presenting themselves. She would have to make a stand. When she left home she could have stayed and helped. But she had to help herself first before she could help others. She was beginning to realize though, with the force of full awakening, that in order to help herself she had to help others. She left Danny in the morning. She jumped from the train wreck she was now witnessing. She hadn't gotten that far when she saw the Cops run into the campsite. She had her Daddy's gun deep in her pack. She loathed the gun, but saw the evil men do to each other. It wasn't just Tyranny and the Hitler side of our being, but we had religions that preached violence. Mankind had turned the world inside out and upside down. Love was a joke to some.

Again Louise was face to face with the world and herself. Another choice another day. It was unavoidable, and she had done everything imaginable to avoid it. She immersed herself in booze. She ran away every time before too long. But here it was again the many varied different colors of choice. This choice went against everything she thought she had learned to survive. But what is truly surviving? Is it just existing or thriving? To take on this obvious harm she wondered how many dragons she would have to slay. Would it be over in a minute, or would she have to confront it again sometime later? What if she failed and lost her freedom? But turning her back how free could she really be? Certainly never free from consciousness and the knowledge of her choices, why she made them, and how they told her who she was. It was only becoming more vicious the circle. The hardest battles were always going to be her own. Once again it was she who was standing in her way more enormous than the last time, and more enormous than any apparent evil. Evil would be a snap to deal with, but her own personal doubt loomed larger, covered in fear. Evil was all flat land compared to the glaciers of moments frozen with fear and doubt with choice, time, intent and consequence.

She watched Wendy cry as those that stood around her seemed so unclear. She could see that Wendy was trying to remove the bait, the hook from her mouth. But which bait, which hook would it be that she would finally bite down on? Her pain and sorrow weld up in her eyes. And Louise cried too. The question was whether to move with forthright force and set so many wheels in motion or to turn and fade away until the moment came back around again, which it would. That time between those moments would be tainted with should haves.

The choice was clear, the results were debatable, and the challenge would reappear. The results did not matter, only the choice to believe and to put out the energy. To send forth the signal and to be challenged in spite of being slammed or thwarted. Most stopped before they started not even trying, and they were sold doubt. She would get up again even if it was without her body. Louise felt she didn't have the energy to try again only to get thrown from another car. But this moment was now. The failure was hard. Slinking away wouldn't make it go away. It would always be with her. She carried her decisions with her everywhere she would go. They would haunt her and define her from moment to moment influencing her very next decision like drifting sand. She would have to search a great deal to find another time where the choice was so large and heroic. But it could never obliterate the fact that she did what she did when she slid away.

No amount of good deeds and wise choices would overcome and wash away the moment of truth. It would be forever present, informing each new moment and coloring every choice. It is what it is, and when the time comes it is known, and what you do stays with you like a skin. It would affect her forever and define her very being. She decided to move forward.

Melon was still gone. The leaves around the captured band rustled. No one seemed to take notice except John. Was it a bird? The police surrounded Wendy still trying to make sense of her words. Louise took flight behind them and flew through the sun-drenched day. The forces of contemplation and intention swirled inside of Louise, churning and overflowing. Johnny Law was surprised this time to find a girl with a gun in his back. Louise picked the youngest. She stripped his gun and tossed it to John in a moment. Four officers caught by surprise by an unsuspecting homeless woman. They were cuffed together, gunless and speechless in a matter of moments. Wendy stopped babbling and her tears dried instantly on the wind of Louise's heroics. This time Wendy knew her choice. In the face of such humanity faith was restored in an instant. Wendy chose to look at it that way and she knew not to second guess it. The only thing they all knew together, the rescued band and the arrested police, was that there were more moments to come. Some feared them. Some ran to them.

THE GREAT SPIRIT

—

The bandmates ran to the police car and gingerly removed Doug and Danny. Eric ran for the jeep. There were no long discussions and no debates. There were no volumes of meaningless political and religious verbiage. Nature was in motion. Action was speaking loudly. The jeep and van had been discreetly parked but not hidden from the police. So Mark was ripping the radios and batteries out of the patrol cars. Officer Melon was deep in the woods planting false evidence. He was taking his time and letting one of the rookies stumble upon the planted evidence. How proud they would all be.

"What are you doing with those batteries," shouted Eric as the Jeep roared to life kicking up the Louisiana dust as it pulled forward. A great pillar of smoke rose up ceremoniously. It signaled the decaying of the justice system and, oh yes, family values. How dare the politicians talk to the poor, down trodden, masses of morals, when the hypocrisy of their decisions are based on money and influence pedaling. Incredibly they speak to us of values and ethics as they gamble, lie, cheat, cover up and exploit each other in their own personal lives. How dare they speak to us of family values when our children are dying of cancer from the pollution spewing, corporations they protect. Would a moral majority choose to only "trickle down" to those who need it most?

"I'm keeping these batteries in the back of the jeep," said Mark.

"What about the van," questioned Eric.

"It's already got the equipment in it," answered Mark again.

"Oh shit," John hollered as he went to the van. Wendy, still filled with plenty of negative energy, got sucked into the impending doom of those two little words. Said right they can crumble mountains. "What do you mean, oh shit, John," barked Mark.

"The keys, the van keys, they're back at the waterfall," John blurted. Everyone stopped cold. There were too many of them to ride just in the Jeep. Doug and Danny were hurt and were already in the back seat. Bonnie had just finished helping them climb in. She turned, reached into her pants, and flung the keys across the dirt parking lot at John. "Can you believe those guys didn't frisk my crotch?"

"I guess Melon didn't like you," said Wendy, after having that nauseating experience herself. John caught the keys and ran for the van. Bonnie now taking charge and looking out for the others hollered at Wendy, "go in the jeep with Eric." There wasn't any time for school girl games. No matter what Wendy thought of Eric, and the situation she was mired in, there was no time to loose. Bonnie had a revelation the night before in her sleep. It was the continuing unfolding of her character and the finding of herself. It was as if the Great Spirit had permeated her soul while she slept under the stars. The waterfall had taken her as if down stream to a place of dreams. She had visions and second sight experiences which were reappearing before her as she spoke. She knew to grab the keys when the cops burst on the scene. The calmness that was bestowed upon her in her sleep was still with her even in the face of adversary. What strange creatures we are that we sleep and dream. Every night we plug back into the great collective consciousness from which we came. Every night we are afforded the soul satisfaction of deep contemplation, and the visionary journeys of the soul. Every night we unplug our conscious minds and fly through the cosmos and experience the other dimensions that are surely out there. Then we awake. What we choose to do with what has unfolded in our subconscious, through our astral travelings, musings and wanderings, impacts our lives in the most extraordinary way, if we let it happen. It was a wise person who paid attention to their dreams and a fool who dismissed them.

The Jeep thundered back out on the road. Eric reached over and grabbed Wendy's hand between gear shifts. "Just let me know when to stop."

"Just get away first," she shot him a mean look back. Danny in the back seat just smiled to himself. Doug next to him yelled, "yeah lets just get away." The van pulled out of its parking spot and stopped. Louise was standing alone in the dirt lot. Everyone had scrambled for their vehicles except Louise. After all she had done her deed. She stood frozen in the moment after retrieving her day pack and bedroll. They were slung over her shoulder. The clay was brown and dusty beneath her feet. A two lane strip of asphalt lay behind her. The road ran in two directions.

Mark threw open the side door of the van and everyone looked back at Louise. She was just standing there. "Louise," spoke Mark softly. Bonnie's eyes from the front seat passenger side were wide with compassion and pleading. Bonnie wasn't going to forget Louise, ever. Louise shot her a glance and then looked at John behind the wheel. John had the look of urgency on his face. This wasn't going to be a long decision. But here was Louise again just moments after making a bold decision to lunge from the forest and rescue the band. She was faced with another huge decision. Mark spoke. "Only you know how long you've been doing this Louise. We've got to try and help each other or what kind of world will we be living in?" Louise's mind was charging through her options. Could she really get away on foot? If she leaves now, the cops chase them, and she gets absorbed back into the street. Or the cops find her first out on the road. It's a long time in the gray bar hotel. Bonnie knew what she was thinking. "Louise don't take the fall. After we get out of Louisiana . . ." Louise didn't let her finish. "Fuck it! I'm no worse off now than I've ever been." With that Louise pitched her pack and bedroll into the van and they all pulled out on the road together.

It was five miles to the interstate. "Slow down," said Wendy from the front seat of the jeep, "we don't want to break the law."

"We haven't yet today," said Danny from the back seat."

"How about resisting arrest," said Doug sitting next to him.

"How about wrongful prosecution," answered Danny.

"If we're innocent, why are we running," shouted Wendy?

"Because you're never totally innocent," confessed Eric.

"No shit," said Doug.

"Where are we going," pleaded Danny?

"Don't worry," answered Eric.

Back in the van things were much the chaotic same. "I'm glad you came with us," said Bonnie turning towards Louise. "What you did back there," Mark started to speak, "was beautiful," he was laughing.

"Where did you get a gun?" asked John incredulously.

"You can get a gun anywhere," stated Louise, matter-of-factly. You can have a rap sheet as long as your arm and still get a gun. Anytime. Then you can go home and kill someone over the neighbor's dog barking. Its a real great world we are making."

"Seriously though I didn't expect you to have one," said Mark.

"No one does," answered Louise, her tone changing. "In the world you guys come from you don't need one. I know because I once came from that world. When I left the Midwest my dad taught me to shoot. He wanted me to stay but understood all too damn well the urge for going. I threw the bullets out before I got on the bus headed east."

"It's not loaded," laughed John?

"Nope. I saved four bullets. If I ever had to use them I'd just go back home instead. It's isolated and lonely and poor, but not as bad as killing someone. Back home you still have the quiet of nature and the stillness of a summer breeze. But it probably takes on a whole new meaning after killing someone. Don't get me wrong. I could have pulled the trigger a dozen times. People just don't get it. They have lost the art of what it means to be a human being. Everyone's lost touch with the wonder of it all. The wonder of people, just people. I mean it blows my mind. You're people with conscious thoughts and bodies to enact them. It's bizarre that we exist that we even walk around or have feelings. Who thought of people? I mean fish are weird enough, but people? How bizarre there are people!

"You're a hero," said Bonnie.

"I don't feel like one."

"Real hero's never do," said Mark. They were on the interstate now and fuel was running low in the jeep. "Good lord, we gotta pull over already," questioned an alarmed Danny?

A MOMENT'S GLANCE

—

They wound their way into a sleepy gas station with a small staff. Eric would have preferred a big station where they would have blended in more. But they needed the gas now. Everyone gathered around the Jeep. "I thought about this last night," said Eric. The stars were dancing with the waterfall and I began thinking about other beautiful places I've been. You know relatively quiet but not isolated. Rural enough not to be too nosy and urban enough to work in and be anonymous. It's beautiful and we can take our time and split up or stay there and disappear. But I don't think any of us can go home again at least not right away. I have a plan but we don't have much time."

"Spit it out," said Doug, "we've got miles ahead of us I hope."

"Yep a long hard way." Eric had the map out, "we're coming off of 996 here, this little connecting highway through the park. We need to jump on 61 heading north and then cross the big muddy. I figure we go south some and maybe give them a little slip. But once we're over the river near New Roads we're gonna head north all the way up route 1 to interstate 71. From there its just a clear shot sort of."

"Where are we eventually going," cautioned Danny?

"Colorado," said Eric proudly. "Near the Poudre River and into the Poudre Canyon. I've got friends up there. By the time we get there maybe they'll have found some other leads in this case and leave us alone."

"Which case is that," said Doug, "the murder case or the drug bust?"

"Or cuffing the cops and bolting," asked Wendy. Eric just shook his head.

"If they don't chase us it's because someone back in New Orleans helped them find the guys that set up Sam."

"I know the place," spoke Louise. They all looked at her. "The place up in the canyon Eric is talking about."

"You do," questioned Danny?

"Yes and its quiet."

"Case closed," asked Eric? Wendy was getting tired of putting her trust in him but there were was no time for discussion. "After 71 what happens and where the hell will we be," asked John?

"71 will take us into Missouri near El Dorado Springs. Were looking for route 54. That's more than a tankful of gas away and we're doing the speed limit sort of." They loaded up and left. Miles of road lay between them and their destination but not miles of conversation. It was time to let it all sink in with what had happened. It was haunting Danny and the others that Adam and Jessica were out there doing who knows what and saying what to whom. Would they try to return home like nothing happened? But could they pull it off and under scrutiny? It would never be the same for them or their relationship. But maybe the bond of their trauma would bring them that much closer. It was after all up to them to decide. But did they have the will power to overcome? "And what about us," said Wendy to Eric, "are we ever going back?"

"Wait and see," said Eric. "At least this is something different and if you go back you'll be a better actor."

"Going back wont be so hard if I don't go back to him."

"Your giving up," asked Eric? "You know he'll be there."

"Peace of mind is hard to come by but it's worth having," answered Wendy.

"Maybe now you'll be stronger but that's not what I'm talking about."

"The Quarter can be magical," she said.

"The magic is everywhere the Quarter has only what you bring to it."

"We have to get clear of this mess Eric. Can we do that?" Deeper into life they went because it was their choice. Dreams fade into goals and become reality.

"I keep dreaming," said Eric.

"I like the sound of that," spoke Wendy, "that's always been my problem too." The miles of road wound by. The white lines shot by one after the other. Day turned to night and night would turn into day. The empty spinning hum of the wheels were no comfort and not at all like home. The road takes it's toll. The road escape is a fantasy and the beating wears your body and your spirit down. Every town looks the same. The echo of Bourbon Street and the barrelhouse jazz and blues were long gone. You have to find the back roads to find the towns true personality. There is a soul out there in the world you just have to dig for it a little. The radio played Roosevelt Sykes, "Viper Drag." It must be a college radio station named after a lake probably. The commercial boys choose not to market Roosevelt Sykes and that was that.

The constant pace of the road dulled their senses. The time and towns slid by. Their hands were endlessly gripped to the wheel. Foot cocked just so and back stiff it was time to change drivers. You pump up the radio or slap in a disc and if your lucky you get to put the window down. Some coffee a drag and your back rolling again. Caffeine's a killer. After seven hundred miles Wendy was driving. The wind was blowing her hair. She never drove to a photo-op with the windows down. She said, "do you think they'll follow us," to no one in particular? Night had seeped in. "It's hard to say," answered Danny from the back seat. Eric reached over and turned the radio down.

"Wouldn't someone had headed us off by now," Wendy asked Eric?

"There's an alert for our tags if they got them," answered Eric.

"That's the big question," said Doug. "Those guys were pretty anxious to bust some heads."

"A camper could have tipped them off about us," interrupted Wendy, "you know thinking we were just some loud party clowns polluting the woods."

"They knew what they were looking for," spoke Danny.

"Eventually were just leaving these trucks in a field somewhere," said Eric. "But not until we rent some wheels," he continued.

"That will leave a paper trail," hollered Doug!

"Not necessarily," answered Eric. "We can't use my card," said Danny, "I used it for the band all the time."

"I've been meaning to thank you for that," threw in Doug as an aside.

"I've got to be hotter than hell." Danny leaned forward.

"Shit is the word that comes to mind now," sighed Eric!

"Deep shit."

"That'll be enough from you," answered Wendy to Doug's deep comment.

"What about you," the bulb went off in Eric's head? "Got any credit Wendy?"

"You bettchya and furthermore they have no connection to me in this. Those cops did everything backwards."

"That's right," said Eric, "they never wrote down the id's they checked."

"They were in too big a hurry to kick our ass," yelled Doug!

"And even if they did get something down back there they'll never pick up mom's maiden name on the credit card she gave me."

"Your mom gave you a credit card?" laughed Doug. "All mine ever gave me was a stick to hang my bag on."

"Mom knew things were wrong with the man I was living with and she was worried. I'm her kid you know the birth canal is real. That's no small deal to her or me." She looked around at her passengers. "This qualifies as an emergency I think but it might not be what she had in mind."

"More like a nice safe trip back to El Reno eh?"

"That's right buddy," she said to Eric.

"Well it sounds like a good option," spoke Eric. "We should go with it. Ditch these wheels get a renter and return it once we get up to the Poudre Canyon."

"We might be able to pull that off actually," answered Eric.

"I hope so," said Doug.

"Where the hell are they going," asked Mark from the back seat of the van?

"I don't know answered John, "I'm just following them.

"Well they better have a real good idea," spoke Mark.

"I think the idea is to run away," said Louise.

"Thank God," answered John.

"I don't know about that," fired back Louise.

"I don't care about the reasons anymore I'm just tired," said John.

"Can't you tell by looking at us why we chose what we did," asked Bonnie?

"Hell no," said Mark, "agendas are secret."

"Agendas are one thing but what about the motives," spoke Bonnie?

"That's no easy trick overcoming your ego," said John.

"What about me? I'm a drifter and a bum. Everyone looks me over for all of two seconds and right away I'm lazy, crazy or didn't try hard enough. They spit on you, laugh at you and all of a sudden it's open season. People used to just turn away. Now they literally set you on fire with righteous indignation. Harshly judgmental they act as trial and jury based on a moments glance. My reasons for my circumstance may be based on an entirely different set of circumstances that they can not even fathom. I'm anything but the stereotypical assumption." Louise paused and turned her focus out the window. "But the last laugh is on me. Their way of life is about to blow up in their faces unless they make some changes. All because of the one rule they were all taught. The one rule they hold so dear and above all others is the very rule they will destroy themselves with." The vans wheels griped the road hard. "Money," spoke John.

"Not just money in and of itself," answered Bonnie.

"Wait let me guess," spoke Mark, "look out for number one." Louise shook her head, "not quite". The van rolled on. "The ends justify the means. The notion that profit be squeezed from every possible situation no matter what the side effects are totally flies in the face of successful long term management."

"And what's the greatest resource," asked John?

"People," answered Bonnie. Mark was surprised.

"Of all the people I know Bonnie you seem to have the highest disdain for the general masses."

"They watch too much t.v.," she quipped.

Said Louise, "I've had more than my share of conflict with people who sound just like the campaign speech I heard last week. Or they act like the punks they think they want to be like. As if anything is better than ma and apple pie. But over all people are the best. And they have a knack of surprising you at the right moment. Right on time like someone wrote the whole damn thing out. Fate's like a fire. It's a miraculous thing. If you look around you can see how nimble it is. It jumps from one life to another forcing and molding events. It's elusive like a current jumping wires and never traceable. The outcome is always so obvious and clear to see after it's gone. Time and how it is measured always seems to hide the connection of inevitability. The true believers keep on believing. The doubters falter. The warriors wade in and fight on both sides and their outcomes and actions have far reaching ramifications. They affect and effect each other countless times over. Life is a never ending array and sequence and series of events that never seems related except to fate. She just keeps on pushing and prodding and weaving her way through all of our lives. And not just in this world but in others. Fate nimbly moves sometimes suddenly and molding the road of reality into a never ending weave of turns and hills and valleys. All things are connected and related and intertwined and gloriously real. It's heavenly and right here on Earth. The battle lines are drawn and each one of us has a hand in the outcome. Whether you use it or not is fate flashing by. Know it, see it, feel it, go with it, and do what inside you feels so very right to do. Only then will you be a complete part of fates wonderful presence and be lucky enough to feel totally alive and for a very long time."

"Fate's bullshit," blurted Mark, "it's a persons choice and the choices that stack up one right after the other. Like a row of dominos going out from the center source in every direction imaginable. Maybe the road you're on is dark and seedy but you chose that road with your decisions and indecisions and you can always choose something else. It's all mangled up and tangled but you can trace it back and untangle it and see exactly how you got where you are based on your choices. Moment to moment day by day it's not fate but your heart and your will power and your decisions that lead you along whatever road you choose to be on. Blaming it on fate is like blaming it on an abusive parent or a bad hair day. You choose to let those actions or circumstances have control over you because you don't want the responsibility of being in the predicament you are in. You are as miserable or as happy as you want to be. In the end you can't face that it all comes from inside of you. The way you look at the world is the way the world looks at you. What you feel from the outside is what you are feeling on the inside and you have no one to blame but yourself. Everything else is an excuse. Fates a cop out."

"No, no," said Louise. We are the circuits that fate travels through. It is up to us and our choices. We and what we think are the conduit in which the creative forces flow and become reality. But not just us life flows through everything. The mountains erupt and slide and move. The waters run teeming with life. The animals move silent and alive. It matters to each one of us what we feel. Are you eaten alive or filled to the top with soul satisfaction? Do you feel consumed or enriched do you feel demise or the sunrise. You're like a switch. Which way you go sends the flow on it's way. Worst of all no mode, no go, no flow. Stagnation is not rest. It is not a recharge of your batteries. It is yourself collapsing down upon yourself. A dead circuit corroding from within being eaten up by your own self. It totally self destructs in a painfully slow shut down. It can be a very long and frightful period."

"You've had a lot of time to think about this haven't you, said Bonnie?

"Silence is a roar," Louise said, "they bomb us with all this crap, stores, advertising, shopping, distractions out the ass because they are in business. But the distractions mount up too high. Whole communities sit still for toxic metal drums in their back yards contaminating their water and families. Without all those distractions maybe the PTA would make a come back. Kids would only have school, sports and each other and maybe do better with all three."

"I don't think people would stand for joblessness, hunger, and poverty without all these distractions," chimed in Bonnie, "it would never be."

"It goes against our very natures," Mark said. "We're all guilty of letting each other down and we know it. That's why no one makes eye contact anymore!"

"Just like maximized profits at any and all cost we bought into survival of the fittest," continued Louise. "Which means in its current translation we are to pummel each other to death until that's it for the other one and take their stuff. Louise stopped speaking for a minute and looked around. They were listening even arguing with her. She wasn't used to that. Bonnie knew first hand about the distractions she was speaking of. How many times did she let love slip away because of them? Mark knew too about distractions that's why he had given up drugs. John knew about distractions that's why he concentrated so hard when they were playing. He loved to play. It was just like driving into the middle of the night through the middle of America. They had structure and they had direction but where it would end they didn't know. Where they were going in their mind set was still developing but thinking made it so. They were riding the wave of life. They were sound in a silent universe. They could feel it and they knew it.

SEARCHING FOR PURGATOIRE

—

W e don't realize we are essentially the same. Only our vague differences of culture, language, wealth, education, talent and strength separate and divide us. A smile's a smile. Some use those differences as tools to eliminate each other. But we are all the same, even with our differences. Our eye color, hair color and skin color are different but it's superficial. We attach some sort of meaning to those differences in our search for identity. Our differences are sought out by our feeble and frightened egos craving distinction and needing defined differences to cling to and be set a part from. We are so consumed by our contrived differences that the globe we reside on doesn't even merit consideration. Certainly we are completely unconscious of the globe as we toss cigarette butts on the ground and fill it with trash. We are laser-locked focused on everything else but the world and our lonely voice in a silent universe. We have all been duped by our organized religions and their lust for power. So much so that all that really matters is the brand name of your particular religion, and not what type of person you are.

We have all we need, and we had it all before the onslaught of product. We ignore our history and heritage and have no real sense of community. We look for handouts and entitlements, but have never read the U.S. Constitution or the Declaration of Independence. We don't vote or dig past the surface to find out how our representative politicians have voted. We mistake compassion and tolerance as weakness. We try to intimidate loudly to get our own way. We holler and argue more intently when we are caught, embarrassed or found out to be wrong. We refuse to think bigger than ourselves and our immediate concerns. We scoff at the very notion. Our defenses are up and hair-triggered. The tension climbs with the neurosis. We must have evidence and we must confirm. Yet we ignore the subtle proof of coincidence and the overwhelmingly fantastic reality of our three dimensional existence. Living on a rock spinning furiously on the outer rim of the galaxy with only a microcosmic layer of atmosphere, is not something we are consciously aware of on a moment-to-moment basis. But we should be. An atmosphere which deflects the withering and deadly radiation of the sun and which protects us all from total annihilation rarely merits a thought, as we stumble through our daily lives. An atmosphere that provides the very air and water we need for survival is taken for granted, as we struggle daily to protect our own interest. Without it there would be no interest to protect. Special interest squawking over tax payer money could never take place without it, and yet we ignore what we are doing to our environment and denigrate those who would bring it to our attention. Within the massive, jumble, tangled string of our individual lives interacting with one another and all our independent choices, runs the thread of the creator. Do we see it? We have been given this world as a great gift. What are we going to do with it? What we do with it defines what human beings are. We are either one step below angels or hideous monsters. We don't deserve this planet and we certainly don't appreciate it.

Unbelievable is the phenomenon that is all around us and that is us. It's unbelievable that we even exist in the first place. Science doesn't define the mystery away. It labels it and defines its mechanism. Religion doesn't define the mystery away. It labels it and reminds us of the phenomenon of the mystery. But organized religion somewhere along the way became more about men and the rules they establish. It became about money and political power and left the awareness and the celebration of existence behind. Gone is the mindfulness of the soul, only to be replaced with the overblown sanctimony of ritual and position. Our earthen reality is ignored and we focus on the window dressing of our cultures and religions. Not cognizant of the movement of the Earth, we are out of sync with our surroundings and each other.

But still there is time waiting patiently for us to realize our very real situation. Utopia waits for those who dare fly in the face of the cynicism, hostility and skepticism. Life is an individual journey we are taking together.

"You have to be a liar and a cheat to make it in this world," bellowed Doug from the back seat of the jeep. It was daylight now and the caravan had been west of the Mississippi for some time. Danny looked at Doug as Doug started up again. "That's why you never made it . . . your little rock and roll fantasy."

"Hey I just like to play music."

"Don't give me that crap Danny. You'd kill for a gig, any gig."

"Yeah that's right, but only with the right guys."

"Bullshit, look how many guys you taught riffs too."

"And songs," Danny answered.

"Where are they now," challenged Doug?

"Working some nine-to-five job and not on the road," said Danny.

"Lucky us," yelled Wendy from the front seat.

"You know I never got to sit up front when I was a kid," said Danny. Doug just looked at Danny and shook his head. "I mean it," Doug charged in again. "You have to be a liar and a cheat to make it. You're too damn honest Danny." Danny gave him the 'I know, so what' look. "You have to beat the other guy to the punch. You have to compete, compete, compete," relentlessly continued Doug.

"Until your blue in the face and fall over backwards," Eric interrupted.

"You mean like have your head blow straight off your head?" asked Wendy.

"Yeah, but think how great that would be," said Eric.

"Or you can have an ulcer the size of Long Island anchored in your gut," said Wendy.

"Ah the true mark of success," said Danny as they chugged up interstate 54.

"When did all this come up," asked Wendy?

"About the time we rolled through Missouri," answered Doug. "I got to thinking about a friend of ours. He was this snot-nosed kid with a hell of a cocaine addiction. No pun intended. Well, he'd hang around our gigs and pretty soon he was coming by practice."

"Not the famous, 'he stole our number one hit'," asked Eric?

"No, not the Fenton Robinson story."

"Well what then," said Eric?

This guy," Danny jumped in, "just lied his way into some auditions and used three quarters of my material. He got a single cut. No big deal."

"Well the good part about the story," interrupted Doug, "is that, yeah, he worked steady for a little while, but he blew his money on hookers and coke."

"No pun intended," Wendy chimed in, "have you told this story before?"

"He plays in a hotel lounge and he wears this funny tux," said Doug.

"And we love this guy," hollered Danny. "You've got to be a liar and a cheat to make it in this world." The jeep rolled along the interstate.

"Where are we going to leave the trucks," asked Wendy.

"Some place that looks good. Maybe in the Arkansas River," said Eric with a laugh. "Most likely outside of Newton."

"Sounds like you've been this way before."

"Well once I was headed to Dodge City. You know wide open spaces, miles and miles to get anywhere." He turned to look at Wendy.

Eventually the morning and sun came back into view. They found their way south of Newton and a gorgeous field of wheat beckoned them. They found an access road and pulled off the highway. It was a perfect morning and they drove right in. Farm land with golden stalks of wheat reflecting the sun, balanced heroically and magically against a blue sky. The wheat rose in the celebration of fertility and creation, which is the life this Earth provides. Together with the sun and the sky the Earth had sustained our very existence from the beginning. The van was right behind the jeep.

"What are they doing now," cried Bonnie?

"Looks like they're ready to make the switch."

"In broad daylight" asked John?

"Well, its not like there's anybody out here," said Louise. The Jeep stopped and they all fell out. The van also stopped beside them and the doors flung open. It was stretch time and they all got out and

found themselves surrounded. They were surrounded by the gentle
breeze and a blue sky that went on for eternity. They stopped their
flight from confrontation long enough to wander into the wheat field
and got absorbed back into the land. They stood silent, breathing in
deeply the aroma of the day, and listened to the gentle rustling of the
yellow stalks. Their hearts and minds were replenished for the
moment as they gazed at a sea of yellow sunshine in the golden wheat.
How separate we are from what sustains us. How magnificent in simple
truth reality is, and beautiful to the human eye. Wendy felt like
weeping. Louise fell over backwards and stared at her new perspective,
framed in yellow and focused on a blue sky. Eric shook his head with
a dopey smile and Doug leaned against the van. There was a small
stalk in Mark's mouth as he peered up the access road. Bonnie hopped
up on the hood of the jeep. Danny ran into the field. He threw himself
face first onto the Earth, rolled over and sprang back up on his knees.
He allowed himself a magnificent stretch. Then took the deepest
breath he could. The fresh air filled his lungs as if God himself
breathed it into him. John waited at the road's edge to give him a bear
hug. The bliss was short lived but it charged up their souls and opened
up their eyes. Let's just stay right here they laughed, but they had to
hurry. Mark started to go for the battery. "Wait Mark," called out Eric.
"We want someone to take it. Help Eric rip the VIN number out. I'll
get the tags."

"Wont somebody just flip when they find the keys in it gassed up
and ready to go."

"As if the crop circles weren't weird enough. Now the aliens are
leaving Jeeps," said Wendy with a huge laugh. "We are the aliens from
outer space," said Eric in a monotone voice, and raising his arms in
classic B-Horror movie fashion.

They had to fit four more people into the van. There was room for
one more in the back. Louise volunteered to squeeze in around the
instruments and so did Danny. Doug volunteered to sit on the floor
between the front and back seats. They stood soaking up as much of
the day as they could. They calmly, jokingly discussed their next move.

"Okay," spoke Eric to John who was going to do his second leg of
driving, "we'll pull over at the first U-Haul or Ryder truck rental store

we see. But not right in front. Wendy here is going to save our asses. Ready for some acting?"

"Save your asses, scene one, take one," she quipped." Of all the changes and events Wendy had been through ten minutes in the wheat field brought it all back into perspective. She had gotten so focused on her career and making the system work for her that she forgot about the reality of it all. The joy ride to the Jaded Lady wasn't just a momentary distraction, but another way to go through life. On a dime she had made the decision she had been building to all her life. She welcomed the unknown and removed herself from the horror that she had placed herself in. For a while fear kept her trapped, but she knew fear was a commodity of man. She didn't wish to trade on that commodity anymore.

"An angel of mercy from the outside world," whispered Louise into Danny's ear. "I'm glad we have a plan," said Doug sarcastically. "What I did on my summer vacation." They methodically made sure the glove compartment of the Jeep had been emptied. They even checked underneath the seats. If the cops found the Jeep they could i.d. the color and make. The VIN number was cut out of the dash. The markings on the door and underneath the hood were altered, stripped and trashed. All the band could hope for were a couple of young men smart enough to have a new jeep and smart enough to make it nobody's business. Things haven't been good in farm country for a long time. But they knew how to survive and the heart of America was much stronger than anyone had ever imagined. The band felt good about their chances and Wendy decided to fall in deeper.

Her decision to come along was made years ago. The opportunity to go was constant. Things can turn around quickly but only after you make that first step. "My life" she thought to herself, "was loaded with disappointment." So much faith was placed in the wrong people, and she had endured what was wrong for too long. It's hard to take a step back when things are pressed right up in your face. Why do we hang onto the bad situations for so long? Why do we trade in soul satisfaction for comfortable? Comfortable can kill. Get the scam running overtime and life looks like Easy Street, but there is always a turn in the river and other people's choices to deal with. "Only after you hang yourself out there completely do you realize what it is you are dealing with," she rambled to herself.

"What are you shaking your head and laughing at," asked John as the van finally pulled back out onto the road.

"This. Look at me. What am I doing here," answered Wendy?

"Can't believe you're in so deep because of a guy," asked Bonnie? Wendy turned around and glared briefly at Bonnie, then a sly smile appeared. "No, I can't believe I literally had to run to get away from one."

"Freedom is a nice thing to have," said Louise to no one but Danny and the guitar case she was leaning against. He nodded his head but he hadn't really known it very long. "When we were headed down the coast," he answered Louise, "on our way to the Jaded Lady I felt it big time. Freedom and the possibilities that laid out before me . . . I really had it then."

"What happened," asked Louise?

"By the time we got there too many dreams became my responsibility."

"Its nice to have dreams of your own," she whispered back.

"But other peoples' dreams," answered Danny, "well, they're too closely guarded and so very important. You never know when you are running counter to them, and that's when your hard fought freedom turns into politics as usual."

"That's why I run alone," said Louise. Danny looked back at her and into her green eyes. "Well, most of the time." Danny kept looking at her. "You've only known me a short while." Danny kept looking. "Look, I just try to make it work no matter what the situation. I try to do the right thing but I end up doing the right thing in the wrong situation. Sometimes that can be lethal."

"Like your last guy," asked Danny.

"Well I was dry, fed and had access to a shower," she paused, "and that's a hell of a lot better than where I am now." They both laughed out loud.

"We wouldn't have made it without you."

"What about Eric," she protested trying to change the focus for a moment. A moment was all she got. For in the next moment he embraced her and she returned his embrace with a warm kiss. It was just a moment. Just another moment followed by another, and then for the moment it was done. Normally under these circumstances the band would have howled. But Danny and Louise were out of view, except to John at the wheel. He spotted the lip lock through the rearview mirror. Even though he and Louise had their moment he didn't say anything. The kiss looked a lot more meaningful than what he got at the Jaded Lady. Besides he wasn't about that now. He had bigger considerations on his mind. The safe sanctuary of life and limb was paramount and he was looking for a U-Haul place or something similar. He was going to leave the acrimony to Doug. But Doug, who didn't miss much, heard the lip lock too, and didn't even turn around.

Doug and Danny went back a long way and their behavior was as predictable as two brothers. He really did care for the guy. He knew Danny realized that. They just went head-to-head when each thought they had the upper hand. A bit competitive verbally, mostly in front of others, but they knew each other for so long they felt like kin. Together somehow they managed. And so it was, Louise and Danny embraced without a hassle. Doug had other ideas. There were things he wanted to do and he just might get on a plane when they came to a stop. Of course he really couldn't go home. But anywhere he landed would be home. He knew that now and it was time for him to go.

Mark had left his drum kit behind. The cops had ripped through it like kids at Christmas. He felt as if he had left his soul behind. Drumming was the one way he knew how to really get at it. There was an emptiness now where before only his friends could have filled. But now all he wanted to do was to get off the van. He almost put his thumb out and split. But he felt he wasn't quite anonymous enough in the wheat fields of Kansas. Satisfied that he still had himself in tacked, he knew he too would be leaving his friends, or his friends leaving him. He loved them. It was all the more reason to go. He worried about Danny. But Mark knew it was time to confront himself fully once again. "It's time to get out," he thought to himself. No shame in that. Knowing when to bail is an art form.

The van was now pulling off the road. It was dusk and they were just outside of Dodge City. "Did we find a rental place," asked Danny? His ass took yet another hit with the van pulling off the street. The packing blankets only did so much. "Eric your coming with me, right," asked Wendy? "They don't know what you look like."

"Go with her Eric," spoke Bonnie from the back seat. They looked at each other and hopped out. John leaned out of the driver's window and started to pull away. "We can't wait here by the side of the road. There are too many onlookers."

"It might be time to get something to eat," spoke Eric from the street walking with Wendy. "Exactly, see that fast food joint on the right? I'll pull around back and we'll get you some burgers. Meet us later." Eric and Wendy nodded their heads and the van accelerated and pulled away. They were alone now and Wendy's heart was racing.

They could easily rent a car themselves and split. Another moment, another decision. The walk up the road was doing them good. "Look Wendy you're not doing anything wrong." He turned and held both of her hands. "We haven't done anything wrong."

"Okay," she heard herself say, "but I'm doing all the talking." No helpless female here and Eric knew that already. "I'll be right next to you," he said.

"Just look pretty," she fired back. Wendy had endured so much pain and anxiety. It always felt like her old man was about to hit her. Now was the real screen test. She had to stop her hands from shaking. They walked through a wooden screened door and an old-fashioned door bell jingled. "We need to rent a truck." The lady at the counter was cordial. In fact she was so damn nice she started asking all kinds of busy-body questions. "Where you going?" Well, that was the question all right. Wendy turned to Eric as if to say, "now's your chance."

"Pueblo," answered Eric. His answer was strong enough to stop Wendy in her tracks. The woman stopped and put her hands on her hips. She wasn't real old, but a little frumpy. Years of dealing with the public polished her smile and sharpened her eye. She needed a shave. As she leaned forward there was an unsettling quiet. Wendy was getting a little squirrelly. Eric's pores were starting to open.

Stomachs were rolling. "Well, we have offices everywhere." Nervous smiles and slight laughter went all around. Wendy pulled her mother's credit card from her wallet. She used up all her training from that bogus class the networks sent her to, "how to be a phoney soap opera ham in ten minutes," and placed the card on the counter. A few more minutes into the transaction and Eric left to go outside and talk to the mechanic. He had to make sure the truck was big enough for the remaining equipment, and big enough for the adults who agreed to ride in the back. Two people in the cab would look a lot less suspicious than eight crammed into one van. Eventually, they would have to get rid of the van the same way the got rid of the Jeep. But they didn't want to leave both vehicles in the same area.

"How's the gas mileage friend?" A thin, handsome, younger guy looked up.

"Oh you ain't taking this one. For your trip into Colorado we got something a little newer." He paused and walked over to a shinny, conspicuous as hell, new truck. "The gas mileage sucks sir," they both laughed. Back out on route 50, with the fast food place behind them, the caravan was rolling again. It was a shame the world was going by so fast. The only way to catch up was to slow it down. You can't make more time, but you can slow down the time you have. "I just want to get to a place and stop for a decade or two," thought Eric to himself. "I'm so damned tired of trying to get everyone together. The harder I've tried, the harder its become. What happened to the times and plans we all had with each other? I thought we'd make a better world for ourselves by now."

Danny was still thinking about the band, and he and Eric were having similar thoughts. It was just too hard to get anything together anymore. Keeping everybody happy was killing him. The understanding on stage was fragile but it was there. However, this latest fiasco was going to make it impossible to get back on or get back off the stage in one piece. The understanding that was needed to form a band was polluted by their personal lives. And if that couldn't be held in check, the band would implode from within. It already had. The understanding that it couldn't be done without each other was there. That each one is vital but never more important than the music, well, they got that. But it was too damn hard to find a group of people who didn't put themselves ahead of the music and each other. Hidden agendas, stroked out egos, unrealistic expectations, and the art of playing a song together were all road blocks that had to be dealt with, let alone finding someone without a Yoko complex.

Imagine, indeed, having no clue, sitting in with the Beatles on the damn piano bench, and you're not a musician. They were trying to record and interact with each other as a band. She was supposed to be the enlightened one. But she didn't understand the impact of an extra dynamic personality on the fragile make up of a band. It's like a painting. All the colors have to blend, and the forms work in relation to each other. The communication has to be between everyone all together, and interacting in a dynamic without a break. Having Yoko there was like nailing a Picasso in the middle of a Van Gogh and wondering why it didn't work. It was John's not-too-subtle way of saying he wanted out and had enough of Paul. Not that John, Paul or Yoko is a bad person, but a band has a dynamic and the players have to respect that. Yoko had to be oblivious or she would have walked out of the studio, and met the boys later. The amazing thing is that people were still relearning this lesson. Axel and Slash didn't get it, and Gun's and Roses disappeared before they even reached full altitude. They were the Lynyrd Skynyrd of their generation. Their personalities came before the music and that was that. Real musicians and artists are only a conduit delivering a stream of conscious. You have to park everything aside, including 'will it sell' and 'what will the neighbors think', and let the creativity have an unfettered flow through the soul. If it's uncluttered by distraction and focused on the essential then the world and the art is pure. Otherwise you just have a bunch of braggarts and egomaniacs running around trying to outdo each other. On stage the band knew and relied on what the other musicians and singers were doing. They were good, if not famous, and realized that those two terms weren't necessarily the same. It was a shame that it got all gummed up by some other motive than creativity. But such is life, with other people's motives driving their choices and impacting our lives. Whether it's the party, the drugs, the booze, the money, the women or the personalities, if anything is put ahead of the music it wont get off the ground. The ground has to be sacred if the music is to be any good, and fun is an imperative. The same could be said for life. Danny turned to Louise and spoke, "when people start taking credit for the inspiration as if they created it because their chops are so good, well that's the very moment they loose the inspiration, loose their place, and the magic is gone."

"That's the same with life," answered Louise.

John and Bonnie were driving the rental, followed by the van with Eric behind the wheel. Wendy sat next to him. She had earned her seat. Doug and Mark were already gone. Oh they were physically present in the van, but this journey had taken them as far as they wanted to go. Doug never wanted to understand all of Danny's mumbo-jumbo, but he did like to jam with him. He would never let on in those rare moments of reflection that he got the basic idea. But Danny knew that Doug was there. How else could he have worked so well within the group? Finally Doug had discovered this about himself and it was time to move on. Mark had always managed to go at his own pace, only getting swept away when he wanted to, or so he thought.

In the back of the rental among the equipment and packing blankets. Danny and Louise were alone. Their time had come quickly although it was passing slowly. Individual decisions that seemed unlikely had joined them together, resulting in the inevitable. The thoughts that were formed in their hearts, and their minds the moment they met, were sidetracked by choice, out of fear, and doubt. Now they took hold in reality. They found themselves feeling each other out by feeling each other up. Like a horse reigned in the bit was beginning to tear at their souls. Her hands roamed freely and uninhibited. She wanted to place her mouth on his crotch. He held her back—not now, not yet. She sat back up. He respected her. Later they would get raunchy. It was Danny and Louise's first opportunity alone and they didn't waste any time. When their legs and arms released they were no longer strangers, and you know you can only get so close before the pushing back starts. Sometimes you push each other as far away as possible, but this time was different. They starred at each other and smiled. There was no tiptoeing, "was it good for you" crap. "If you gotta ask, it sucked," Doug was fond of saying and he was right. They fell asleep in each others arms.

Hours later, crossing into Colorado along the Arkansas River, the van was searching for Purgatoire. They were driving steady all alone, south of the John Martin Reservoir in the quiet southeastern side of Colorado. Danny and Louise awoke from their sleep as the truck came to an abrupt halt. The road noise subsided and it got quieter. Their mood changed for the worse. Alone in the back they couldn't see. They both had known plenty of bad times. They knew enough to recognize the vibe and knew good times could turn on a dime. They held onto each other and listened and expected to go down together. "Cops," whispered Danny? Louise didn't blink an eye. They were as trapped as two rats could ever be. "Cornered in this damn box truck," Louise thought to herself. There was no way out. The handle on the back of the door clanked around, steel on steel. The rolling door screamed along the rails as it was flung open. The truck echoed and rocked and there were lights in their eyes. "We're at the Purgatoire River boy, wanna take a last look?"

LIVING THE
DREAM

—

Life as it seems never stops becoming a dream. Only to the casual observer does it seem out of control and beyond reach. The life force just rolls on, catching us as we fall and as we fly. It never lets on and the design is so subtle that it remains hidden. We all lack faith in the unseen. So why look to the unseen for faith? The Earth is our provider. What we do to it and upon it says everything about ourselves. Do we care for it or rape it? Our choice demonstrates our understanding of our real place in the universe. See clearly the spot we are on and know it for what it is. Be immersed in the moment and the next one is new. Set a course and watch it ricochet. It doesn't have to be mundane. We may be in a world of trouble or it may be the holiest ground we have ever walked upon, but only we can move it forward or backward alone and together. The option is yours. Even if it breaks all the rules, and totally goes against everything we have ever understood or recognize, we still have that option to move. Take your steps one at a time. Pick up your feet, one foot at a time. Place one in front of the other and amazingly we go on our way, alone and together. Break the freeze of indecision and move on to decide later. Carefully feel, and inspiringly the right mindfulness is gained. It wasn't the Cops opening the truck door. It was Doug, Mark, John and Bonnie, the band was saying goodbye.

They pulled Danny and Louise out of the back. They weren't afraid to hug each other. They were hugs built from years of friendship, love and laughter. They weren't the hugs of fear from the past few days. They were beyond that at this point. The band stood in view of the river fully immersed in their collective and individual adventures. The night was clear and cool, and a million mountain stars greeted them.

"We'll follow the Purgatoire, said Doug."

"Lets see where it goes," answered Mark.

"It goes from here," spoke Bonnie and she lightly touched his heart.

"Follow your heart," agreed Louise. She was the embodiment of the wandering spirit they had all become. Exodus. It was time to move on again. Only this time they knew where they were going. They were going not so much as to a promised land, (people break promises), but rather to another place. It was a place not so much on a road map. But rather a place where they thought they could begin again. It was a place that would remind them that everything they needed was inside of them, and their journey home was found. That how the world responded to them was how they responded to the world. A new place that was the same old place, but that their feeling toward it would be forever amazed, and awed by its mere presence, and magnitude. A place that would remind them of the world, and what it was that was simply themselves, and the Earth on which they came. Time was waiting for them patiently. It was there all the time waiting for them to find the place that would remind them of what they already knew, but had forgotten. A place that would galvanize in the core of their very being where they were, and what they are.

They wanted to go where they could make it work. Maybe not with music, although Danny knew that would always be in his life, but rather with the truth of the full consciousness of where they were, and immersed in each moment. The truth that they could accomplish, they could help, they could do, they could be free and living the dream. If only for a moment that feeling was worth a lifetime of experience to feel. The fact that we could feel freedom was the most gifted feeling we could ever have. What we do with that freedom depends on how we value it. Throughout life we are a reflection of what we have been taught and told. We are what we choose to believe, and have learned from experience. But real freedom teaches us that we do not need to blindly accept wholesale what we have been told. Freedom teaches use to look behind the curtain for the strange little man at the controls. To see things as they really are is to stand there and define what we see on our own terms. If we see bullshit then it's bullshit, and in the face of all odds call it that way. Come up with a view of your own, and don't let anyone sell you. Draw your own conclusions and realize what is going on, not in the newspaper, but what was in your eyes, your heart and your voice. Our own view is our own road, and our own journey home back to the source, which is ourselves. However you picture that home or that heaven to be it will meet you full force in your soul, and the music you hear will be your own.

This life on Earth does not have to be so negative. We choose to act and see it that way. It is perhaps the fashion of the times. The hype is there to sell us. Nothing replaces what the actual reality is for very long, no matter what its product placement. No mater how caught up we get in the definition or the playing of the game, what is so simply all around us, and so plainly to see are the lessons of nature and the universe. It is beautiful and rare and horribly unforgiving if we are out of balance. The lessons of nature are there to guide us. You can't ignore it. You can't define it. You can't explain it, and you can't deny it. Danny and Louise did not want to miss their opportunity to realize fully the here and now.

The woods spoke loud and clear. The animals hear and are attuned to their inner drives and outer environment, solely and completely. What we are trying to tell ourselves doesn't need to be said. We don't need mystics allegedly walking on water if we understand we are already floating in space. An innate knowledge of our surroundings reveals a temple of reality, a temple of consciousness, giving voice to a silent universe. Heaven is on Earth. The infinite and the finite mingle. It is our temple along with our body, and heart and mind at play. Every moment is there for realization, and time is the greatest forgiver of all. Man-made systems are just tools and not divine. They are an outcrop of our imagination, and a mixture of horror and beauty of our own doing. We are the witnesses who huddled together in the darkness. We harnessed fire and created our reality out of our fear. We try to define what is around us and why, and try to simply understand what it is that we see. That understanding is what we make it. Even if life is just an accident of science it still exists and deserves a holy place of understanding for its uniqueness, and the opportunity it brings. Nihilistic the Earth is not. It sustains us. We need to be careful. For what we imagine it will be will come to pass. Life is but a dream. Choose a good one because we all have to deal with each other's nightmares.

Danny was puzzled by how the band had met its end and how their journey had been blown apart. Not lost on him was the strange manner and way in which he and Louise had met. Both of them were looking for relief, and on the interstate they had found it. They seemed to be in the right place at the right time. What to make of that, and the punctuating revelation of a falling star? It was all around them, sign posts waiting to be seen. Their focus had been too narrow when the big picture needed to be front and center. And their focus wasn't sharp enough to be in the here and now. Doubt and fear fogged their lens, and it heaped upon them so many roadblocks. They had to overcome themselves, and their particular manifested struggles. Danny, in spite of everything, hung on with resolve just happy to be here and a witness to all that he saw. He wasn't an idiot. He felt pain, but he knew it helped shape his understanding of all that is around. Louise had known this thing called forever. It was a feeling of eternity that floated through her soul as subtle as a luffing sail in a gentle breeze.

And the Earth just kept on spinning. After long looks deep into each other's eyes Danny and Louise said goodbye to Bonnie, Mark, Doug and John. They moved the band gear together for the last time. It had been moved into the rental truck and placed out of view, in case the van got pulled over. Roadies once again they moved the equipment back. They were sick of moving it around, and bellowed at their own buffoonery with enormous laughter. Working side by side their true commonality came back home to full realization. They were just people working to survive. It was a lot easier when they were pushing the road boxes in the same direction.

Danny kept his guitar and amplifier in the box truck. He held out hope he would find new bandmates as good as his true friends turned out to be. It was time now. The band split up, and they went their separate ways from Purgatorie. Hanging on to a few remaining packing blankets Danny watched his old van carry his old friends away. The tour had a life of its own, and now it was snuffed out. He fought the tears terribly as they rolled from his eyes. He and Louise reluctantly climbed back into the box truck. But as they turned, the van now gone from their sight, they afforded themselves a smile. They could still hear Bonnie hollering one last, "we love you mannnn . . .," into the night. A new beginning was dawning, and so it was they climbed aboard. Eric and Wendy were smiling feeling privileged to be a part of all that was that night. The box truck door shut yet again on Danny and Louise. They drifted back off into each others arms, clinging to the future, dreaming again, a dream of their very own. With Eric at the wheel the truck rumbled away. Wendy felt the melancholy of the bittersweet moment. They headed North towards the Poudre Canyon. Behind them the Purgatoire River was as beautiful as it ever was. To the south the van rumbled away from them. Inside the van Bonnie, Mark, Doug and John chose not too get too comfortable. They kept plugging along into the night, and agreed upon a destination. There were literally miles to go, and they were headed to Austin with a pretty good sound system.

EPILOGUE

—

The Poudre Canyon was enormous. Here is where the vastness of reality really dwarfed the ego. We gain true appreciation of our humbling reality in light of what surrounds us. It was not created by man. The ego gives way to an avalanche and flood of awe. The soul is immersed by the mountains. The rocks are hard and they fall. Swept away on a torrent of floods the snow melts, and rushes through the vastness. Your life and limb is at risk, and you are at the mercy of creation. Man only conquers himself. He limits his growth and falls short of his dreams and understanding. Buried heads of ego miss the enlightened revolution of spirit. The development of soul rafts down the river of enlightenment. It realizes it is a part of everything, and everything is a part of it. Effortlessly it goes, whereas man's ego is knocked about with fury. We stand apart from nothing but our own awareness and actualization.

Winding their way through a misty gray mountain pass the quiet stilled their souls. As human beings they recognized all this beauty and it filled them with life. Eric was grinning a grin that ripped right off his face. He knew what separated them all from themselves was in the past, and beyond Rustic and the Cameron Pass. He was going to start reconnecting by planning a long slow date with a hot tub, and resting by a wood burning stove. He'd invite his friends to join him for a dip, and some serious stargazing in the cold gray mountains at night. He knew just where the cabins were as the truck pulled into a gravel lot. They freed Danny and Louise one more time from the back of the truck. This time they weren't scared by the stopping. They all got out, and marveled at the vastness of the universe that surrounded them. It spread itself out before them for all their eyes to see. The quiet natural energies of the steely mountains was something to be known and felt. It was universal and indescribable. Danny and Louise embraced under the stars. Wendy and Eric could see so clearly. They scrambled to check in and get a bite to eat.

The night sky went on for an eternity. The wind and the woods and the animals moved, and called to one another in the summer breeze. They made an intricate symphony of sound that Mozart spent a lifetime trying to capture. Man had his place too, and when working with creation, instead of against it, nirvana was had for all. An opening in a dark silent universe was our Earth. A home, where heavenly sights were seen, and heavenly sounds were heard, and heavenly air was everywhere to breath. Earth is as mythical and mystical a place as any in all of literature or eternity, and it is our home. Its intricacies are beyond imagination, and to this day not fully known. It is a place inaccessible through the vastness of space, except for those who are born unto it. How should we treat it, with reverence or disdain? What are we doing with it?

We are the only voices in a silent universe. How will we use those voices? What are the words we choose to say? What are the thoughts we choose to convey? We are the only bodies forcing our will upon the Earth, and acting upon it. What do we choose to do in light of its rare and precious reality? Our thoughts carried by our voices are the foundation of our deeds. They are more powerful than we understand. We build our communities and nations based upon our premises, on a world, in a universe, not of our making. The Earth is a gift and an opportunity completely beyond anything we could imagine or create for ourselves. Do we recognize the magnificence, and implausibility of it all as we measure our daily decisions? What are we trying to make for ourselves on this lonely, tiny whisper of air, in the vastness of a borderless universe? Will it be heaven or hell or something puny, undecided, and in-between? We don't have to believe in some man-made religion, some hocus-pocus, mumbo-jumbo. We just have to see the Earth, and our place in the Universe for what it really is. Earth spins on. It is an amazingly, incredibly, infinite, tiny opening of sight, and sound, and consciousness. It began as an empty vessel of fire and rock and sea. We can either fill it up with hate or heroics.

The trees swayed slowly with creaking rhythm and rustling leaves. The crows called out in numbers, and filled the sky. On some beach the gulls laughed and dove for food. The blue jays called in some meadow, and the song birds answered with staccato notes each different in response. In the mountains the coyote howled to hear the vastness of it all. Hung by a changing room, near a hot tub, behind some cabins, a set of wind chimes were played by a light breeze. They brushed gently together. Soaking wet in the hot tub Wendy popped open a bottle of champagne, while Eric looked on. Louise giggled at Danny. These were sounds worthy of the uniqueness of this world. Billions and billions of stars, and they were lucky enough to have one of their very own. They were given eyes to see and ears to hear and heads to think and senses to smell, taste and feel. It was theirs to choose what to do with and a gift from God straight up, and each one a life to live. Just then a sixty-nine Thunderbird came careening off a mountain pass, and pulled along side a brand new rental truck. The gravel kicked up and two young lovers leaped out, grabbing their guitars and back packs. They were looking for something to eat, a place to stay, a cabin to rent, a tub to soak in, and a place to jam. They settled on these simple cabins in Rustic. They knew that in the mountains at night they would need a wood burning stove.

Printed in the United Kingdom
by Lightning Source UK Ltd.
120863UK00001B/312